LIGHT *in the* EMPIRE

MORE THAN HONOR

CAROL ASHBY

CERRILLO PRESS

MORE THAN HONOR

Scripture quotations marked (ESV) are from the Holy Bible, English Standard Version, copyright © 2001, 2007, 2011, 2016 by Crossway Bibles, a division of Good News Publishers. Used by permission. All rights reserved.

Cover and interior design by Roseanna White Designs

Cover images from Shutterstock.com

ISBN: 978-1-946139-27-6 (paperback)
       978-1-946139-28-3 (ebook)
       978-1-946139-29-0 (hardcover)

Cerrillo Press
Edgewood, NM

But in your hearts honor Christ the Lord as holy,
always being prepared to make a defense to anyone
who asks you for a reason for the hope that is in you;
yet do it with gentleness and respect.
1 Peter 3:15 (ESV)

So Jesus said to the Jews who had believed him,
"If you abide in my word, you are truly my disciples,
and you will know the truth, and the truth will set you free."
John 8:31-32 (ESV)

And we know that for those who love God
all things work together for good,
for those who are called according to his purpose.
Romans 8:28 (ESV)

To my children, Paul and Lydia,
for their love, support, and encouragement.
And especially to my husband, Jim,
who's better than the best of my heros
because they're modeled on him.

And most of all, to Jesus.

Soli Deo gloria.

A Note from the Author

Sharing our faith. Once we know the peace and joy that come from being children of God through our faith in Jesus, we want to share it with those we love most, with friends, and even with casual acquaintances we're sure will be interested. But how can we share when we expect a hostile response?

Perhaps it's easier for those who were old enough to remember what it was like to live without Him to explain their faith in Christ, those who chose as adults or mature teens to believe Jesus is their savior and then received the Holy Spirit. If we know what led us to faith, we can share the path we took. We would know how the choices we've made put a barrier between us and God, one we couldn't cross ourselves. We would know we need a Savior. We would remember the joy of becoming a child of God when we first believed Jesus paid for our sins.

But even those of us raised from childhood in a Christian home need to embrace the Truth with mature understanding. It's harder to pinpoint exactly when that happened. But we still know that it did happen, and we can share how we've grown in the depth of our relationship with God as we love and follow Jesus as Lord.

The choice each person makes about Jesus has eternal consequences. We don't know ahead of time how best to share, but the Holy Spirit will guide us. How we live sets the stage. When someone sees us treat others with the unnatural kind of love God commands, it can start them wondering. It might start them asking why. When they do ask, we need to be ready to explain what and why we believe. That's why the apostle Peter wrote that we should always be prepared to explain the reason for the hope that is ours and to do it gently and respectfully, speaking at all times with a spirit of love.

In *The Legacy*, Publius Drusus died for his faith in a Roman arena

i

before he had the chance to tell his son how he came to believe in Jesus as his savior. He wrote a letter to explain his choice and asked his best friend Torquatus to read it before sending it on to his son. Torquatus studied it with their mutual friend Lenaeus and his daughter Pompeia, and the letter that was first written to lead Publius's son to faith led three others as well. In *More than Honor*, Publius's written legacy bears unlikely fruit as a man who scoffs at religion decides to believe in the Truth that can set him free.

That's how sharing our faith still works today. The apostles and earliest disciples told others, those others told more, and we believe in Jesus because someone more than 1900 years later told us. I hope you enjoy the story of Titianus, Pompeia, and their friends as her courage to live the faith and share the truth changes the future for all of them.

May we always be open to the Spirit's revelation of those in our own lives who are just waiting for us to tell them about Jesus. May we all know the joy of opening the door that will lead another person to salvation, peace, and joy as a beloved child of God.

Characters

The Roman familia is the Roman family unit consisting of the pater-familias, his married and unmarried children regardless of age, his son's children, and his slaves. Wives and freed slaves (freedmen) are sometimes included in the familia.

Romans took names and what they said about family connections very seriously. The three-part name (like Manius Flavius Sabinus) meant you were a Roman citizen of the clan Flavius and family Sabinus. Using a three-part name if you weren't a citizen was actually a crime. Which name of the three you called someone depended on the closeness of your relationship. There were only 20 male first names in common use, and one-in-five Romans was named Gaius. Only close friends and immediate family called you by your first name. Others used your last name, both your second and third names when being formal, and sometimes your first and third names.

When a male slave was freed by a citizen so he became a citizen, too., he took the first and second names of his former owner with his slave name added as his third name. Women were named the feminine form of their father's clan and family names. Married women kept their maiden names because they stayed part of their father's familia, not their husband's.

FLAVIUS TITIANUS FAMILIA
> Titus Flavius Titianus (29): tribune in XI Urban Cohort, nephew of Quintus Sabinus
> Probus (55): manager of Titianus's warehouse and shipping business
> Sciurus/Melis (15): youth Probus is training to replace him someday

POMPEIUS LENAEUS FAMILIA
> Gnaeus Pompeius Lenaeus (54): owns school of rhetoric, friend of Publius Drusus
> Pompeia Lenaea (24): single daughter of Gnaeus, teaches in her father's school
> Kaeso Pompeius Lenaeus (18): son of Gnaeus, also a teacher
> Corax (45): house steward and manservant
> Ciconia (40): housekeeper and cook, married Corax 12 years earlier

Lilia (17): Daughter of Ciconia, housemaid and lady's maid to Pompeia

Theo (11): Son of Corax and Ciconia, door keeper

FLAVIUS SABINUS FAMILIA AND SLAVES

Quintus Flavius Sabinus (63): senator and ruthless Roman power broker

Manius Flavius Sabinus (42): Quintus's second son

Septimus Flavius Sabinus (18): Manius's second son

Tutelus (25): Manius's Syrian bodyguard, former gladiator bought out of the arena

Festinus: agent for Quintus Sabinus who runs his spy network

Brummbar, Barin, and Pardus: more of Manius's bodyguards

MANLIUS TORQUATUS FAMILIA

Appius Manlius Torquatus (61): prominent senator, best friend of Publius Drusus

Appius Manlius Glyptus (34): freedman working as Torquatus's personal secretary

CORNELIUS RUFINUS FAMILIA:

Faustus Cornelius Rufinus (42): politically ambitious senator whose freedman commits murder

Gaius Cornelius Rufinus (15): second son of Faustus Rufinus

F. Cornelius Arcanus (36): freedman who oversees Rufinus's questionable businesses

F. Cornelius Lupus: freedman of Rufinus, embezzler who dies in the fire

PUBLIUS CLAUDIUS DRUSUS FAMILIA

Publius (deceased): patriarch who was killed in the arena for his faith in AD 114

Lucius (29): grandson of Publius, Titianus's best friend from age 15 onward

Marcus (deceased): younger brother of Lucius who tried to kill him in AD 122

Antonius Brutus familia

Marcus Antonius Brutus (42): wealthy equestrian owner of gladiator school, Ludus Bruti.

Africanus (40): Brutus's favorite gladiator as bodyguard, sparring partner, and best friend

Lanista Felix: head trainer over the Ludus Bruti

Fortis: gladiator used as second-level trainer of young men

Pugnus: gladiator used as beginning level trainer

Miscellaneous people

G. Aurelius Longinus: centurion of the Vigiles who fought the fire

Speratus: overseer of carts going into Rome for a wineseller; reported the fire

Gellius: an optio who reports to Titianus

Tertius Valerius Flaccus: Gaius Rufinus's best friend who overheard the conversation

Marcus Fabius Quintilianus (AD 35–95): celebrated orator, rhetorician, Latin teacher, and writer

Khepri, Rezia and Taliba: Pompeia's Egyptian students

Vulpis: assassin for hire, real name Marcus Siricus

M. Lollius Paullinus Valerius Saturninus: Titianus's commander, urban prefect AD 124-134, also consul in 125

G. Julius Victorinus: less-than-competent tribune of the Urban Cohort

Aulus Secundus: rescued Pompeia from kidnapper 8 years earlier

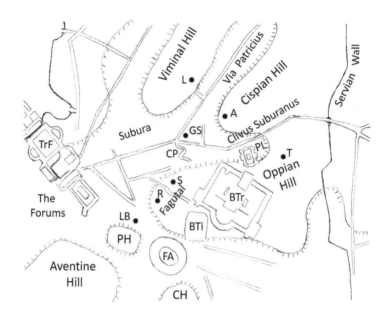

Locations in Rome

(A) Arcanus town house: on the Cispian Hill

(L) Lenaeus town house: on the Viminal Hill

(R) Rufinus town house: in the Fagutal district of the Esquiline Hill

(S) Sabinus town house: in the Fagutal district of the Esquiline Hill

(T) Titianus town house: on the Oppian Hill

Ludus Bruti (LB): near the Flavian Amphitheater (FA)

Guard station (GS): near the intersection of the Clivus Pullius, Clivus Suburanus, and Vicus Patricius

Clivus Pullius (CP): shortest road from guard station to Sabinus town house

Baths of Titus (BTi): imperial bath complex

Baths of Trajan (BTr): imperial bath complex on the Oppian Hill

Porticus of Livia (PL): Art galleries and Shrine of Concordia

Trajan's Forum (TF): Rome's "shopping mall"

Palantine Hill (PH)

Caelian Hill (CH)

Beyond the Boundaries of the Map

Praetorian Fortress: outside the Viminal Gate on the Via Patricius
Lupus estate: south of Rome near the Via Ostiensis
Torquatus estate: north of Rome

This is Carol's map of important locations in the story derived from "Ancient Rome," made by S.B. Platner for his book *The Topography and Monuments of Ancient Rome*, published in 1911. You can access the full map online at http://bit.ly/DetailedMapofRome.

Chapter 1

THE FIRE

The warehouse district of Rome, AD 126, Day 1

The smoke-gray stallion snorted and tossed his head. Titus Flavius Titianus, tribune of the Urban Cohort, leaned forward and patted the skittish animal's neck.

"Calm down, boy. The fire's out. It's only smoke now."

The horse froze with front legs spread as it leaned back. Titianus couldn't blame him. He'd seen the aftermath of too many fires in the city. Like his horse, he'd rather turn and leave. Even with the best efforts of the firefighters of the *Vigiles Urbani*, too often someone died in the flames. Sometimes they made it out, so badly burned they'd die in agony before the week was out. Given a choice, he'd pick the quicker death.

Titianus stroked the horse's withers a few times before scratching lightly with his fingernails. With each pass of his fingertips, he spoke gentle words. As the stallion relaxed, tension drained from Titianus as well. After several cycles of strokes and scratches, both were ready to go on. Nudged by Titianus tensing his calves, the horse moved forward.

When word of the fire in the storehouse district spread through the fortress shared by the Praetorian Guard and the Urban Cohort, he'd called for his horse. He was not a man who could sit and wait for bad news.

The warehouse and shipping business built by his father and grandfather sat on the Tiber's edge where the fire was burning. As he'd trotted down the Vicus Patricius through Subura, skirted the Forums and the Circus Maximus, and passed through the Porta Trigemina to reach the storehouses by the river, worry had gnawed at him.

1

Probus, warehouse manager since Titianus was a boy, lived in an apartment above the office. Had the man who always had a honey roll for a hungry boy been trapped inside? Had the flames just consumed half his family's fortune? Had the dowries of his two younger sisters turned to ashes and smoke, ending their chance for a good marriage?

Relief swept over him when the Titianus property came into view. Half a block past it, he reached the smoldering remains of another man's prosperity.

Charred beams lay at odd angles atop piles of bricks where the walls had collapsed. Wisps of smoke still rose from the rubble, and the soldiers manning the fire engine pumped a stream of water onto whatever was smoldering.

"Tribune." Longinus, the centurion who'd directed the battle against the blaze strode toward him. "There's something you should see."

Titianus dismounted and tied his horse to a ring on the fire engine. He wove his way past the soot-stained men who poked at rubble piles with their shovels and dowsed any embers they found with water from their pitch-sealed rope buckets.

Before Titianus reached the centurion's side, Longinus pulled in a deep breath and coughed. "It's good you came. I was going to have to send for you."

"What is it?" Did he really want to know? The sun was almost down, and when the vigiles called him to a fire scene, it could be hours before he left.

Longinus tipped his head toward the one small corner of the building that still stood, smoke-blackened but intact. "I'd rather not say until after you see it."

Titianus rubbed his mouth. Would it be minutes or hours before he could ride back to the fortress? The tightened lips of the centurion whispered "hours" without speaking a word. When Longinus stopped short of the wall, waved him on, and crossed his arms, that whisper became a shout.

On the ground lay the body of a man. Blackened roof timbers had fallen on his lower torso and legs. But it wasn't smoke or flames or falling debris that had killed him.

Titianus squatted beside the corpse and drew a breath between clenched teeth. A blow to the head had ended this life, but the fire that was supposed to hide that fact had been spotted and extinguished too soon.

The fire was an arson, and the death a murder. As the tribune commanding the cohort that policed this part of Rome, he'd make certain the killer stood in the arena and paid for both.

The Porticus of Livia by the Baths of Trajan, late afternoon of Day 1

The afternoon in the library at the Baths of Trajan had been close to perfect. Pompeia Lenaea and her brother Kaeso had drifted along the wall of cubicles in the historical section, looking for scrolls that might be new. But it was getting late, and walking back to their small town house would be dangerous after dark. It was in a decent neighborhood on the Viminal Hill, but no one without a bodyguard walked the streets of Rome at night, not even in the most elite areas. Especially not a young woman with only her unarmed brother, despite his claim that he could protect them. She knew too well what could happen.

They had almost passed the Porticus of Livia to the east of the bath complex. Through the arched entrance to its inner courtyard, Pompeia could see the network of walkways among the flowers and the Ara Concordia with its altar for offerings to the Roman goddess of agreement in marriage and society. It would be a beautiful place to stroll if not for that pagan shrine.

"Kaeso!

She turned to find Septimus Sabinus striding toward them.

"I didn't expect to find you here, but your timing is excellent." Septimus directed his smile at both of them. "There's a new display in the Porticus of paintings of the mountains of northern Italia. Magnificent country. If I get to serve in a frontier legion in Germania, I'll get to see it myself."

Pompeia raised her eyebrow. "I've heard about the displays there. Some of the paintings show people doing things I don't want to see."

Septimus waved away her objection. "I walked the galleries yesterday, and I can take you to the ones of the *Alpes* without passing anything like that."

He fell in beside Kaeso, and they resumed walking. "The gardens are lovely, and you'd find the temple pretty as long as you don't dwell on what it's for."

"There's a much better way than sacrificing here to have a peaceful marriage. Love and respect between husband and wife"—she lowered her voice to a near-whisper—"that's what God says will bring harmony to a home."

"It would, but not many have that." Septimus's shrug accompanied a wry smile. "My grandfather always chooses pretty young wives who are too weak to disagree with him openly. But when it's time for me to marry, I want to choose a woman who values what I do. That should naturally lead to agreement about anything important." He grinned. "Now I just have to get Father to agree to let me choose."

"Even the closest friends don't always agree on the most important things, like whether there's a god who's real." With his knuckles, Kaeso tapped Septimus's arm. "But I expect I'll convince you someday."

Pompeia slid her hand up, then down her upper arm. "There's only one thing I will insist my husband agree about, and that's God."

Septimus drew his breath through his teeth. "That might mean you never marry. The only Christians I knows are in your father's *familia*. How will you ever find a Roman man who worships only your god?"

Septimus's question pricked too close to Pompeia's heart. How, indeed? "Maybe I will. Maybe I won't. But if it's God's will for me to marry, He'll bring the right man into my life. God can work all things for good for His children, whether I can see the way or not."

Three men in togas walked toward them, and one pointed at the sky above the bath complex. Pompeia turned to find a wide column of black smoke spiraling upward from the storehouse district by the Tiber.

Kaeso blew his breath out between pursed lips. "I hope that doesn't belong to one of our students' fathers."

Septimus sucked a breath in. "Or my cousin Titianus. He's equestrian, but not by much. Losing his warehouse would drop him below the minimum fortune to stay in that order."

"We should pray everyone gets out safely and no one gets hurt fighting the fire." Pompeia turned her gaze from the smoke to Septimus. "Titus Titianus?"

Septimus nodded.

"He was one of Father's students when I was a girl. He always seemed so serious." She slipped her fingers under the palla draped across her shoulder and adjusted the edge where it brushed her neck. "He was quieter than most, but Father liked him. He expected Titianus would do well in life."

"I think he has, even if my father doesn't. He's been a tribune of the Urban Cohort for several years. He wanted to serve in a frontier legion, but he stayed in Rome because his father was sick and his sisters were small. He's been *paterfamilias* for a few years now. A true man of honor. That's what Marcus Brutus called him. Brutus said I should try to be like him."

Pompeia rubbed her arm again. "Brutus of the Ludus Bruti?"

"The same. I still train at his *ludus*, but he's not there very often since he remarried in Germania. He and your father taught me the importance of honor. I wanted to become good enough with a gladius to spar with his best trainer, but Africanus is in Germania with him. Brutus said he was his good friend and a man of utmost honor, even though he was a slave. A man's true worth isn't decided by his family ties, his social rank, or his wealth. It's his honor."

"I met Africanus." Pompeia traced a line in the dirt with her sandal.

Septimus's eyebrows rose. "How? Even Kaeso hasn't." He grinned at her. "I would never have expected you to be one of the giggling girls who come to the ludus to watch gladiators."

Pompeia turned her eyes toward the column of smoke. The memory still pained her. "He came with Aulus Secundus and Marcus Drusus to rescue me when I was kidnapped. He's the reason the man who bought me was afraid to refuse their demand that I be freed. I prayed so hard for deliverance, and God brought them to get me before the worst could happen."

Septimus's eyes narrowed. "But how can you be certain your god brought them? Didn't they come because they thought Aulus's sister was there?"

"That might be why they thought they came, but God can use people to accomplish something they never intended." She pursed her lips, then let them curve into a smile. "Maybe He's even using you now, and you don't know it yet."

Kaeso choked back a laugh.

Septimus elbowed him. "I'll concede that might be possible, if your god does happen to be real. But you haven't convinced me of that."

"As Father always says, 'The man of honor will accept the truth when he finally faces it.' I don't have to convince you. Someday God will." Pompeia offered her warmest smile to her almost-brother. "Can you join us for dinner?"

"Not today. Father is giving a banquet for Grandfather and some senators, and he wants me to join them. The food will be delicious, but the affairs of the Empire and the men who direct them will be the main topics of conversation." He ran a hand through his hair. "I always want to say something they don't want to hear, but I know better than to speak about honor in the presence of power."

"Father also says, 'When speaking truth to power can draw its wrath, the prudent man chooses silence.'" Kaeso offered his arm that held up his toga, and Pompeia rested her hand there. "We need to go. I don't want it to get dark before we reach home." He tapped the dagger that always hung at Septimus's side. "We don't have an armed escort if you can't come with us. Do join us tomorrow, and dine where truth is always welcome."

"I'll try."

Pompeia glanced over her shoulder at Septimus as she and Kaeso headed toward their modest home that also housed the Lenaeus School of Rhetoric. Septimus's family was richer than most kings, but Septimus was still her second little brother. With a ruthless grandfather who pulled the strings on powerful men and a father who wanted to follow in those footsteps, how could he safely remain a man of honor, one who, despite his skepticism about God, was worthy to be Kaeso's best friend?

Chapter 2

FORTUNA'S FROWNS

The warehouse district by the Tiber

Surrounded by more than a dozen other men who'd been drafted into the water brigade, Arcanus set the bucket at his feet and arched his back. It had been years since he'd done real labor himself. He had the muscles of a man who lifted wax tablets, not barrels and crates. He would be sore tomorrow.

Fortuna had frowned on him too many times that day. He'd only come to deliver a reprimand to Lupus for selling substandard goods to the government and cheating Faustus Cornelius Rufinus, the senator who was patron of them both. A reprimand and a demand that Lupus repay what he'd stolen. Since Lupus had made the business highly profitable, Rufinus was willing to give him a second chance to serve honestly.

But the arrogant embezzler had laughed at Arcanus and made his own threat. Senators were forbidden by Roman law from owning that kind of business. Rufinus could never risk the damage to his noble reputation if that ownership was revealed. Especially now, when Rufinus was positioning himself to be elected consul. If his patron wanted his silence, he'd better let Lupus run the business however he wanted. He should be grateful Lupus shared any of the profits with him.

Insolence was not something Rufinus tolerated. Not from a freedman like Lupus, not from anyone. The tilt of Lupus's head to look down his nose, the sneer twisting his lips, the eyes filled with contempt…it was only right that Arcanus should have slapped the side of Lupus's head as he con-

7

demned the thief's plan to defraud the man whose father had bestowed Roman citizenship and financial security when he set Lupus free.

How was he to know Lupus kept a club in his desk drawer? That the thief would pull it out and strike him? That it would turn into a wrestling match and a stand holding a dozen lamps would be knocked over before Arcanus wrested the club from Lupus's grip and struck him back?

He hadn't meant to hit Lupus so hard. He'd meant to knock him out, not kill him. But once he had, there was no bringing him back.

The clay lamps had been freshly filled with oil and some were lit. When they shattered, flames followed the oil wherever it went. If he'd tried, he probably could have beaten them out with Lupus's cloak that hung in the corner. But a fire could make the death look accidental. Had anyone seen him well enough to describe him after the body was found?

While he hesitated, the thin drapery that served as one of the office doors had caught fire as well. Flames raced up the fabric to the ceiling, where the tongues of fire licked the wood planks and set them ablaze.

Any chance for stopping the spread was gone. Rufinus would lose his warehouse, but if that was the cost of silencing Lupus, the senator would be willing to take the loss of such a small part of his wealth.

Arcanus had used a broom handle to push the burning fabric aside and squeezed past, his own tunic getting singed as he slipped through the doorway. As he raced to a door that opened onto the riverbank, the fire crackled and popped behind him. He slipped outside, and rested his back against the closed door. But only for a moment. He couldn't be sure, but he'd seen no one watching as he entered. He wanted no one to see him as he left.

He'd walked up the river some distance before returning to the road—just in time to be ordered to join the chain of "volunteers" who would bring bucket after bucket of water from the river to keep the three fire engines' reservoirs filled.

Teams of soldiers stood on each engine and worked the pump handles to wet down each of the buildings next to the burning one. But they also turned the stream from the nozzle onto the parts of the burning roof closest to the adjacent buildings. The roof above the office where he'd left the corpse was being cooled by the same water he'd been forced to carry. When the last of the flames flickered out, the corner where his temper had flared as hot as those flames still stood.

When one of the soldiers signaled for the centurion to come to that corner, Arcanus's stomach knotted. But the centurion would be called to look at anyone who died in a fire. Would he see anything suspicious? When he only glanced and then walked over to the man directing the nozzle of one of the fire engines, Arcanus released the breath he hadn't realized he'd been holding.

He'd lost count of the number of times he passed a full bucket forward or an empty one back. But even with the last flames quenched, the centurion in charge of the fire brigade had ordered the water carriers to stay. Perhaps he only wanted them there in case a smolder turned back into a flame. Arcanus might do that himself if he was in charge. But as the time stretched out with no sign they could leave, he had to push back harder on a growing urge to run.

Then a tribune rode up, and Arcanus's stomach churned. The last person he wanted to see was Tribune Titianus of the Urban Cohort, a man both praised and feared for his dogged determination to uncover the truth before he would stop an investigation.

The centurion immediately strode toward Titianus, calling out and summoning with raised arm and curling fingers. Then the two men in armor, one darkened by soot and one in polished brass that reflected the beams of the setting sun, headed toward what Arcanus had hoped to hide. When the tribune squatted by what was left of the thief, Arcanus's heart rate rose. When the officer stood and turned toward the centurion, Arcanus swallowed hard. That scowl—Titianus thought it was murder.

Arcanus had worn a plain tunic that was too clean for him to be a warehouse slave, but it still let him blend in near the docks. It was filthy now. He looked like the men who labored there. Perhaps he would escape the tribune's notice. If only the centurion would release them all to go about their own business, he could slip away before Titianus recognized him.

Fortuna's frown had become a scowl as well. What had started as a necessary threat toward a man who'd cheated his patron had turned into death and fire. But Titianus would call those murder and arson. The killing Arcanus might explain away as self-defense. He had the bruises to support that. But arson was a capital crime, and Titianus's stubborn pursuit of what he considered justice would never stop until someone burned on a stake in the arena for it.

◆

With Centurion Longinus beside him, Titianus returned to his horse and withdrew a wax tablet from the satchel attached to its saddle. "Who reported the fire?"

Longinus pointed to someone standing with the men drafted to make the bucket brigade. "Speratus oversees the carts going into Rome each night from the wine merchant a half mile down this street. As he was riding past, he smelled something burning. He came to the barracks to get us."

"Does he know who the dead man might be or if others were in the building?"

"It's far enough to where he works that I wouldn't expect it. But he helped my *aquarius* gather men for the bucket brigade by going into the nearby warehouses to ask them to send men out while my man recruited those walking the streets. Then he tied his horse over there and carried water himself."

"Tell your tribune I said an official letter commending him should be sent to the wine merchant." Titianus finished writing down what Longinus said and snapped the tablet shut. "Speratus might not know the name, but my warehouse manager will." He pointed at Probus, who stood, shoulders drooping, with several of Titianus's own workers who'd brought buckets to join the fight. "Don't let any of the others who helped leave until I talk to them."

Longinus strode away to pass on his order, and Titianus headed toward his own men.

Probus greeted him with a sooty face and a warm smile. "It's good to see you, Master Titus. It's been too long."

Titianus removed his helmet and tucked it under his arm. "You tend my affairs so well I don't need to come often." He tipped his head toward the ruins. "There's a dead man in what was probably the office. Do you know who that might be?"

The smile vanished. "The warehouse belongs to Faustus Cornelius Lupus. It would have been closed for the night when we heard about the fire, but Lupus often works late."

"Where does he live? In the warehouse?"

"I sometimes see him ride past toward Rome, but more often he heads the other way."

"Are there others who live there?"

"Twenty or so. Most nights they're there, but Lupus sometimes lets everyone go to the circus and the baths. Then he's there alone. I didn't see any of them carrying water, so he probably gave them today off."

A fit of coughing racked Probus, and when it ended, the older man wiped at the sweat on his forehead, making streaks of soot.

Titianus placed a hand on his manager's shoulder. It had been too long since he'd come. He should have seen right away that Probus wasn't as strong as he remembered him. "Can one of your men write down what I tell him?"

"Sciurus." Probus summoned a short, scrawny, dark-haired youth with a curl of his fingers. He placed both hands on the young man's narrow shoulders and squeezed. "I've begun training Sciurus to help me. I bought him cheap three years ago from a wine merchant who was eager to dispose of his slaves before moving back to Corinth. He could read and write Greek already, and he's learned to write Latin well. He's good with numbers, too."

He smiled down at the boy, who had glanced at Titianus and then kept his eyes lowered. "It's good to have some young legs to run errands faster than I can go myself."

"Sciurus." When Titianus spoke his name, the boy raised his head. "Someone was murdered before the fire, and it's my job to find the murderer. You'll be helping me as I question people. I want you to write down what they say, whether Greek or Latin. Can you do that?"

The boy's eyes widened, then grew somber. "Yes, master. I can write fast so you'll have everything they say."

"Good. You'll stay with me until I finish here. Get a tablet and stylus from the bag on my horse."

The boy scurried away, and Titianus turned to the rest of his men. "You did well helping today. Probus will arrange for a special meal tomorrow for it. You can go home now."

His workers headed toward his warehouse, but Probus stayed. "Is there anything I can do to help?"

"The murder isn't all. The fire might have been set to cover it. I'll know after Centurion Longinus decides where and how the fire started. If it was in the office, then it could be both murder and arson." Titianus replaced his helmet. "I'll be back tomorrow to talk with you about who might have wanted Lupus dead, but I don't want you asking around. I don't want you dead and this warehouse burned as well. In fact, until I catch the one responsible, put a man or two on guard at night, and send me word right away about anything suspicious."

"As you wish. But I won't be alive forever to tend to matters here. Sciurus is one you can trust to serve you as I would. In time, he'll be able to manage the business as I have."

"As you'll continue to do for many years. But it's good you're training him to help. Now, go home and rest."

Titianus watched Probus as he trudged back to the family warehouse. He was ready to go back to the fortress and rest himself, but first he would gather enough information from the men who'd been on the street when the aquarius gathered his volunteers so he could find and talk to each of them later.

"Sciurus."

"Yes, master."

Titianus startled and turned. The boy had walked up behind him, tablet in hand, silent as a hunting owl. "Listen carefully, and write down all you can. Watch the men as I talk to them, and if you see anything suspicious, make a note of that, too."

"Yes, master. I'll watch the others as well as they watch you question someone. Truth leaks out of dishonest men when they don't think someone important is watching." The boy opened the tablet and gripped the stylus, its tip hovering just above the wax. He stood erect, shoulders squared, reminding Titianus of the first orderly he had.

"There are a lot of them, master. I'll need a second tablet."

Titianus held out his hand. "I'll hold that one. Go get another."

Before Titianus reached the cluster of men, Sciurus was back at his side.

When he cleared his throat, all eyes turned on him. "Rome thanks you for your help in keeping this fire from spreading. Since no one in charge of the warehouse is here to report what started it, I'll be talking to all of you in the next few days." From the corner of his eye, he caught Sciurus moving a little to the side so the boy could watch the men without them realizing as Titianus spoke with each.

"For the record, I need your name, whether you are citizen, free, or slave, and where I can find you during the next three days. You can leave after I get that information. I'll start with you." He pointed at the overseer who'd first reported the fire. Then, one by one, the men filed past him, providing the information he required.

A handful of the slaves who weren't from the nearby warehouses seemed tense, but not beyond what he expected if they were in the area without specific orders from their master. He had six to go when Sciurus approached, hand out for the blank tablet. Titianus exchanged it for the full one, and the boy stepped off to the side and kept writing as the final few spoke.

As Titianus watched the last man walk away, the snap of a tablet closing drew his gaze back to his helper. "Did you get everything?"

"Yes, master."

"I have one more thing for you to do before you go back to Probus."

A quick nod and a hand held out to take the second tablet was the boy's answer. As they walked back to his horse, Sciurus cleared his throat. "I noticed something unusual, master."

Titianus glanced down at him. "Did you write it down?"

"No, because I'd already given you the tablet with his name."

"What is it?"

"I looked at all their hands."

Titianus's brow furrowed. "Their hands."

"Yes. To see if their hands matched what they said."

"Matched?"

"Yes, like whether someone who said he worked down here had hands to show it. Cuts, callouses, scars."

Titianus raised an eyebrow. "Did they?"

"Mostly. Speratus didn't, but he's a free overseer, so that no surprise. But there was another who said he worked the docks south of here—Tenax. He was dressed like he might, but his hands looked…soft. When you talked with him, he put his hands behind his back, and when he walked away, he made sure you wouldn't see the palms. Maybe he had fresh blisters."

One corner of Titianus's mouth rose. After a first glance, few would give the nondescript Greek youth a second thought. But the quick mind behind those dark brown eyes had spotted something even he had missed. A tribune in uniform could never watch unobserved, but a youth on an errand for his master…that was a different matter. Probus always planned ahead and took advantage of a good deal when he saw it, but whatever he paid for Sciurus, his manager got more than he bargained for.

When they reached his horse, Titianus traded the two tablets filled with names for two fresh ones. "I have one more task for you before you go back to Probus. Centurion Longinus knows fires well, and he'll be inspecting the rubble before he returns to barracks."

He led Sciurus to where Longinus stood, arms crossed, watching his men check for hotspots that might reignite.

"Did you need something, tribune?"

13

"As you make your inspection, Sciurus will follow you around to write down anything you think I should know. If anything is even slightly odd, I want that in my records. Have one of your men escort him back to my warehouse when you're through. Watch to see if they're followed. Whoever started the fire might still be close. I'll be back tomorrow to start the investigation."

Longinus glanced at Sciurus, and his lips twitched. "As you wish, tribune."

When Titianus returned to his stallion and mounted, he scanned the small crowd that had gathered to see the aftermath of the fire. Did any of them know someone who was involved? If they didn't know, did they suspect? Would they tell anyone if they did?

Too many didn't want to get involved, and the guilty too often escaped when the innocent chose to do nothing.

Honor above all else, honor no matter the cost...that's what he'd learned from Gnaeus Lenaeus, the good man who'd tutored him in the ways of a scholar, and from Marcus Brutus, the equestrian who'd mentored him as he learned how to fight like an officer of Rome.

He kicked his horse into a trot. He'd wash off the soot and the smell of smoke when he got back to the fortress. But more important than a clean body was a clear conscience, and only a man of honor could claim that.

Chapter 3

SOMEONE TO BLAME

The Lenaeus town house, Day 2

When Pompeia entered the library with an armful of scrolls and a wax tablet in her hand, her father was already there. One arm cradled some scrolls he'd used with his students as he returned each to its cubicle. She set her smaller stack on the desk beside the rest of his and picked up the Latin primer she'd created for foreign women who wanted to learn the Imperial language.

Father greeted her with his warmest smile. "How did your newest student do?"

She returned the primer to the cubicle where she stored the other scrolls she'd created. What suited young Romans wasn't useful for teaching Latin and Greek to the wives and daughters of wealthy foreigners and freedmen. Some wanted their women to speak the two common languages of the Empire, but a man could never spend so much time with the females of their family without triggering vicious gossip. As a well-bred Roman maiden with impeccable manners, the daughter of a teacher of rhetoric who trained the Roman elite, Pompeia was no threat to anyone's virtue, real or imaginary.

"Khepri is so eager to learn. Better still, her enthusiasm rubbed off on Rezia and Talibah. Until today, I was thinking Talibah's father couldn't have chosen a less suitable name. 'Seeker of knowledge' was the last way I'd describe her. I've been praying that she wouldn't be held up as an example of how poorly I teach."

Pompeia's eye roll broadened her father's smile. "I hope you're not teaching her that face as well." He kissed her forehead. "Your brother and I find it endearing, but most men wouldn't."

"I don't do it where students will see. Anyway, Khepri is only a little older and so pretty." Pompeia chuckled. "She married only a month ago. When she told them her husband was so handsome the gods would be jealous, so strong he could do anything, and so eager for her to learn Latin because every wife of a wealthy merchant should know it, they both focused on the lesson like they never had before."

She opened the tablet and held it out for her father to read. "Before Khepri left, she wrote out my name in hieroglyphics. She showed me how each glyph is really a sound, like our alphabet, and she's going to teach me how to write with them."

Carrying several scrolls in a cylindrical basket, Kaeso came through the door, humming. "I learned something today as well. You know that fire we saw yesterday?"

Pompeia nodded.

"The shipping overseer for Gaius Norbanus's father was the one who reported it to the Vigiles. Then he stayed to help fight it. He overheard the centurion and a tribune talking about a man they found inside, and it looked like a murder. They suspect the fire was arson to cover it up."

Pompeia's hands flew up to cover her mouth as she gasped. "That's terrible! Was anyone else hurt?"

"It burned to the ground, but it seems no one else was in the building. The men who work there weren't even around to help fight the fire."

"With the warehouse gone, what will happen to all the workers?"

Father patted her arm. "Any who are free can find work with someone else. The slaves...if he isn't going to rebuild, the owner might keep a few, but he'll probably sell most of them right away. Men have to eat whether they're working or not, and that expense will lead to prompt sales."

"That's so sad. It will separate men who've become friends and maybe even families."

Father wrapped his arm around her shoulder. "Most Romans don't consider that. The slaves of their familia aren't true family. They aren't brothers and sisters in Christ, like we are in this house."

"I'll pray that their owner is more merciful than mercenary, or at least that the next place they serve will be as good or better."

"Sometimes changing owners is a blessing." Kaeso placed his first scroll back in its cubicle. "God can work all things together for good, even for those who don't yet know Him."

The Cornelius Rufinus town house, Day 2

The golden light of early morning had driven back the shadows from one side of the street as Arcanus made his way to the Rufinus town house. But after last night, it felt safer to walk on the shadowed side. It was almost an hour before Rufinus's secretary would open the front door for the salutation to begin, but at least twenty men stood waiting when Arcanus rounded the corner. Normally, he would have joined them and listened for gossip to share later with his patron, but today was not normal. Life might never be normal again. He retraced his steps along the wall and knocked on the stableyard gate.

By now, Tribune Titianus would know the dead man was Faustus Cornelius Lupus. Lupus's full name would reveal he was a freedman. Faustus was rare enough as a first name that the tribune would easily narrow the list of potential patrons to one man: Faustus Cornelius Rufinus.

It was vital that Rufinus knew what had happened before Titianus came sniffing around with questions. It might be lethal for Arcanus if Rufinus let slip that he'd been sent to the warehouse before his patron knew where that could lead.

A small panel slid sideways to reveal an eyeball; then the gate swung open enough for him to slip in before it closed again.

Rufinus might be in the triclinium finishing his breakfast, but it was more likely that he'd be reading in the *tablinum* before receiving the first client. Arcanus came often enough to see his patron about business that no one would have given him a second glance as he walked through the peristyle garden. But today the garden was empty.

The tablinum's door for clients opened into the atrium, but its back wall was made of sliding panels that opened into the peristyle, turning the room into an extension of the garden. Today, one of the panels was partly open, and Arcanus's patron was visible as he stood by a side table where he'd placed some scrolls.

"May I speak with you, *Patronus?*"

Rufinus's head turned toward Arcanus, and the senator's eyebrow rose. "Come in."

Arcanus slid the panel halfway across the entrance. One clay lamp still burned on the bronze lampstand, and a few small openings across the top of the peristyle wall let in light as well. What he had to say was better spoken in a dimly lit room than in bright light. He crossed the room to close the atrium door.

He returned for one quick glance to make certain the peristyle remained empty before he pulled the panel the rest of the way. As he pressed his back against it, he cleared his throat. "When I went to talk to Lupus, there was a problem."

"What kind of problem?" Rufinus turned to half-sit on the table and crossed his arms.

"I gave him your message, and then he laughed. He said he'd keep doing whatever he wanted because you couldn't risk him telling anyone what you've been doing. You'd never become consul if your ownership of an illegal business was known."

A clenched jaw was Rufinus's only response.

"You gave him everything. What he said, the way he said it...it angered me. I slapped the side of his head." Arcanus rubbed the back of his neck. "He pulled a club from his desk drawer and hit me here." He barely touched the bump above his ear that was concealed by his curly black hair. "We fought. I took the club and hit him back." He dropped his gaze to Rufinus's feet. "I didn't mean to, but I killed him."

Rufinus inhaled sharply. "Did anyone see you?"

"No." He raised his eyes and drew a deep breath. "A stand with a lot of clay lamps on it got knocked over as we struggled. Some were lit. The oil went everywhere, and the flames followed it. Maybe I could have put it out if I'd started right away. But I'd just killed Lupus, and I panicked. I waited too long. Before I could do anything, the door curtain caught fire and then the ceiling." He swallowed hard. "Your warehouse burned to the ground."

Rufinus's eyebrows plunged as his mouth curved down. "Everything?"

"Not the office. A tribune of the Urban Cohort saw Lupus. He and the centurion think it was murder and the fire was arson to hide it."

"Which tribune?"

"Tribune Titianus."

A string of curses erupted from Rufinus, each made more potent by the chill overlaying a voice too quiet to penetrate the closed doors. Arcanus clasped his hands so Rufinus wouldn't see them trembling. He lowered his head and stared at his feet. In all his years serving Rufinus, first as master and then as patron, he'd never seen him lose his temper.

The softly spoken words faded into silence. Harsh breathing quieted. Arcanus sneaked a glance at his patron and found him leaning against the table, arms still crossed.

"You were a fool to let the fire burn without trying to stop it. You added what looks like arson to what could have been excused as self-defense. I could have arranged the right judge to ensure a self-defense ruling."

"I'm sorry, Patronus. I got so angry when he threatened to reveal you owned the business when you shouldn't. He owed you everything, and he was ready to betray you. I wasn't thinking about the fire when we were fighting, and when I did, it was too late to do anything."

Rufinus drew a deep breath and huffed it out. "What's done is done. I would say it was over, except Titianus will be the one investigating. The man never quits until he solves a crime and brings someone to justice. So, before he can blame you and therefore me, we might have to arrange for him to blame someone else."

Arcanus rubbed his chin. "We'll need to choose someone who might have had a reason for killing him and setting the fire. Then we can put in place whatever is needed to make him look guilty. Maybe someone Lupus underbid for a government contract. He was selling shoddy goods for only a little less than well-made ones. A few people died because of that, so maybe you could choose someone who'd want revenge." Arcanus ran his hand through his hair and cringed when he touched the bump. "But any records probably burned."

"Only if he kept everything at the warehouse. He was probably wise enough to keep the important ones at his house. That will give us a chance to remove them and add something to serve our purpose. Maybe a record of him sharing the illegal profits. Forge some letters to look like he dabbled in extortion." One corner of Rufinus's mouth rose. "He planned to try it on me, so he was already an extortionist."

The flicker of amusement vanished from his eyes. "Lupus's strongbox is in his library. I lent him a number of my scrolls. When you take a chest to retrieve them, you can plant what we want Titianus to find." Rufinus's brow furrowed. "Can you pick a lock?"

Arcanus shrugged. "I've gained many skills in the years I've served you. A lock is no problem."

As the fear of discovery drained away, Arcanus felt his smile grow. It was no surprise that Rufinus would soon be a consul of Rome. "I can write something based on what Lupus did himself, but with other men blamed. Perhaps some senator who has opposed you too often?"

"You know who those are. Pick one or two and take care of it today."

"Let's go." The voice of Rufinus's son Gaius came from the top of the wall, making its way through the small openings that let in light…and let out sound.

Arcanus's heart pounded like the hooves of a chariot team straining to cross the finish line first. There had been no one in the peristyle when he pulled the open panel shut. When had someone come in? Had they been close enough to hear? If so, how much?

"No one was out there when I came in, Patronus." His whisper felt like a shout.

Rufinus raised one finger to his lips. Arcanus clamped his lips shut. Then Rufinus pushed off the table and walked to the first panel that would open. He slid it open just enough to see down the garden toward the entrance to the stableyard. Arcanus moved behind him for a view, but he stayed back in the shadows.

Gaius and another young man were passing through the archway. As they did, the boy Arcanus didn't know looked back over his shoulder. He blinked twice as he paused, and his lips twitched before he followed Gaius and disappeared from sight.

"Who was that?" Arcanus's whisper echoed around the room.

Rufinus closed the panel. "Tertius Valerius Flaccus. He's Gaius's close friend. They both study rhetoric with Pompeius Lenaeus and train at the Ludus Bruti."

"Do you think he heard?"

"I don't know. I was well away from the wall, and we weren't speaking loudly like Gaius was. So, perhaps not."

Arcanus took a few deep breaths, trying to slow his heartbeat. Rufinus was at the table near the opposite wall, far from the openings, but he'd been standing right below them.

With steepled fingers, Rufinus rubbed both sides of his nose. "But I can find out tonight. Tertius is supposed to join us for dinner, and boys like him can never hide their thoughts well enough to fool me."

He squared his shoulders. "Go prepare those letters. Titianus moves quickly, so there's no time to waste. They should be in Lupus's strongbox no later than tomorrow morning. I have a tablet listing what I loaned him in my library. Everyone saw the smoke yesterday, so I expect someone will tell me during the salutation that Lupus died in the fire. Return this afternoon for the list, and you can pick up my scrolls and lay the false trail for Rome's relentless tribune before sundown."

Chapter 4

THE HYPOTHETICAL QUESTION

The Lenaeus School of Rhetoric, morning of Day 3

With his eyes focused on the open scroll, Gnaeus Lenaeus walked into the room where he taught rhetoric to a mix of equestrian and senatorial youths. The theme of Book VI of Quintilianus's *Institutio Oratoria*, was the use of laughter as a tool of persuasion. It was one of his favorites to share with his students.

"Rhetor Lenaeus."

At the sound of a human voice, Lenaeus jumped. None of the boys should have arrived yet, but Tertius Flaccus stood in the darkest corner of the room.

"Flaccus. You're early today."

"I wanted to ask something before everyone got here." Flaccus's voice had mostly lowered to the pitch of a man's, but a trace of the boy's voice edged his words.

Lenaeus set the scroll on the side table and half-sat on the edge. "What's your question?"

The youth cleared his throat. "It's about a moral quandary…hypothetical, of course."

Lenaeus nodded once, his usual way of giving permission to speak.

Tertius rubbed his hands on his thighs, then adjusted his toga after the folds slipped down his left arm. "Suppose someone overheard a conversation about a man who was found dead after a fire, and there was a tribune who thought it was murder and arson. Suppose the men were talking about how a business one of them shouldn't own but did had sold shoddy goods and how when they didn't work right, some people died. Suppose the dead man was part of that, and he was killed so he wouldn't tell anyone."

Tertius dropped his gaze to the floor. "They talked about making it look like someone else sold the goods that led to those deaths. They planned to make it look like the dead man was making that innocent man pay to keep him quiet. Then the tribune would think the innocent one had the dead one murdered." He shifted his gaze back to Lenaeus. "If a man of honor heard that, what should he do?"

The story had shifted from "suppose" to a plain statement of what they said and did, as if it had really happened. The haunted look in Tertius's eyes—that could only mean this was no hypothetical question, and some of the people involved were important to him. Was it his father? The father of a close friend? There were many businesses that were illegal for a senator to own, but with so much profit to be made, some ignored the law.

"I see three issues here. First is the selling of defective goods that led to people dying. Second is killing to hide that crime and the arson to cover up the killing. Third is the plan to shift the blame to an innocent man to avoid punishment." Lenaeus crossed his arms. "So, what do you think the one who heard should do?"

Tertius drew a deep breath, then held it without speaking. He rubbed the back of his neck. "Well…I see two things he might do. The first is to tell someone in authority that he suspects the deaths of a few people were due to money-saving shortcuts where full price was charged but full value wasn't delivered. That the man found after the fire was killed so he couldn't reveal who else was part of that. That the guilty men planned to make an innocent man look guilty."

He massaged the back of his neck. "But if a man of honor thought telling the authorities would be too dangerous, especially if he's wrong, he might warn the man they planned to blame. That's assuming he knew who that was."

"But is warning the one they would frame enough? The crime still goes unpunished."

"Yes, but what if he knew one of the men in the conversation, and he's a really good man? What if he can't believe that man would ever do such a thing deliberately? Maybe he misunderstood. Reporting what he thought he heard could destroy that man and his family."

"Wrong choices always affect other people, even innocent ones. What about the man they intend to blame and his family?"

"But if the one they blame really hasn't done anything wrong, surely that would come out in the investigation. Or at least it should if the tribune is as good at investigating as they think."

Youthful laughter echoed in the atrium before three young Romans entered the room. Tertius's eyes widened; then he pasted on a smile.

Gaius Rufinus sat at the table he and Tertius usually shared. "I stopped by your house to get you."

"I wanted to ask Rhetor Leneaus about something from yesterday." The smile Tertius offered Lenaeus didn't match the worry lingering in his eyes. "I think I understand now, but if I don't, I'll ask again later."

Tertius took his chair by Gaius, but the sidewise glance he cast at his best friend spoke more than words.

If it was Gaius's father, extreme caution was required. Senator Rufinus moved in the highest circles and had the Emperor's ear. Rumor had it that he might become consul soon. Any accusation would be dangerous for a person of lower standing to make, and even more so for a youth.

The name of the man who would be set up to take any blame—Lenaeus didn't know it. It was unlikely to be someone he knew personally. How would any senator respond to a boy or his tutor telling him a fellow senator planned to blame him for murder?

Gaius nudged Tertius. "Where were you last night? We expected you for dinner."

Tertius shrugged. "My father had something else for me to do."

"What?" Gaius rolled his stylus between his fingers.

Tertius opened his tablet. "I can't tell you."

Lenaeus cleared his throat. "You two can talk later. It's time to begin."

As Lenaeus taught about humor as a tool for an orator, the boys laughed at all the usual places. They were still smiling when he rolled up the scroll. "That will be all for today."

As the boys placed tablets and styluses into their satchels, Lenaeus strolled to Tertius's side. "Did you still need some help?"

Tertius swallowed. "Not today." He slung the satchel on his shoulder and joined Gaius and the other two boys who went from his school to the Ludus Bruti to train with swords.

He walked beside Gaius as they passed out the door. "I told Father I'm moving up to Fortis today. He said he'll come watch me next week."

As the boys' voices faded, Lenaeus rubbed his jaw. Perhaps it wasn't Rufinus, but was the senator in Tertius's story the father of one of his students?

If they'd killed one man already to hide what they'd done, was Tertius in danger, too?

Afternoon of Day 3

When Pompeia's handmaid knocked on the door to their town house, the girl's brother opened it.

"You should have seen him. Sanura's boy is so cute." Lilia tousled Theo's hair as she walked past, and he ran his fingers through it to get it back in place. "Almost as cute as you were."

His eye roll was his only answer.

Pompeia mussed his hair as well, but she smoothed it before taking her hand away. "Ciconia and I thought you were the cuddliest baby in the world. But mothers are known to be biased, and you were the first baby I ever held. That was more than ten years ago, and now that I've seen the children of several of my students, well…you're still in the top three."

Another eye roll from the curly haired boy was accompanied by a grin.

Sanura's baby was beautiful, and Pompeia couldn't have been happier for her. But as she she held someone else's child, Septimus's words played at the back of her head. She would never marry a man who didn't follow her Lord, and that meant she'd probably never marry. The joy of a new mother might never be hers.

Lilia set down the basket that had held the small blanket Pompeia wove for the new baby and a loaf of Ciconia's honey-and-rosemary bread that Sanura loved. It always delighted her Egyptian students when Pompeia taught Roman table manners. Lilia took one end of Pompeia's palla, and Pompeia turned to unwrap the long rectangle of fabric. As her maid folded it, Pompeia strolled to the door of her father's classroom and froze in the doorway.

He sat at one of the student tables, eyes closed, hands clasped against his forehead. Why was he praying in the public part of the house while Kaeso still had students with him?

"Father?" His eyes opened, but the smile he gave her looked forced. "Is something wrong?"

He waved her forward. "Close the door."

She swung the door shut and slid the bolt. "What is it?"

"I face a quandary. One of my students told me about something the father of his friend was doing. He started with a question about what would be the moral thing to do, but as he spoke, I could see the problem was real, not hypothetical, as he claimed. If what he said is true, someone is already dead, and innocent people might be blamed for the crime."

Father rubbed his jaw. "I've been asking God for guidance. I don't know enough to act yet, but I'm not certain what I could do that wouldn't endanger our familia." He squeezed his neck. "He was starting to give me details when the other students came. After class, he seemed in a hurry to leave. He said I'd answered his question, but I know I hadn't. I think he didn't want one of the other boys to hear."

"Are you certain what he described really happened?" She pulled over a chair and sat, facing him across the table.

"Almost, but it is possible that it was simply a tale well told. He's good at that. But if it is true, I must do something. The question is what." He massaged the back of his neck. "If he won't or can't report it, should I? If so, to whom? The father of his friend would either be high in Roman political circles or a wealthy equestrian. If I talk with anyone in authority and that man learns I raised the question…that poses a serious risk, whether the story is true or not.

He ran his fingers through his hair. "I'd have made a powerful enemy, and most of the Roman elite wouldn't think twice about speaking evil of an ordinary citizen like me. They often do it to each other. Any lie might damage my reputation so badly that men who want a Quintilian education for their sons would think me unsuitable to have charge of them."

Pompeia took his hand. "Can you talk to the one who might be hurt directly?"

"If I knew names, I could warn the one who's in danger. But if it's someone I don't know personally, why would he even listen to a mere tutor when I accuse a senatorial colleague he doesn't suspect is his enemy?"

She squeezed his hand before leaning back. "He probably wouldn't."

He traced a wiggle in the grain of the tabletop. "I don't want to draw attention to our family from any who might consider me a problem to be disposed of. That's especially true because of our faith. If that became known, others beyond our familia could be put at risk as well."

Pompeia placed both palms on the table as she stood. "It's more important to do the right thing than the safe thing."

Lenaeus's hand covered hers. "But there might be an honorable path that can protect the innocent without endangering us. Before I learn more, I probably shouldn't do anything."

She walked around behind him and kneaded his neck muscles until they relaxed. "There's no point in worrying about this until you're certain it's something real. Remember what Jesus said about worry. 'Therefore don't be anxious for tomorrow, for tomorrow will be anxious for itself. Each day's own evil is sufficient.'"

"This evil would be sufficient for several days if it's not hypothetical. But as you say, worrying about it now is fruitless." Father patted her hand and smiled up at her. "Thank you for reminding me. On a more pleasant topic, how were Sanura and her new baby?"

"She looked tired, but her smile when she looked at her son...I've never seen her look more beautiful." One final squeeze, and she lowered her hands. "But love can do that to the plainest faces."

Father's eyes saddened, and he sighed. "As your father, I should have already found you a good husband. You deserve the joy of loving your own children."

"But you don't know anyone who follows our Lord who's suitable, and nothing else will do for me."

"I could ask Torquatus. Maybe he knows someone."

"He has to be as quiet about his faith as we do, maybe more since he's a senator. Even his own wife doesn't know, only Glyptus."

"But what will happen to you when I'm gone?"

"I can make a living teaching with Kaeso, just as I've done with you." She rested her cheek on the top of his head. "Truly, I'm content as I am. If it's God's will for me to marry someday, He'll arrange the match Himself." She kissed his cheek before straightening. "But I expect to oversee your household for many years yet."

"If it's God's will."

"I'm sure that it is." She opened the scroll that lay on the table and scanned it. "Quintilian's teaching on laughter for persuasion. I expect the boys loved that lesson."

Father rose. "It's my favorite, too. Tomorrow they'll get a chance to practice on each other."

"I may listen at the door. Laughter fills the heart with joy." She bent to kiss his cheek. "And a good meal fills the stomach with contentment. I'll go see if Ciconia needs help with anything."

As she left the room, she looked over her shoulder. Father was praying again, but the furrows were gone from his forehead, and his mouth curved up, not down. Worry over what might be had been replaced by peace for this moment in God's presence.

She rested her hand on her stomach. Would she ever feel her own babe kick, as Sanura's boy had the day of her final lesson? Only a husband who loved her Lord as much as she did would do. Was such a man waiting for her somewhere? Or was Septimus right that she'd never find one?

She shook her head to chase away the doubts. God could work all things for good for those who loved him. What that would look like in her life, only time would tell.

The Rufinus town house, evening of Day 3

When Rufinus entered the triclinium, his son Gaius was already sitting on the edge of the dining couch...alone.

"Where's Tertius? Since he didn't join us last night, I expected him tonight."

Gaius shrugged. "Something came up that he couldn't."

"Did he say what?" Rufinus sat and swung his legs up on the couch and leaned on his left arm. A nod to the slave serving at dinner sent the youth scurrying toward the kitchen for the hot portion of the first course.

"No." Gaius copied his father's movement and reached for a slice of cheese. "But we didn't get to talk much. When I reached his house this morning, he'd already left. He was talking with Rhetor Lenaeus when I got to the school, so we didn't have time before the class started."

"Was he asking for help with a speech? I could offer some advice when he dines here."

"I don't think so. He does better than most of us. When Rhetor Lenaeus asked if he needed to finish their conversation after class, Tertius said he had the answer he needed." Gaius leaned forward to get another slice of cheese. "I think he didn't feel well today. We learned about laughter as a tool of persuasion, so we were trying to make each other laugh as we walked to the ludus. I thought Lucius was hilarious, but Tertius didn't laugh much." He popped the cheese between his teeth. "He didn't go to the taberna after we finished sparring, either."

"Hmm." Rufinus tapped the lip of his goblet, and the wine slave came from the wall to fill it. "Perhaps he'll feel better tomorrow."

As a string of slaves carried the platters of the salad course in and arranged them on the low table between the three couches, Rufinus's gaze settled on the empty one where Tertius usually reclined. There was little doubt the boy knew too much. The only questions now were how much he heard and what did he tell the rhetor.

Chapter 5

What Should He Do?

The Lenaeus School of Rhetoric, morning of Day 4

Three sharp knocks drew Lenaeus's gaze from his scroll to the door. But it wasn't Tertius, as he'd hoped. The slave who often came with the boy stood before him instead.

"I beg pardon, Rhetor Lenaeus. I come to tell you Master Tertius's grandfather asked for him to come to his estate immediately, and he left shortly after dawn."

"When do you expect him to return?"

"I don't know, Rhetor."

"Is his grandfather well?" There were few coincidences in life, and a small voice inside whispered this was not one of them.

"No one said, Rhetor, but I think he is."

"Thank whoever sent the message. Tell him Tertius will be missed, and we all hope he'll soon join us again."

"Yes, Rhetor." The slave bowed and left.

This news of Tertius's departure triggered Lenaeus's frown. Had Tertius talked with his father already? If so, was Flaccus sending his son out of Rome where he wouldn't be able to do either of the things an honorable man would feel compelled to do?

He ran his fingers through his hair. If Tertius was now unable to do anything to protect the innocent, what was the right thing to do himself? Could he be certain what Tertius said really happened? Had the boy misinterpreted what the grown men were saying?

If it was true, he couldn't keep silent. But it would be dangerous to go to the authorities. Even an anonymous report could lead to revealing his name and making an enemy.

God, what should I do? I don't know the details of the crime. I don't know who the targeted men are. I don't know if it's Tertius's father or someone else who's involved.

His lips tightened. If he were a betting man, he'd bet it was Gaius's father. Rufinus's ambition to become consul was well known, and rumor was he'd achieve it soon. He might do anything to avoid even a whiff of scandal about himself...or to create a lingering odor around his opponents.

He rolled the scroll to reveal the next panel. He'd read only the first line before his mind looped back to Tertius's revelation. What he could report was only second-hand information from a youth who was no longer in Rome to confirm it. Besides, no one should make an accusation without solid proof, and he had none. No proof and no idea who the men might be that Rufinus or Flaccus had targeted to blame.

All he could do was pray that the one investigating the crime was wise enough to see through the lies so only the guilty would pay.

The Rufinus town house, Day 5

Arcanus sat on a bench in the atrium, and it was all he could do to keep his leg from bouncing. Rufinus's secretary always made him the last person to speak with his patron during the salutation. He'd been waiting at least three hours ago, and just when he thought it was his turn, four more men came to curry favor with the patronus.

As the last one strolled out of the tablinum, the secretary waved him over and escorted him in.

"Arcanus." Rufinus lounged on the throne-like chair he used while listening to petitions from clients. "Are you the last?"

"I am, Patronus, and I'd like to speak with you..." He pointed up at the openings near the ceiling. "In a room without those."

"Come upstairs." Rufinus rose and led him to the room at the head of the balcony stairs.

As Arcanus closed and bolted the door, Rufinus strolled to the window overlooking the marble and concrete buildings in the center of Rome.

Arcanus joined him. "I prepared some letters and accounting tablets and planted them in Lupus's strongbox. When Titianus sees the names, he'll focus his investigation on G—"

"Stop." Rufinus raised one hand. "I don't want to know whom you picked. When the gossip starts, I'd rather be genuinely surprised." One corner of his mouth lifted. "There are limits to my skill as an actor."

"As you wish, Patronus." Arcanus cleared his throat. "I've been thinking about whether Gaius's friend overheard too much. Does he act like it?"

"I haven't had the opportunity to watch him." The corners of Rufinus's mouth dipped. "Gaius said he found Tertius talking with their tutor when he got to the school. He didn't join us for dinner last night, but Gaius didn't suspect anything amiss. He thought Tertius simply didn't feel well."

Arcanus took a deep breath and willed his heart to beat slower. "When only you and I knew what happened, your secrets were safe. But if he heard us and talked with his tutor…who knows what that man will do."

"Lenaeus?" A frown accompanied the shake of Rufinus's head. "He follows Quintilianus's approach to teaching rhetoric. I've found the Quintilian style of plain speaking to be more persuasive than the flowery style used by others, and Lenaeus has done a good job teaching Gaius. As for Quintilianus's insistence that a good orator must first and foremost be a man of honor, I think that's true to a point as well."

Rufinus glanced at Arcanus before returning his gaze to the white buildings in the distance. "When Tertius joins us for dinner, he often quotes Quintilianus. He quotes Lenaeus as well."

"That's not good. Would the boy tell him everything he heard?" Arcanus cleared his throat. "Or how you're involved?"

"A good question." Rufinus pinched his lower lip. "Even if he did, I don't think Tertius would mention any names to him. The boys both understand the obligations of friendship. Revealing my name would cause great harm to my son, and I don't think Tertius would choose to do that."

Rufinus's shrug wasn't what Arcanus expected. "He's a respectful son as well. He'd ask his father before he said anything to someone else. Flaccus is under obligation to me. He'd tell his son to say nothing. In fact, he sent word this morning that he'd taken the boy to visit his grandfather in Campania for a while…no doubt to remove the temptation to talk with anyone else about it."

"But the tutor…" Arcanus sucked air between his teeth.

"If Tertius described what he heard without any names, Lenaeus will suspect Flaccus, not me."

"But you can't be certain the boy didn't name you. Tutors don't make much. He might want to add to that with extortion money to keep quiet."

Rufinus snorted. "A Quintilian scholar? I doubt it. He'd be more likely to tell someone in authority what he suspected. But Tertius didn't overhear enough details to be credible. Surely Lenaeus would realize the danger of making such an accusation against any powerful man without proof. If one of my clients spread rumors about his honesty, he'd never get another student, no matter how honorable he really is. No Quintilian rhetor would risk that."

Arcanus fought to keep the amazement off his face. Rufinus had no idea how easily a poor man gave up his scruples when doing so might make him rich. The teacher might think it worth the risk to get enough to live well without working. Thinking any man would only do the honorable thing when he could become wealthy by doing something dishonorable... that was delusional. Rufinus's own illegal businesses were proof of that.

"How many others in Gaius's class? Would his friend have told any of them what he heard?"

Rufinus rubbed the underside of his jaw. "There are six more, all sons of men I know. They usually go to Brutus's ludus when Lenaeus finishes midday, grab a quick lunch after their training, and go to the baths. Gaius would have overheard if Tertius had spoken to one of them on the way to the ludus, and Tertius didn't join them at the taberna after. I'm not concerned about them."

Arcanus lowered his gaze to the floor. Not concerned? How could Rufinus not see the risk? But it wasn't Rufinus whom Tribune Titianus would be accusing of arson. The elite covered for each other, and they wouldn't hold the patron responsible for the death and fire his freedman had caused without being told to.

"That's a relief, Patronus. Titianus's reputation worries me, but he can only find out what someone who knows something can reveal."

"Exactly. He'll believe what he finds hidden in a dead man's strongbox over the suspicions of a teacher, even a respected one." Rufinus turned from the window. "I'm expected at the baths shortly. Anything else?"

Arcanus dredged up a smile. "No, Patronus. Nothing else needs your immediate attention."

Rufinus left the room first, turning along the balcony toward his dressing room, and Arcanus descended the stairs.

As Arcanus left his patron's town house in the wealthy Fagutal region atop the Oppian Hill, he heard the distant roar of the crowd gathered at the amphitheater below. It was almost lunch time. Were those cheers for the last of the *venatores* fighting with beasts? Or were they for the first executions? He'd watched those often enough. Something to fill the time between the beast fights in the morning and the gladiators in the afternoon.

Mostly it was slaves and criminals. They provided some diversion while he waited for the professionals to appear. It was often laughter, not cheers, that greeted those sentenced to *damnatio ad bestias*, especially when Christian men with their women and children died for their ridiculous faith that was treason against Rome.

Or had the fire just been lit in the fuel piled around the feet of an arsonist? Were the screams of a man engulfed in flames being drowned out by the cheers of men applauding that death?

He swallowed hard. Would that be his fate if Rufinus was wrong and the tutor went to the authorities with what he knew?

Chapter 6

THE RIGHT WAY

The Lenaeus town house, Day 5

I t was midday when Arcanus reached the block where Lenaeus taught. He'd timed his arrival to when Gaius and his friends should be leaving for their training at the ludus. He stopped a short way up the street, opposite the direction they would be walking. When a cluster of youths, followed by their attendants, stepped into view, he counted the striped tunics signifying the two noble orders. Seven. With Tertius gone to his grandfather, that was the whole class.

The rhetor should be alone.

He wiped damp hands on the folds of his toga and adjusted the silver signet ring that Rufinus had given him the day he freed him. One deep breath, and Arcanus approached the entrance to the Lenaeus School of Rhetoric. He'd never been inside before, but he'd escorted his patronus's son to the doorway a handful of times when the nine-year-old boy started there. Nothing seemed to have changed in the intervening six years. With a weaver in the shop to the right of the narrow entrance and a potter and shoemaker to the left, no one would suspect so many equestrians and senators wanted their boys schooled there.

But even the best tutors with a well-regarded school needed many students to earn a decent living. Rufinus was naive to think Lenaeus wouldn't try to make extra with what he knew.

No matter how well Lenaeus taught, it was wise to finish a young man's training with an orator who also argued cases in the Roman courts. Gaius would have finished here within a few months. He'd just be moving on sooner when the rhetor died.

Arcanus glanced down to check the draping of his toga. He looked like a wealthy man in the finery bestowed by Rufinus, who appreciated Arcanus's business acumen as he stewarded the patronus's less-than-legal investments. His life had been harder as a boy under Rufinus's father, but what he'd learned as the elder Rufinus's houseslave was what he needed today.

Quintus Flavius Sabinus moved in more exalted circles now, but he came often to dine then. Arcanus had been told to take some stew and wine to the stableyard for Sabinus's bodyguards. As he approached the armed men, they were arguing about the best way to kill someone quickly and un-observed. One favored a cut starting behind the ear and continuing along the jawbone while the other argued for a thrust at an upward angle under the rib cage and into the heart. The heart man insisted that would kill so fast the victim wouldn't cry out, and there was no risk of blood splattering on you like cutting the throat might do. You could make it look like suicide as well.

Arcanus set down the platter on the stack of crates behind them, and as he turned to leave, a meaty hand clamped across his mouth and jerked him against a brawny chest. Before he could utter a sound, the man who liked cutting throats drew the edge of his hand across Arcanus's neck. Then he shoved Arcanus away. As Arcanus scurried back to the kitchen, the body-guard bragged there'd be no blood on you and no sound if you did it right. He'd reached the safety of the kitchen door before he looked back. They were laughing as they tore off some bread to eat with the stew.

One corner of his mouth lifted. Who would have thought that was a lesson he'd find so useful now? Maybe he could cut a throat without sound or blood, but he wouldn't risk it. The heart was a safer choice.

He wouldn't risk being caught with a bloody dagger, either. By leaving it behind, it might even look like suicide...if Fortuna smiled.

He stepped into the alcove and knocked. It was several long moments before the door swung open, revealing a boy who had not yet started his growth spurt.

"Is Rhetor Lenaeus in?"

The boy nodded and invited Arcanus to enter with a sweep of his hand.

Only a few steps took Arcanus through the vestibulum and into the small atrium.

"Tell him Gaius Holconius Macer is here to speak with him privately about my son attending his school."

"Class is over, and he can see you now. Please follow me." The boy led him to the first door on the left. "Master, Holconius Macer wishes to speak with you."

Lenaeus sat at a table by the wall, reading a scroll. At the boy's first word, he looked over his shoulder, then stood. "*Salve*. Do come in."

As he entered, Arcanus closed the door. His gaze settled on the bolt. Locking it would ensure privacy for the deed, but would it seem suspicious? He'd be finished and gone quickly enough. He could risk leaving the door unlocked.

A well-worn toga draped a thin man with graying hair. Crinkles formed at the edge of the rhetor's eyes as he approached, his mouth curved in a welcoming smile, his right arm extended.

Arcanus clasped the offered forearm. As his right hand fell away from that friendly greeting, he slipped it into his toga to reach the dagger on his left hip. Some things were best done quickly.

Lenaeus's hand swept toward a chair by the closest students' table. "Please sit. As you may already know, I teach using the methods of Quintilianus, with his clear style of oratory and an emphasis on becoming a man of honor to become a good orator."

"So I have heard." Arcanus's hand tightened around the dagger's hilt. "You come highly recommended." He withdrew it from the sheath slowly, silently, and kept it hidden inside the toga's folds.

Then he pulled it free, and with one quick thrust, it was done. He left the dagger in place as he stepped back. The trusting eyes widened as the tutor's mouth opened.

But no yell came out. Only one whispered word escaped with his dying sigh.

"*Ignosco…*"

Lenaeus crumpled to the ground, and Arcanus turned away. The bodyguard had been right about where to strike.

As he opened the door, he glanced back. "Thank you for your time, Rhetor. I'll let you know what I decide." He pulled the door shut. With unhurried steps, he walked away.

The boy was sweeping the atrium, and he scurried ahead of Arcanus to open the door to the street. As the door closed behind him, the breath

Arcanus had been half-holding released. Any threat the tutor posed died with him.

No risk now that he'd be hoisted on a pole with flames licking at him.

Rufinus owed Arcanus for taking care of the teacher, even if he thought it unnecessary, but it would be better to never tell his patron just how much he owed.

He lengthened his stride. He'd walked fifty feet before he turned right onto a side street that led down to the Vicus Patricius. He'd gone less than a block when the shakes hit. He seized one hand with the other and pulled both against his chest as he fought to stop them.

He'd made a terrible mistake. He'd left a witness. He should have kept the dagger and killed the boy on his way out.

His stomach roiled, and he clamped his mouth shut to keep from spewing anything down the front of him. The last thing he needed was for Titianus to find people talking about the well-dressed man who didn't look drunk but threw up on himself. Several deep breaths, and everything settled.

Rufinus had killed in battle. Scarcely more than a youth when he struck down his first enemy, had the same weakness hit the young master as he moved away from that kill?

One foot in front of the next...slow breath after slow breath. No one more than glanced at him as Arcanus walked down the slope.

He couldn't go back and do it himself. It had to be silent, swift, just like the killing of Lenaeus had been. The boy would never open the door to him. Most likely, he'd call the men of the house to come catch their master's murderer.

He swallowed hard. He'd done it himself so no one could link him to the murder. But it was clear he needed a professional, someone the boy wouldn't recognize so he could get close enough.

Professional removal of unwanted persons. He'd never used that kind of service before, but he had a good friend who had. It was time to pay him a visit.

Gaius lived on the Cispian Hill, not far from Arcanus's own modest town house. He could drop in with an invitation to join him at the baths. They could discuss it on the way when no unwelcome ears listened.

Then they could relax in the hot water and find some other friends who would remember him being there should the tribune start asking where he'd been when the rhetor died.

It was a steep climb up the path at the end of the street to the brow of the Cispian. The easiest climb from the valley to the top of the Oppian Hill where Trajan's baths sat was up the Clivus Suburanus, and most people went that way. It was easier, but it took a lot longer; that extra time worked to his advantage. With the quick route, most would think he must have been soaking in the hot water when the poor unfortunate rhetor died.

Chapter 7

WHAT FRIENDS ARE FOR

Pompeia placed a ribbon in the codex to mark where she stopped. Apostle Paul had just prayed for the boy who died when he fell out of the third-floor window in Troas. She would finish copying the story later.

She closed her eyes, and a contented sigh escaped. To see that healing power of the Holy Spirit when all were certain their loved one was lost forever…who could doubt they worshiped the One True God after that?

She closed the codex and traced the fish drawn on the cover—two curved lines, touching at one end and crossing near the other to make the tail. For twelve years she'd been making copies of the precious words written inside.

Twelve years ago, Appius Torquatus first shared with Father the letter Publius Drusus wrote his son from the cell under the amphitheater. Drusus made Torquatus promise to read it before sending it on to the condemned man's son. It was the only legacy he could give after the *praetor* confiscated everything before Publius died in the arena for calling Jesus his only Lord.

The two scholars longed to understand why their brilliant friend would choose to die when a meaningless offering to the Roman gods would have spared him. They sought out the writings that guided those who believed like Drusus. Torquatus was rich enough to buy copies, but he was a senator who couldn't risk that interest fueling malicious gossip among Rome's leaders. Even his own wife couldn't be trusted with the secret. So Glyptus,

40

who'd waited in the cell to bring Publius's letter to Torquatus, became his secret agent and later his brother in Christ.

It was safer to study them at Father's house than his, so the gospels written by the apostles Matthew and John, the letter Apostle Paul wrote to the Roman believers, and the gospel by Luke and his book about what the first apostles did remained at the Lenaeus house.

How many copies of those scriptures and the Epistle of Publius had she made in the last twelve years? Dozens, but where they all went after Glyptus took them, she didn't know.

She placed the codex and the papyrus she'd been inscribing into the unadorned chest with the others. She locked it and draped the key chain around her neck before sliding the box under her bed.

Humming a song they sang during worship, she headed downstairs.

Kaeso leaned against the doorframe of his classroom, smiling at the boys he tutored. One waved farewell, and he raised a hand in response. Theo pulled open the door and stood at attention as they passed. Chattering like squirrels, they entered the street with their accompanying slaves, and peace descended in their wake. Kaeso raised his hand again to greet her as she started down the stairs; then he re-entered his room to prepare it for tomorrow.

Father's door was closed so she tapped on it with the pattern of knocks she saved just for him.

Silence. She repeated the sequence, knocking harder. She waited for Father's usual response, "Enter and brighten my day."

More silence. She opened the door enough to stick her head in. Father was lying on the floor, facing away from her.

She shoved the door open so hard it slammed against the wall and ran to him. She dropped to her knees beside him. "Father?

She rolled him toward her. A dagger pierced his chest, a crimson blotch stained his toga, and the eyes that always warmed at her approach stared at her, unseeing.

A scream pierced her ears before she realized it was hers.

Theo dashed into the room and froze. "He killed him! Why did he kill him?" his face crumpled, and tears flooded his cheeks.

Kaeso was three steps behind the boy. He grabbed Theo's arm and spun him around. "Who did this?"

His hands gripped the slender shoulders.

"He said he wanted to talk with Master Gnaeus about his son coming here." Hiccupping sobs racked the boy, and he fought to stop them. "He looked like all the other fathers. He said goodbye to Master as he closed that door." His hand shook as he pointed.

Corax, Ciconia, and Lilia filled the doorway. As a river of tears washed Theo's cheeks again, Ciconia slipped forward, arms open wide. Kaeso released him, and he ran into his mother's embrace.

Pompeia lifted Father's hand to her cheek. Still warm. So many times, he'd cupped her face and stroked her cheek with his thumb.

Never again.

Kaeso knelt beside her, wrapped an arm around her shoulders, and drew her into his side.

His eyes mirrored the anguish in her heart.

With her free hand, she closed Father's eyes. He was seeing Jesus face-to-face now. So many times, he'd told her how he looked forward to that. That death had lost its power over him since the day he believed. That death would separate them here on earth, but someday he'd be with them all forever in the presence of their Lord, where sorrow and tears were no more.

But even though she believed that with her whole heart, even though she knew the truth of it above all other truths, she'd give anything to have that separation in the distant future, not now.

Right now, sorrow was ripping her heart to shreds, and waves of pain swept over and through her, carried by a torrent of tears.

It wasn't every day Septimus had something exciting to share when he joined Kaeso for dinner, but he did today. Lanista Felix had just assigned him to one of the top tier trainers at the Ludus Bruti. It had taken three years of dedication at the ludus and many hours of practice at home with one of his father's bodyguards. But when Felix commented that he would likely become good enough for Africanus if the retired Class 2 gladiator wasn't in Germania with Brutus —it was all he could do to keep from grinning like a fool.

He stepped into the alcove and knocked on the door. One hand was ready to ruffle Theo's hair. That always got an eye roll and a smile as the boy smoothed it.

Instead of the sound of a bolt drawing back, he was met with silence. He knocked again.

After the third time with no answer, he pounded on the door.

He was about to strike again when the door swung inward, and Kaeso, ashen-faced, stood before him.

"What's wrong?" Every muscle tensed, and Septimus froze with his fist in the air.

Kaeso shut his eyes and dragged in a breath. They opened as he let the breath out. "Someone just killed Father."

Septimus stepped inside, bolted the door, and wrapped his arm around his friend's shoulders. Kaeso's eyes closed again, his jaw clenched, and silent sobs shook him.

How long they stood like that, Septimus couldn't tell, but it felt like hours. What should he say? What could he do? No one he cared about had died before. To have a loved one murdered? That was a horror beyond imagining.

He clamped his own jaw as he fought the start of tears. Kaeso was more his brother than Father's other sons were, and Lenaeus was more second father than friend. But the last thing Kaeso needed was for him to let emotion sweep away his ability to think clearly, to make good decisions, and to act.

At last, Kaeso drew a slow, deep breath and stepped away. He squared his shoulders and wiped his eyes. "Pompeia needs me strong." Another deep breath, released slowly. "They all do. I'm paterfamilias now." His jaw started to quiver, and he clenched his teeth. "God help me. I don't know what to do."

"We'll figure that out…together. Take me to him." Septimus draped his arm across Kaeso's shoulders as they walked through the atrium and into the room where his dead friend lay.

Pompeia knelt on the floor by her father, eyes closed, lips moving silently. He'd bet she was praying to the Christian god, for all the good that would do. Dead was dead, and no amount of prayer, even to a god who might be real, could change that.

Corax stood by the wall with his family, and Septimus summoned him with a curl of his fingers. "The first thing we should do is report it." He focused on Corax. "Do you know the guard station where the main streets meet at the edge of Subura?"

"Yes. Where the street to the baths starts up." Corax swiped at the corner of his eye.

"Go there and report someone has been killed, but don't say your master's name. Tell them Septimus Flavius Sabinus, grandson of Quintus, wants Tribune Titianus to come with you right away."

"Titianus?"

"Yes. He's my cousin and the best investigator Rome has. If anyone can find the man who did this, it's him. Say my grandfather's name, and they'll get him for you."

Corax nodded. As he walked past his weeping son, he placed his hand on the boy's shoulder. "Come bolt the door behind me. I'll be back with the tribune as soon as I can."

Septimus squatted beside Pompeia. Her eyes opened, and he took her hand. What to say? "I'm sorry" was what you said when you broke something accidentally or bumped into someone or hurt their feelings. But Lenaeus had taught him when words fail, a friend can hear all you want to say in the silence. He squeezed her hand, and when she squeezed back and looked into his eyes, he knew she heard.

"When Titianus gets here, he'll want to see how he was when you found him."

Pompeia's shoulders slumped. "I looked in when he didn't answer. He was on his side, and I turned him to see what was wrong." Her hand shot up to her mouth, and fresh tears pooled in eyes already red from crying. "Kaeso was still teaching and I was writing upstairs when whoever did this came. I closed his eyes, but no one's touched the dagger." She jerked as she silenced a sob before it escaped. "I held one hand for a while before I put both on his stomach."

Septimus squeezed her hand again before releasing it. "That shouldn't be a problem for him seeing what he needs to. Just tell him what you did."

"He was one of Father's students before we decided to follow Jesus. I was only a girl then, so I never got to know him." She wiped a tear from her cheek.

"Father says he's like a wolf on a blood trail. Nothing stops him until he takes down his quarry." Septimus took her hand and stroked the back with his thumb. "He'll be all business when he comes, but he's not as stone-hearted as he'll seem. He settled for a tribuneship in Rome because his father was dying and his little sisters would need him. He was younger than you when his father left this life. I'm sure he remembers how it felt."

A tentative smile accompanied Pompeia's single nod.

"After your cousin has seen Father"—Kaeso swallowed before a sigh escaped—"I don't know what to do with his body."

Pompeia reached for Kaeso's hand. "Ciconia and I know. I helped her do it for Mother." She bit her lip and swept aside a teardrop.

"But after people pay respects...then what?" Kaeso massaged his neck.

"I don't know." Her brow furrowed. "Father took care of all that."

As Pompeia fought back tears again, Ciconia came forward and wrapped an arm around her. "She didn't believe. He let her relatives do a Roman funeral, like she would have wanted."

After a shuddering breath, Pompeia squared her shoulders and stepped back. "We'll ask Torquatus. He'll know, and he'll help us do it." She swept another tear away.

"Manlius Torquatus?" Septimus's eyebrows rose. Why would one of the leading senators whose wealth rivaled his grandfather's get involved with the funeral of a dead teacher? Torquatus's sons were as old as his father, and his grandsons went to more famous tutors.

"Yes. He and Father have known each other as long as I can remember. They've been closer than brothers for years. He comes...came here often." Her eyes turned toward her father but returned to Septimus after the briefest glance. "He and Father liked to study the same things."

"Write to him, but only tell him your father died suddenly. Say nothing about how, and don't mention your faith. I can have one of Father's slaves deliver it as soon as I get home, but I can't guarantee it won't be read before he does."

Septimus rubbed his jaw. What kind of man came into a house in the middle of the day, killed without anyone knowing, and walked out as if he'd done nothing wrong? A paid assassin. But who would have hired one to kill the kindest man he'd ever known?

He swallowed hard. If they wanted Lenaeus dead, would they kill his children, too?

"Until my cousin figures out who wanted your father dead and why, you can't stay in this house. The murderer might come back to get you."

Kaeso's lips tightened, and he shook his head. "We can't leave. Father's legacy...it won't be much money. All we have is the school. We don't even own the house. I have to keep teaching here. If I don't keep getting paid, I can't pay the rent, and our familia will be out in the street with nothing to live on. If I quit even for a short time, my students will find other teachers."

He squeezed the back of his neck. "Father was the sought-after teacher of rhetoric. The parents of the boys I'm teaching are pleased with their progress, but it was Father's reputation that drew new students."

His shoulders drooped. "Being good at what I do isn't enough. Reputation is everything in this business. I have five people relying on me to support us. Six if you count me. I can't lose the students I have right now."

The sad smile he directed at Pompeia collapsed into straight lips. "What Pompeia and I make together is less than what Father made. I'm not sure how we're going to get by on less than half."

Septimus straightened to his full height. He was four inches taller than his friend, and he knew how to use his size to get his way with his friends at the ludus. Then he relaxed. This was Kaeso, and they always dealt straight with each other. No power games like with the sons of other rich men.

"I understand, but you can't stay here unprotected." He tapped Kaeso's upper arm. "Where would I find a friend to replace you? Or a sister to replace Pompeia? So, for friendship's sake, let me help. Come spend nights at my house. Father has armed men on every entrance and several bodyguards who trained for the arena. You can come back here to teach in the daytime. Father will lend me one of his guards to escort you and watch over everyone while you're here."

"I don't know…" Kaeso scrunched his nose.

"It will let you keep your students, and it will keep you two safe as well." He rubbed under his jaw. "Since reputation is everything, you should tell the students your father died suddenly, but don't say he was murdered in the classroom while you were all in the house. Romans who believe in the gods are superstitious about such things."

Pompeia released a delicate snort. "You wouldn't have to be superstitious for that to bother you, but we have to be truthful."

"That wouldn't be lying. He did die suddenly." Pain clouded her eyes, and he wished he hadn't spoken those words.

"But what would we say when they ask how?"

"Say you can't talk about it yet. That should satisfy. But if they keep asking, say it was his heart. That's completely true."

"But if whoever it was comes back, wouldn't they be in danger?"

"I'd bet against it. It was a professional. He came deliberately to kill your father. Assassins don't kill someone for no reason, and he doesn't pose a threat to your students."

Her eyebrows lowered, and Septimus heard her silent disagreement. He'd never convince Kaeso if he couldn't persuade Pompeia. "Besides, if you're at my house, you'll bring a bodyguard back here with you, and he'll protect everyone in the household, students as well as all of you." He swept his hand toward Ciconia and Lilia. "Your whole familia will be safer while you're here, and Corax can lock everything up tight at night to be safe then."

She still frowned, but her slow nod said she saw his point.

Kaeso shook his head. "Living at your father's house...are you sure he'll want that?" He glanced at Pompeia. "We're not the kind of Romans he's used to."

"Let me worry about convincing him. The only thing is you'll have to hide your faith. He does the regular Roman rites in the morning, but it's a big house. You won't have to be there." A wry chuckle escaped. "He doesn't believe the Roman gods are real any more than I do. Just don't mention you think there's a god who is."

Chapter 8

THE LAST THING HE NEEDED

Guard Station of the Urban Cohort, Day 5

Titianus closed the wax tablet that lay on the desk before him and leaned back in his chair. He usually ended his day at this station that served both the best and the worst parts of Rome: the Baths of Trajan and the elite Fagutal neighborhood just west of it, the Amphitheater and the slums of Subura just north of it, and the mixed residential and business neighborhoods on the western ends of the Viminal and Cispian Hills. His six centurions were good men who watched over their assigned parts of Rome with experienced eyes, but the only way to be certain all was as it should be was to sometimes walk the streets himself and to check the reports regularly. The stack of tablets was tall today.

Petty thefts from cubicles at the baths, a handful of muggings of men who'd drunk too much and stayed out too late, a three-way fight over a taberna waitress who'd made two men think she was available and taken their money before heading toward the door with the third man—it had been a normal day in this part of his domain.

His centurion would assign some men to the baths to catch the thief. He'd contact his Vigiles counterpart to increase night patrols where the muggers were active. As for the fight—they'd paid the taberna owner for what they broke, the owner had refunded the money to the two his slave had cheated, and what happened to her was her owner's business, not Rome's.

He leaned forward to place both elbows on the desk and rubbed his forehead with his fingertips. All was normal for this part of Rome. Not so for the warehouse district where a dead man had been left in a burning building to hide his murder.

Faustus Cornelius Lupus was the owner of the building that burned. Centurion Longinus had still been inspecting the charred remains with Sciurus at his side when the dead man's slaves returned from the baths. Longinus had taken them to Titianus's guard station near the Circus Maximus, the one that oversaw the races, the Forum, and warehouse district. He'd left them in the cells there for Titianus to interrogate.

Titianus could smell the fear when he got there the next morning. Under Roman law, when one slave killed his master, every slave in the household could be executed to send the message that they should have prevented the murder. He'd talked with them one by one, and as each denied any part in the killing and swore Lupus had been well and in his office when they left for the baths, he saw the truth in their terrified eyes. They'd all sworn Lupus was a fair master that no one would have wanted to kill. Several had belonged to much worse men, and their worry over what the next would be like supported his already-formed opinion about their innocence.

But if it wasn't the act of a disgruntled slave who panicked and burned down the building, who wanted Lupus dead and why?

"Tribune." The *optio* who was second in command to his centurion at this station stood in the doorway. "Someone is asking for you by name. Septimus Flavius Sabinus sent him to fetch you."

Titianus lowered his hands to the desk and clasped them. "Sabinus?"

"Yes, tribune."

"Bring him here." Titianus's eyebrows lowered. Why would Manius Sabinus's son be summoning him?

A man of at least forty followed the optio into the room.

"Leave us."

The optio saluted, spun on his heel, and returned to his desk near the station entrance.

Titianus crossed his arms as his gaze raked the man. His tunic was clean enough but far from new. Definitely not the quality Manius put on his house slaves.

"Why did Septimus send you for me?"

The slave clasped his hands at his waist and looked down. After a blink that lasted several times normal, he cleared his throat. "A man has been killed, tribune, and Master Septimus said to come get you." He raised his eyes to Titianus for a moment, then quickly lowered them. "He said you were the best man to find the one who did it."

"Who is this dead man?"

The slave's glance at Titianus was fleeting. "I beg pardon, tribune, but Master Septimus said I wasn't to say the name."

"Where is he?" Titianus was through with the reports. It might be simpler to ride directly back to the Praetorian Fortress after seeing the dead man.

"This end of the Viminal Hill. Not far."

Titianus raised an eyebrow. Viminal Hill? Manius Sabinus mostly stayed at the Sabinus town house in the Fagutal or on one of the family estates northeast of Rome. Why would his son be with a dead man on the Viminal?

"The dead man—a natural death, accident, or murder?"

The slave kept his eyes lowered. "Murder, tribune."

Titianus lifted his helmet from the corner of the desk and settled it on his head. "Take me to him."

As he stepped through the doorway, he glanced toward the common area where at least two dozen soldiers waited to replace the ones who would return from patrol shortly.

"Gellius."

The optio straightened at his desk. "Yes, tribune?"

"Give me four men who can find out whether some shopkeepers saw anything suspicious."

The optio's eyes narrowed. "Asellus, Barbus, Juncus, Lentinus." Four men stood. "Go with the tribune."

Titianus waved his hand toward the outer door. "Lead the way."

As the slave turned east and started up the Vicus Patricius, Titianus's normally straight lips curved down. He already had one murder to solve. The last thing he needed was another that involved a favorite grandson of his ruthless uncle who wielded too much power behind the scenes in Rome.

The Lenaeus town house

Titianus and his men followed the slave up a side street that climbed to the top of the Viminal Hill. When his guide turned off the street onto one

Titianus remembered too well, unease grew behind the impassive mask he wore when leading his troops. He seldom smiled, and his men mirrored his seriousness. That was a deterrent for anyone with bad intent who saw one of his soldiers.

Smiling and laughing implied friendly, and friendly didn't scare people into behaving as they ought. Almost nine years of cool eyes and straight lips on duty had carried over more than he liked with family.

He was barely twenty-two when Father died, making him paterfamilias for his half-sisters, girls of six and eight. With his duties as tribune, it was hard to get away to spend any time with them at the estate south of Rome. Not that they seemed to care. The nurse who'd mothered them since Father's second wife died in childbirth was the only person they loved.

He rarely saw his sisters now they were fourteen and sixteen. They lived with his aunt and her husband at their estate east of Rome. Soon they would move to a town house in the city and enter Roman society to find a husband. That would be much easier in the company of an affable middle-aged man and his warm-hearted wife than with him. All he'd need to do was provide their dowries.

That was fine with him. He never knew what to say to them. He didn't understand why girls were so silly, so moody, so unpredictable. He didn't understand grown women any better.

When the man turned in at the Lenaeus School of Rhetoric, Titianus's jaw clenched. Gnaeus Lenaeus was one of the few men he admired without reservations. No matter who lay dead inside, it would cause problems for his school. And if it was the rhetor himself…

Three knocks, and a boy who'd been crying opened the door. His guide squeezed the boy's shoulder as he passed. Titianus and his four men followed him into the atrium. The clunk of a bolt sliding shut followed the thud of the door closing behind them. The boy slipped past and joined a woman in her forties, a younger one probably under twenty, and his guide by the atrium wall.

On a chair like the one Titianus had used years ago, Septimus sat facing two people on one of the wall benches. The pretty woman…was she Lenaeus's little girl all grown up? Was the young man who sat with his arm around her the small boy she'd splashed in the atrium pool as he squealed with delight?

Their red-rimmed eyes and stricken faces proclaimed what he'd feared. The man who'd shaped his understanding of life more than any other was the victim. He forced himself to slow his breathing as the fire of his anger smoldered, flamed, and licked at the mask of detachment he wore when he asked questions.

Septimus turned his gaze from the pair and rose. "Titianus. I'm glad Corax found you. Gnaeus Lenaeus deserves Rome's best."

"What happened here?"

"Someone came after Lenaeus released his class for the day. He went in to talk with him privately. Then he killed him and walked out without anyone realizing what he'd done."

"How long ago?"

"Right after lunch." Septimus ran his fingers through his hair. "It was three hours or so before Pompeia found him."

Septimus glanced over his shoulder at the grieving pair. "I'm trying to convince Kaeso and Pompeia they should come home with me and be under Father's protection until you catch whoever did this."

Titianus walked over to stand before the young man. "I'm Titus Flavius Titianus, tribune of the XI Urban Cohort. I'll be investigating the murder of Rhetor Lenaeus, and I assure you that I will find the man who did this." He flexed his jaw to loosen it. He'd find the murderer for himself as much as for them.

"But until I do, you should go with Septimus. You'd be fools to reject his offer. Whoever did this walked into a house full of people, killed, and left without raising suspicion that he'd done so. That suggests he's a professional. If he was hired, you don't know whether the one who hired him will decide he needs one or both of you dead as well."

He cast a glance at the woman before focusing his gaze on her brother again. "Until I arrest the man and learn who hired him and why, you can't be certain you aren't targets as well. The Sabinus town house is guarded like a small fortress. There's no safer place in Rome than there."

His mentor was dead, and he'd catch the killer. But if he could also protect the children Lenaeus loved, he would. Staying with Manius was a step in that direction.

Pompeia took her brother's hand, and his eyes turned from Titianus to her. "As long as we can come back here to teach, perhaps we should. Septimus says it's best, and the tribune agrees."

Kaeso squeezed her hand before releasing it. "Very well."

Those words drew a smile and a nod from Septimus. Titianus kept his eyebrow from rising. Maybe it was just habit for the new paterfamilias to defer to his older sister. He'd learn to be in charge soon enough.

"The murderer—can you describe him?"

"Typical Roman. Brown hair and eyes. He wore a plain toga. He said he was looking for a school for his son. Nothing unusual compared to the other men we serve." He looked at the boy with raised eyebrows and got a nod in return."

Titianus turned to his men. "Spread out and ask at the shops for three blocks in all directions. Did they see anyone wearing a toga who caught their attention shortly before or after lunchtime? Anyone who was acting odd in any way. If you find someone, see if you can find another farther along that street or the ones coming off it. Tell those you find I'll speak with them tomorrow."

His men saluted and headed out the door, closing it behind them.

He turned to Kaeso. "I would like to see your father now."

Like was not the right word. The sight of a dead person was never something he liked, and he recoiled from the thought of what he might see when he looked at Lenaeus. He'd rather remember his tutor as he last saw him, not much older than Titianus was now, with a smile and a hand raised in farewell as he asked Fortuna to smile upon the boy who would soon be a man. But as tribune, he'd learned long ago to show no sign of disgust or regret while he examined a corpse.

Pompeia rose. "I found Father." Her eyes closed, and she squared her shoulders before they opened. "Kaeso was dismissing his students when I came downstairs. I'd ended my class early today, or I would have been in the room next to him."

"You help your father teach?"

"Kaeso teaches the younger boys, and I instruct Roman girls in literature, philosophy, and history. I also teach peregrine women who want to learn Latin and how to behave in Roman society."

He nodded without commenting. The little boy in the atrium pool now worked at the family trade. The laughing girl who splashed him had grown into a pretty woman, even with her eyes puffy from crying. She was at least six years older than when most Roman girls were married. But her still living in the Lenaeus's household made some sense if she was working for her father.

She led him into the classroom, and everyone filed in behind them.

Lenaeus lay on the floor, covered by a sheet. His daughter stopped three feet short of it.

"Father was facing away from me when I entered. I knelt and rolled him on his back." She hugged herself as her gaze lingered on the sheet. Her chin quivered until she clamped her teeth. "His eyes were open, and there was so much blood around the dagger."

He bent over and pulled back the sheet. "Did you touch the dagger?"

She squared her shoulders again and blew out a slow breath. "No. It was obvious he was already dead. I closed his eyes and held his hand for a while before placing them like you see there."

Lenaeus's face had wrinkles he didn't remember. Some by his eyes, others by his mouth, and they looked like the traces left by smiles and laughter. He'd seen too many faces after a violent death. For the most part, they weren't much different from those who left this life in the normal way. But something about Lenaeus looked…strangely peaceful. No injuries to the head, no sign of a struggle. Titianus squatted beside him for a closer view of the dagger. It entered the chest at an angle, pushed up from below the ribcage. The placement was right for either a suicide or an expert thrust for a quick kill.

One final view of the face of an old friend, and he drew the sheet back over the body of the man who'd encouraged and guided him.

When he stood, she was looking straight at him, and in those honey-brown eyes he saw the pain of deepest loss. The next questions—they must be asked, but he wished he didn't have to.

"Have you seen the dagger before?"

Her head drew back, and her brother slipped an arm around her. "We don't keep weapons in the house."

Titianus scanned the pair. He wouldn't expect a sword, but any man of Lenaeus's status who was out at night carried a dagger for protection. Rome after dark was a dangerous place, and the vigiles were too few in number to guarantee safety.

"Is there any reason to think he might have ended his own life?"

Her eyes widened. Then her lips curved into a sad smile. "No, tribune. There's not a man in Rome less likely to kill himself."

He stared at her. That question usually brought fresh tears or anger to the women he asked. He'd never before seen a smile.

Kaeso covered his face with steepled fingers, then drew his hands down his cheeks before dropping them to his side. "If only I'd seen the one who did this, maybe I could have prevented it."

Titianus spun on him "You didn't see him?" His frown deepened. Had he sent his men out looking with a worthless description from a man who'd seen nothing?

"No."

"If you didn't, then how do you know what he looks like?"

"I saw him." The soft voice came from behind him. The four from the atrium wall had moved to the wall just inside the doorway.

His cheeks wet with tears, the boy drew a shaky breath. "He said he wanted to talk to Master Gnaeus about his son coming here. I brought him to Master's classroom."

The boy swiped a tear aside and pointed at the doorway. "He stood right there and told the master he would let him know soon if he was going to send his son here. Then he closed the door on Master Gnaeus, and I went to the street door to let him out." His lips quivered. "I didn't know what he'd done." More tears dribbled down his cheeks.

Titianus scanned the boy. Well fed, decent but plain tunic like the man who came for him. "Does Lenaeus own you?"

"Yes."

Chapter 9

The Tutor's Daughter

Titianus turned his gaze on the older woman when she sucked air between her teeth. The man who came to the station blanched as he put his hand on the boy's shoulder.

He turned to Kaeso. "Which are slaves here?"

Kaeso opened his mouth to answer, but before he could, Pompeia stepped between them.

"That isn't something you need to know. I can vouch for the honesty of everyone in this household. You will not be taking anyone away to question them. I will not have our people tortured for evidence when they will tell you everything they know because they loved my father. No one wants you to catch whoever did this more than they do."

"I only enforce Roman law, and—"

"And you will not be enforcing that barbaric rule against any of our people." She jammed her fists on her hips and locked a determined stare onto him.

He blinked first. This was not the sweet, laughing girl he remembered. Why she was still unmarried was no longer a mystery.

No one who wasn't his military superior could speak to him that way, but he'd let it pass this time. She'd just lost her father, and his men weren't there to see his response to her defiance. "If I believe they are telling me all they know, that will be enough for now."

With a curl of her fingers, she summoned the boy. Then she stood behind him, her hands resting on his shoulders. "Tell Tribune Titianus everything you can remember."

She squeezed, and the boy looked back at her, his head nodding.

Titianus took a wax tablet and stylus from the satchel he carried on every investigation. It was too easy to forget details if they weren't written down.

"What did the killer look like? Hair, eyes, how tall?" Titianus's lips tightened. The description had better match what Kaeso had said, or his men were wasting their time.

"Brown hair, darker than Master Kaeso, and a little curly, like part Greek, but his nose was like a Roman." The boy touched the corner of his forehead. "Gone from here" He tapped the top of his head. "Thinning a little here. Dark brown eyes, like the dog at the butcher shop. Height… maybe halfway between Master Kaeso and you."

"Beard?"

"No." Small fingers stroked a cheek that wouldn't need shaving for a few years. "His chin was like yours, but no shadow beard like you have."

Titianus's mouth twitched. His beard grew too fast, and its outline was obvious even with shaving that morning. The boy noticed more than most witnesses, like Sciurus did. "How old?"

"Like most of the fathers."

"How did he speak? Like a native of Rome or with an accent?"

"No accent."

"Was his voice high or low?"

The boy's brow furrowed. "High or low?"

"High like yours, middle like your Master Kaeso, or low like mine?"

"Between Master Kaeso and you."

"Did the killer sound like an educated man?"

"Educated?"

Pompeia leaned over until her lips were by the boy's ear. "Did he use the right endings on his words? Were the words in simple order or moved around like the boys do when making a speech?"

"Right endings, simple order."

With a smile, she squeezed his shoulders before straightening.

"What exactly did he say?"

The boy closed his eyes. "Is Rhetor Lenaeus in?" His eyes opened, and he looked over his shoulder at Pompeia. "I shouldn't have let him in, but I didn't see anything wrong with him. He wore a good toga." His lips quivered.

"I would have let him in, too. You couldn't have known." Two pats with one hand accompanied her fleeting smile.

Titianus wrote toga on the tablet. Citizen or pretending to be one. "What made it good?"

"Newer than Master wore. More folds. Good like the fathers wear."

"Were there stripes on his tunic or toga?"

"No stripes."

By the word toga, he wrote not noble order but good quality.

"What did he say next?"

He squinted. "Tell him Gaius Holconius Macer wants to speak with him privately about his son attending the school."

"Are those his exact words?"

"Maybe not, but close."

Titianus wrote the name. "Is that the exact name he said?"

The boy nodded. "Yes. I repeated it to Master when I stood at the classroom door."

"And then?"

"Master was reading, but he came over and asked him to come in. The man closed the door when he did." The boy's eyes brimmed with tears as a soft whimper escaped. "If I'd opened it and stayed there, maybe he wouldn't have killed Master."

Pompeia stepped nearer behind him and wrapped her arms around the boy's chest. Then she pulled him close and whispered in his ear. "It's not your fault. It's a good thing you didn't stay. If you had, he might have killed you, too, and my heart would be aching even more from losing both of you."

Titianus drummed on the tablet frame with the stylus. Such kindness from a mistress was rare. When he'd studied in this house, her father had been undemanding of his slaves. Good masters could expect some loyalty in return. His gaze swept the other three where they stood against the wall just inside the doorway. Grief could easily be faked; most slaves learned young how to lie well to a master. But in this household, the grief he saw might be real.

"Is there more?"

The boy sniffed. "When the door opened, he thanked Master for his time and said he'd let him know what he decided. He closed the door, and

I led him out." He wiped the corner of one eye. "I didn't know he'd killed Master until Mistress Pompeia screamed."

Titianus glanced at Pompeia as he scanned his notes. She was right about one thing. At least one of Lenaeus's slaves did love him.

His jaw clenched, and his eyebrows plunged. It had been fourteen years since the last time he'd been in that atrium. Lenaeus had rested his hand on Titianus's shoulder. He'd said he was proud to have been his teacher and expected great things of him when he became a man. Honor and duty—Lenaeus had helped form him into a man of principle who knew their value and lived his life by them.

If it was the last thing he did, he'd see the one who drove in the dagger executed, and if anyone hired the murderer, that man would pay with his own blood as well.

◆

Pompeia watched the tribune's face as it hardened into a straight-lipped scowl. Not as stone-hearted as he would appear—those had been Septimus's words, and all she could say was she hoped they were true.

Her experience with military men was limited. Torquatus had fought with a legion in Germania in his youth. But even before he and Father became Christians, he'd spent many years in the Senate. There it was persuasion, not issuing orders, that got others to do what he wanted.

The serious boy she vaguely remembered had grown into a stern man with unsmiling lips and unreadable eyes. Perhaps that's what he needed to deal with the criminals of Rome.

But there was no excuse for his coldness in this house where he'd traded childhood for young manhood. He'd studied with Father for five years. How could this man not be feeling sadness or anger or something at Father's death?

How could he suggest that the man who'd taught him to face life with courage and honor would have surrendered to despair and killed himself?

How could a man Father had taught to value truth and fairness even consider torturing a child to get evidence because he didn't happen to be free? She bit the corner of her lip. Was it too late for Kaeso to free Theo if it looked like Titianus planned to take him from their house for questioning?

Her breathing sped up, and she forced it to slow. The tribune had said he wouldn't need to if he thought he'd been told everything. Surely he could see Theo loved Father and told all he knew.

Steely eyed and stone hearted—a perfect description. But there had been a moment before he drew the sheet over Father…had he displayed a trace of affection and a shadow of regret?

"Is that all you can tell me?" The tribune's face softened as the straight lips curved into the hint of a smile.

Theo swallowed, then nodded.

"If you think of anything more, I want you to tell your master. He can let me know right away. The more I know, the quicker I'll catch the killer. Will you help me do that?"

"Yes, tribune." With shoulders squared, Theo managed a smile.

A real smile and approving eyes accompanied Titianus's nod. "Good."

There was warmth in that last word. She considered his features as they turned serious again. Maybe Septimus was right, and this tribune wasn't as unfeeling as he seemed.

Pompeia moved her hands back to Theo's shoulders. "You did well. That should help the tribune find Macer." He smiled across his shoulder as she gave it a final squeeze. "You can go to your mother."

"The rest of you." Titianus turned to face her people. "Did any of you see Macer?" His mouth twitched as three heads shook. "Then you can go back to what you should be doing."

As Corax and his family filed out, Pompeia rejoined Kaeso.

Titianus closed the tablet. "Do you wish to go to a different room for my questions?" He'd put a softer edge on his voice.

"Yes." Kaeso's eyes turned toward the sheet. "My classroom would be better."

Titianus's hand swept toward the door, and Septimus lead them across the atrium. The soft thud of the door closing followed Titianus as he came last.

Kaeso pulled a chair out for Pompeia before sitting on the edge of a table with Septimus beside him.

Titianus lifted off his helmet and placed it on the desk. "Do you have any idea who might have wanted your father dead?" He rubbed his jaw. "I remember him as a patient man who never lost his temper. It's unusual for someone like that to make a mortal enemy."

With tightened lips, Kaeso shook his head. "I can't imagine who could possibly want to harm Father."

Titianus was looking at her brother, but the moment Pompeia cleared her throat, the steel-gray eyes turned on her.

"Father was still like you remember him. I can't think of anything he ever did to hurt anyone." She wiped at a tear just beginning to escape the corner of her eye. "But he was concerned about something one of his students asked him."

"What was it and which student?" He opened the wax tablet and held the stylus above it, ready for the name that would launch him in the right direction. If only she had one to give him!

"He was vague with the details. He didn't tell me enough for me to figure out which student or exactly what the issue was."

"What did he tell you?" The cool voice of the interrogator was back as he snapped the tablet shut.

"One of the boys asked a hypothetical question about what to do if the father of a friend did something wrong, but Father thought the question was personal and real. He didn't tell Father details, but he said someone was already dead, and innocent people might be blamed for the crime."

"Do you have any idea who that might be?" The eyes that had warmed as he encouraged Theo were the calculating eyes of the hunting wolf again.

"No. The other students came before the boy said, and after class, it was as if he didn't want one of the others to know what he'd asked."

"Your father's students—are they all from the noble orders?"

"They were." Speaking that past tense pricked Pompeia's heart, but she held back the tears. "He couldn't be certain, but he thought the father of his student's friend was either high in Roman political circles or a wealthy equestrian." She closed her eyes, and Father's worried face came into focus. When she opened them, Titianus steel-gray eyes bored into her.

"He said there would be serious risk if whoever it was thought he'd talked with anyone in authority. Father's reputation is why we get students. All someone would have to do is spread lies about him, and no one would send their sons here."

Titianus's eyebrows dipped. "Your father's integrity was beyond question." One corner of his mouth curved up. "But he was right about truth being no defense if the wrong senator goes after a man." He glanced at Septimus, and Kaeso's friend looked away. "I don't consider a man's rank an excuse for letting the guilty go free."

The twitch of his jaw convinced her of that.

"Your father taught the sons of important men. If one of them was involved, this could become dangerous for you all before I'm through. But no one is above the law except Hadrian, and it's safe to assume the emperor wasn't involved."

"Are you sure about that? He is back in Rome now. Grandfather just dined with him." Septimus's attempt at humor drew an eye roll from the tribune. Her brother bumped his friend with his shoulder to silence him. But if it wasn't Father lying in the other room, it would have been funny.

"Father wanted to protect the innocent one who might be accused, but he didn't know who that was...or who was guilty."

"And you think someone might have killed him because they thought he did."

"I wouldn't have thought it possible when Father first told me, but now...yes."

"The murderer doesn't know what Lenaeus told you. That makes it doubly important for you to go to the Sabinus town house tonight. You'll be safer under Sabinus protection than you'd be in the imperial palace. No one wants to draw Quintus Sabinus's hostility, and the enmity of Manius is almost as feared. They know too much about too many, and they can be ruthless in how they use it."

His lips curved into an almost-smile as his gaze settled on Septimus. "But thanks to your father, Septimus is a man of honor. Manius is proud of him, and he will protect you if Septimus asks."

Septimus stood. "He will. He's a better man than some might think." He raised his chin and met Titianus's gaze. "Maybe a better man than he thinks himself. He knows honor when he sees it. Sometimes he even speaks well of you."

A full smile accompanied Titianus's amused snort, but it vanished when his gaze returned to her.

Perhaps his flint-like features were only a mask. One he wore as an officer of Rome. Behind it, there might be a man who knew the blessing of good friends and the pain of loss.

Titianus opened his tablet again. "Give me the names of Lenaeus's students and their fathers' names."

As Kaeso began the recital, Pompeia's gaze drifted from the tribune's moving hand to his emotionless face. The best investigator in Rome. That's what Septimus called him. A wolf on a blood trail who would never quit. A true man of honor.

Father had liked Titianus and expected him to do well. Would he like what the quiet boy with the serious eyes had become?

The open doorway framed her view of Father's classroom. Beyond that now-closed door, Father had loved sharing what he knew with boys like Septimus and this tribune, preparing them for lives of honor and service. Only yesterday, she'd leaned against the doorframe and joined in their laughter as he taught how to use humor to persuade. How long would it be before she could laugh again?

God, I know You said I have to forgive, but how will I ever be able to forgive this? I know I should try, but right now, I can't even do that.

She closed her eyes, but the memory of Father's lifeless stare forced them open in time to see the tribune, stone-faced even if not stone-hearted, put his helmet back on.

Whoever killed Father probably killed before, and he might kill again. Please use this man to catch him before he can. I know vengeance belongs to You, but I ask You, please, use Titianus to avenge Father's death as well.

Chapter 10

THE TRIBUNE'S SUSPICIONS

Titianus scanned the list of names, then slipped the tablet back into his satchel. "I need to get the dagger, but that will be all for now. I'll know the next step when I hear what my men have learned."

It might seem an odd skill for a military man, but years of investigations had made him expert at gauging wealth as well as rank from a person's clothes. This household of citizens had enough but not a surplus.

The sister's tunic was linen, but it was simple cords, not decorative chains that wrapped around her to give shape to her tunic. It was held together at her shoulders by plain brass clips, not decorated with colored glass or stones, not shaped like animals or flowers.

As a teacher, Kaeso wore his toga, but the wool was light-weight and unbleached. Lenaeus's had been the same. The togas of the wealthy were made of twenty feet of woolen fabric to allow elegant folds. A senator's toga was almost twice as long as that of a poor citizen. The Lenaeus togas were long enough to make adequate folds, but not more. It was likely they only had one apiece.

Titianus pinched his lower lip. Lenaeus would be laid out for viewing in his toga, and that blood stain would scream "murder or suicide" to any who saw it. If they were to keep any students, that wasn't what this brother and sister needed.

"You can get the blood out of his toga by soaking the spot in white vinegar for half an hour, rinsing in cool water, and repeating a few times. If there's still a stain, you can flip the toga before you wrap to put it underneath him."

Her eyebrows rose; then surprise was replaced by a flicker of amusement before sorrow returned to her eyes. "Thank you for telling me. We've never had this problem before." A sad smile lifted the corners of her mouth. "But I suppose you've seen it too many times and learned many things you wish you didn't know."

He had, but this was the first time he'd given laundry advice to anyone. What made him do it?

"The good a man has done, not the way he died, is what he should be remembered for." He cleared his throat. "I want to look at your father one more time and get the dagger before I leave you to your preparations."

"If you're going back to the station, I'll walk with you." Septimus slipped off the table. "I need to get one of Father's bodyguards and a litter to fetch whatever they'll be taking with them."

"The letter to Torquatus—I'll write it now so you can send it to him as soon as you get home." Pompeia looked back over her shoulder as she walked toward the room that served as the library when Titianus studied there. "It will only take a moment."

Titianus watched her as he crossed the atrium himself. The Torquatus he knew was an important senator, like Septimus's grandfather except honorable. Maybe it was one of the senator's sons, but why would she be sending an urgent letter to any of them with Septimus as intermediary? If it was only a formal death announcement, what was the rush, and why was she writing it instead of her brother as the new paterfamilias?

She disappeared into the library, and he stepped into Lenaeus's classroom. He dropped to one knee to lift back the sheet and pull out the dagger. He wiped it off on Lenaeus's toga at the edge of the bloodstain before adding it to his satchel.

One final look at the face of the wisest man he'd known, and it was time to go. This wasn't the only murder he was working. Add in the arson, and Lupus's death was a crime that had caught the urban prefect's eye. His commander had asked about it already, but it wasn't clear why.

Marcus Lollius Paullinus Saturninus, prefect for the last two years, consul as well for part of last year—that a man of such importance would be so interested in a dead freedman and his burned warehouse was unexpected.

Unexpected by Titianus, at least, and he was better than most at piercing the veil that hid odd connections among Rome's elite.

But for Titianus, Lenaeus's murder mattered more. Was it a coverup for a nobleman's crime? Were the son and daughter in danger as well?

The helmet's neck guard prevented the massage that would release the tension at the base of his skull, so he rubbed his stubbled chin. One corner of his mouth lifted. His shadow beard the boy had called it. A description he'd use himself in the future.

He pulled the sheet up, pausing for a final view of the man who'd prepared so many for manhood. It had been months since he'd thought about Lenaeus, years since he'd seen him, so why did this death feel so personal? Not since his own father died had he felt this hollow ache.

Duty had helped him weather that loss. It would help with this one. It was within his power to bring justice to the worm who'd done this, and he wouldn't stop until he did.

When he returned to the atrium, Septimus sat beside Kaeso on the bench where he'd first seen brother and sister. No words were being spoken, but in the silence, much was being said.

Titianus leaned against the doorframe and waited. His cousin knew these people well, and he'd get Septimus talking as they walked. If there was a reason for the murder other than what Lenaeus's student had revealed, Septimus might be the key to finding it. Something felt different in this household, and it centered on the sister.

Pompeia emerged with a wax tablet wrapped in both directions with cord, the ends trapped in wax in the leaf-shaped seal box. Why would the reporting of a death to a friend need to be kept private? Or was there something more in that letter?

She offered it to Septimus. "We'll try to be ready when you come back for us."

He squeezed her hand before taking it. "Take however much time you need. I'll be armed, and I'll bring a bodyguard. Even if it's after dark, you'll be safe with me."

"Bring two." Titianus's words drew her gaze and raised her eyebrows again. "The Germans if your father isn't using them tonight, and tell them an assassin already killed their father today. You want them on high alert."

He straightened in the doorway. "Let's go."

With Septimus beside him, he approached the outer door. As the boy opened it for them and stepped back against the wall, Titianus paused. "After you bolt this door, don't let anyone in you don't know for certain to be safe. If your master or your father doesn't approve the one who wants in, don't let him in."

The boy's eyes widened. "Yes, tribune." He glanced back at the atrium, where Kaeso stood with Pompeia, and his lip quivered. "I'll keep everyone safe from now on."

Titianus placed his hand on the boy's shoulder. "I know you will."

A fleeting smile curved the boy's lips as he nodded, and Titianus led Septimus into the street.

The door closed, and the click of a bolt sounded behind them.

◆

Pompeia watched the tribune as he walked through the *vestibulum*. Despite what she'd said, Theo was blaming himself because he'd let Macer in. For Titianus to say he knew the boy would keep them all safe—nothing could have helped Theo more.

That act of kindness toward a slave boy was the last thing she expected from this man. Perhaps the heart inside that brass cuirass was more human than he let show.

But he'd looked too closely at the tablet when she handed it to Septimus. Those wolf eyes had locked onto the seal box, then turned on her. She'd only sealed it because Septimus said someone at his house might read it. It was none of their business that she asked a family friend to help with the funeral. If she'd considered how the tribune would react, she would have left it open. Nothing in it would reveal their faith to the casual reader.

She drew her breath through her teeth. Titianus wasn't a casual observer. The seal box triggered his suspicions. What he suspected, she couldn't be certain, but suspicion of any sort was bad.

What if he started watching them too closely? What if he insisted on being present at Father's funeral to see if anyone's display of grief was faked? It wouldn't be the standard affair invoking the Roman gods. Father deserved a Christian burial and a celebration of his new life with Jesus, even as they all mourned his separation from them. Exactly how they would do that, she didn't know, but Torquatus would arrange something.

What would Titianus do if he discovered they were Christians? As a senator, Torquatus had to keep his faith secret. He'd managed to do it for years. Even his wife didn't know. But if Titianus was as good as Septimus said, would he learn too much about them all?

She tipped her head back and closed her eyes. *God, please let him find Father's killer quickly without finding out we all follow You.*

Chapter 11

To Keep Them Safe

For the first block, Titianus walked in silence beside his cousin. Seeming too eager could put anyone on guard. "It's a good thing you told their man to ask for me."

"Kaeso's my best friend. I wanted the best for him." He offered a sad smile. "And for Lenaeus. You studied with him, too, so you know he deserves justice. He might not get it if you weren't hunting his killer."

With his thumb, Titianus rubbed his lower lip. "I appreciate your confidence in me. I'll try to deserve it."

As they turned the corner and started down the sloping street to the Via Patricius, Titianus pointed at the wax tablet in Septimus's hand. "Is that for Appius Manlius Torquatus?"

Septimus nodded. "Why do you ask?"

Titianus furrowed his brow. "I heard he planned to inspect his estates in Campania soon. Will you be able to get that to him as quickly as Pompeia seemed to think necessary?"

"I can try. If he's not at his town house, they can tell me which villa he's at. I'll send someone there on horseback."

"Why does your friend's sister think Torquatus will help them deal with this?" Titianus shifted the satchel on his shoulder. "He's a busy man."

"I thought it odd when she said he'd help, so I asked. As scholars, he and Lenaeus have been friends for years. She said he came often, and the two of them studied things together."

"At their home? Why not at Torquatus's town house in the Fagutal? I've heard his library is exceptional."

"Even scholars need more than that." One corner of Septimus's mouth rose. "Maybe Torquatus finds it relaxing to get away from being a senator to spend time with people who don't play power games. Grandfather and Father often want me to join them at their friends' houses for dinner. I've learned a lot at those meals, but I wouldn't call them enjoyable."

Titianus let his mouth curve into a wry smile. "It would be safe to bet a month's wages that you've learned more than your father or grandfather intended."

Septimus's smile mirrored his own. "True. The food is beyond delicious, but I'd rather eat a simple meal among friends where I don't have to watch every word, and no matter what I say, it will go no further."

"I agree." Titianus smiled at the memory of days long past. "I had a friend like that at your age. Lucius Drusus, but his father's house was not a place to let your guard down." His smile faded. "But Lucius married in Judaea and he's posted in Thracia now. He won't be coming back to Rome to live until his father dies and maybe not even then."

Septimus rested his free hand on Titianus's shoulder. "You'll always be welcome at my house when I get one. If it's genuine and trustworthy you want, I can invite Kaeso and Pompeia." His mouth twitched. "Sometimes I can talk freely with Father when it's just the two of us. When there's company at dinner..." He tightened his lips and shook his head. "He and Grandfather take me to dine with people who watch each other as carefully as they do."

He tapped Titianus's arm. "I wouldn't expect you to be on those guest lists, but you wouldn't want to be. Honor and truth are never main courses at a Sabinus dinner or at those of the men Grandfather calls friends."

The conversation had drifted away from Pompeia and Torquatus, but Septimus knew so little about their relationship that he probably couldn't answer the questions that remained. If Lenaeus had been killed for knowing too much about the affairs of an important man, Torquatus wasn't a suspect, anyway. When a flatterer called him "the honorable senator," he was speaking truth.

At the station, they parted. Septimus headed up the Clivus Pullius to his father's house in the Fagutal. The guard at the door struck his chest as Titianus passed him. There were still a few hours of daylight. He could finish the reports and return to the Praetorian Fortress well before sunset.

The Prefect had made more than one snide remark about him choosing the officers' quarters over his own town house. None of his other tribunes had. But when a man spent so little time at home, it was better to put property to work earning rent than to leave it a useless expense. He'd moved his whole library to his quarters, and he enjoyed the solitude. Most of the time, anyway.

He nodded in response to the optio's salute. "Have any of the men I took returned?"

"No, tribune."

Titianus strode into his office and removed his helmet. After setting it on a side table, he settled into his desk chair and took the dagger from the satchel.

The blade was long, thin, and sharp enough to shave with. It was an ordinary steel blade with a brass hilt, but it was engraved with a complicated design of vines entwined with each other as they wrapped around the handle. It was not a poor man's weapon. Tomorrow he'd ask his troops if any had seen one like it before. For now, he'd lock it in his drawer, safe and secure for when he'd need to present it as evidence against Lenaeus's murderer.

He flexed his jaw to relax it. That day couldn't come soon enough. He didn't often watch the executions in the arena, but for this one, he'd make an exception.

The Sabinus town house, Fagutal section of Rome

As Septimus stepped out of the office of Father's secretary, he blew out a slow breath. Pompeia's letter to Torquatus was on its way to his town house, and if he wasn't there, the letter would return with directions for where a horse courier should take it so Torquatus would get it by tomorrow.

That had been the easy part. Now to convince Father to welcome Kaeso and Pompeia into his home and protect them for as long as Titianus thought necessary. On evenings when Father wasn't being entertained by some senator or hosting a banquet himself, he was usually in his library, so Septimus crossed the atrium to the room next to the tablinum.

So many came to curry Father's favor there each morning, and he might not want strangers to see who came. But Kaeso and Pompeia would leave to go teach more than an hour before the salutation started, so they wouldn't see what Father wanted to hide.

When Septimus strolled into the room lined with cubicles filled with writings that actually got read, Father looked up from the scroll he had spread on the desk. "I didn't see you at the baths with your friends from the ludus today."

"I'd planned to dine with Kaeso, but when I got there, someone had just killed Lenaeus."

Father's head jerked back as his eyebrows plunged. "How did that happen?"

"Someone came to the school pretending he might want Lenaeus to teach his son. He stabbed him in the classroom and left him for Pompeia to find. I got there just after she did. I sent for Titianus right away."

With an approving nod, Father leaned back in his chair. "I'd hate to have your cousin hunting me for murder. He's the best man Saturninus has, whether he likes Titianus or not."

"The prefect doesn't like him?"

"A man who makes no allowance for rank or friendship or family connections—that can put his politically ambitious commander in a difficult position."

"But isn't that what it takes to get justice?"

His father's chuckle raised Septimus's eyebrow. "You're assuming justice is what the prefect wants. That's not always the most desirable end."

"It is for Kaeso and his sister...and for me."

"That's not something to tell your grandfather."

"I know."

Father crossed his arms. "Why was he killed?"

"Titianus thinks it's because one of his students told him about a murder done for a friend's father, and that man wanted to silence him before he could report it."

"Why does he think that?"

"Lenaeus told Pompeia what his student said, but she didn't know which student."

"If someone killed Lenaeus for what he knew, it might not stop there."

"That's what I fear, and Titianus agrees. So, I came to get a bodyguard and a litter to bring Kaeso and Pompeia here." Septimus pulled a deep breath and forged ahead. "He said I should ask for your two Germans if you weren't using them tonight."

"I'm not, and you can take them." Manius's eyes narrowed. "But I'm surprised your cousin knows so much about my guards."

Septimus fought a smile. "He probably has an opinion about the guards of everyone who lives in the district he polices."

Manius snorted. "Maybe I should ask him which I should buy next time I need a new one."

"He'd probably tell you." Septimus chuckled. "After all, you are his cousin."

Manius scrunched his nose. "He doesn't care about family connections."

"I think he does, but he cares about justice, too. I like him. You would, too, if you got to know him."

"It's probably better for both of us if I don't."

Septimus responded with a broad smile. It was time to ask for what he really wanted, and Father might not be so quick to agree. "There's no reason to believe the killer won't come back for Kaeso two days or two weeks from now. I'd like him and his sister to spend nights here until Titianus catches the killer and whoever hired him."

Father's slight smile flipped into a frown.

"They won't be here all the time." Septimus picked up the gold-and-ivory stylus and kept his gaze on it as he rolled it between his fingers. "They'll have to return very early to their town house to teach, and they won't return until late afternoon. And they can eat with just me or by themselves in the smaller dining room when you host a dinner here."

He returned the stylus to the desk and focused on his father's eyes. "They won't learn anything they shouldn't. They wouldn't tell anyone you care about, even if they did. I trust them completely."

Father rubbed his lower lip with his middle finger but said nothing. Silence was not a refusal, so maybe that was a good sign.

"I'd like to borrow one or two of your guards to escort them and maybe stay at their house while they teach."

Silence was also not a yes, and the longer it lasted, the less likely it would become one.

"If they don't teach, they'll lose everything. But if you'd rather not help me protect them so they can keep earning their living with the school, I'll figure something else out." He massaged his neck. "I can rent a bodyguard from Brutus's ludus or do it myself. I can move in with them to make certain they're protected at night."

As Father's lips tightened, Septimus tensed. Silence was about to become an answer and probably not the one he wanted. "That's ridiculous. Of course your best friend is welcome here while it might be dangerous for him to be at his house, and his sister is welcome as well. But as for you being the bodyguard...you have other things to do." Father's mouth relaxed into a wry smile. "You knew I'd say yes, but you are getting better at manipulation to get the answer you want. Your grandfather would approve."

Septimus gave his father the grin he expected.

"Not the Germans, but you can use one or two of the others to escort them to and from their school or wherever else they need to go. Have one stay there while they teach. Their father was murdered in broad daylight with others in the house. No one should enter without the guard inspecting them." He rubbed his jaw. "Take the Syrian as one of them." One corner of his mouth lifted. "Or whichever one Titianus recommends."

"Thank you, Father. Kaeso and Pompeia are important to me. I'd hate to lose either of them." Goal achieved...and easier than it might have been.

"This Pompeia...how old is she?" His father's eyes narrowed. "Is she betrothed?"

Septimus drew a breath at the question he hadn't expected. "She's six years older than Kaeso. Still unmarried, but she loves teaching young women at the school. Lenaeus praised her skill."

Father's frown returned. "I don't want anyone getting the idea that I'm making marital decisions for you by hosting her in this house. You'll make a political marriage, as I did and as your grandfather did for his first marriage."

Septimus chuckled, which raised his father's eyebrow. "Pompeia is like an older sister to me. I have no interest of that sort in my best friend's sister. She'd laugh if you suggested it. She looks on me as another little brother. You'll see that after they come."

Father leaned back in his chair again and crossed his arms. "I will see, and I'll keep watching. She and her brother are welcome to stay as long as you both continue to think of her as a sister."

"Thank you, Father. I'll take the Germans and the litter now. It might be late when we come back. Did you want to know when we arrive?"

Father rolled the scroll to display the next panel. "That won't be necessary." He flicked his hand toward the door. "Go rescue your friends. I hope they appreciate how lucky they are to have you."

Septimus replied with a nod and strode from the room. Father might think Kaeso and Pompeia were lucky to have him as a friend, but it was he, not they, who was truly the lucky one.

The Arcanus town house on the Cispian hill, evening of Day 5

Behind the closed door of his library, Arcanus paced. Four steps one way. Turn. Four steps back. Gaius had told him a man would be coming who could solve his problem, but it was an hour later than he was supposed to be there.

Like most freedmen, Arcanus had trained himself to project both authority and superiority in the presence of his own slaves. He'd masked his worry as they waited on him at dinner, but the pork cutlet with apples and leeks in a red wine sauce that was one of his favorites sat like a lump in his stomach now.

A soft tap on the door stopped him midstride. "Enter."

The door opened to reveal an ordinary man in a clean tunic wearing a polite smile. "Gaius said you wanted to speak with me."

Arcanus returned an identical smile. "I do. Come in and close the door."

He settled into his desk chair and offered the other chair to his…what should he call a man who killed for money? "With whom am I speaking?"

Gaius's solution to his problem tightened his lips to stop a cynical smile. "What's my name? Since this is a one-time arrangement, you don't need to know that. What should you call me?" He rubbed his jaw but cocky arrogance, not uncertainty, described him better. "Vulpis will do. Tell me what you need, and I'll tell you if I can provide it."

Arcanus wiped his palms on his tunic before crossing his arms on his desk and leaning on them. "A door slave saw something I would rather he hadn't, and it's important that he not be able to give evidence in court."

"That should be easy enough. What did he see?"

"What did Gaius tell you?"

"What I told you already." Vulpis leaned back in his chair and crossed his arms. "Tell me who, where to find him, and how soon you need him removed."

"The boy's eleven or twelve. He's the door slave at the Lenaeus School of Rhetoric, and the sooner the better."

"That should be easy enough. Is tomorrow or the next day soon enough?"

"That would be excellent." Arcanus leaned back in his chair and mirrored Vulpis's posture. "What do you charge?"

"To replace a live boy that age, you'd pay 250 or 300 denarii. Normally, I charge half the value of the property I'm destroying, so 125 is my regular price for this." He rubbed his jaw. "But because Gaius vouched for you, I'll give you a dead door slave for 100, paid in advance."

"In advance." Arcanus brow furrowed. "How do I know you won't take it and not do the job? I'd rather pay after."

"How do I know you won't have me do the job and then not pay me?" Vulpis mimicked Arcanus's face and tone. His mouth relaxed back to the cocky smile. "If you don't like my conditions, you can shop elsewhere."

He put his hands on the chair's arms and started to rise.

Arcanus raised his palms toward the killer-for-hire. "Sit back down. I trust Gaius. Since Gaius recommends you, I'll trust you as well."

Vulpis settled back into his chair. "Good choice. Now, tell me everything you can about the boy, where he works, who else is there."

As Arcanus launched into his description, the pain in his stomach faded. He'd always found you got what you paid for, and Vulpis's price was high enough he should be satisfied with what he was buying.

Chapter 12

A Promise to Keep

The Lenaeus town house, morning of Day 6

Vulpis approached the entrance to the Lenaeus School of Rhetoric from the north. A knock on the door, a dagger under the ribs to impale the boy's heart, and a casual walk down the street as if nothing had happened—that was all it would take. An easy 100 denarii for a moment's work. He pursed his lips to erase the smile. He'd find a way to thank Gaius later.

But...walking up the street from the south was Tribune Titianus, dressed in full armor but without any soldiers behind him. Vulpis stopped at the bakery four stalls up and across the side street that led down to the Vicus Patricius. Four people stood in line ahead of him, waiting to hand their dough to the worker who would put them in the community oven.

Titianus should assume he was waiting to pick up his already-baked loaves and walk by without a glance.

Instead, the tribune stopped at the school's entrance and knocked.

"Your loaves?" The grouchy voice of the baker's helper startled him. His gaze snapped back on the sweaty man who'd been loading the oven."

"I want to buy one." He dropped a *dupondius* into the open hand and received a round loaf in return.

He slipped the loop of the string that had been baked into the loaf as a handle over his wrist. Then he sauntered down the street, stopping at the shoemaker who was two doors from the Lenaeus doorway. He pretended to look at the sandals piled there.

The boy should have opened the door already, but two more times knocking brought no response.

Vulpis moved to the potter's stall next to the door and stopped to watch a lump of clay becoming a goblet on the spinning wheel.

With closed fist, the tribune pounded on the door and almost hit the woman when she opened.

She was definitely not a slave. Her hair was braided and wrapped at the back of her head, but the pins holding it had colored glass heads. The dyed linen tunic matched both the necklace of glass beads and the pins.

"I'm sorry we kept you waiting, but we didn't expect you. Theo had to find one of us."

The boy who was his target partly hid behind her. "I beg pardon, tribune."

"None needed. You obeyed me completely. Next time, you can let me in without asking."

A fast nod, and the boy slipped past him to close the door, leaving Vulpis with a nagging question. Why was Titianus there? If it was official business, why didn't he have his usual squad of four men trailing behind him? If it was personal, the risk had just gone from almost none to possibly major.

With the tribune behind the closed door, Vulpis settled onto the bench built into the wall across from the school and tore off a piece of bread. How long the tribune stayed and who else came would decide just how big that risk was.

As he ate and watched, a parade of people entered. A well-to-do man brought a high-quality toga and a basket of boughs. A house slave came out to spread the greens around the doorway, then disappeared back inside. The rich man left without basket or toga. Then more than a dozen students trickled in. They stayed no more than a quarter hour and came out looking distressed.

The tribune was still there.

Even if the boy opened the door, he'd be a fool to kill him with Titianus there. The strike was usually silent, but not always.

He needed to leave before the tribune came out. The man was said to miss nothing. After the boy was dead, he might remember that he'd seen Vulpis nearby.

It was time to go back to Arcanus and find out why he really wanted the boy dead. If he'd been hired to kill the witness to a murder that Titianus was investigating, the fair price for the job just doubled.

Titianus raised his hand and rapped on the school door. One of the students had unintentionally caused Lenaeus's death. Observing the reactions to the news of the passing of their teacher should be illuminating. Boys weren't skilled at hiding their thoughts well enough to fool him.

No one answered, so he knocked again.

The eight students in Lenaeus's class were sons of senators, and the list had already provided food for thought. Three he knew to be honorable men. They even qualified in Marcus Brutus's eyes to buy his superb vintages that he sold only to men of unquestioned honor. As the man whose gladiators had trained half the senatorial sons in swordsmanship, himself included, no one was better equipped to pass that judgment.

The other five were good men...as far as he knew. But what he knew already was like the mirror surface on a lake at sunrise. You had to dive into the water to find what rocks and snags and sometimes skeletons were hidden beneath.

Where was that boy who should be at the door? He rapped on the door panel, but this time harder.

There was an odd coincidence...if it was one. Faustus Cornelius Rufinus was the father of Gaius. Faustus was an unusual name, and he'd already seen it that week...attached to the man who died in the warehouse.

Faustus Cornelius Lupus—was he a freedman of Rufinus? If so, how was the freedman still serving his patron? Before Titianus left the station last night, he told his optio to search the records of Roman citizens to find other men who shared the first two names with the senator. There was always someone in a network of freedmen who would reveal something their patron concealed.

His fellow tribunes looked on the monthly dinner hosted by Saturninus for the Praetorian Prefect and his tribunes as a chance to forward their careers. For him, it was a useful source of gossip about who was doing what to whom among the elite of Rome. Rufinus was rumored to be positioning himself to be elected consul soon. Snags and skeletons under the water could sink any possibility of that.

Tomorrow he'd visit Lupus's house and see what was in his strongbox. The records at the warehouse burned, but things meant to be secret were often kept locked away far from the business itself, secure in a place where prying eyes couldn't see them. He already had a key that hung on a chain around the murdered man's neck. But a tribune of the Urban Cohort could demand the key to any lock when a crime was involved.

What seemed a coincidence seldom was, and someone who'd murdered a wealthy freedman would have no qualms about murdering a teacher, freeborn citizen or not.

With closed fist, he pounded on the door. He'd told the boy not to let any anyone in without asking his father or Kaeso, but it should have been obvious that didn't include him.

His hand was moving forward again when the door swung in, and Pompeia leaned far back to avoid the fist.

"I'm sorry we kept you waiting, but we didn't expect you. Theo had to find one of us."

Nervous eyes in a pale face peered out from behind her. "I beg pardon, tribune."

"None needed. You obeyed me completely. Next time, you can let me in without asking."

A fast nod, and the boy slipped past him to close the door.

"So, why have you come so early?" Pompeia swept her hand toward the atrium inviting him to go first.

Once in the atrium, he turned to face her. "To watch your students as they arrive. I need to know which boy told your father the story. He shouldn't act normally if he suspects his teacher's death relates to their conversation."

"If you're in your armor, no one will act normally, and you won't learn anything." One corner of her mouth curved. "One look at your eyes will remind the boys of Plutarch's description of Sulla."

His eyebrows dipped. The prefect had quoted that at the monthly dinner, and with as much wine as the others had drunk, they all found it hilarious.

The second corner joined the first to make a subdued smile. "You know the one. 'His personal appearance, in general, is given by his statues; but the gleam of his gray eyes, which was terribly sharp and powerful, was rendered even more fearful by the complexion of his face.' That description fits when you're in armor."

He disliked the comparison, but she was right. "I can take it off if you think it makes me too frightening for your students. Where shall I put it?"

"You can remove it in the library, but the students go in there sometimes. We'll store it upstairs in Kaeso's bedchamber so they won't see it."

With the back of her index finger, she stroked the underside of her chin. "If you're going to learn anything, you want to blend in with our familia. So…if anyone asks about you being here, we can say you're a former student who came to offer his help." She glanced at her father's classroom, where some student tables had been moved together to hold his body. Her eyes moistened, and she tightened her lips to stop a quiver. "That is true, after all, and watching the boys is the best way for you to start helping."

"As you wish." It was true and deceptive at the same time and what he would have proposed himself. This teacher's daughter would excel in deflecting the innocent-sounding but malicious questions among the wives of the elite.

Her fleeting smile declared their conversation over. Palm up, she motioned toward the library, then walked into her own classroom.

As he walked by the *lararium* that used to hold statues of Lenaeus's household gods, he paused. They were gone, as was the brass incense burner, and what had taken their places were two small busts of Augustus and Trajan. He drew his middle finger across the floor of the niche, and it came away dusty. Maybe it had been Lenaeus's now-dead wife who'd used the shrine. Some scholars who took part in the state rituals didn't worship any gods in the privacy of their homes. He didn't believe in any himself.

He glanced over his shoulder to find Pompeia watching him. Any hint of amusement or grief had vanished. She instantly broke eye contact and whispered something into the ear of the houseslave who stood beside her. A quick nod from the girl, and she disappeared down the narrow corridor that led to the back of the house. Pompeia sat down at her desk, rested her elbows atop it, and covered her face with her hands. Her shoulders jerked, and he turned his gaze away from her silent tears.

He took his helmet off and set it on the small table before running his fingers through his hair. He lifted the scabbard strap over his head and wrapped it around his sheathed sword. As he undid the clasps that held breastplate to backplate, his eyes were drawn toward her classroom. She was standing by an open cabinet, straightening a stack of papyrus sheets before she closed and locked it.

Women were hard to understand, harder still to predict, but Lenaeus's daughter was an enigma. From perceptive to witty to practical to…what she said next would likely surprise him. Uncontrolled sobbing and floods of tears were what he expected from a loving daughter, but she bore her grief like a man, and he had to admire her for it.

The cuirass swung free of his torso, and he stood it on the floor. After removing the apron of leather straps and the padded linen vest, the last thing that made him look like a soldier was his dagger. It would stay. He never went anywhere without it.

But Septimus always carried one, too, so as long as he only wore his red-striped tunic, he could pass for an older version of Kaeso's friend, whom the students had probably seen often.

When his gaze returned to her classroom, she was gone. A deep male voice he'd not heard before drew him to the doorway, but not through it. Observe before you're observed was a motto that served him well. It served even better when he wasn't in uniform.

He stuck only enough of his head out to see who the voice came from.

A man a little older than himself stood at the doorway of the vestibulum with Pompeia wrapped in his arms and his cheek resting on the top of her head. With curly black hair and the face of a Greek, he wore the bleached toga of a man with enough money to buy high quality. To the side stood Corax, holding a folded toga at least as white and at least as expensive. Kaeso came out of his room, and the man lifted one arm away from Pompeia to make room for him to join the hug.

A basket sat near his feet, piled high with the cut cypress branches that would declare to passersby that this house was in mourning. Ciconia popped out of the narrow passage to the peristyle and scurried over to join the group. She scooped up an armful of branches and, after receiving a sad smile and a nod from the newcomer, disappeared into the vestibulum to spread them just outside the door.

Titianus would have preferred she wait until after the boys came. He wanted to see their first response to the news of Lenaeus's death. But it was the custom, and this family deserved what they could have of the rituals of a normal death.

"Your letter came to us last night." The visitor's words drew Titianus's frown. This wasn't the Torquatus to whom the letter was sent. "I've sent it on, and he should arrive at the estate by evening. I'll make all the arrangements for taking Gnaeus there tonight when the city opens to wagons. He'll lie in the family mausoleum."

Perhaps this friend was Torquatus's secretary or house steward.

Pompeia stepped back and smiled at the man through tears. "Thank you for coming so quickly. I didn't know what else to do besides contact Appius."

The Greek rested his hand on her cheek. His thumb swept aside a tear...too familiar a gesture from a man not more than ten years her senior.

Titianus relaxed the frown he'd formed without thinking and silently laughed at himself. Who was he to say what was too familiar between this stranger and the woman he'd known less than half a day? Why had he even cared?

The stranger called Lenaeus by his first name of Gnaeus, so they must be close friends. But she'd called Torquatus by his first name as well. Appius Torquatus was old enough to be her father. No, her grandfather, and that level of familiarity was definitely odd.

"You did exactly what you should. I brought my spare toga. Before any come to view your father, let's trade it for his old one." He bent over and picked up the basket. "And I brought something else you need here."

Titianus pulled his head back as the Greek started his way. The moment he revealed himself, their visitor would start acting more formally, and he'd lose the chance for an accurate impression of how this man fit in the family's life.

Footsteps stopped short of the library door, then a few clinks like metal bumping metal. A moment of silence, and the footsteps retreated toward where he'd left brother and sister standing.

Silence filled the atrium. It was time to reveal himself. Titianus stepped out of the library to find Kaeso and Corax had gone to change Lenaeus's toga. The stranger had one of his arms around Pompeia's shoulders as they walked toward him.

"Appius Manlius Glyptus, this is Tribune Titianus of the Urban Cohort." A slight smile appeared so fleetingly he almost missed it. "He'll be looking for the one who killed Father."

Glyptus's arm dropped to his side. "I've heard of the tribune whose very name terrifies the criminals of Rome. I never expected to meet you, especially not under these circumstances."

They had reached the lararium, and she glanced at it. When Titianus's gaze followed hers, he saw two changes. Between the busts of the two great emperors was a small statue of a household god. In front of it sat a brass incense holder. Were those two additions the something else Glyptus thought she needed?

Glyptus's mouth assumed a friendly smile, but caution filled the eyes of this freedman of Torquatus. "With you as investigator, the one who killed one of the best men in Rome will soon pay."

"He will." His gaze shifted from the freedman to the freeborn woman beside him. "I give Pompeia and her brother my word as a Roman that the secrets that led to his death will be revealed and the man responsible for this punished."

"Whether he is or not, I'm sure you'll do your best, and that's all I can fairly ask." Her eyes warmed as she spoke, and that almost made him smile.

Although she was nothing to him but the daughter of the man who once taught him, that was one promise he was determined to keep.

Chapter 13

More Questions Than Answers

Pompeia expected Titianus to scrutinize her dear friend and Christian brother. Glyptus was as skilled as Torquatus at hiding his faith, so that didn't worry her. His additions to the lararium would conceal their refusal to worship idols like the pagan Romans. When word of Father's death spread, there would be visitors. The statue and incense holder would keep curiosity over their absence from leading to questions she'd rather not try to answer. She wasn't a skilled liar.

Father's funeral would be a private affair where their familia, Glyptus, and Torquatus could both grieve and celebrate him joining their Savior in heaven without worrying who would see them. But keeping it so private could raise questions among their neighbors and the parents of their students. The incense holder and meaningless piece of metal would prevent casual visitors from suspecting the real motivation for the privacy.

But Titianus was no casual visitor. The piercing eyes worthy of Sulla shifted from the idol to her face almost before she could mask her concern. Without doubt, he'd noticed what was in the niche when he fingered the dust there. Would he comment on the additions Glyptus had made? Would he ask for the reason?

But he said nothing about it. His unreadable eyes turned on Glyptus as her friend expressed confidence that Titianus would catch the killer, but it was only a moment before they focused on her again.

His promise that he would find the secrets that led to Father's death—

that was a frightening thing. When a man like him started looking for secrets, would he uncover the secret of their faith?

But in the depths of those steely gray eyes as he gave her his word, a flicker of warmth said it wasn't just duty. He actually cared.

◆

When Kaeso and Corax emerged from exchanging the togas, Titianus joined them. "What usually happens in the morning?"

"Our students go to their rooms, and we begin teaching." Kaeso's shoulders drooped as he sighed.

"I'd like to watch your father's students when they arrive. I can do that best if I'm in their room. They can pay their respects to him while you speak with your students first, and I'll watch and listen."

Corax held the old toga against his chest. "Theo usually opens the door as they arrive, but I'll do it today." He glanced at his son, slumped on the low stool by the door.

Kaeso reached for the toga. "Tell him he can help in the kitchen today. He's too young to mask his grief."

With Glyptus beside her, Pompeia came to stand next to Titianus. She lifted the toga from her brother's hands and stroked it before raising her eyes to Titianus's face. "I want to thank you, tribune. We almost got the stain out doing what you said. It would have been sufficient if Glyptus hadn't brought another."

He answered with a nod. He'd never washed anything himself.

The Greek slipped one arm around her shoulders and drew her to his side. The smile he received as he held her spoke her affection more than mere words would. But was theirs a simple friendship or something more?

Titianus's lips tightened. That was irrelevant to the investigation. It was only curiosity that made him wonder.

"You don't need me here when your students come." Glyptus's voice had softened. "I'll return tonight with the wagon."

She leaned her head against his shoulder. "Thank you for everything."

Glyptus glanced at Titianus before giving her a quick squeeze. He stepped from her to Kaeso. A light slap on the brother's arm accompanied a reassuring smile.

Kaeso's nod launched the Greek toward the door, and Corax followed to release the downcast boy from his post there.

Titianus watched Glyptus until the door closed behind him. The mystery of why Pompeia contacted Manlius Torquatus was solved, but why Torquatus would host the funeral at his estate and give Lenaeus a place in his own mausoleum remained unclear. What Glyptus did at their family shrine made no sense, either.

Two young voices came from the vestibulum. The first students were arriving. Without a word, Kaeso and Pompeia went to their classrooms. He entered the room where Lenaeus lay. Soon he'd know which boy told the story that got his tutor killed. It should be a short step from there to finding the killer.

He sat on the edge of Lenaeus's desk as each boy entered, grim-faced. One by one, they approached the grouped tables where their teacher lay. Seven sad faces, but the eighth never came.

Each took a chair and sat, eyes upon him, as if expecting something. If he was to learn more, they needed to talk to each other, not watch him. Perhaps a few words of encouragement, and he'd retreat to the wall by the door and wait for Kaeso to come.

"Rhetor Lenaeus was my teacher years ago. I was fortunate to have the opportunity to learn from him, as you have been. He taught us all about honor and how important it is. How only men of honor can become truly great orators. He taught us how…"

It had been years since he'd made a speech to a group. He'd always preferred writing to speaking without any preparation. But the boys listened as if his words were pearls of wisdom. Perhaps Lenaeus had done a better job of teaching him than either of them ever thought.

But he was glad when he finished and walked to the door. They soon lost interest in him, and he watched what they did as he listened to their words.

As quiet as a deer entering a forest glade, Pompeia slipped into the room to stand beside him. The faint aroma of roses came with her. She fixed her gaze on her father's desk, and he felt the tension that held her upright beside him. If Glyptus was here, her friend would wrap his arm around her. It was what she needed.

But as tempting as it was to offer her support as her friend had, she'd have to ask before he could. She wrapped her arms around herself and closed her eyes. Her shoulders squared, and a hint of a smile softened her face.

When Kaeso finally entered and announced his father's death, Titianus saw no sign that any were trying to mask feelings of guilt. They made clumsy attempts to offer condolences, and then they left.

Kaeso adjusted his toga and came to them. "For the boys we still have, I'll add a lesson on conventional things to say to those grieving a death. Even young men need to learn that, for you never know when death will come unexpectedly. The right words can be balm, and the wrong ones can cause more pain than they can know."

Pompeia nodded, then her face crumpled. As tears flowed down her cheeks, Kaeso pulled her into his arms. He locked his jaw and donned a stoic mask like a Roman man should. But he couldn't quite stop every stray tear. He guided her into the atrium before he returned to cover their father.

Titianus ground his teeth as he followed her. One man had caused this woman such grief. This anger…it was a strange feeling. What was it about her that was breaching his usual detachment from the victims of the crimes he investigated?

She was pretty enough but not stunningly beautiful, and he could resist a woman's physical allures. He never let a pretty face, curvaceous body, or flirtatious manners cloud his judgment. She only had one of the three.

Why did she attract him?

His wealth was not exceptional by equestrian standards, but he was paterfamilias so he owned what he had. It was enough to make him a desirable husband in most fathers' eyes. Before they realized he wasn't close to his powerful uncle and his cousin Manius, even some senators had considered him suitable.

Women much prettier than Pompeia with substantial dowries were within his grasp, if he wanted them. But he was waiting to marry until he finished his years as tribune and settled into private life. That was still his plan.

Perhaps it was only because she was the daughter of the man who'd help make him what he was…that had to be it. He wasn't angry for her sake. He was angry for himself.

"You said Lenaeus had eight students, but only seven came today."

Pompeia swept the teardrops from her cheeks. "A messenger came two days ago to say Tertius Flaccus had gone with his father to his grandfather's estate for a visit."

"Which Flaccus?"

"Valerius Flaccus. Tertius's older brother Marcus studied with Father, too."

"Did he leave before or after your father shared his concerns about the student's question with you?"

"After." She bit her lip. "You think he's the one, don't you."

"It's likely. Which of the other boys was he especially friendly with?"

"You'll need to ask Kaeso. He helped teach the youngest ones who are fourteen and fifteen. They leave here midday in a group, and most go to the Ludus Bruti to train with his gladiators." Her nose scrunched. "If they're going to serve in the legions, I realize they need skill with swords. But knowing the gladiators personally makes them eager spectators at the arena. They all enjoy watching other men die."

His eyebrows lowered, but he tried not to frown at her. "I trained with Brutus's gladiators. The skills they learn there will keep them alive in battle, and Brutus prides himself on helping raise young men who value honor and devotion to Rome. Your father did the same."

"Septimus has said that Father and Brutus are why he chooses the honorable way instead of…"

She clamped her lips shut and looked away as pink washed over her cheeks.

Embarrassment was becoming on her. He squashed the wry smile before it fully formed. "Instead of the way his father and grandfather do things. Your observation is just, and it will go no further than me. Manius and Quintus Sabinus are my cousin and uncle, and I know what kind of people they are. Septimus has chosen better men to emulate."

Earnest eyes turned back to him. "But Manius Sabinus is a generous man. He did welcome us into his house for as long as you think we need protection, and one of his bodyguards is eating in the peristyle right now. He'll stay here while we teach and escort us back and forth every day."

"One of the Germans?"

"No, I'd guess he's from the eastern provinces, maybe Syria."

The corners of his mouth lifted, but only for a moment. "He gave you his third best man. He's taking your safety seriously."

Her smile was warmer than he'd seen before, and it took effort to keep his mouth straight. "As you do, and we truly appreciate it."

"What Septimus says about your father and Brutus…I can say the same. Bringing any murderer to justice is my duty, but making your father's killer pay will be my pleasure as well."

"I want the killer caught before he can kill again, but I expect no pleasure from it. I'm trying not to hate him. Father always said hatred poisons the one who hates, and forgiveness is the only cure for this pain. Even murder must be forgiven, no matter how hard I find that. The greater the injury, the more important it is, even when the one who hurts us isn't sorry."

He stopped his jaw from dropping, but he couldn't keep his eyes from widening as he stared at her. He never heard Lenaeus say anything about forgiving horrible deeds by unrepentant men. It was Seneca's words—To forgive all is as inhuman as to forgive none—that her father always quoted. But if Seneca had seen all the damage from the selfish acts of evil men that he had, the philosopher wouldn't have been that forgiving.

He'd seen anguish in her eyes but not anger. Rage and a desire for revenge was what he usually saw when a loved one had just been murdered and rightly so. There was more sadness in her eyes than anything. But expecting the usual from her…he'd seen enough already to know that was a mistake.

He turned his eyes toward the atrium to get his gaze off her. "It's time I should go. I learned what I could already. It's better to leave now before others come. They might wonder whether I'm here officially, and that could lead to gossip about what happened."

"Thank you for the special attention you're giving to this." Her voice was soft and coated with sorrow. "For your concern about our safety and our reputation. For everything."

Even with the lingering sadness, the warmth of her eyes as she smiled declared how real her gratitude was. She was more than welcome. He'd done very little so far, but that would soon change.

"I'll keep you posted on my progress."

Kaeso gestured toward the stairway. "I'll take you to your armor. It's up in my room."

He followed her brother across the atrium and up the narrow stairs to the balcony. Before stepping into the bedchamber, he looked over the railing. With her head hanging, Pompeia's slow steps carried her toward the back of the house. Her fingertips brushed the corner of her eye before she disappeared into the narrow hallway.

His jaw clenched. Whoever killed Lenaeus would pay with his life. The nobleman who hired him would pay as well.

Chapter 14

TITIANUS RAISES THE RISK

The Rufinus town house, evening of Day 6

When Rufinus's son entered the dining room, the boy's shoulders drooped. With mournful eyes, Gaius sank onto his couch. "Rhetor Lenaeus died yesterday."

Rufinus froze with a raisin halfway to his lips. "Has he been ill?"

"I didn't think so. He taught us about humor as a tool of persuasion in the morning, and he seemed like he always did. We all laughed a lot. It's too bad Tertius missed it. Too bad he missed this morning, too. He really liked Lenaeus. He'll be sorry he missed paying him honor."

Gaius blinked several times. "I never saw someone dead before. He didn't look...real. I'd heard the dead looked like they're sleeping but..." He shook his head. "He always listened like what we said mattered. And when I did something really well...he'd smile at me like you do." His eyes swam in tears.

Rufinus swung his legs off the dining couch. "Come here, son." He patted the cushion next to him. Gaius came and sat. "Life is full of unexpected partings. I was older than you at my first, but it's hard no matter how old you are." He wrapped his arm around his son's shoulders. "We honor those who die by remembering the good times we had with them, not by grieving too long. A few tears are appropriate, but a Roman bears his grief without showing it too much."

Gaius nodded, sniffed, and swallowed hard. "I'll try, Father." He wiped the corner of his eye. "One of his old students was there. He talked to us a little while Tutor Kaeso talked with his own class first. He said we were fortunate to have had Rhetor Lenaeus teach us how honor was what made the difference between being a skilled speaker and a great orator. The lessons Lenaeus taught him had made him the man he was today, and he wished the same for us. He said to choose honor and duty and live in a way that would make Lenaeus proud to say he'd been our teacher."

"Was he a rhetor, too?"

"No, he was equestrian. Someone called him Titianus."

Rufinus tensed. "How old was he?"

"Thirty, maybe."

"What did he look like?"

"Hair cut like a soldier, no beard. What you said about not letting grief show...he was good at that. Almost like a statue. His eyes were gray and felt cold when he looked at me."

"A tribune?"

Gaius shrugged. "Maybe. His belt and the sheath for his dagger were like Tertius's brother wears with his armor."

Rufinus forced a smile. "His words about how to live are worth remembering."

He lifted his goblet from the table and took a sip. As he rolled the wine around in his mouth, he glanced at his son's bowed head.

Why had Titianus been at Lenaeus's house without his armor the morning after the teacher died? Why was he watching Lenaeus's class and lecturing them on honor?

Maybe Arcanus had been right to worry about what the rhetor knew. But if his freedman had anything to do with the teacher's death, Arcanus had turned Titianus's investigation from a matter of duty into a personal quest for retribution.

A shiver ran up his spine. Where would that end if he didn't do something to stop it? He pulled a deep breath, and when he let it out, tension left with it. Perhaps he could do nothing, but he knew the man who could.

The Arcanus town house, late evening of Day 6

For the first time since the fire, Arcanus had enjoyed a relaxing dinner followed by a leisurely goblet of wine in his library. It was almost time to retire, and tonight's sleep should be sound and sweet. By now, Vulpis should have killed the slave who could tie him to Lenaeus.

He rolled the scroll and placed it in the cabinet.

"Salve, Arcanus."

He spun at the voice behind him. A frowning Vulpis stood in the doorway, arms crossed.

Arcanus swallowed hard. He'd paid in advance. Why had the assassin returned?

Vulpis stepped into the room and closed the door.

"Is it done?" To his own ears, Arcanus's voice sounded higher than normal. Could Vulpis tell?

"No. You didn't tell me everything you should have." Vulpis sat in the guest chair by the desk and pointed at Arcanus's own chair, as if he were the master of the house.

"What do you mean?" Arcanus lowered himself into his chair in a way he hoped looked stately. He tipped his head back slightly, like his patron often did with his clients. He was the employer, and Vulpis shouldn't think himself in charge.

"I was about to make the kill, but Tribune Titianus reached the door half a block ahead of me. The domina let him in, and he was still there when I left."

He picked up the goblet and sniffed. "Decent vintage." He set it in front of Arcanus and tipped his head toward the table where the flagon and another goblet sat. "Pour me some. Take some more for yourself, too."

"Tribune Titianus?" Pretending ignorance was sometimes the safest approach, and sharing some wine might be wise.

"Don't pretend you don't know about Titianus's reputation. He was there by himself, so it could have been a personal visit. A woman spread cypress boughs around the doorway after he got there."

Arcanus handed him a goblet. "So?"

"So, someone already died in that house." Vulpis took a sip. "Not bad." Predator eyes locked on Arcanus. "Or maybe they were murdered. If I'm supposed to kill someone who might matter to Titianus, the risk to me is many times higher." He took another sip. "Price depends on risk. It's going to cost more than a hundred."

Arcanus let his goblet untouched on the desk. His hand might shake if he picked it up. "How much more?"

"That depends on what the boy saw."

Vulpis had picked his fake name well. Arcanus felt every bit the mouse being watched by a fox.

"There was a murder, and the boy could identify the one who did it." He fought the urge to rub his lips.

"Then it's double…in advance."

Arcanus's head pulled back. "That seems a lot."

"It's not your head at risk if Titianus catches me." The feral smile that sent shivers up Arcanus's spine appeared. "But it might be yours if he catches you. I can return what you already paid if you want to risk that."

Arcanus swallowed hard before he could stop himself. Perhaps two hundred denarii was not too much if it ended the threat to his own life. "Very well. Finish your wine while I get it."

Vulpis set his goblet on the desk, stretched out his legs, and rested his hands on top of his head. "Why the first murder?"

"The teacher knew something he shouldn't, and he was killed to prevent him reporting it."

Vulpis chuckled before taking another sip. "Unless what he knew about was murder, arson, or treason, whoever killed him was a fool. He has Titianus hunting him now, and you can't even be certain the teacher didn't tell someone before you killed him."

"I didn't kill him."

Vulpis snorted. "No one hires me like you have to kill a witness who saw someone else. Who else might have seen you?"

"Lenaeus might have told someone else what he knew, but the son and daughter don't know it was me who killed him. They were in their rooms teaching. Only the boy saw me."

Vulpis drained the goblet and returned it to the desk. "I give repeat customers a discount."

"I won't need you to kill his children."

Vulpis's sneer relaxed into the feral smile. "Gaius can reach me if you do."

Arcanus got four *aurei* from the strongbox and dropped them into Vulpis's open palm. The killer rose with the grace of a hunting cat and left the room.

When Arcanus closed the door behind him, his hand started shaking. He grabbed his wrist to stop it. Then he returned to the desk, rested his elbows on it, and buried his face in his hands.

Chapter 15

WOLF ON A BLOOD TRAIL

On the road to the Torquatus estate north of Rome, Day 7

As each wheel in turn rolled off the stone paving of the Via Flaminia onto the dirt road to Appius's estate, the carriage rocked. The jostling tossed Pompeia into Kaeso where they sat on the heavily padded back seat. With his family filling the bench at the front, Corax had chosen to ride up top with the driver. If she'd known what the trip would be like, she might have claimed that seat herself.

This was her first time in a raeda, but that wasn't the only first. It was her first time in anything pulled by animals. Her first time outside the walls of Rome, where villas larger than a whole block on the Viminal Hill could be seen in the distance. The first time where sheep dotted the hillsides, where rows of grapevines on racks stretched out across a field, where huge gardens were worked by dozens of people with an overseer watching from the back of a mule.

Any other day, she would have been transfixed by all she saw. But today they were going to a funeral. Glyptus had brought Father over this road last night, wrapped in a shroud. Had Father ever seen what she was seeing now?

She shook her head to drive those thoughts away before they ended in tears. When she closed her eyes, a disturbing image replaced them. Cold gray eyes above thin straight lips, muscular arms crossed against a brass cuirass—Tribune Titianus contemplated her. A wolf on a blood trail who never stopped until he took down his quarry—Septimus's description fit perfectly. She shuddered at the thought of seeing him again.

Talking to him about forgiveness…that was a mistake. The shock on his face…she must have made him suspicious. He'd only known what Father said before he knew the Lord. Unconditional forgiveness wasn't the Roman way. Justice, not mercy. Retribution, not forgiveness. Those were what she'd expect from a man like the tribune.

She turned her face toward the window so Kaeso wouldn't ask what was wrong. Perhaps the tribune had all the information he needed to start his investigation without talking to her again. But he'd said he'd report on his progress.

She drew a breath and blew it out slowly. He'd be back. She'd be more careful in the future, and maybe he'd forget what she said. One corner of her mouth lifted. Maybe the sun wouldn't rise tomorrow morning. That was about as likely.

God, protect us from Father's murderer and from the man hunting him.

Septimus claimed his cousin wasn't as stone-hearted as he seemed, and there had been a few times she'd seen a hint of the man behind the emotionless mask. He was angry about Father's death, and that seeped through the tiny cracks in his frigid façade.

At some level, he'd cared about Father. Because of that, he cared some about her and Kaeso, or he wouldn't have insisted they go with Septimus. But if he found out they were Christians, would he care enough to tell no one so they could stay alive?

The Lupus villa south of Rome, Day 7

Titianus's gray stallion tossed his head and snorted. He would give the animal the gallop it wanted if he were alone. But an army mule walked beside him, and this was the first time Sciurus had ridden anything. The youth had been leery of mounting the beast, but he'd clenched his jaw and tossed his leg across the mule's back after Titianus showed him how. Forcing him to ride a gallop on the first day would scare almost anyone half to death. He'd rather keep his special assistant alive.

He'd borrowed the mule at the Praetorian Fortress before riding by his warehouse to pick up the youth. Lupus's villa was southeast of the warehouse area toward the Via Ostiensis, and he had plans for Probus's observant assistant.

When the modest villa came into view, he reined in. "I'm going to leave you in the stableyard while I go inside to search Lupus's strongbox. We'll pretend you're there to watch my stallion, but you're really there to watch the workers and ask questions about their dead master that would never be answered if I asked. Any known enemies, unusual visitors, suspicious trips he took, who visited in the last couple of weeks. You'll know what to ask when someone starts talking. After we leave, you'll tell me all you learned, like you did the night of the fire."

Sciurus's energetic nod accompanied bright eyes. "No one will suspect I'm there as your spy. I'll borrow a curry comb from one of the stable slaves. I'll tell him my master likes his horse well cared for and we left too quickly this morning for me to finish. If I work near where he's working, I can get him talking."

His words triggered Titianus's wry smile. "Probus chose well when he brought you into my familia. He's planning for you to be my future warehouse manager, but while I'm still tribune, you'll sometimes be my eyes and ears where a man might turn into an actor or a statue if he sees the uniform or even my tunic stripes."

"After I learn what I can, I'll do my best to watch without being seen and listen without being heard." Sciurus grinned.

Titianus tightened his lips to keep his own grin from leaking out. "I've built a reputation of lacking human emotions, so don't be surprised if I seem cold. I'm starting now." "He drew his hand down his face, leaving behind cool eyes and straight lips.

Sciurus's eyes widened. "That's scary. Should I act like I'm afraid of you?"

"No. Emotionless means no anger. You can act like I'm safe to serve but not a man who lets anyone see his thoughts or affections. So, careful respect is the right tone."

Sciurus nodded. "That's easy. The merchant who owned me last was like that."

They crossed a shallow stream. "Stay behind me now." Titianus tensed his calves, and the stallion walked ahead. A quarter mile down the road, the gate to the stableyard stood open. Titianus donned his interrogator's mask and led them into the villa where the identity of one, maybe two murderers might be revealed.

He dismounted, and Sciurus slipped off his mule to take the reins. Titianus strode toward the arch leading to what should be a peristyle garden.

When he reached the portico, he summoned the girl sweeping the tile floor with a curl of his fingers.

"Bring me the house steward."

"Yes, tribune." She dipped her head and scurried into the house.

He crossed his arms and scanned the stableyard. Sciurus was already talking with one of the stablemen. Titianus kept his mouth straight, but inside he was smiling. Probus was proud of the boy. He'd be even more so when Titianus told him about Sciurus's ingenuity and enthusiasm for this assignment.

"I'm Steward Celeris. How may I help you, tribune?"

Titianus turned at the voice behind him to find a too-well-fed man of fifty-something with a fringe of gray hair.

"I'm investigating your master's murder and the arson of his warehouse. I'll need to see the contents of his strongbox and any other business records you may have here."

"I wasn't told to expect this." He cleared his throat. "Perhaps I need to talk with his patronus before I can do that."

"Faustus Cornelius Rufinus is well aware of my authority to inspect whatever I deem necessary during the investigation of murder and arson." Titianus crossed his arms. "Did he tell you to obstruct an officer of the Urban Cohort in the performance of his duty?" He raised one eyebrow. "If he didn't, do you think he'll be pleased that you chose to cause a problem yourself?" Titianus kept his voice soft, but he was a master of delivering a quiet threat with a menacing undertone.

The steward drew himself to his full height. "The patronus is an important senator, and he'll soon be consul. He supports the rule of law in Rome and the honoring of the rights of her citizens."

"As do I, especially the right of an innocent man to have his murderer caught and punished. For that to happen, I need to see the contents of your master's strongbox. If Lupus's patron takes issue with that, you can tell him to complain to the urban prefect about Tribune Flavius Titianus. But he will have to explain why he didn't want Lupus's murderer found."

Celeris blanched, then swept his hand toward the doorway. "This way, tribune. What you seek is in the tablinum."

After leading Titianus to the strongbox, Celeris withdrew a key from beneath his tunic and opened it.

"Remain with me while I inspect the contents." Titianus dropped to one knee beside the large chest.

"Yes, tribune." Celeris moved behind the chest and rested his hands on the open lid.

A pile of wax tablets and a stack of papyrus sheets lay at one end with bags of money at the other. One by one, he lifted out the documents, inspected them, and made stacks on the floor. He found some estate deeds, Lupus's record of manumission, and his will, which left half to Rufinus. It also left the proceeds of the sale of the destroyed warehouse business to his patron. Nothing seemed odd.

He replaced everything in their original locations and stood. "Is there another strongbox in the house?"

"Yes, in the library. Master Lupus kept his business records separate from the household records."

"Who has keys to the strongbox in the library?"

"For that one, only Master Lupus."

Titianus mouth twitched. A box with only one key often held the answer to a case.

"Has anyone been left alone in the library since your master died?"

"Only a slave who came to reclaim some scrolls Patronus Rufinus had lent to Master Lupus."

"Had you seen the man before?"

"No, but he had a tablet from the patronus saying he was authorized and listing the scrolls he'd be reclaiming. I recognized Rufinus's signet mark."

"Did someone watch him while he collected the scrolls? Did he take only what was on the list?"

Celeris's head drew back. "There was no need. I trust someone sent by the patronus."

From inside his tunic, Titianus pulled a key on a chain. It was the one he'd found hanging around Lupus's neck. "Is this the key to the library strongbox?"

"It looks like it."

"I'm going to inspect that box now. Have you seen the contents?"

Celeris mouth turned down. "No. It was the master's private letters and business records that went into it. That's the only key."

"Take me to it."

The steward led him across the atrium to a strongbox in the back corner of the library. When he opened it, Titianus took out the tablets and papers and stacked them on the desk. "We'll both count these. When I finish looking at them, you'll make certain the number we return to the box plus the number I take with me are the same as what we've just taken out."

It took more than an hour to sort through the box, but his patience was rewarded by several tablets showing crimes by Lupus and two senators. Some were evidence Lupus sold substandard goods and foodstuffs packed to look like they were larger quantities than they were. One tablet listed a summary of sales where Lupus had shorted an imperial customer.

Three letters from each senator revealed why they might want Lupus dead. There were accusations that he'd made illegal investments for them and held onto their profits. Then warnings about trying to extort money to keep quiet about them breaking the law. Finally, veiled threats about getting justice outside Roman courts if he didn't pay what he owed them or if he exposed their partnerships.

But they posed a problem. Someone smart enough to commit such crimes undetected wouldn't be stupid enough to keep written records of them. The two senators would have to be utter fools to put in writing such wrongdoing.

But even if they had, these tablets weren't proof. The wax tablets looked like they came from the same craftsman. The handwriting was too similar. The shape of the letters, the depth of the impression in the wax, how close to the frame the starting and ending letters of a line were…a single hand had prepared these, and he'd bet a week's wages two senators would never use the same scribe to write incriminating documents, even if they were stupid enough to write them.

He rubbed his chin. They did fit the story the student told Lenaeus about killing someone and trying to shift blame. Neither of the senators had boys at the Lenaeus school, but Pompeia had said the question was about the father of a friend, and circles of friends went far beyond a single school.

As a youth, he'd been content with his own company most of the time. His own circle of friends had been small, and none of them had Lenaeus as tutor.

He'd met Lucius Drusus when he started at the Ludus Bruti. They shared a training time, and Lucius had invited him to join a group that went to the taberna after they trained. That had grown into a friendship where honesty and trust made them feel like brothers, a friendship like Septimus and Kaeso had. The rest of the men from that group were now friendly acquaintances, nothing more.

It would help narrow down suspects if the boy had been mostly solitary, like him. Perhaps Kaeso could help him figure out the circles for his father's students beyond the boys at the school. The oldest would have been just starting when Kaeso was finishing, and the youngest he would have taught himself.

If Lupus wasn't the real owner of the business that was cheating the imperial government, then Rufinus probably was. The grain ships involved were not something a senator was allowed to own. There might be more to the business that a senator wasn't allowed as well. If someone who was only fronting for the real owner decided to cheat him, a senator had no legal recourse. Rufinus couldn't take his agent to court for cheating him while doing something illegal.

If Rufinus was involved, there was risk in exposing him, but there was greater risk if he didn't. Lupus had died for his cheating. Lenaeus had died for knowing almost nothing. Pompeia knew even less. How great was the threat to her? Any at all was too much now that he'd promised to protect her, even if that promise was only to himself.

"I'm taking these and leaving the rest. Count them now and record the numbers on that." He pointed to a stack of papyrus sheets on the desk. "Sign and mark with your signet."

As the steward wrote, Titianus tucked the sales records and senatorial letters into his satchel. They were meant to be proof of illegal transactions and evidence of attempted extortion and counterthreats. The illegal transactions he believed. The threats and extortion were fakes. He'd locked the dagger in his desk, but he'd lock all this up in a place only he knew, a place for which only he had the key.

Chapter 16

CATCHING THE SCENT

The Torquatus estate, Day 7

At the end of an avenue of neatly trimmed shrubs, the Torquatus villa sprawled before them. But it wasn't the white villa walls sparkling in the sun or the row of columns with carved floral capitals holding the portico roof that held Pompeia's gaze. It was Appius Torquatus and Glyptus walking out to meet them before the raeda even stopped.

While Kaeso held her hand to steady her as she climbed out, Appius spread his arms. She stepped into them, and they wrapped around her. She rested her cheek against his tunic, and he moved his hand to the back of her head.

"How are you, child?"

Those four words, spoken so often by Father after her mother's death, were the battering ram that finally breached the wall that held back the grief. Sorrow welled up, and he held her as sobs shook her slight frame and teardrops washed her face. Until the torrent turned into a trickle, he simply held her. Since the moment she turned Father over to see his sightless eyes, this was what she'd needed most.

He rested his cheek atop her head. "This, too, shall pass." His near-whisper was thick with his own grief. "And someday we'll know such joy together again."

She stepped back from his embrace and wiped the last of the tears from her cheeks. "I know, and 'all things work together for good to those who love God.' I must have copied those words a hundred times. In my head I know it's true, but in my heart…I can't see how good can come from this."

"Nor can I."

Glyptus had taken the others to the portico, and Appius placed her hand on his arm for the walk to join them.

"I didn't know whether you'd left for the southern estates yet. I'm glad you hadn't gone too far for Glyptus to find you." She rested her head against his shoulder. "I don't know what we would have done without him."

"We were staying a few days at the Tusculum estate. On horseback, it's an easy one-day journey. I brought only the two bodyguards I sent down with the raeda. When I got here, Glyptus already had your father prepared to be placed in my mausoleum, and he has the chef making a funeral meal for the eight of us under the trees beside it."

"Kaeso, come here." He stopped walking and waited for her brother to reach them. "I have something to ask privately." He steered them toward a circle of chairs under a carob tree.

After they settled in, he cleared his throat. "Will you have enough to take care of your familia?"

Kaeso rubbed his jaw. "I think so, as long as we don't lose the students Pompeia and I have now. If it got out that Father was murdered in his classroom while I was teaching, their fathers might be afraid to let them stay."

Torquatus's head drew back. "How have you managed to keep it quiet?"

"The tribune Septimus sent for thought he had a better chance of catching the killer if no one knew for a while."

"Who was that?"

"Titianus. He's Septimus's cousin. When he sent Corax to the guard station to fetch Titianus, he told him not to say it was murder."

Appius sucked air through his teeth. "There's not a man more likely to find the killer than him, but you need to be careful. When it comes to enforcing Roman law, he sees only black and white. For him, there are no shades of gray. Sometimes that's good. Even if it was a consul of Rome who killed your father, Titianus would still arrest him for it. Rank and wealth and family connections shouldn't decide whether justice is done, and with him, none of that matters."

He leaned back in the chair. "I've seen him make even men I thought honest become nervous when he crosses his arms and watches them. At the moment, Hadrian isn't interested in arresting Christians, but the proscription is still in place. Watch what you say around him."

Pompeia fixed her gaze on Appius's pasture. A lamb bleated, then sprinted toward its mother. "I already said more than I should about for-giving the one who did this. The shock on his face…it was the only time he reacted to anything."

Jesus had said his people were lambs among wolves, but she'd never felt like that before meeting the tribune.

"He promised to keep us informed about his progress. I hope that doesn't mean he comes every day. There's something about him, about the way he looks at you. Cold gray eyes like Sulla's." A little shiver ran through her.

Kaeso took her hand. "We'll be careful, but I don't think it will be a problem. He studied with Father before we became Christians. He remembers us as children. For Father's sake, I think he'll protect us. He said we weren't safe until he catches the murderer and finds out who hired him. Then he told us to move in with Septimus until he does."

"Be careful there, as well." Appius blew his breath out between pursed lips. "Septimus is a fine young man, but his father and grandfather…"

"It's a large house." Kaeso shrugged. "Neither of them will want to waste their time with a couple of Quintilian teachers."

Appius rested his hand on Kaeso's shoulder. "It's when the deer lets its guard down that the wolf takes it. Just be careful."

The road back to Rome

As they headed back to Rome, Titianus rode ahead until they crossed the hill and were out of site of the villa. Then he dropped back beside Sciurus. "Report."

"Stabularius sees almost everyone who comes there. It gets boring wait-ing around after he's groomed the horses, and he likes to talk."

"What did you learn?"

"That I wouldn't want to belong to Lupus. He didn't want to spend more than he had to on food. Some freedmen are mean to prove they're better than their slaves; he was one of those. Stabularius isn't sorry he's gone, even though changing owners is scary."

He shot a sideways glance at Titianus. "Sometimes it turns out really well, but you don't know beforehand."

He cleared his throat. "Lupus had a mare that couldn't carry a foal to birth. He told her buyer that she was the mother of a yearling he'd bought that was the same color."

"So, he was miserly and dishonest. What else?"

"He didn't have many visitors. No one came regularly. So maybe no close friends. He rode to the warehouse each day, and he usually rode home at night. But not always. Some nights he wouldn't come home, but wherever he went, someone groomed his horse. So, it wasn't someone poor he visited."

The stallion tossed his head, and Titianus leaned forward to stroke its neck. "Rufinus sent a slave to get some scrolls he'd lent Lupus. Did your new friend see him?"

"Plain tunic but not cheap. Rode a bay mare. Nose like a Roman, hair like mine, so maybe part Greek. Losing his hair here." He touched his temple. "And here." He patted his crown.

Titianus's eyebrow rose before his smile grew. Had he found the link between two murders?

"Rufinus's slave…what did he take into the house?"

Sciurus's smile vanished. "I didn't think to ask." He lowered his head.

"Sciurus."

When the boy's dark eyes focused on him again, Titianus tipped his head as the corners of his mouth curved. "You did well. You can expect to do this again in the future when I need a good spy."

A grin split the boy's face, and Titianus almost returned it before nudging his horse into a faster walk.

Satisfaction settled in his chest. He had little doubt there was a connection between the fire and Lenaeus's murder, and somehow Rufinus was part of it.

Nothing in the will was unusual for a freedman. Nothing was odd about sending someone to retrieve borrowed writings.

But what he found in the private strongbox was too much like what the boy had told Lenaeus to be coincidence. The record of illegal trading, the letters from the senators…without what Pompeia told him, he'd be pursuing two innocent men, bent on bringing them down. What he had so far was too vague to be used as evidence in court, but it would have been enough to make him interrogate both senators to get to the truth.

He stopped a frown. One was a cousin of Saturninus. It took no imagination to know what the prefect would have said about that.

Pompeia…if he let them, thoughts of those honey-brown eyes wormed their way into his consciousness. They'd flashed with fire when she thought he would hurt the boy. Lenaeus's sweet little girl had grown into a smart, strong woman. He'd bet a week's wages she had made her father proud.

Was she in mortal danger now because a murderer thought she knew what her father did? She was only his old tutor's daughter, but something twisted inside when he thought of her dying because he failed to prevent it.

He glanced at Sciurus, so obviously enjoying his first ride on a mule. Tertius Flaccus, the absent boy, was about the same age. How far from Rome was he now? Had his father taken him away before he said anything to anyone other than Lenaeus? Was that boy also in danger because of what he heard?

He nudged his horse into a slow trot, and the mule kept pace. Sciurus's eyes widened as his mount picked up speed, but his tightened lips quickly relaxed. Titianus had been five, not fifteen, when he learned to ride. If he was going to keep using the boy as his spy, he'd need to teach him to ride fast and far.

He rubbed his jaw. How far had Pompeia had to go for Lenaeus's funeral rites? Would she and Kaeso be back at Manius's house tonight? His mouth twitched. Waiting until tomorrow to see her was too long.

He could stop in and tell her...tell them about his progress on the way back to the fortress. Nothing would bring Lenaeus back, but even the anticipation of justice could be an antidote to grief.

He flexed his calves, and the stallion trotted faster. One glance at Sciurus's grim face as he bounced too much declared the need for a lesson right then.

Titianus slowed to a walk. "Move with your mule, don't fight him. Don't squeeze your knees so tight, don't lean forward, and let your body float as he goes up and down. Relax into the motion, and you won't bounce."

"I'll try." The boy swallowed hard, then straightened from the crouch over the mule's neck that he'd assumed.

As the two mounts switched from walk to trot and back several times, he watched the boy. "Straighten, relax, float." As the boy settled into the rhythm of the trot, Titianus began increasing the speed.

"Comfortable now?"

A quick smile and nod gave the answer he wanted, and he urged the stallion into a distance-swallowing trot. He'd leave the mule at the warehouse for a few days. No one would suspect a youth holding a horse and a mule of doing anything but waiting while his master took care of business.

The next step was to learn who talked to Lenaeus. Kaeso should know which boys were close friends. He might know which families dined together. Another conversation should reveal whether the Rufinus boy was involved. If he had Pompeia join them, perhaps she would remember some nuance of what her father said that would confirm the friends' identities.

Tonight would be better than tomorrow. He'd seen women who'd borne their grief bravely for a while, then collapsed, totally overwhelmed by emotion. Hysterical women were no use at all when he wanted trustworthy information.

One corner of his mouth lifted. A woman who would defy Roman law as she challenged its chief enforcer over a slave boy wasn't likely to turn hysterical. But even if she wouldn't, he needed to check on her, to make certain she was all right.

He'd promised to keep her posted on his progress. She should be pleased he had a solid lead already. She'd been grateful even before he'd done anything. Even if she wanted to forgive the brute for what he'd done, he'd give her justice to make it easier.

The half-smile had almost become a whole one when he stopped it. The hunt was on. He'd caught the scent, and he'd bring down the prey.

Chapter 17

SEEING THINGS DIFFERENTLY

The Sabinus town house, evening of Day 7

As Titianus rode into the Sabinus stableyard, he congratulated himself on his decision not to wait. Septimus was talking with a stableman by his stallion's stall, so the brother and sister would be there. Titianus reined over and dismounted.

"Titianus." Septimus's eyebrows rose. "To what do I owe this visit?"

"I told Kaeso Lenaeus I'd update him as I made progress."

"They aren't back yet. I expect them tomorrow."

"I thought, since you're here..." He frowned, then narrowed his eyes to mask the disappointment he hadn't meant to show. "You're like family to them. Even for the smallest gathering, I expected you there. When do they return?"

"I'll be riding out with Father's Syrian tomorrow to escort them back."

"They didn't take the bodyguard?" His frown deepened. "That was foolish."

"They're safe. Tutelus and I escorted them to the edge of town to meet Torquatus's raeda. He provided guards himself for the rest of the trip. We'll meet them tomorrow afternoon and walk them back to the school."

"Walk?" His lips tightened. "That's a long way for her to walk."

Septimus's chuckle raised his eyebrow. "They don't have a litter, so anywhere she wants to go, she walks. They both do. I'm not sure Kaeso even knows how to ride."

"You can tell them I'll come tomorrow." Titianus fingered his reins. At the fortress, a quiet evening alone with a new history of Trajan's conquest of Dacia awaited him. He enjoyed solitude, so why the disappointment?

Septimus leaned forward and slapped his arm. Titianus's head drew back at the familiarity.

"Since you're here, stay for dinner. Father has gone to a banquet with Grandfather, and I could use your company. We can play some tabula or latrunculi after we eat." He smacked his lips. "I chose the menu, so I can guarantee it will be good, and even Father says I make him work for every win at latrunculi."

"It's a safe bet that any cook your father would keep can do better than garrison food." Titianus relaxed enough to let a half-smile escape. "Time will tell if you're as good as one of the Praetorian tribunes. We play many nights at the fortress because he lives there, too."

Septimus's brow furrowed. "But you have a town house not far from here. Why would you live at the fortress?"

"I've rented it out for several years. My sisters live with their aunt now, and I hardly used it. By the time I've finished everything I want for the day, there's not a lot of day left. All I need is a place to read and sleep, and I can do both at the fortress, plus find a good partner for a board game."

"You can have that anytime if you want to eat with me. Until you catch the killer, Pompeia will be here, too." Septimus bounced his eyebrows.

Titianus's eyebrows lowered in response before he thought to stop them. He relaxed his face. "And her brother."

"Yes, but she probably gets bored when the two of us play. Kaeso's good, and he says she beats him as often as she loses. She'd probably enjoy playing you. You could help get her mind off what's happened." His teasing smile vanished. "She really needs that. She and her father were very close."

"I'll stay for dinner. The last time I had food prepared by a chef instead of a cook was the prefect's monthly dinner with the Praetorians." He pursed his lips. "It's not wise to say much there. It's better to listen."

He barely knew Septimus, but his cousin chuckled like they often shared jokes.

"I know what you mean. I dine with Father and his friends. Instructive, but not relaxing. Truth and honor are often not welcome in a room filled with power. We can talk or not as long as you promise me a good game afterwards."

Septimus took Titianus's reins and summoned the stableman. "Dinner should be ready. The sooner we eat, the more games we can play before you have to leave."

As he walked beside his young cousin into the peristyle garden, Titianus glanced at Septimus. His father and grandfather were powerful men. They mostly used their power for the good of Rome, as they saw it. But how they saw it and how he saw it often differed. No one wanted them as enemies, but neither was a man he'd want as a friend. Septimus seemed different, and if he truly was, might his young cousin become one?

Dinner had been excellent, and Titianus had enjoyed the companionable silence. Now they were setting up for the second game of tabula. It was time to satisfy his curiosity while no one else could hear.

"The man who brought a clean toga, Glyptus—they all seemed so glad to see him. What was his relationship to Lenaeus?"

Septimus's chuckle wasn't what he wanted to hear. "Do you mean what's his relationship to Pompeia? You sound like Father. He wanted to make sure I had no interest in her for a wife before he agreed to let them stay here." His cousin fought a grin. "Well, Glyptus doesn't, either. He's been a family friend since she was still a child. He's Torquatus's secretary, and both of them were good friends with Gnaeus Lenaeus."

Titianus's eyebrows dipped. "I asked the question I wanted to. It's the whole family, not just her, that I want to understand." His cousin's eyebrow rose. "There could be other motives for the murder."

"Of course you do." Septimus rolled a game piece in his fingers. "Kaeso says it's a mistake to let her go first. She usually beats him then. But maybe you play better than he does." He placed it on the board. "Do come for dinner tomorrow. She could use the distraction."

"If I can."

Titianus made his first move. It was the whole family he wanted to help and not just the pretty daughter who was unlike any woman he'd met before.

Septimus played, and it was his turn again.

But a man of honor must be a man of truth as well. He did want to help the whole family, but what he wanted for her…he wasn't sure what that was. What he wanted for himself…he wasn't sure about that, either.

"Ooh. That scowl—not what I like to see on my opponent." Septimus placed his piece. "But you left your sword over there with the helmet and cuirass, so I'm safe enough."

It was a good thing they played tabula and not latrunculi. Titianus didn't like losing, and his cousin played well enough that winning the harder game would take focus, more focus than he had when Septimus kept mentioning her.

He started to shake his head, then stopped before Septimus commented on it. There was no good reason why she'd captured his interest so strongly. He felt sorry for her because she'd lost her father; that was all. More than he usually felt for a dead man's daughter, but surely that was because he remembered the little girl who brought her father lunch and closed her eyes when she hugged him before leaving.

He'd make certain he came back tomorrow. The best way to get over fascination with something was to see enough of it that it lost its novelty. There was no reason that shouldn't happen with her.

The Torquatus estate, evening of Day 7

As Pompeia leaned against the marble column of the portico to watch the sun set, she bore the ravaged heart of a beloved child newly orphaned.

Appius Torquatus had overseen the funeral, and he'd shared Jesus's words about eternal life with her familia and Glyptus. She'd copied them so many times she knew every one by heart. Now Father lay in a niche in the Torquatus family mausoleum. She wiped the corner of her eye. Father's body, not Father. He was joyous in the presence of Jesus now, and she knew she'd see him again. But that didn't dull the ache or stop her tears.

The flaming orb had just disappeared behind the hills when she felt a hand on her back. She turned away from the setting sun to find Kaeso with troubled eyes.

"I need to talk with you…away from the others."

"Of course." She slipped her hand into his. "Let's go over there."

A low wall surrounded the rose bed with its profusion of red and yellow flowers, and she pointed at a bench on the far side. As they strolled past each bush, the fragrance around them shifted between sweet and spice and musk.

She sat, and he settled onto the bench beside her. "What is it?"

He leaned forward to put his elbows on his knees. Then he cradled his head. Her own heartache was mirrored on his face.

Silence stretched out between them, but finally he straightened. "I didn't want to say anything where Theo or Lilia might hear. I don't want to distress them any more than they are. I don't want their faith shaken just because mine is."

He turned anguished eyes on her. "But I'm struggling with how God could let this happen." His jaw clenched.

She slipped her arm around his shoulders. "I know. I've asked God why so many times I've lost count. I can't believe Father's gone, but as least we know he's with God." As the quaver started, she cleared her throat to stop it. He was hurting enough without her own pain adding to it. "I keep reminding myself what Jesus said. How He was going to prepare a place for those of us who love Him. How He told the robber crucified beside Him that they'd be together in Paradise that very day. How those of us who believe in Him can never truly die."

"I know all that, but why did Father have to die now? Why that way?"

"You were too young to remember, but I was twelve when Publius Drusus wrote his letter as he waited to die in the arena because his son had betrayed him. It was that letter that started Father and Appius wondering whether God was real, whether Jesus was His son whose death reconciled us with God. I studied it with them."

"What's that got to do with Father being murdered?"

"Father knew that following Jesus doesn't mean horrible things won't happen to you. They did to Publius. But it does mean that on the other side of the horror there's a life wonderful beyond anything we can imagine while our bodies still live."

"I know that, too, but Publius died a martyr, and it led others to follow Jesus. Father's death doesn't serve God. It doesn't serve any purpose." He rubbed his jaw. "I know I shouldn't let it, but what happened makes me so angry." He drew a deep breath. "Angry at God. I just keep asking why, and maybe I shouldn't because there's no answer. It's like He isn't listening, like He isn't there."

Pompeia tried to draw him closer to her side, but he shrugged off her arm instead. "But we know He is. We've felt His presence when we worship. Can you even count how many times we've seen Him answer our prayers? I can't." He looked away, and his silence frightened her. It was only trusting God that was holding her broken world together.

"He already knows you're angry. You can ask why as many times as you need to. He isn't shocked by our anger or our questions. He knows how much we're hurting. We're His children, and He loves us. Someday, maybe it will all make sense, and if it doesn't..." She rubbed both sides of her nose. "Well, Father always said part of faith was accepting things we don't understand now, trusting that someday God will make it clear." She pushed back a strand of his hair, as she'd done when he hurt as a little boy. "Even if that isn't until we join Him in heaven." A slow, sad smile curved her lips. "Father's questions are all answered now. Ours will be someday."

Kaeso's sigh was deep as he slowly nodded. "I understand everything you say in my head, but I don't feel it in my heart."

She took his hand and interwove their fingers. "I'll pray for you to find peace with this. I'm still praying for peace with it myself."

"And there's one thing more." He withdrew his hand. "Something worse."

"What is it?" The guilt on his face stopped her next breath.

"I'm struggling with hating whoever did it. I know I should be trying to forgive him like Jesus said, but I can't. If he was standing right here and I had a dagger, I don't think I could stop myself from driving it into his chest like he did to Father." He rubbed his forehead. "I'm not sure I'd even try."

"But we have to keep trying. I know we can't forgive this on our own. At least I can't." She wiped the corner of her eye before a tear could escape. "But we don't have to. It's only with the Spirit's help that we'll get past this. Forgiveness isn't a feeling. It's a decision, and Jesus told us we can't refuse to give it if we want God to forgive us."

The next tear got halfway down her cheek before she caught it. "Each time I start to feel the anger and hatred rising up within me, I ask the Spirit to take it from me, to help me as I try to forgive. And each time, I feel my anger cool, and the hatred fades. I want whoever did this caught and punished, but not just for vengeance. I don't want him to ever do this to someone else."

She drew a deep breath and released a shuddering sigh. "I keep reminding myself Jesus asked the Father to forgive the soldiers as they were crucifying Him. He asks us to forgive those who hurt us." She sniffed. "Commands, actually, not asks. I'll keep trying, and with the Spirit's help, I'll be able to obey."

She wrapped her arm around him again, and he let it stay. "But we'll both struggle with that for a while. I'll keep praying for us both to succeed."

He stared into the distance before he slowly nodded. The sky fire had peaked while they talked, and it was fading now.

"Ready to go back?" She glanced at the portico, where Corax sat with his family.

"Back to the villa, yes. Back to our house, not really. But no matter what happened there, we have no choice. We have to keep teaching, and we have no other place to do it." He blew a breath out slowly. "I don't know how I'm going to be able to look at Father's room and not see him lying there, bloody on the floor or dead on the tables." He squared his shoulders. "But death isn't the end, and life must go on. We have good memories in that house, too. Perhaps in time, those will outweigh the bad."

As they walked back, the perfume of roses hung in the air around them. An enchanting scent from a beautiful flower, but every rosebush bore skin-piercing thorns.

God, please get us past these thorns to the beauty of life again. Please replace this pain with peace.

Chapter 18

A Difficult Man

Near the Lenaeus town house, midday of Day 8

Of the four soldiers Titianus had sent out to look for a witness, Asellus alone had been successful. He'd found a weaver who'd seen a man fitting the description who'd looked like he was going to throw up, then he didn't. Even professional killers sometimes reacted that way in the aftermath of the deed. Today Titianus would speak with her himself.

He walked past Lenaeus's door and turned right on the next street up. The woman's shop was three blocks ahead where the slope down to the Via Patricius steepened.

She was working at a loom on what would probably become a cloak. He stepped up to her counter and cleared his throat.

"What can I he—" Her eyes saucered as she turned, then veiled. "help you with, tribune?" A nervous smile appeared, then steadied. She stood halfway at attention.

Some spoke truth more freely when he projected authority. Others did better when he was less frightening. This one...she'd be the latter. He took off his helmet and set it on the counter. "Asellus spoke with you yesterday. He said you told him about something suspicious that might help us clear up a problem."

He drew his fingers across a small beige table runner among several she had displayed. A green vine with red flowers was embroidered along the center. "Hmm. Nice." He focused his gaze back on her face. "I'd like to hear what you told him and ask a few questions about what else you might have seen."

He let his eyes warm and the corners of his mouth turn up. She relaxed and stepped closer to the counter. "He asked if I saw anyone like what he described who was acting strange. I said maybe."

Titianus held one arm against his stomach so he could rest his elbow on it. Then he rubbed the underside of his jaw. "Tell me about it."

"A dark-haired man in a toga looked like he was going to throw up, but he didn't. Then he kept walking that way." She pointed downhill toward the Via Patricius.

"That might be the man we're looking for." He fingered one of the flowers. "I can see you have an eye for detail." He let his eyes turn friendly. "Tell me as much as you can remember."

"His toga and tunic...whiter than most. I know wool fabric, and he'd paid a good price for those."

"What exactly did he look like?"

"Dark hair, a little curly. Thin up here" She tapped the crown of her head. "And going back here." She touched her temple. "Not muscled like you, but he was still a man to catch a woman's eye."

"Did you see any red spots on his clothes? Or mud or dirt?"

"No, very clean."

"Was he wearing a dagger that you could see?"

Her laugh was not what he expected. "No, but he covered his mouth when he fought with his stomach, and he had a silver signet. Wouldn't a man like that without a bodyguard wear a dagger?"

"He would." Titianus let a smile warm his eyes further. Friendly definitely got more information from women like this. "My job would be easier if everyone noticed things like you. Anything else I should know?"

"I watched him awhile to see if he threw up." She shrugged. "He didn't."

"Did you see where he went?"

She pointed down the street. "He went straight down to the Via and crossed it. Then he started up that path to the Cispian Hill that you can see to the left."

"Excellent." He gave her a full smile. "If you see him again, I'd like to know all about it. You know the guard station on the way to the baths?"

She nodded.

"I'm usually there. If I'm not, Optio Gellius will be glad to have someone find me for you. I'm Titianus."

She nodded, this time more slowly. She wouldn't come without owing him a favor.

"This runner." He stroked the flower again. "I have a friend who'd like it. How much?"

Her merchant-eyes took his measure. "Two sesterces?"

He took a denarius from his purse, twice what she'd asked. "It's worth more, and I always pay a fair price."

Her eyes widened, and her smile grew to match them. "Thank you, tribune. If I see him again, I'll let you know."

He put his helmet back on and scooped up his purchase. "I appreciate that." With a nod and a smile, he started back up the hill. When she could no longer see his face, his lips relaxed to their normal straight line.

Asellus had done well in finding the weaver. He'd commend him to both optio and centurion the next time he spoke with them.

He glanced at the runner he still carried. It was rather pretty, but he had no use for such things. However, the Lenaeus house was his next stop. He'd give it to one of Pompeia's people for them to give to her later. Surely, she could find something to do with it.

He reached their door and knocked. The boy should let him in without delay this time.

No answer. He knocked again. Still no answer, and the cypress branches hadn't been replaced with fresh ones. It was not what he expected, but it looked like they all might have gone to the funeral. Septimus hadn't mentioned that, but the way she claimed they loved her father, maybe she decided to take them along.

Even the most loyal slaves would normally choose a day of little work because the master was gone over a bumpy road trip to funeral rites. But there was usually good food after, and Torquatus would feed them better than they were used to. So maybe it made sense.

He folded the cloth and tucked it in his satchel. He would take Septimus up on his standing offer for dinner. His cousin played tabula well, and he'd enjoyed their dinner the night before. He'd even enjoyed the companionable silence when they exhausted the few things they had to talk about.

It wasn't because Pompeia would be there, although he could give the cloth to her then with an explanation of how he got it. It was proof he was making progress. The dinner would give him an opportunity to ask her and Kaeso questions without students or servants hearing.

He stopped the smile that was trying to grow. It would also let him judge for himself whether she played tabula as well as Septimus claimed. He'd be willing to bet a week's wages she did.

The Lenaeus town house, late afternoon of Day 8

Since negotiating the new fee-for-service, Vulpis had tried twice yesterday and once this morning to kill the boy, but each time his knocks brought no answer. This morning, no one had replaced the dried-out cypress boughs with fresh ones. Where they'd all gone… he had no idea. But that didn't matter since he didn't care. They'd be back sometime, and the longer it was since the murder, the more likely the boy's guard would be down.

But this time as he approached the door, the smell of fresh-cut cypress greeted him. Three knocks on the door and he fingered the hilt of his dagger as he waited. He'd brought an old one he wouldn't miss if he had to leave it behind.

The door swung open, and his hand dropped away from the blade. In the place of a small boy stood a massive Syrian, hand on his own dagger and a scowl on his face.

"What do you want?" The voice was deep, the words were icy, and the eyes were cold.

Vulpis put on a smile. "I'm here to see Rogius Varus."

"He doesn't live here." The bodyguard took a step back, and the door closed in Vulpis's face.

He retreated up the road to the corner where a bench was built into the wall. He sat and tried to blend in. Why was a bodyguard on the door instead of the boy? Where had the Lenaeus familia been, leaving the house totally empty as if they weren't coming back? If the bodyguard left, would the boy open the door if he tried knocking again?

His musings were interrupted when the door opened and the bodyguard, an armed young nobleman, a pretty woman, and another young man emerged.

The last man turned back. "Don't open the door to anyone until we return tomorrow."

"Yes, master." A man's voice, not a boy's. Someone not likely to disobey and open, no matter what Vulpis said.

The foursome started down the street, the two young men together, the woman beside the bodyguard whose gaze swept the area around them, even looking behind them.

Vulpis followed, staying well back. These two were the son and daughter. It was worth knowing where they would be spending the night. Odds were good that Arcanus would be needing his services for more than the boy.

If Titianus was personally involved with this household, he might show up where they were going tonight.

He trailed them off the Viminal Hill and down the Vicus Patricius to the switch-backing shortcut that led to the elite Fagutal neighborhood. When they entered a stableyard, armed guards flanked the gate, scabbards hanging from the straps draped across heavily muscled chests.

Where guards could see him was not a good place to loiter, but they'd passed a taberna with tables a few blocks back. If Titianus was coming up from the guard station at the edge of Subura, he'd be coming by there.

Vulpis backtracked and sat at a street-side table. When the servant girl came, he ordered some stew and bread.

It wasn't long before the red crest on a brass helmet came into view. The tribune rode past without looking at him and turned at the side street that went to the house where the brother and sister were.

As his teeth tore off another bite of bread, Vulpis's smile grew. He had his answer, and it would double what Arcanus would have to pay when he made another request for a kill.

The Rufinus town house, evening of Day 8

When Rufinus ran into Prefect Saturninus at the baths, Fortuna had smiled upon him. The ex-consul had accepted his invitation to dine with appropriate expressions of pleasure. Now they lounged on couches in the private dining room beside the peristyle garden, the water spouting from the marble dolphin's mouth making watery background music. Soon the salad course would come. As an appetizer, Rufinus wanted an assurance that the prefect would rein in his overzealous tribune.

"You may have heard that I'll be proposed for consul next year. It's a heavy responsibility, and I hope I can count on your sage advice, both before and during my term of service. You were consul last year, even while being urban prefect. How did you manage the burden of both so well?"

Saturninus leaned over and picked up a raisin from the bowl of fruit. "Delegation of lesser tasks. I have enough senatorial and equestrian clients with solid administrative skills to cover that."

"I suppose you have the same as urban prefect. Were your tribunes as helpful? I've heard your most senior man—Titianus?—is extraordinary in his attention to every detail." He chose a slice of dried apple. "Of course, that can make a man less efficient if he doesn't choose his focus wisely."

"Hmph." Saturninus scrunched his nose. "I'm glad Titianus will be hitting his tenth year as tribune shortly and returning to private life. It will be good to have a man less likely to cause a political scandal when someone important does something a little outside Roman law."

"A scandal?" Rufinus bit the end off a dried fig. "What is he working on at the moment?"

"Two politically unimportant cases…a dead freedman with an arson to cover it up and a teacher killed in his own classroom when no one was watching."

"Those do seem a waste of time for your best investigator. Neither sounds important."

Saturninus shrugged. "They aren't, but he thinks they are. He doesn't like any murderer to go unpunished. If some crime of importance occurs, he works that first, but he doesn't drop the others. When I replace him in a few months, I expect the new tribune will close much of what Titianus is keeping open."

That was a few months too long from Rufinus's perspective. "He'll be a difficult man to follow."

"I'll choose a replacement who won't want to. He was installed by Annius Verus. Verus didn't know what he was getting. He picked him as a favor to Titianus's father. The son needed to stay near Rome as his father was dying."

Rufinus chose another apple slice. "Why do you keep him?"

"If your enemies raised the question in the Senate, would you want to explain why you got rid of the best investigator Rome has?" Saturninus's ironic laugh raised Rufinus's eyebrow. "Would you risk someone demanding that he investigate you for trying to get rid of him?"

He gave Saturninus the wry smile he expected rather than the frown his words deserved. He'd get no help reducing the Titianus risk from the prefect. "I have nothing to hide, but the opposition can always create the appearance of wrongdoing, even for an innocent man."

"Exactly." Saturninus tapped his goblet, and the slave came forward to fill it. He inhaled the complex aroma and took a sip. "Excellent Falernian. I like to serve Brutus's special vintage, but I'm out at the moment. It's harder to get since he moved to Germania."

"It is extraordinary, but like you, I need to replenish my supply."

As Rufinus took a sip, he watched Saturninus over the goblet's rim. Neither he nor Saturninus had access to Brutus's vintage for the honorable, and pretending they had it meant they never would.

Chapter 19

Guests in the House

The Sabinus town house, evening of Day 8

From the station to the Sabinus house in the Fagutal was not a long walk, but this evening Titianus chose to ride. He always rode back to the fortress at the end of the day. If he'd walked, there would be unspoken questions about where he'd gone. His men didn't need to be wondering about what he did when off duty or how late he was doing it.

Dinner with Septimus had been pleasant, but tonight Kaeso and Pompeia would be there. In his satchel was the runner from the weaver who'd seen the murderer. It was soft and pretty; most women would like it for those reasons alone. But it was more than that. It was an assurance that he was making progress and that the one who killed Lenaeus would pay.

When he rode into the stableyard, a boy approached from the portico. "Master Septimus hoped you would make it tonight. They're waiting for you. Follow me." He bowed and led Titianus to the small dining room off the peristyle that they'd used yesterday.

Septimus swung his legs off his couch and came to greet him. "I'm glad you could make it. I told them you were here yesterday and might be back."

Titianus took off his helmet and set it by the wall. After lifting the satchel and scabbard straps over his head, he undid the latches on one side of his cuirass and stood it by the helmet.

Kaeso and Pompeia reclined on the center couch, and Septimus returned to his. Satchel in hand, Titianus approached her.

"I went to your house today, and no one answered my knocking."

"We all went to the estate. Like I told you before, our people loved Father. It would have been wrong to keep them from his funeral rites."

Her words could have seemed harsh, but her eyes and voice softened them into an explanation, not a rebuff.

"I stopped by your house for a reason. I had to buy something from a weaver to get her to tell me everything she knew." He pulled the cloth from the satchel and held it out.

She didn't take it. She stared at it like it might bite her.

He felt like a fool.

◆

It was the first time a man had offered her a gift like that. Even folded, she could see the embroidered roses were exquisite, but why would he give it to her?

She shifted her gaze from the needlework to his face. The gray eyes hadn't changed...cold, unreadable even while they seemed to read what you were thinking.

"If it's not something you want, just give it away." A trace of disappointment colored his words.

He had feelings she hadn't thought existed, and she'd hurt them. But she didn't want to encourage any interest he had in her by taking his gifts.

Still, she took it. "Thank you. It is lovely, and I can use it in my classroom when I'm teaching. If you buying it helps you catch my father's killer, I'll remember that each time I use it."

With a quick tip of his head, he took his place on the empty couch.

The salad course came, and the room fell silent as they ate. Too silent. At her house, Septimus usually talked during dinner.

The tribune...every time she cast a glance his direction, he was watching her. After that gift, she didn't want him to think she wanted any attention. But she'd never dined with a strange man who showed interest before; how should she send that message? She taught her students Roman dining etiquette, and here she was, flustered like a young girl at her first banquet. She felt her cheeks heat, and she could have kicked herself for blushing. Surely the tribune saw it. What would he think?

He cleared his throat. "Where did you all go?"

She'd never been so relieved to be asked a routine question. "We went north of the city. I'd never been outside Rome before. Some other time, it would be a beautiful place to visit."

Septimus turned toward her. "What did you like best?"

"I'm not sure I could pick one thing. None of us had ridden in a raeda before. It jostled a lot until we got off the stone road onto the dirt. But with the big window and the open door, I saw so many new things…vineyards and huge gardens and grain fields. The flocks on the hills…I loved the lambs. Theo had never been on a horse, and one of the bodyguards let him ride with him for a while."

Kaeso hadn't spoken a word since the tribune came. She looked over her shoulder to find him brooding.

Septimus's gaze shifted to her brother. "What about you, Kaeso? What kept your attention?"

"The future…what that means with Father gone." He rubbed his forehead. "We should know within a week or so if we've kept enough students to pay the rent where we are. If we lose too many, we might have to move. Depending on where we go, we might lose even more. Even if they all stay, I have to figure out how to add new students as the boys we have move on. Long term…I just don't know."

She shifted to rest her hand on his arm. "Don't worry about the evils of tomorrow. Today has enough evils of its own."

Her brother placed his hand on hers. "Keep reminding me."

In the silence that followed, she heard the tribune move on his couch. She glanced his way to find him looking at Kaeso, lips tight and brow furrowed. Then his eyes focused on her, and the anger vanished, replaced by… she couldn't be sure. Then his mouth curved into the closest thing to a smile she'd seen on him yet. It was only polite to return it.

◆

He'd come to ask some questions tonight, but Titianus could see he'd have to come again. It would be cruel to make them focus on what had happened when he could feel her grief so close to the surface and her brother was worried about how they'd be able to live.

He prided himself on controlling his emotions, but he couldn't completely quench the anger that flared when he looked at them. They'd lost their father and might lose the school because some nobleman had broken Roman law, had a man murdered because of it, and killed Lenaeus to hide the crimes.

What if whoever had killed to silence her father came back to silence her brother or her? If he failed to get the one who hired the killer, she would never be safe. Manius Sabinus wouldn't let her stay at his house and provide a bodyguard forever. If the killer was patient, she'd be unprotected again and an easy target.

Failure wasn't an option this time. He'd find the ones responsible, and the shadow-smiles dimmed by the grief in her eyes could become bright ones again.

Flanked by his two Germans, Manius rode into the stableyard. An unfamiliar smoke-gray stallion stood tied to a ring on the wall, unsaddled and munching hay. Ridden by one of Septimus's friends, no doubt.

He entered the peristyle and headed for the private triclinium. Depending on what Septimus was eating, he might join them. Keeping track of his son's social contacts was important, even if the boy had said more than once he wouldn't take advantage of a friendship for political reasons.

As he approached the door, a brass cuirass and red-plumed helmet came into view. When he stepped inside, his head drew back. Titianus reclined on the couch opposite Septimus with the Lenaeus siblings between them.

Manius pasted on his political smile. "Cousin Titus. To what do we owe the pleasure?"

"Manius." Titianus tipped his head to acknowledge the greeting. "I stopped by with some questions for Lenaeus and Pompeia."

"And I asked him to stay for dinner." Septimus wiped his mouth and dropped the napkin on the couch beside him. "I've heard so many stories about how bad military food is that I thought I'd give him a reprieve from it tonight." He sucked air between his teeth. "I'm dreading what I'm going to be eating when I go to my first posting in two years."

"You train with Brutus's men to be prepared for battle." What Manius started as a half-smile turned into a full grin. "I can ask the chef to make you some special meals if you want to prepare for garrison-style cooking."

Septimus's snorting laugh was what Manius expected. "I can wait. A few surprises make life more interesting."

Titianus swung his legs off the couch. "Thank you for the dinner, Septimus. If you want to try real garrison food, I'd be glad to return the hospitality." He stood. "I need to ride back to the fortress now."

"Is that wise?" Septimus's brow furrowed. "Stay the night. Traveling alone in Rome this late—it's too dangerous. Go back in the morning."

Titianus's chuckle was closer to a laugh, and it left behind a smile that looked human. "If a tribune of the Urban Cohort in full armor can't ride safely through Rome at night, no one can."

Manius rubbed his lower lip. It wasn't every day he was presented with an opportunity to talk privately with a man who knew the underbelly of Rome as well as Titianus. "Come back tomorrow when I can join you for dinner. You can entertain us with stories about what you're investigating."

Any warmth vanished as his cousin's mouth reverted to his usual slight frown. "I don't discuss cases with people who are not involved with them."

When his eyes turned on Pompeia, his face softened. "But Septimus mentioned that Pompeia teaches lyre and singing to young women. Perhaps she would entertain us with some music."

"I don't know what Septimus told you, but I'm not as skilled as he might have implied. I only teach beginners, and you don't have to be an artist yourself to do that." The smile she directed at Titianus was lukewarm. "But if you think it would give you pleasure and there's a lyre I can borrow, I would be willing to play."

"Good." He slipped on his cuirass and began fastening the latches. After the second, he paused to look at her. "Anticipation of that could make a man want to come often." After hanging a satchel and sword across his chest, he donned the helmet. "If you'll excuse me..."

"Of course." Manius offered his cousin a cool smile.

"You'll come again soon?" Septimus's eagerness received a nod before the tribune vanished into the peristyle.

Titianus had been entertaining to watch, but Manius found Pompeia even more so. His cousin's clumsily expressed interest in seeing more of her didn't make her blush, as he half expected, but the way her eyes widened at his suggestion and veiled when he said he'd return just to hear her showed she was aware of the attraction. Aware and not quite sure how to encourage it. Or was she less naïve than she seemed?

Most girls at this point would flirt to draw more compliments, but the tribune who read motives too well wouldn't play that game. Maybe she was smarter about men than Manius had thought. That lukewarm response was precisely what would fire the interest of a man who thought himself immune to women's wiles.

"It's been a long day, so I'll leave you to enjoy yourselves without me."

A chorus of goodnights sent him from the room and up the stairs. As he reached the balcony, he couldn't help silently laughing at Titianus.

The tribune famous for letting nothing sway him in his pursuit of justice seemed captivated by the teacher's daughter. It was too soon since her father's death to tell if she shared the feeling.

It would be amusing to encourage them. If she returned his regard or even if she only let him think she did, she wouldn't be trying to lure Septimus into making her his wife. As the daughter of a teacher of noble sons, she should already know senators married for political advantage while equestrians could marry for love.

Chapter 20

WHAT MORE COULD GO WRONG?

The Rufinus town house, Day 9

Arcanus was usually the last to speak to Rufinus at the morning salutation. Often there was something his patron wanted him to look into after meeting with his other clients. He used to relax on a bench, watching and listening to pick up information that might be of use. But since Lupus died, he found himself fidgeting when someone who was waiting looked at him too long. His leg would start to bounce, and the people sitting near would begin to stare. Today had been worse than yesterday.

At last, Rufinus's secretary escorted the final petitioner out, and Arcanus entered the tablinum, closing the door behind him. He strode to the panel providing access to the peristyle, and stuck his head out. Nothing stirred, but he still took a place against the wall where he could keep an eye on the garden to be certain that didn't change.

Rufinus rose from his throne-like chair and joined Arcanus by the opening. "I have good news."

Arcanus's gaze shifted for a moment to his patron's face. "What is it?" Then he turned his eyes on the garden again.

"A message came from Lupus's house steward. Titianus came to inspect the contents of the strongboxes. He took some tablets with him." Rufinus's mouth slowly curved. "He found some records of suspicious sales and some letters from a couple of senators in the library strongbox. Celeris said our tribune seemed pleased, as best as he could tell with a man who shows less emotion than one of Trajan's statues."

He slapped Arcanus's upper arm. "Whatever you prepared, it appears to be fooling Titianus. He'll be trying to tie the two senators to the murder and arson, but they're important enough he'd have to have an eyewitness to them doing it to prosecute the crime."

Satisfaction oozed from him like a cat that had just taken a mouse. "I can fan suspicions behind their backs that will weaken them when they try to oppose me."

He walked to the wine cabinet and withdrew flagons of wine and water and two goblets. To each, he added water and some of his best Falernian, then handed one to Arcanus.

He raised the goblet. "To the gullibility of Rome's finest investigator."

Arcanus lifted his own before they both took a sip. He savored the golden liquid, but his enjoyment was tempered by a twinge of regret. Perhaps killing the teacher hadn't been necessary. But it was still better to kill the teacher than to risk dying himself.

The Baths of Trajan, afternoon of Day 9

The water of the hot pool wrapped around Rufinus like a nanny's embrace. His eyes were drifting shut when Saturninus slipped into the water beside him.

"We don't often run into each other here. I'm expected at a banquet tonight, or I'd return your hospitality of yesterday. My new chef is excellent."

Rufinus shifted on the underwater bench to make it easier to watch the prefect's face. "I'll look forward to it. It's been some time since I so enjoyed an evening of games and conversation."

"Men who will serve Rome as consuls are always welcome at my table. Only such men understand the burdens we bear for the good of Rome."

"Like too many demands on your time and underlings who hinder instead of help."

"Quite. But sometimes even they turn up something worthwhile." Saturninus spread his arms along the pool wall.

"Has your overzealous tribune focused on something more worthy of his talents?"

"Yes and no. He has better instincts that I gave him credit for. Those two cases I thought unimportant…"

"The arson and the teacher?"

"Yes. I met with each of my tribunes for reports on their top cases yesterday. Titianus said he's collected evidence of someone trying to incriminate two innocent senators for illegal businesses and killing the freedman Lupus, and that the murder of the rhetor Lenaeus is linked to covering up the murder and arson."

Rufinus stomach churned. "I'm amazed. No, shocked." He shook his head. "I knew Lenaeus died a few days ago. He's been my son's tutor in rhetoric for a few years. He came highly recommended, and I was impressed when I talked with him before I started Gaius there. He gave excellent training in Quintilian-style oratory. I had to move my son on to someone who argues in the courts early because Lenaeus died suddenly. But Gaius never said Lenaeus's death was a murder. I thought his heart stopped."

"It did…" Saturnius smirked. "But it was a dagger that stopped it."

"If it was a warehouse by the Tiber that burned, the dead man was my father's freedman. I don't know much about Lupus's business because it isn't one that senators get involved with, but he'd been honest in all he did for the Rufinus family before my father freed him in his will."

"An interesting coincidence—both men having ties to you." Was that amusement or suspicion in the prefect's eyes?

"If it is one." Rufinus rubbed his mouth. A half-truth could be better defense than a lie. "Was I one of the senators someone tried to incriminate? As you well know, when a man runs for consul, many lies get told about him by his enemies."

Saturninus chuckled. "Do you have any enemies who would go that far?"

Did suspicion still linger in those laughing eyes?

"Does a man ever know before they strike?" Years ago, Rufinus had mastered the art of answering a dangerous question with a question. "If not me, who are the senators?"

"You ask two good questions. As for the first, not always. As for the second, I don't have an answer for you. Titianus wouldn't say who they were. He said it was premature to reveal details until he had the murderer in hand."

"Saturninus." The call and wave came from a group of five senators near the hallway to the changing rooms.

The prefect rose and climbed out of the hot water. "Watch your back, and let me know if you need my help doing that."

130

The nod and grateful smile Rufinus directed at the prefect were returned before he strode toward the door to join his senate colleagues.

Rufinus slipped lower into the water and rested his head against the hot pool's wall. He closed his eyes and blanked his face. He wanted no one to try to strike up a conversation, and feigning sleep should give him some moments alone to figure out what to do before something else went horribly wrong.

Chapter 21

THE MAN UNDERNEATH

The Sabinus town house. evening of Day 9

Pompeia rested her elbows on the dressing table, steepled her fingers, and buried her face in her hands. Only six days ago, she'd held Sanura's son and shared the joy of new life with one of her favorite former students. Five days ago, she'd stood at the door of Father's classroom, laughing as he demonstrated how humor could persuade and then had his boys try. Life had been sweet, and then…

She bit her lip to stop the quiver.

And then she found Father.

For what seemed the thousandth time, tears washed her cheeks. She opened the drawer to get a dry handkerchief, and the embroidered rose sitting next to them mocked her with its cheerfulness.

She dried her cheeks, then took the runner from the drawer and spread it on the tabletop. Someone had spent hours making the leaves and tendrils, buds and blossoms that stretched across its length. It was a thing of beauty, and if Kaeso or Septimus or one of the girls she taught had given it to her, she would have loved both the runner and the thought behind it.

But it came from the tribune she'd rather not see again until the day he could tell her he'd caught Father's murderer. He'd given a believable reason for having it. Maybe he did have to buy something to get the weaver to tell him everything, but why this and why give it to her?

Womanly instincts whispered words she didn't want to hear…he liked her. Why he would was a mystery. They hadn't spoken fifty words before she challenged him over what he might do to Theo. He hadn't liked that one bit. Until he gave her the runner last night, she'd seen scarcely a hint of human emotion in his eyes or heard any in his voice. But it had mattered to him that she accept it. What else could explain that?

Too often when she glanced his way during last night's dinner, she found him watching her. And when she caught him, he didn't look away. The slightest hint of a smile would curve those straight lips, and a trace of warmth softened the steel-gray eyes.

Why had Septimus told him to come every night if he wanted to? Why had his father specifically invited him to join them tonight?

Why had her second brother promised him an evening of music so Titianus could claim a good reason for wanting to come?

She glanced at the elegant instrument lying on her bed. The arms were carved with vines wrapping around them. Paintings of matching vines adorned the soundbox. Intricately carved roses in full bloom adorned the ends of the crossbar where the strings attached, and each tuning key was a rosebud. It was a thing of rare beauty for both eyes and ears.

She fingered the largest embroidered rose. It could be the pattern for her students to copy. She'd told him she could use it in her classroom, and he'd seemed pleased…or at least not displeased. He frowned more readily than he smiled.

Maybe she should be thankful Septimus had volunteered her to play. Tomorrow she'd be teaching again, and she'd have something to focus on beside the void Father left. Today she had music to practice, and as long as she didn't play one of Father's favorites, she could forget for a moment there was a hole in her universe that only time and prayer would fill.

With anticipation beyond what he would have expected, Titianus rode into the Sabinus stableyard. Manius's chef was superb, and Pompeia would provide some music. Either would be better than the garrison stew and an evening by himself. Together…the thought almost drew a smile.

The stableman came to take his horse even before he dismounted. "Master Septimus said to come into the peristyle whenever you arrive, today and in the future."

As he walked under the archway, he heard his cousin's voice coming from the room where he'd already enjoyed two good meals. Tonight should be another one.

When he stepped into the room, Septimus was setting up a new game of tabula with Kaeso. Another gameboard sat on a second small table. His cousin was proving more valuable as an arranger of his social life than he expected.

"Titianus. Welcome. Dinner won't be ready for a while, but I expect you'll enjoy playing a game of tabula more than watching us play." With a curl of his fingers, he summoned the girl who was putting clean covers on the couches. "Go fetch Mistress Pompeia. She's in her room."

A quick dip of the head, and the girl scurried up the stairs.

Titianus moved to the corner, where he shed his armor and the padded vest. Almost her first memory of him was in that armor, kneeling by Lenaeus's body. Was that why she was so cool toward him every time they met? Did that wretched memory always rise each time she looked at him?

He glanced at his dagger. It was too much like the one locked in his desk at the station, but the sheath attached to his belt in a way that made it too difficult to remove and replace, and that belt was all that kept his tunic from hanging like a sack.

His gaze turned on Septimus. A dagger also hung at his side, so maybe his wouldn't cause her too much distress, either.

He ran his fingers into his hair and swished them to loosen what the helmet had flattened. Then he stood by Septimus's table and waited for his opponent to arrive.

◆

With the lyre balanced on her hip, Pompeia entered the dining room. She started to sigh when she spotted the second table set up for tabula, then stopped. Titianus stood beside Kaeso, his eyes fixed on her rather than her brother's moving hand.

Septimus picked up his game piece, but before he placed it, he tapped his cousin's arm. Even that didn't shift Titianus's gaze off her.

"You're in for a treat. I heard her practicing." Septimus turned a pleading face toward her. "Father will want to hear you later, but maybe one for us now?"

She weighed the options. Conversation with the tribune or playing the lyre. The better choice was obvious. "If you wish."

"I've looked forward to this all day." The statue-like countenance of the tribune warmed into something more human.

"I'll try not to disappoint." She seated herself on a couch and plucked the first note. A glance revealed Kaeso and Septimus focused once more on the board. That left her a rapt audience of one, who had moved to sit on the adjacent couch.

When she finished, Titianus's eyes proclaimed his approval even though he wasn't smiling. "I'm not expert in music, but that seemed better than what Orpheus himself could play." Then one corner of his mouth started to lift. "But perhaps no mortal could expect to surpass the son of the muse Calliope and a Thracian king who was the son of Ares himself."

She nearly choked stopping the laugh. "I would never have expected that a man as intelligent as you seem would think the Greek gods and goddesses had any part in giving birth to real people."

Perhaps she should have let the laugh out. Questioning the intelligence of a man like him should offend his pride and end his interest. "If Orpheus was even real. Pindar claimed he was, but he's the one who named that goddess as Orpheus's mother, so I don't take his word for anything."

She tried for a mocking smile that should repel him, but instead of anger, something akin to laughter danced in his eyes.

"And you'd be right. As Seneca said and your father so often reminded us, 'Religion is regarded by the common people as true, by the wise as false, and by rulers as useful.' But since many speak of Orpheus as if he and his lineage were real, I didn't expect you to call me on it."

"When you were Father's student, he did say that often." The tribune was the last man she should tell that Father later decided one God was real and Jesus was God's only begotten son.

"I saw your friend Glyptus add the incense holder and the statue of a household god to your lararium. I assumed it was for appearances for the less-than-wise visitors who would be coming to pay respects. I suppose the ones that were there when I was a boy were for your mother." He cleared his throat. "I should have paid respects when she died, but boys of eighteen don't always understand what's important or why. Youth isn't known for its wisdom."

"If any boy could understand, it would have been you. You were always so serious. You never were young like Kaeso and Septimus."

◆

Titianus's brow furrowed before he could stop it. Was that a compliment or an insult?

"Like Kaeso was." The shadow of grief that enveloped her told him it was neither, only an observation like he was prone to make without considering its effect on the listener. "He's paterfamilias now. No one is prepared at eighteen for that."

He barely stopped himself before he reached for her hand. "I know. I was twenty-two with sisters only six and eight. Every new tribune wants a frontier post, a chance for glory and honor in battle for Rome. I asked to serve here, catching criminals in the city because I knew Father was dying and someone needed to lead the familia."

"I'm sure your sisters were glad."

"Half-sisters and they didn't care. I was too old when they were born for us to be close. They live with their aunt now. She's been a good second mother."

He rubbed his jaw. Why was he telling her his family history? It was no one's business except his, and since Lucius Drusus went to Judaea eight years ago, there'd been no one he'd chosen to share it with.

He tipped his chin toward her brother. "He looks toward the future. He'll do well, even at eighteen." He smiled down at her. "And he has you to help him until he can carry the load alone."

He stood and gestured toward the gameboard. "Septimus spoke truth about your musical skills. Shall we see whether you find me a suitable opponent in tabula, as he claimed?"

She set the lyre aside and rose beside him. She'd never been so close before. She only came to his chin. She'd seemed much taller when she stood, fists on her hips, and challenged his right to interrogate the boy in the normal Roman way.

Talent, wit, strength, and kindness…not what he expected to find in any young woman. All those plus beauty and intelligence were there in abundance in Lenaeus's little girl all grown up.

◆

When Pompeia set down the lyre, she would have preferred to retire to her room to await Manius's arrival. Still, playing tabula with Titianus had been better than talking. Accidentally revealing secrets wasn't possible when silence prevailed as they maneuvered for advantage in the game.

But playing with him wasn't comfortable like it was with Kaeso. Instead of concentrating on the board, Titianus had watched her with an intensity that was rather unnerving. But his eyes had warmed when she glanced at his face, and the slightest hint of a smile had relaxed his lips from the thin straight line that would make anyone he hunted tremble.

There might be a decent man underneath his professional mask, but finding out was too dangerous to consider. Too many lives were at stake if she accidentally said something to Rome's top investigator that exposed their faith.

Chapter 22

Exactly What He Needs

A few hours at the Baths of Trajan with his father had been fruitful but tiring. After circulating among small groups of senators, cultivating relationships and harvesting gossip, Manius was ready for an evening with his guard down.

When he walked into his stableyard, the gray stallion was there again.

His guard could be mostly down. Titianus had accepted his invitation. There were many things his too-honorable cousin shouldn't know, but his presence was still welcome. Manius rubbed his palms together. It should make for an entertaining meal. A chance to observe Septimus with his friends. A chance to watch Titianus slip closer to the loss of self-control that was typical of falling in love.

As he walked toward the peristyle triclinium, where Septimus fed the tribune before, he saw his cousin's armor by the wall. Beside helmet and cuirass were the padded vest he wore under it, his gladius, and his satchel.

Seated at a tabula board was the man himself, but he wasn't likely to be playing his best. Leaning over the board across from him was Pompeia. Her gaze was locked on the playing pieces. His eyes were on her.

Even with tightened lips, Manius couldn't stop the smile. The host's couch on the left would hold Septimus and him. Titianus would take the center couch for honored guests. Pompeia and her brother would take the right-side couch as befitted their lower status, but that would place her very close to his cousin...close enough for him to smell the rose scent she wore and to touch her hand as they reached for the same dish. The only thing better for a man who was captivated by a woman was to actually share the couch with her, but he couldn't arrange that with Kaeso present.

Most men turned foolish when they grew too fond of a woman. Would the man rumored to feel little more than Hadrian's statues succumb to this unassuming woman's charms?

His cousin watched the tutor's daughter with more than casual interest, even though he seldom spoke to her. Manius couldn't blame him. She was pretty and graceful. From what he'd seen in the few days she'd been in his house, she treated everyone with kindness, and her interest in each person seemed genuine. She was nothing like the manipulative women who were the wives of the senators and other important men with whom he and his father dined.

Just the sort of woman to attract his scrupulously honest cousin, and she seemed barely aware of the effect she had on him. She was doing nothing to encourage him except be herself.

The day Titianus tells her he wants her, if he ever does, she's going to be shocked by the revelation. Would she accept him for the security he could offer her and her brother, or decline because she has no feelings for him? He'd bet on the latter, unless that's only a peaceful façade and underneath there's a passionate woman who wants his handsome cousin, too.

She made her play and raised her eyes to catch Titianus staring at her. "If you don't keep your mind on the game, I'll beat you again."

He rubbed his jaw and placed his next game piece. Then he sat back in his chair, crossed his arms, and fixed his gaze on her once more. "Your turn."

His move hadn't been the wisest choice. If she didn't make a mistake, she had him now. It was time to step in before his ego was bruised. Winning a game wasn't worth losing an admirer.

Manius clapped, and the girl replacing the pillows after changing the couch sheets stood at attention. "Tell the chef we're ready to eat now."

As Manius seated himself and swung his legs up, Septimus joined him. Kaeso went to the lowest-rank couch, leaving Titianus to take the couch between. But he failed to lie as close to Pompeia as Manius would if he liked the girl. His cousin had much to learn about sending messages to women.

The salad course was carried in, and each was handed a plate with their portion.

Although meals often started with silence, that seldom lasted long. By the second course, most people would be chatting with total strangers reclining near them. Manius had cultivated the skill of listening to everyone while making the ones to whom he was speaking think they had his full attention.

That skill was unused tonight. If a spy could only hear their words, he'd report three people dined. After Manius started the conversation with a question, Pompeia shared her opinions about some of his favorite philosophers and poets. That grew into a discussion of the situation in Parthia and the disagreements between several histories of the Dacian war. Septimus only asked a few questions, Titianus spoke little, and Kaeso said nothing at all.

By the end of dinner, Manius had seen enough to know that he liked this sister of Septimus's friend. She was like a younger version of his Julia. Well informed, confident in her opinions, yet not aggressive in how she spoke. That a young woman not of the noble orders would be so poised and knowledgeable about history, philosophy, and current events around the empire —that was beyond what he'd experienced. She was exactly the type of woman who should appeal to his serious younger cousin.

It was pleasant having a woman at his table who had no intention of manipulating anyone. That was not what his friends married, not even what he married. But his wife had turned into one, and if she were to die, he'd settle for nothing less.

When he married Julia, they were both young. His father had selected her well, and she reveled in the banquets with other senators and their wives. When she helped him watch the men, she was as good as he was at spotting shaky alliances and potential betrayals. She was even better at predicting when a divorce was about to break political unions as well as personal ones.

No woman alive was better at teasing information out of unsuspecting women while making them think she was a trustworthy friend. She excelled at spotting which woman might be used to make an opponent vulnerable.

But she wearied of that as their number of children grew, and they moved out of the town house to the villa. After twenty years, she told him she had tired of the political games in Rome, and they agreed to some changes. She could choose to attend each social event or not, and he would do nothing to cause her embarrassment with her female friends.

He mostly stayed in town, but when he did join her at the estate, it felt good to spend time with someone who knew him so well and accepted him as he was. If someone were to ask if his marriage was a happy one, he would say yes without hesitating.

If he could help Titianus to the same happy state, his cousin would owe him no end of favors. This teacher's daughter would suit his cousin well. But would both see it that way?

"My son promised a musical finale to this meal." Manius tapped his goblet and indicated half full with finger and thumb. "At least two of us are ready to be delighted." The wine slave refilled the goblet, and Manius lifted it toward Titianus, whose jaw twitched.

"Ready to be delighted…again." Titianus shifted to move closer to Pompeia. "And as often as you're willing to delight us."

She rubbed the back of her neck. "A Quintilian scholar should know he'll never persuade someone when his speech violates the spirit of truth by gross exaggeration." The smile that started froze half-way. She raised her chin. "Father would have been disappointed to hear you speak such flattery."

Titianus's smile changed to a slight frown, then returned even broader. "He wouldn't be disappointed with your performance or my words. I spoke only the truth, and I didn't exaggerate."

The blush swept across her cheeks, and she looked away.

What started as a chuckle turned into a laugh as Manius watched her. "Tribune Titianus is renowned for his dedication to truth. You might as well abandon your false modesty and believe him."

Her lips tightened. "It's not false modesty when it's true." She was even prettier when her eyes flashed, and a glance at Titianus revealed he thought so, too. "I play well enough for my own enjoyment and for friends, but enjoyment and delight are quite different."

Manius raised one eyebrow. "Perhaps for most, but for a lover, they're often the same."

Red swept across her cheeks and up to the tip of her ears. Titianus's scowl triggered Manius's chuckle.

It was masterfully played on her part if she wanted to snare him, but was she playing that game?

"You haven't met my wife Julia yet, but she can still delight me. For a few of us, wife and lover are the same woman." He directed a too-knowing smile at Titianus. "I hope you find a woman who does the same for you, cousin."

Septimus cleared his throat. "I have some good news."

Titianus and Kaeso looked at him, but Manius kept watching Pompeia. If a woman could hug someone with her gaze, she'd just wrapped Septimus in an embrace. The game of teasing his cousin had been ungracious toward his female guest. It was time to stop...for a while.

"What is it, son?"

"I moved up to Brutus's top trainer today." He squeezed his neck. "It's not quite like fighting Africanus, but it's almost as good."

"Is Brutus returning to Rome soon?"

"Lanista Felix said he planned to come check his estates here while the pass is still open."

"If he brings Africanus, maybe you can spar with him then." Manius chose a jam-topped pastry. "Did you ever spar with him, Titus?"

"No, but Lucius did." Titianus chose a pastry as well. "I became tribune before I reached that level." He bit off the corner. "Not many made it, and I wasn't going to be one of them."

Titianus glanced at Pompeia, no doubt to measure her response to that admission. Her indifference to what that failure meant was obvious.

"There are more important things than skill with a sword." Pompeia's words warmed his cousin's eyes.

"Like honor." Septimus picked up the last pastry. "Brutus told me being good enough to spar with Africanus was a worthy goal, but being a man of honor like my cousin Titianus was a better one." He toasted Titianus with the raisin-topped tidbit before popping it into his mouth.

Manius lifted the goblet to his lips to hide his grin. He would have bet any amount that he would never see his stoic cousin flush with embarrassment. He would have lost.

"Lenaeus and Brutus shaped us both." Titianus turned to Pompeia. "We could keep debating the difference between enjoyment and delight, or we could experience them as you play again."

"I dislike arguments, so I'll play more to end one. But only if you promise not to start again when I finish."

Not a hint of playfulness colored her voice. Manius rubbed his lip. She wasn't trying to excite his interest. She wanted to douse it. But why? He was everything a woman like her should want.

"You have my word." The smile Titianus gave her was as disarming as any Manius had faked himself. Perhaps his cousin wasn't as ignorant of how to please women as he seemed, but he got no smile in return.

She slipped off the couch and moved to a chair. As she plucked the first string, Manius tipped his head back to drink the last of his wine.

He wouldn't tell Father yet, but soon cousin Titus would owe him for many evenings spent with his houseguest. Time would tell what came of it. Persistent attention could win over most women, and Pompeia should be no different. She knew how to captivate him, and she might be exactly what he needed. But would Titus ever figure out what would please her?

Chapter 23

TIME FOR A REPLACEMENT

The Lenaeus town house, morning of Day 10

As Pompeia approached the door to the school, a shiver coursed through her. It would be their first day teaching since Father died. How could she bear waiting in the atrium for the students to arrive without Father there beside her? How could she walk past his classroom to reach hers without remembering how she opened his door to find him dead? How could she fill the silence that would never have been there if someone hadn't murdered him?

"Mistress? Are you all right?" Tutelus, Manius's Syrian bodyguard, walked beside her, like Septimus walked with Kaeso, armed with a dagger and scanning each person they passed. She should feel safe, and she did. But that was probably because she mostly felt numb with an occasional stabbing sense of loss.

"Yes, it's just hard coming back where Father was killed. But I suppose everyone feels that after someone dies."

He nodded, but his eyes declared he didn't understand. But how could he? Septimus had told them he was bought out of the arena, the son of a gladiator and his owner's cook, born and raised in a ludus where death was no stranger and never a surprise. What was he going to think of this house where master and slave were true family?

Kaeso knocked the agreed-upon pattern, and the door swung open. Theo stood at his post, and she tousled his hair as she passed. His eyes were red and puffy, but the swish of her hand through the curls brought a grateful smile before he closed and bolted the door.

144

Ciconia, drying her hands on her apron, came from the kitchen with Lilia beside her. Pompeia spread her arms, and first Lilia, then Ciconia joined their three-fold embrace. Three sets of tears wet three pairs of cheeks, and the ache in her heart calmed a little.

When Pompeia finally stepped back, her eyes were drawn to Father's classroom. Someone had closed the door, blocking the view of where Father had lain. If only she could block out the images in her mind…but that would come with time.

"Tutelus, wait in the library until after our students arrive. Then you can sit where you want in here." Her hand swept the atrium. "If you put the desk chair outside the library door, that should be more comfortable than the benches."

A silent nod was his answer before he disappeared into what had been Father's favorite room.

Ciconia squeezed Pompeia's upper arm as she and Lilia headed back to the peristyle and the work awaiting them in the kitchen.

Pompeia closed her eyes and breathed in the familiar scent of home. The Sabinus town house was elegant, but it was good to be back here with the people who loved her, the people she loved. They shared the grief today, and they would share the reunion someday. But for now, they would all take one day at time.

Still, grieving for her mother had been so much worse. Mother never chose to follow Jesus, and she was gone forever. Father…she would see him again.

A breath of air brushed her as the front door opened behind her. She turned to see her three Egyptian students arriving. Septimus slapped her brother's arm and raised his hand to her in farewell before heading through the still-open door. Kaeso gave her a quick hug and an encouraging smile, and it was time to teach.

Palm up, she gestured toward her room and followed her students in. Khepri had stopped to let the others pass. Her most eager student touched her arm. When Pompeia paused, Khepri drew her into her arms for a quick hug before sitting at her table.

Pompeia moved to the front. It was good to be back doing something worthwhile with her time, something to hold her focus on the present, not the past.

Like a soldier marching into battle, she squared her shoulders. "Today we're going to talk about how the words for what we do change when we're going to be doing it in the future."

Outside the Lenaeus town house, early morning of Day 10

The cloudless sky overhead drew Vulpis's gaze and triggered a smile. A few of the merchants had opened their stalls, but most had not. Yesterday, he'd taken some dough to the baker and learned at what hour the school opened and when the students came. He'd spent the day watching from different spots along the street, never too long at one place.

Now he knew when the son and daughter came in the morning. He'd learned when they left in the late afternoon. He knew they returned to the fortress-like house in the Fagutal and Titianus joined them for dinner.

Armed with that knowledge, he'd come early today. The boy, not the gladiator should be guarding the door now. It was a good time for a kill.

But as he walked the half block from the bakery to the school, the wavy black hair of the gladiator could be seen above the heads of the other men walking up the road toward him. Vulpis shortened his stride. He was almost to the school entrance when the same group of four that went to the house in the Fagutal reached the school and turned in.

Vulpis kept walking. A quarter block past the school, he leaned against the wall to watch. The armed nobleman came out and walked past him, retracing their steps.

The bodyguard had stayed. Muttering curses under his breath, Vulpis rubbed his jaw. It was too risky to knock on the door now. The boy might answer, but so could the bodyguard. Asking for someone who didn't live there raised no suspicions when done the first time. If the guard answered his knock again, he'd need a believable reason for being there.

He was a man who could blend into a crowd, but no one whose job made him naturally suspicious could fail to recognize him.

He'd return later to watch the foursome leave. Maybe the boy would be guarding the door again. Maybe young Lenaeus wouldn't tell him to let no one in. And if he failed to give the order, he would need another door slave tomorrow.

The warehouse district, midmorning of Day 10

As the door to the wine warehouse closed behind him, Titianus held his hand out to the side. He didn't need to look or speak a word to know the wax tablet containing the names of the men who fought the fire would be placed into it.

Sciurus had been at his side as he worked through the first three-quarters of the list yesterday, finding each man where he worked in the warehouse district and asking what he'd seen before the fire started.

He checked off the last name and handed tablet and stylus back to go into the satchel slung from the boy's shoulder.

"Your thoughts?"

The youth moved up beside him. "Nothing to do with the fire, but…"

"But what?"

"We take wine from the large amphoras that come up from Portus on your riverboats and put it in smaller flasks to sell cheap enough for most people. They were doing the same, but what they measured it out with…it was smaller than it should be for the flasks they were using."

"Why is that important?"

"Their flasks looked just like ours: color, size, shape. Just before the fire, someone came to complain that there wasn't as much wine in one of our flasks as there should have been. Probus gave them one of the smaller flasks for free to make up for what they said was missing."

Sciurus squeezed the back of his neck. "What I wonder is whether they're shorting merchants who think they're buying your wine. When the steward saw you enter, he looked scared. Then when you asked for Batillus he was so eager to help you."

Titianus pulled his hand down his face, leaving his interrogator mask behind. "I do tend to frighten people."

Sciurus's chuckle came with a grin. "True, but only the ones who've done something they shouldn't. I think he's passing off his wine as yours because everyone knows yours is worth what you charge, and he's only partly filling his flasks."

Titianus placed his hand on the boy's shoulder. "Discuss this with Probus, and the two of you decide what we should do about it." He squeezed before lowering his arm. "Now, your thoughts about our search."

"We found the best lead yesterday. Tenax had hands too soft to be working the docks, and the steward of the warehouse where he said he works claimed he'd never heard of him."

"Do you believe the steward?"

"I think so."

"Why?" Training Sciurus in Titianus's own way of thinking was one of the pleasures he'd had this week. That, and reporting his progress to Kaeso and Pompeia each night. Also, the games of tabula and listening to her play the lyre or talk with Manius.

She was more relaxed and friendlier with his older cousin than she was with him. Not the wrong kind of friendly, like some women were with wealthy, powerful men. The kind that let people get to know each other.

The kind he wished she'd be toward him.

He forced his attention back on Sciurus's words.

"I watched his mouth and eyes like you said to. They were always agreeing, not like when people lie."

He slapped his helper's shoulder. "I believe him, too. We also know whoever Tenax really is passes through this part of Rome sometimes, or he wouldn't have known the right name of the warehouse where those roads cross."

He rubbed his lower lip. "But I don't remember exactly what he looked like. It was too dark by the time I got to him, and they all had sooty faces. Nothing stood out about him. Did his hair match the description of the slave who picked up the writings at Lupus's house?"

"I don't know. I'm too short to see the top of his head, and I didn't pay attention to anyone's temples." He lowered his face. "I'm sorry."

"No one can notice everything when they don't know what they're looking for. You've done well." He almost tousled his helper's curly hair, as he'd seen Pompeia do with the boy Theo, but he stopped himself. "Tomorrow you can work with Probus, but I might need you again before this case is through." He settled for a warm smile, which the boy returned. "And for other cases."

Sciurus's eyes lit, and Titianus led them back to his warehouse to get his horse. He'd definitely be using Sciurus again.

He didn't have anything special to report to Pompeia tonight, but he'd join Septimus for dinner anyway. Nothing at the fortress could compete with an evening in the company of the friendly young cousin with whom he'd never spent time before this case and the woman who didn't yet want to spend time with him. But perhaps, if he visited often enough, she would.

The Rufinus town house, late morning of Day 10

As Arcanus awaited his turn as the last client of the salutation, he stretched out his legs and crossed his arms. Today he'd been able to focus on the conversations around him, and he had a few choice bits of gossip to share with Rufinus.

He let the satisfied smile leak out. He'd fooled the best investigator Rome had, and he and Rufinus were safe.

At last, the final client emerged with a smile and a small sack of coins. Arcanus sauntered into the room, and the door closed behind him.

Rufinus was at the doorway to the peristyle. He stepped out, and a distant voice drifted through the door. "Good morning, Father."

He raised his hand in greeting and reentered the tablinum. "We have a problem." He pointed at the small windows that had leaked their conversation to Tertius. "Follow me."

As Arcanus trudged up the stairs behind his patron to the room where they talked before, his heart beat faster with each step. Rufinus walked to the window, then turned to face him. "Shut the door and come closer."

Arcanus did as told. When he stopped three feet away, his heart was thudding so loudly Rufinus must hear it.

"I spoke with the urban prefect at the baths yesterday. The tablets you made that Titianus took…they didn't fool him. He told the prefect he had evidence someone was trying to implicate two senators in unlawful business deals and Lupus's death."

Arcanus blew his breath out between pursed lips. "That's unfortunate, but it's probably not much of a problem. Titianus can think what he wants, but he won't be able to tie any of it to us without the Flaccus boy or Lenaeus. One is no longer in Rome, and the other died."

"It is a problem." Rufinus's eyebrows plunged. "Titianus also told the prefect he thought Lenaeus was killed to cover up the murder and arson. Gaius told me his teacher had died from a heart problem. But he hadn't been sick." His scowl deepened. "Did you kill him?"

To dry sweating hands, Arcanus slid them down his thighs. Rufinus had never before looked ready to kill someone himself.

"I did. The surest solution to a problem isn't to ignore it and assume it will go away." He straightened to his full height. "You can't rely on the honor of a poor man to keep him from doing something dishonorable that will make him wealthy. Many will do it just to get enough that they don't have to work for a while. Extortion could have set him up for life."

He fought the urge to rub his neck and won. "And if he was truly honorable, he'd report you. I decided it was too dangerous for you if the teacher knew what the Flaccus boy overheard. The way Gaius's friend avoided you before leaving town...I was certain that was what he was discussing with the teacher when Gaius got there. So, I took it on myself to keep the story from spreading further."

Rufinus rolled his eyes. "But you don't know if Lenaeus told anyone else. What's to stop them from saying something?"

"I could—" He got no further before Rufinus raised his hand.

"Stop. I don't want to know anything about what you could or could not do. What I don't know, I can't be held responsible for or accidentally reveal. Right now, everything Titianus thinks is only speculation. He can't be certain those tablets are forgeries. Even if he could, he wouldn't know who did them. He has no evidence strong enough to take to court for any of his suspicions. Don't give him anything else that might tie us into any crimes." Anger flamed in Rufinus's eyes, hotter than any Arcanus had ever seen.

"Yes, Patronus. I understand. He'll have to give up at some point if he gets nothing more." He cleared his throat. "I overheard some useful things as I waited today."

Rufinus pointed at a chair and lowered himself into a second one. "What?"

As Arcanus shared the day's gossip, his path forward was clear. Titianus was the only one bullheaded enough to keep investigating when he had written proof in hand that someone else might be guilty. So, it was time to force his replacement by a less able, less dedicated man. He'd already hired Vulpis to take care of the boy. Getting rid of the tribune as well should be no problem.

Chapter 24

WORTHY OF TRUST?

The Sabinus town house, evening of Day 10

Manius lounged in his favorite library chair, reading Pliny's *Natural History* for a change of pace. It was relaxing to think about planting new grapevines after spending the afternoon cultivating an alliance with a newly elevated senator who was too impressed with himself. Father had asked him to do it because he couldn't stand the man himself.

A flash of brass drew his gaze to the door just as Titianus raised his fist to knock.

"Come in, cousin. Are you paying respects on your way to entertain my pretty houseguest or is this official business?"

"Both." Titianus stepped into the room and closed the door.

Manius's eyebrow rose as the latch clicked.

Titianus cleared his throat. "First, I want you to give me your word you will not tell your father what I'm about to ask."

"Will it cause Father a problem if I give that promise?"

"As long as he had nothing to do with a crime I'm investigating—and I don't think he does—he should have no problem from my request." A half-smile curved his cousin's mouth. "Although it will keep him from knowing something about someone that he'd like to know but has no business knowing."

Manius met half-smile with half-smile. "I don't tell Father everything, despite what you might think. There are many things he doesn't need to know. This can be one of them."

A quick dip of his head marked Titianus's acceptance of his promise. "I need to know who might want me to investigate two particular senators."

"I can see why you don't want Father to know you asked this." Manius rolled his scroll and set it aside. "I might have some ideas. Who are they?"

"Gaius Valerius Paullinus and Lucius Fabius Gallus."

Manius's brow furrowed. "Isn't Valerius Paullinus a cousin of the urban prefect?"

"Yes."

"Hmph." Manius covered his mouth and rubbed his face. "If you start an investigation of him, you'll get no end of grief from your commander."

"I know, and whoever put his name where I'd find it in a forgery trying to implicate him was probably counting on that."

"Well…" Manius sucked air between his teeth. "Both are well-respected men in the Senate. There are always rivalries and arguments, but I can't name anyone who hates either enough to put you on their trail, let alone both." He leaned back in the chair. "But Father might."

Titianus shook his head. "I don't want your father to know I'm even asking. I don't want any rumors started, and I don't want anyone put on their guard that I'm looking at them. The evidence that I need to find the truth might be destroyed."

"If you tell me why you want to know, I can probably figure out a way to ask Father that won't get him suspicious and won't get back to any of the people involved."

Piercing gray eyes locked on Manius as Titianus contemplated him, mouth straight, thoughts unreadable. Manius fought to keep a smile from betraying his inner laughter. Titus really did look like Sulla when he put on that face.

Another quick nod showed his word had been accepted. "It's about the dead man we found after the warehouse on the Tiber burned ten days ago…and Lenaeus's murder. The person trying to get them into trouble might know something about who killed Pompeia's father."

Any inclination to laugh fled. "I'll see what I can learn, and I won't let Father know you have any interest in the answer."

"Thank you." The straight lips curved into a grateful smile. "I'll see you at dinner. It's time to go see if I can win one for a change. She beat me two straight yesterday, but she distracts me."

Manius's laugh filled the room. "Women can do that when they want to."

"It appears so." Titianus returned a grin and walked out the door.

And even when they don't want to. Manius's smile dimmed. His cousin always got the men he hunted, but would he get the woman he wanted?

As he picked up his scroll, he couldn't keep from laughing at himself. Why did he feel so honored that the incorruptible Titianus decided to trust him with something so important?

He'd do whatever he could to help. He liked Pompeia and her brother, and he wanted to get justice for them and their father.

And for Septimus, who loved them all.

Outside the entrance to the dining room, Titianus removed his armor. It might not be what kept her cool toward him, but why take the risk? When he stepped into the room, brother and sister were there with Septimus, but Kaeso was already playing with Pompeia.

With a wave and a curl of his fingers, Septimus called him to a game at the second table. Without a word, Titianus settled into the chair opposite his cousin. But while he fingered his game piece as Septimus made the first move, his eyes were drawn from the board to her.

She talked very little while they played, but the change of opponent was still a disappointment. More so than he expected. He scanned the couches and found no sign of the lyre. If Manius didn't join them at the table and get Pompeia talking so he could join their conversation, the whole evening might be disappointing.

"So, what progress did you make today?" Septimus played his next piece.

"It was my second day tracking down those who helped fight the fire."

"Any good leads?"

"None remembered seeing anything odd before the fire started."

Pompeia had turned in her chair and watched him instead of Kaeso's next move. A definite improvement, even if her eyes didn't bestow a warm welcome. "Nothing at all?"

"The vigiles drafted someone to help carry water who didn't live in the neighborhood, but he was familiar with it. He lied about his name and where he worked, so he was probably doing something wrong before the aquarius pulled him into the bucket brigade. But whether that had anything to do with the murder and arson or another crime, I don't know."

Kaeso tapped her hand, and she played another piece before turning back to Titianus. "What are you going to do next?"

"I'm telling you this because it seems tied to your father's murder, but it doesn't go further than us."

She nodded as his finger pointed to each of them in turn.

"The hairline of the man Theo saw and that of a slave who took something from the library of the murdered man…the descriptions match. So, someone is a freedman or higher passing himself off sometimes as a slave, or a slave is pretending to be a citizen, which is a crime in itself. The slave at Lupus's estate presented authorization to reclaim borrowed writings that bore the signet mark of Rufinus."

She inhaled sharply, and her eyes widened. "The father of Gaius Rufinus?"

"Yes. Tomorrow I start checking into a list of freedmen of the Rufinus familia. Someone with access to a Rufinus signet got into the Lupus library and maybe into the strongbox where I found forgeries like what your father described."

A quick glance at her brother caught Kaeso and Septimus exchanging satisfied smiles. He wanted to smile himself. He might be only days away from getting justice for Lenaeus.

"I know what he left there. I don't know what he took out of the library. Before I go further, I need to talk with the men who would know the Rufinus signet well enough to make a copy that could fool Lupus's steward. The killer could work for Rufinus or for one of them."

"Hmm." Her straight lips curved into a smile. "Septimus said you were good at this." She directed her smile at his cousin before turning it back on him. "I wouldn't want to be someone you were investigating."

"How do you know I'm not?" As he did with Sciurus to make the boy laugh, he drew his hand down his face, leaving his interrogator's mask behind.

Her eyes saucered as the color drained from her face. Septimus sucked air between his teeth; then the room grew as quiet as death.

"I'm only joking." He drew his hand up the other way and restored his smile. "You don't need to worry that I'll be uncovering any of your personal secrets or those of your family." One corner of his mouth lifted. "I can't imagine what Lenaeus and his children could possibly have done that would interest an officer of Rome, anyway."

Kaeso's chuckle broke the silence, but there was a nervous edge to it.

"You might as well give up trying." Septimus's grin looked forced. "I've eaten at the Lenaeus table so many times in the past three years that I'm unofficially family, and there's nothing about them that would ever be a threat to Rome. There's no good reason for Rome's best to be a threat to them."

"I can't see one myself." But should he look? Why was Septimus in such a hurry to vouch for the family when he'd only been joking?

"Why don't we change partners?" Her words were louder than normal, and her eyes were unnaturally bright.

His head drew back. She'd never seemed eager to talk or play with him before. But he wasn't about to question her proposal. Anything that could make her warm up toward him was welcome.

"An excellent idea. You beat me twice yesterday. I need revenge today." She rose and came to his table. As soon as Septimus moved off it, she slipped onto the chair.

"Or perhaps I'll make it three in a row." She flashed him a quick smile before focusing her full attention on the board.

"Are you sure you want to flaunt your wins so openly?" He placed his first piece.

She responded without words by placing her game piece and picking up the one she would play after his next turn.

"Some men don't like their failures pointed out. None of us like to lose, but when it's a pretty young woman…that can make it harder to bear. Harder to play our best, too."

She should have said something, but when she didn't, he put his piece on the board. "But truth must be acknowledged, and you can play better than me when I don't focus."

"Women need to focus, too. You distract me from the game by talking. If you persist, I'll have to assume that's deliberate and you don't want to play fairly with me."

From where she placed her game piece, it was obvious he'd done nothing distracting.

"Point taken. We'll just play." He made his move and leaned back in his chair. More than a few young women had flirted with him. He wasn't the most skilled at playful banter, but he knew it when he heard it. This was definitely not it. There was nothing playful about her tone, and she had no trouble focusing when she talked with Kaeso while playing.

Had she suggested they play only to divert his thoughts? Was there a family secret that he should be looking for? Was that why she was so cool toward him?

He liked both her and her brother. But could he trust his favorable impressions of them, or should he doubt his analysis? Was it only because he knew their father? Or because he was so drawn to her? Had past and present affections blinded him to something he should see?

He glanced at Septimus, focused in silence on the game with the friend he loved like a brother. Could a conversation with Septimus reveal if she deserved his trust, or would his cousin hide whatever they were hiding to protect his friends?

He crossed his arms. But no matter what it was, the urge to protect her from harm, to help her feel safe and enjoy life again, to become more than her brother's friend's cousin was something he couldn't deny.

And he wasn't sure he wanted to, even if he could.

Chapter 25

TOO DANGEROUS TO IGNORE

Near the Sabinus town house, evening of Day 10

People were predictable, most of the time at least. Vulpis had relied on that in his years of removing problematic people. Lenaeus's children were no exception. They were escorted to the school in the morning, taught all day, and returned under escort to the Fagutal town house in the late afternoon.

What had surprised him was how predictable the tribune was. What he did during the day was barely a matter for curiosity. But what he did in the evening…maybe he only joined them for dinner, but she was a pretty woman. Any tribune was rich, and this one was handsome enough to draw any woman's eyes.

With a chunk of bread, Vulpis sopped up the last of the broth and wiped the sides of the bowl. If the last two nights were any indication, Titianus should be riding by shortly.

The rapid thuds of trotting hooves raised Vulpis's eyes from the bowl. The smile of anticipation on the tribune's lips as he hurried past suggested more than a good meal awaited him.

Vulpis glanced at the darkening sky. Perhaps the tribune would stay later tonight for some after-dinner entertainment. How late Titianus left didn't matter, anyway.

Arcanus wasn't paying him for stalking brother and sister…yet. He'd learned what he needed. With a quick tip of his head, he drained the wine cup.

The day had started early; tomorrow would as well. With a yawn, he headed home.

The Arcanus town house, late evening of Day 10

The sun had set some time ago, and the oil lamps on the rack in Arcanus's library had been lit to drive back the darkness. But he could never look at the small flame of each clay lamp without thinking about how a knocked-over lamp stand had given an accidental killing the appearance of murder and made an accidental fire look like arson.

He rolled the scroll and set it to the side. Elbows on the desk, he rested his forehead against his clasped hands and closed his eyes. He'd let Gaius know he needed to speak to Vulpis. He got a stare in return until he remembered the assassin had used an alias. But Gaius said he'd pass on the message and to expect a visit tonight or tomorrow.

"Gaius said you needed to speak to me about something too dangerous to ignore."

Arcanus half jumped out of his skin when that voice came from the guest chair not three feet away.

He faked a confident smile. "I did. Titianus…I need you to kill him. I want you to figure out where and how to do that as soon as possible."

Vulpis's chuckle sent a shiver up Arcanus's spine. "Fortuna has smiled on you, Arcanus. The bodyguard was serving as doorman again, so I wasn't able to dispose of the boy yet. But I've been watching the son and daughter for you. Your tribune has eaten dinner with them the past two nights. Odds are good he's doing it every night right now."

He leaned forward and reached across the desk to pick up Arcanus's goblet. He inhaled the fruity aroma, then took a sip. When he settled back into his chair, he took the goblet with him.

"I know where Titianus will most likely be tomorrow night, and each time I've seen him there, he's been alone." He took another drink. "Killing the tribune will require three men. I'll arrange the other two. The cost will be a thousand denarii."

Arcanus blanched. "That's a lot of money for one dead man." His voice came out squeaky.

"It's Titianus. He's not an ordinary man, and what you want is high risk." He tipped his head back to drain the goblet and returned it to the desk. "One thousand in advance."

A couple of deep breaths were not enough to erase Arcanus's feeling that he was an easy-to-cheat weakling in Vulpis's eyes. But it was time to change that. "Only a third upfront. I paid upfront for the boy, and he's still alive."

"A gladiator bodyguard is watching over the boy." Vulpis's words were ice-coated. "I'll dispatch him when they get careless and the boy goes somewhere unprotected. As long as he's dead before a trial, it's a timely kill."

He pointed at the strongbox. "But since you're turning into a regular customer, I'll settle for half upfront." The cruel smile matched his predator eyes. "He'll be dead by tomorrow, and I can wait a day for the second half."

"Very well." Arcanus went to his strongbox and put twenty aurei into a small sack. Five hundred denarii was a lot of money. But maybe Rufinus would pay back part of it...if it was ever safe to tell his patron that he'd taken care of the problem of the tutor. If it became necessary to kill the tutor's children, he'd need Rufinus to share the cost.

Arcanus held out the sack.

Vulpis took it, and the coins jingled when he bounced the sack in this hand. "I'll be back tomorrow for the rest."

Arcanus nodded, and the assassin left as silently as he'd come.

He sank into his chair and buried his face in his hands. Then he flopped back in the chair. How many would have to die and at what cost before he was safe once more?

Nearly midnight of Day 10

Moonlight shadows of the bars on her bedroom window moved slowly across the wall, and Pompeia had watched them for hours. Manius's house was a fortress, as Titianus had said, but she didn't feel safe in it now.

She'd made Titianus suspicious again. Over and over, her mind rehearsed every word she'd spoken to him that night. What had she said or done that made his eyes change from those of a dog wanting its head scratched to a cat watching a bird at the fountain?

Septimus's efforts to defend them had only made matters worse.

For what must be the hundredth time, she released a shuddering sigh.

If he looked for what he thought she was hiding, would he find Glyptus's and Appius's secrets as well? What would he do if he did?

She rolled on her side and pulled the sheet over her head.

Why hadn't she let it rest after Septimus asked if he had any leads and he said no one saw anything before the fire started. More than likely, that was all he would have said until Manius joined them and teased his cousin into joining the conversation...with her. One foolish question on her part got Titianus talking again, and then he wouldn't quit.

Why had she complimented his investigative skill? He was impressive, but he already knew that. When he hinted at investigating her, she should have seen it for the joke it was.

Fear can seem like guilt. The thought of him looking at their lives too closely made her stomach clench and her heartbeat ramp up. He probably could smell fear. He triggered it in so many people. He sensed hers, and that aroused the hunter in him.

Why did Septimus ask him to come so often? Why did Manius encourage him as well? She flopped onto her back and draped her arm across her eyes.

Manius wasn't that hard to understand. He liked to tease people, to see if he could get a reaction from one as he teased the other. It was a sport with him, and he usually stopped only after he made her blush.

But Septimus should have known better. He knew his cousin's reputation...the wolf on a blood trail who never stopped until he brought the quarry down. A shudder coursed through her. Septimus should have known what that could mean if the tribune learned their family's greatest secret.

But it was too late now. If Septimus discouraged him coming, he'd just dig harder to find the truth about them. What if he didn't stop even after he caught Father's killer?

Tomorrow she'd send Corax to tell Glyptus where the tribune's interest in her was leading. Maybe he'd know what she should do. At the very least, he could warn Appius that they both should be on their guard.

When Mother died and Pompeia had to take on her roles, the grief and responsibility had overwhelmed her. Appius had taught her a promise from the Jewish scriptures given through the prophet Isaiah. She'd said it to herself over and over. Each time through, a tiny part of her heart healed and a little more strength came.

She forced herself to take slow, even breaths, and her heart rate slowed.

Fear not, for I am with you; be not dismayed, for I am your God. I will strengthen you, I will help you, I will uphold you with My righteous right hand.

What God promised then was just as true now. She closed her eyes and released a deep sigh.

God, I know Titianus is a good man, but what he might do frightens me. Please let him find Father's killer soon so he'll leave us alone. And please don't let him discover we belong to You before he leaves.

Chapter 26

The Cost of Justice

The Sabinus town house, evening of Day 11

It was later than normal when Titianus rode into the Sabinus stableyard and handed his stallion off to the stable boy. After an afternoon of visiting freedmen of Faustus Cornelius Rufinus, he was ready to shed his official role and relax among friends.

Not all had welcomed his visit. The current Rufinus's father had freed a dozen men over the years, half of them early, half in his will. Some Rufinus had set up in businesses, while some kept serving him much as they had before they were freed. For the most part, those businesses were not forbidden to senators, but a handful were, including the one that burned.

He'd picked up Sciurus and his mule before the first one, and the boy's observations from the stableyard or the street in front of a business had mostly fit with what he'd learned from each freedman himself.

Outside the tablinum, he took off his armor. As he lowered the satchel to the ground, one corner of his mouth lifted. In one wax tablet, he had seals made with each man's signet, and some of them were very similar. Probably slight variations of the seal of their former master. Maybe close enough to fool a steward who only saw it occasionally.

But of the six men he tried to see today, two had eluded him. It was afternoon, so they should have been back from Rufinus's salutation. Whether they left or hid when he was announced or whether they really were away... he couldn't say. He'd left a message that he'd be back tomorrow afternoon. Sciurus would try to find out if they left to avoid him today.

He'd taken to leaving the apron of leather strips with the cuirass and helmet. Maybe he imagined it, but she seemed more reserved when he wore any of the uniform in her presence. He'd blamed that on memories of their first meeting, but after yesterday's discussion of secrets, he wasn't so sure.

One step into the room, and his smile faded. Only Kaeso and Septimus sat at a game board.

"Where's Pompeia?"

Kaeso finished his move and turned his eyes on Titianus. "Upstairs. She had some writing to do."

"And you weren't here to entertain her." Septimus leaned back in his chair after playing. "She'll join us for dinner." He bounced his eyebrows. "You haven't ridden up here for nothing." He looked past Titianus into the atrium. "Here she comes now. I told Famula to let her know when you got here and then serve dinner."

He stepped through the door to await the woman who intrigued and baffled him.

With her gaze on the floor, she walked slowly, like soldiers after a twenty-mile forced march. When she raised her head, a cordial if not enthusiastic smile greeted him.

"Did you have a good day?"

"Satisfactory. Tomorrow should be better."

Her smile and nod as she walked away ended their conversation before it could start.

The first tray of food appeared, and each settled onto their usual couch.

"Where's Manius?" Without his cousin to get her talking, what topic would make her comfortable?

"Father and Grandfather are dining at one of the newest senator's houses tonight. Father would have rather eaten with us, but duty called." A chuckle accompanied Septimus's grin. "He never used to, but now he understands why I ate at Kaeso's so often. As soon as you catch the killer, I'll be able to do it again."

"Maybe." Kaeso's deep sigh stole Septimus's smile. "If I can find some new students. One of my boys has moved to the same school where his older brother went after Father died. I need to replace him as soon as possible. If one more leaves, I'm not sure how long we can stay where we are."

"Why?" Titianus tried to make it sound like curiosity, not interrogation.

"We don't own the town house. We've always rented it. If our landlord decides to sell it, the new owner might raise the rent or move in himself."

He squeezed the back of his neck. "The current owner…he's rented to Father since before I was born. His son was one of Father's first students. But with Father gone…he might raise the rent on me."

"Perhaps he won't. Good renters are hard to find. I don't raise my rents until I get a new tenant moving in."

Septimus's sigh echoed Kaeso's before silence filled the room. Manius would have known how to keep words flowing. But with his cousin not there to do it…

"Pompeia, how is it working out with Manius's bodyguard escorting you and staying all day?"

Gratitude at him breaking the silence warmed her eyes. "Very well. Tutelus is a nice man, and I think he likes being with us. While he sits in the lobby, Theo is teaching him how to read and write."

Titianus stopped his eyebrow from rising. He knew Tutelus's history. In the arena, he was called the Savage Syrian, and it described him perfectly off the sand as well as on it. But maybe he'd mellowed since Manius bought him.

"Does Manius approve of that?"

"Of course." Septimus had found his voice again. "Many who work in the town house can read. Father doesn't make them, but those who want to are allowed to learn. Aren't yours?"

Her eyes turned on him, and there was no expectation of a yes in them. "What my warehouse manager and estate stewards do…" He shrugged. "They're reliable men, and I don't keep track for the most part. But they know I don't approve of cruelty. I expect my people to be treated fairly. I don't have any of my own people at my town house. I rent it out."

"You rent out your town house?" Pompeia slipped a raisin between her lips. "Where do you live?"

"Officers' quarters at the Praetorian Fortress." Her eyebrows rose. "My sisters live with their aunt, and I was almost never there. It would be foolish for a man like me to pay all the expenses of keeping a town house when I can make money from renting it. But I'll reclaim it as my home when I finish being tribune."

"Can the great Titianus stop hunting criminals?" Septimus's chuckle brightened the room. "What will Rome do without you?"

"It did fine before me. It will do fine when I'm gone."

"Will that be soon?" Was that regret or hope coloring Pompeia's question?

"A year or so." He offered her a smile. "I have plenty of time to get justice for you."

She looked down, then back at him with sad eyes. "I'm sure you'll do your best, but even if you don't succeed, we appreciate all you've done."

"Your father helped make me what I am. He deserves justice, and so do you. I won't quit until I succeed."

"I'm not sure I want Roman justice. Sometimes the cost is too high. Innocent people can get hurt, not just the guilty."

Conversation died out, and they ate the main course in silence.

But silent lips can speak volumes, and he'd heard what she didn't say. She meant Theo.

Titianus had no doubt he'd find the man who used Rufinus's signet or one like it to plant the tablets. But if he was also Lenaeus's killer, how could he prove that without Theo being hurt? As the only one who saw the murderer, the boy's testimony would be required, and Roman law dictated that only what a slave said under torture could be used as evidence.

With her spoon, she was pushing the last of the fish around her plate. She hadn't eaten much since she spoke the painful truth. She'd hate him if catching her father's killer meant suffering for Theo. She loved that boy.

He'd get Sciurus tomorrow and take him along as his extra eyes and ears. The eager eyes, the infectious grin...he'd only worked with the boy for a week, and already he was fond of him. He wouldn't want to see his investigative protege hurt by what she'd rightly called that barbaric rule.

The dessert course came, but other than a handful of comments on how tasty the jam-filled pastries were, silence still reigned. He could be silent alone at the fortress without watching her sadness or suspecting condemnation in her eyes.

He swung his legs off and stood. "I have some things to complete before I retire. I'll leave you now."

Septimus raised a hand. "Come back tomorrow. Father should be with us."

"I will." Titianus entered the atrium and donned his armor. After slipping both satchel and scabbard straps over his head, he draped the red cloak over his shoulder and settled the helmet in place.

It was built to deflect the blows of swords and battle axes. It wasn't comfortable, but at least he could leave the chin strap unfastened, except during formal inspections. The strap was meant to keep a helmet on in battle. He wore his only for the authority it proclaimed.

He strode through the archway into the stableyard. Tied at the wall by a manger, his stallion lifted its head, tufts of green hay hanging from its mouth. As he walked toward it, the stable boy untied it and bridled it.

With a nod of thanks, he mounted and rode out the gate, away from the woman who attracted and frustrated him more than any before her.

Maybe there was no point in coming. She didn't welcome his attentions. There was no reason to expect that would change, but he'd be back tomorrow. Somehow, he couldn't stay away.

◆

Septimus listened to the rustle of the apron of leather being fastened around Titianus's waist. The snap of each clasp locking announced when the cuirass encased his chest once more. The sword, the satchel, the helmet made no noise as he donned them, but the fading clicks of hobnails on marble told Septimus it was time to excuse himself and leave his friends for a private discussion.

Kaeso was in trouble. How much their rent was, Septimus didn't know. What else the familia needed to stay where they were—he didn't know that, either. But he had an allowance from Father that he mostly didn't need, and his equestrian cousin had enough that most people in Rome would call him rich.

A man would have to be blind not to see Titianus liked Pompeia, even with her doing her best to discourage him. He'd want to help.

But his friends mustn't hear him ask. The answer might be no, and even if it was yes, Titianus might want to do it secretly so she wouldn't feel indebted to him.

"I'll be back." He rose from the couch and followed his cousin toward the stableyard. He got there just in time to see the red cape and crest disappear through the gate.

"Bridle my horse. I won't need the saddle." He fidgeted until the stable boy led his mount over. Gripping the mane, he threw his leg over and settled onto the horse's bare back. Titianus wouldn't be far ahead. He'd enlist his help and be back before they finished the last of the pastries.

It might take a little arguing. Kaeso wouldn't want to take advantage of their friendship, but Pompeia would tell him to accept the help for the sake of the familia. They could pay him back later.

He tensed his calves and the horse went through the gate. One more nudge, and he settled into a trot. He'd have Titianus's answer and return before they started wondering where he'd gone.

The surprise on Kaeso's face when he brought back the answer to their problem would be priceless.

The nearly full moon in a cloudless sky gave plenty of light, but Titianus didn't see it coming. It was only a man leaning against the wall near a taberna and two drunks swaying as they walked toward him, laughing. But when his horse drew abreast of them, the lone man stepped out and grabbed his stallion's halter. Before he could draw his sword, the other two grabbed him, dragging him off and pinning his arms. His helmet came off, and one kicked it aside.

He saw the short club as the horse-grabber drew his arm back.

In slow motion, it descended toward him. When the thug slammed it into the side of his head, first came an explosion of pain and flashes of light. His knees buckled, but the men held him upright. With the second blow, everything went black and pain turned to…nothing.

Septimus spotted Titianus's crest half a block ahead, and he nudged his horse into a faster trot. He was still a quarter block away when three men jumped his cousin. A hundred feet when the first blow hit Titianus's head and he hung limply between two men while the third drew back his arm for another strike.

He urged his horse into a canter.

The thug struck again while thirty feet still separated them. But before he could strike a third time, Septimus rode him down. The impact of the charging horse sent the would-be murderer flying. He hit the pavement headfirst and didn't move again.

He reined in hard and whirled toward the two holding his friend. Twenty feet away and he slung one leg over his horse's neck to slide off and run beside the animal. With dagger drawn, bellowing like a Germanic chieftain charging his enemies, he'd almost reached them when they released Titus, grabbed his satchel, and ran.

As he dropped to one knee beside his cousin's limp form, he sheathed his dagger. He stared at the face, now strangely peaceful, of one of the best men he knew. Blood matted his hair. Some trickled from his ear.

He felt under the jaw. A pulse still beat.

"Titus. Can you hear me?" No response.

If he could get him home, they could send for a doctor and…

He chewed his lip. What could a doctor do? Maybe there was something he didn't know about. Titus was still alive. Maybe there was still hope.

He jumped when the gray head appeared beside him. Titus's stallion nickered and nudged its master with its nose. If he could just get Titus on the horse, he could get him home.

In front of the taberna just down the street, a crowd had gathered.

"Come help." He scooped up the horse's reins and stood. "I need to get him on the horse with me."

Two men came forward. Between the three of them, they got Titus astride the horse facing backward, and Septimus mounted behind him. One scooped up the helmet and offered it to Septimus. He put it on his own head and pulled Titus against his chest, head resting on his shoulder. A trickle of blood warmed his cheek, and he shifted Titus's head to his other shoulder to take pressure off the wound. He wrapped one arm tightly around his cousin's back, but with the reins in his hand, his second arm couldn't hold much weight.

The brass was smooth and cold against his bare arm. Holding a limp body in place would take more strength and a firmer grip than he had. If Titus started to topple as the stallion moved, he'd never be able to hold him.

"It's a short distance home. A denarius if you'll stay beside me so he doesn't fall." The two who'd helped nodded, and they started for home.

Chapter 27

NOT HIS TIME TO DIE

The Sabinus town house

Thereʼs another one." Pompeia pointed at the shooting star as it passed across the sky above the peristyle garden. "That makes five."

Kaeso shot out of his chair when the stable boy sprinted through the peristyle and disappeared into the atrium. "What the…"

She was already to the archway before he could finish.

Her hands shot up to cover her mouth. Septimus, wearing the helmet, sat on Titianus's gray horse with the tribune slumped in his arms. Two men walked beside them, their arms raised and hands resting on the cuirass. Titianus's head rested on Septimus's shoulder. His eyes were closed and the side of his head was bloody.

While the two men held him, Septimus slipped off the horse's rump and jumped sideways to avoid the kick. Kaeso strode past her, and the four of them pulled Titianus off the horse and laid him on the ground.

She knelt beside him and rested her hand on his cheek. It was the first time she'd touched him, and his day's growth was prickly against her hand. "Titianus, can you look at me?"

So many times, his steel-gray eyes had looked into her own, sometimes cool, sometimes warm, always making her uncomfortable. If only he'd look at her now.

"What happened?" She looked up at Septimus, standing beside her with anguished eyes.

"Three men jumped him. I rode into the one who was hitting him, and

169

the others ran. He was alive when we started home." He squatted and felt under Titianus's jaw. "He still is, but he won't be for long."

Kaeso squatted on his other side, looking almost as miserable as Septimus.

She stood. The steward had come and several of the men of the household were with him. Titianus wouldn't be alive much longer, unless she…

"Four of you, carry him up to the room next to Kaeso's. My brother will show you, then leave them."

Kaeso's brow furrowed, then his eyes widened. He started to open his mouth, then shut it.

He rose. "Follow me."

A servant took each limb, and they vanished into the house.

One of the two men who'd helped bring him cleared his throat. "The denarius?"

Septimus turned to his steward. "Give each two."

She touched Septimus's arm. "Can you find a physician quickly?"

"Brutus's lanista could get one, but where he's bleeding…I think it's too late."

"Go get him." She knew too well how the claws of despair dug into you, where you wished you could do something, anything, to change what had happened. But it wasn't time to give up yet.

"He didn't deserve to die like this." His jaw clenched, and he wiped at the corner of his eye.

"Perhaps he won't." She rested her hands on both his shoulders, stood on tiptoes to reach his ear, and lowered her voice to a whisper. "I know the Great Healer. Kaeso and I will ask Him for help. Death hasn't won while Titianus still lives." She gave him a gentle shove. "Now go. Find the physician and hurry back."

Septimus strode to Titianus's horse and remounted. As he looked down at her, hope wrestled with despair in the depths of his eyes, and hope won. He swung the stallion and trotted out the gate.

Back inside, as she climbed the stairs to the bedrooms, visions of the risks to which she was about to expose them all swooped through her mind like carrion crows. If God healed him, how could Titianus not ask what they'd done? Even an ordinary man would if he'd been almost dead and after their prayers he was fine. When he asked which god healed him, she'd have to tell him. The heartless investigator who made no allowance for rank, family, or friendship…what would he do when he learned they were Christians?

God, give me courage to do what's right, no matter the cost.

When they were small, she and Kaeso had loved to play in the sheet of water that poured off the top basin of Appius's fountain. Her brother would giggle and fling handfuls of water as she stood, eyes closed, with the water-fall bathing her face. Just like those long-ago showers, peace washed over her from the tresses piled atop her head to the soles of her feet. Whispered words filled her mind and wrapped around her. *Trust Me, My child, and all will be well in the end.*

She closed her eyes and held her breath. And when she released it, she knew what she must do. *Not my will, Father, but Yours. Not my fear, but the courage You give me. Please listen to our prayers and save him, no matter what that brings.*

Pompeia slipped into the room where Titianus lay and bolted the door behind her.

Kaeso stood by the bed, shoulders drooping. "When we took the cuirass off, I wasn't sure he was still breathing. It's so shallow…it's hard to tell." He put his finger in Titianus's outer ear. It came out wet with blood. He offered it for her inspection. "I think his skull is broken."

The powerful man who took control of a room whenever he entered looked so fragile now. She bit her lip to stop the quiver. While he still lived, hope remained.

"Are you ready to pray?" She stroked Titianus's stubbly cheek and drew her thumb across the lips that had been so stern the first time she saw him. If only God's answer to their prayers would be yes, perhaps she'd see them smile again.

From the corners of both eyes, she wiped away tears. *I know nothing can be broken that You can't heal, Lord. Please don't let his life end like this. Please spare him, and then please protect us all.*

"I guess so. He looks too far gone." His mouth curved down. "God let this happen to him. Maybe He doesn't care if Titianus dies. Maybe He doesn't care if any of us do."

Her breath caught as fear for her brother shot through her. "You can't mean that. God cares about everyone, even a stone-hearted tribune like he seemed when we met him." She pushed a strand of hair off Titianus's forehead. "He's still breathing, and where there's breath, there's hope."

She reached across the bed and took Kaeso's hand. "Remember the time when Apostle Paul was preaching late into the night, and the young man sitting in the window went to sleep and fell to his death on the ground outside? He would have hurt his head, too. Paul prayed, and God restored him to life. This isn't as extreme as that. Titianus is still alive."

He pulled his hand free and rested it on Titianus's shoulder. "But Paul was an apostle. He healed lots of people. We've never healed a single one, not even from something minor."

She placed her hand on Titianus's other shoulder. "It wasn't Paul who did the healing. It was the Holy Spirit, and He listens to our prayers just like He did to Paul. There's nothing to lose and everything to gain in asking God to heal."

"Maybe you're right." His sigh revealed both doubt and sadness, but he reached across and took her free hand. "Start praying."

She took a deep breath and closed her eyes.

"Father, we ask you to heal our precious friend Titianus. He doesn't know You. He's never seen Your healing power. He's never felt Your loving presence with him. Please keep him alive so he has a chance for all of that. Please heal his body now; then open his heart and mind to love Jesus and be filled with Your Spirit. In Jesus's precious name, we ask this."

"Amen." Kaeso's response was almost a whisper.

From so shallow she could barely see it to deep and slow, Titianus's breathing had changed to that of a man enjoying his sleep at the end of long day.

She moved her hand to the center of his broad chest. The slow rise and fall and the beating of his heart were proof of God's power and love for this man who frightened her even though he wanted to help them. She tipped back her head and rejoiced in God's presence and mercy.

"Did you feel it?" Kaeso's smile started small and grew into his biggest grin.

"The heat?"

"Yes. Up to my elbow as we were praying, and then he started breathing normal." He squeezed the back of his neck. "I never expected to see the power of God like that, to actually watch as He healed while we prayed."

"Neither did I. I've copied the stories of miracles that Luke recorded so many times, but to be part of one…" The joy of it all coursed through her. What could she say? What she felt—in Latin or Greek, she knew no words to express it.

With her eyes closed and her arms raised, she thanked God again, not just for healing Titianus's injuries but for restoring Kaeso's faith. He'd no longer be questioning whether God cared or whether He listened to their prayers.

"I'll be right back." From her own room two doors down, she brought a pitcher and basin. With a small wet towel, she wiped the blood and dirt off Titianus's forehead and temple. The blood in his hair he could wash out later. He didn't open his eyes, but she knew what they'd look like if he did. She used to clean up Kaeso the same way when he was small. Titianus's shock at her treating him like her brother would have provoked her to laughter, even if she tried to stop it.

But he wasn't her brother. One last wipe, and she set the towel aside. She would have laughed if Septimus had predicted it, but when she knelt beside him in the stableyard, the thought of him dying hurt more than she expected. She'd wanted him to leave her alone, but the fear of never seeing him again tore into her. Without intending to, was she starting to care for this unusual man?

She fought the smile as she laughed at herself. Surely not. He was the last man she would want as a husband. But maybe as a friend. That must be it. Septimus loved him that way, and Kaeso liked him. Perhaps she was starting to like him as well.

But a problem lay ahead. What should she say when he asked why he didn't die? Septimus was sure to tell him how bad off he was when he went for the physician, and Titianus would ask what they did to help him.

She rubbed both sides of her nose. Jesus had said not to worry when called before governors and kings to explain the hope all Christians had. The Holy Spirit would give them the words they would need. She'd have to listen for what the Spirit wanted her to say and then have the courage to say it. But before that conversation, she would pray that he would want to know more about the God who spared him.

For at least half an hour, Pompeia sat on a chair near Titianus's bed, watching him breath. With each rise and fall of his chest, she thanked God again for restoring him to them. As Septimus had said, he didn't deserve to die that way.

Kaeso had carried the chair in from his room and sat beside her. She wanted to be there when Titianus awoke so he wouldn't panic about where he was. But being alone in the bedroom with him—that didn't seem right, so Kaeso sat with her.

At last, Septimus's voice drifted up to them. He was talking to someone when he entered the peristyle below the balcony. A voice she didn't recognize answered. Lest the physician assume she was more intimate with the tribune than she was, she moved her chair back against the wall and stood beside it. Kaeso moved his back and returned to Titianus's side.

"Is he dead yet?" Resignation echoed in Septimus's words as he entered the room.

"No. Just sleeping." Kaeso's reply raised Septimus's eyebrows. Kaeso replied with a shrug and a smile.

It triggered the physician's frown. "So, it's not as urgent as you claimed. The night ride will cost you extra." When he reached the bedside, he crossed his arms and watched the chest move up and down a few times. "You made it sound like he'd reach the Styx before we could get here."

"I thought he might." Septimus's shrug drew an eye roll.

The frown deepened when the physician touched the dried blood in Titianus's hair. He bent over for a view behind Titianus's ear, and his brow furrowed. "This purple halfmoon behind his ear…that's a sign the skull is broken." He wiped some dried blood off the ear. He worked his fingers into Titianus's blood-matted hair and parted it for a better view of his scalp.

"Hmm." With thumbs resting on the underside of his jaw, he steepled his fingers and tapped his lips three times.

"I've heard Tribune Titianus is as hard-headed as they come." One corner of his mouth lifted. "Looks like they were right. That halfmoon, bleeding from the ear…that usually means broken skull and dying man."

With his fingertips, he shook Titianus's shoulder. The eyelids fluttered, then opened. Then Titianus squinched them almost shut as he looked away from the lamp Septimus was holding for the physician. He draped his arm across his face to partly block the light. "Where am I?"

"Back at my house." Septimus moved the lamp to put his shadow on Titianus's eyes. "I got there just in time, but I was afraid I hadn't." He turned his eyes toward Pompeia, and Titianus's gaze followed his. One eyebrow shot up, and his restrained smile declared both surprise and pleasure at her being there.

Her cheeks heated, and she silently scolded herself for letting that happen. Though what she could have done to stop it, she had no idea.

"I know you." Titianus's brow furrowed as he looked at the physician. "I've seen you at Brutus's ludus after the games."

"Galenos. Felix sent your young friend to find me to help you. The way he described you, I expected a corpse."

Titianus gingerly touched the blood-caked hair. "I expected to be one, too."

"How do you feel now?"

"I've felt better, but I don't feel too bad. But..." He squeezed his eyes shut, then blinked several times as he peered at Galenos. "I'm seeing two of you."

"That's not unusual after a blow to the head. You may find you get dizzy when you stand. If so, have someone beside you when you walk. The problem usually lasts a few hours, sometimes a few days, rarely a few weeks, but it should pass soon enough."

"Some things I don't mind seeing two of." Titianus's gaze rested on her only briefly, but it was enough to heat her cheeks again. "But me seeing two of you doesn't mean you should charge Septimus double."

Galenos's amused snort accompanied Septimus's chuckle. "No, but I'll gladly pay extra for the night ride."

"A few more tests before I leave. Move your arms and legs. Wiggle your fingers and toes." With arms crossed again, Galenos watched Titianus do what he told him.

"Fortuna has truly smiled on you, tribune. There's nothing else for me to do here. Rest, and I'll be back tomorrow to check on you."

"Thank you for coming so promptly." Titianus's eyes narrowed. "It was promptly, wasn't it?"

"Half an hour or so." Kaeso moved to Titianus's side. "Pompeia and I watched over you while Septimus got Galenos."

Galenos scanned Pompeia, and she offered him the kind of smile she taught her young women to use with strange men at banquets.

A suggestive smile accompanied his bouncing eyebrows, and her cheeks heated. That wasn't the response she expected from a respectable man. "Have someone keep an eye on him through the night…but make it someone who'll let him rest."

Titianus looked at her with his unreadable eyes, and she felt the heat to the tips of her ears.

Kaeso crossed his arms and frowned at the physician's insinuation. "I'll make sure of that. My sister and I also thank you for coming to help our family friend."

When she glanced at Titianus, she read a wordless apology for what the man said. If Titianus corrected him, that would only make him believe it more. It might make him start spreading rumors. She smiled her thank you.

His eyes drifted shut, and his mouth relaxed into the straight line she knew so well. His breathing returned to the slow, steady rhythm she'd watched before.

Septimus waved toward the door. "We'll find our steward and get you paid for tonight."

With another too-knowing smile and quick lift of one eyebrow at her, Galenos followed him out.

She joined Kaeso at the bedside. "I'll watch over him until morning."

He took her hand. "What Galenos said…it's better if I watch."

"He's seeing double, so he's not completely well yet." That had surprised her. When God did a miracle, why wouldn't He heal everything?

"I'll get you if he needs prayer again." He squeezed her hand before releasing it.

With a featherlight touch so she wouldn't awaken him, she pushed a strand of hair back from the tribune's forehead. She lowered her voice to a whisper. He didn't need to hear her next words. "He's a good man. I wonder if it was the one who killed Father who did this. I'm glad Septimus got there in time. I'd hate for him to die because he was seeking justice for us." She tipped her head back and raised her arms. "Thank you, God, for sparing him and for letting us be here as You did."

Kaeso wrapped an arm around her. "Amen."

"I'll close the door so no one disturbs him." As she stood in the doorway, hand on the handle, she looked at Titianus one more time. He was a good man. Might he be someone she could love if he followed her Lord?

It was inevitable that he would learn of their faith since God had healed him. Discouraging his interest in her was pointless now.

Her mouth curved into a smile she was certain he'd like. She'd be praying for him until he was restored to full health, but it would be the healing of his heart and soul she'd be praying for even more. He'd never suspect it, but even if he knew, there was nothing he could do to stop her.

Chapter 28

A Good Friend

The Sabinus town house, morning of Day 12

F ather."

Manius was on his way to the tablinum for the salutation when Septimus spoke behind him. Then he trotted up beside him and matched his stride. "There's something I need to ask you." He pointed at the library. "In private."

As soon as they entered, Septimus closed the door and leaned against it.

Manius sat on the edge of his desk. "When I returned last night, I discovered I have a new houseguest under my protection. Is this about adding yet another one?"

"No…" A shadow veiled his usually cheerful son's eyes.

"The ones you've chosen so far have enlivened this place, so I have no objection to more of the same."

"There is another problem, a big one, but it doesn't belong to someone new."

Manius crossed his arms. "Is it my wounded cousin or the endangered brother and sister who need something?"

"Kaeso and Pompeia, but only for a while."

"What's their problem?"

"When their father died, the school lost all his students. That was more than half what they all earned. Kaeso's worrying about how he's going to find and keep enough students to support him and his sister and their slaves. He's worried about whether he can make the rent."

Septimus drew a deep breath and held it.

"Go on."

"So, I was thinking you could buy the building and lower their rent by half."

A snort was Manius's first response. "Why would I want to do that?"

Septimus's brow furrowed; then he shrugged. "If you don't want to, that's fine. I'll use some of my allowance to pay part of the rent for them. They need to stay in that building to keep running the school. Kaeso will argue with me over that because he doesn't want to take advantage of our friendship, but he'll listen to reason if that's what it takes to keep their familia together."

Not looking at Manius, Septimus walked to the desk. "But..." He straightened a stack of tablets before turning to face his father. "If you buy the town house, you can charge them less by deducting part of the rent from my allowance. They won't have to know I'm helping. Then make their town house part of my inheritance someday so I can keep it affordable for them."

"Would he even be able to pay the lower rent now that Lenaeus is gone?" Manius tipped his head to look down his nose. "How many slaves do they have? Selling some will reduce their expenses."

"Only four, and that's the last thing he'll do. Their familia is like real family, not just a household."

The hopeful look on Septimus's face was something Manius couldn't resist. Not that he wanted to. Pompeia and Kaeso were fine young people who deserved his help.

"Talk to my steward and have him take care of it. But don't tell your friend I've done it. I don't want him assuming I'll help any further."

Septimus's chuckle was not what Manius expected. "He won't, and you've just saved me from having to argue with Kaeso until Pompeia finally tells him to let me help for a while for the sake of the whole familia. She'd say they can work on paying me back later when they build up their number of students or she figures out some other way to supplement their income." He grinned. "And then Kaeso would take her advice and see the wisdom in my proposal."

"She's all woman when it comes to winning over a man, brother or otherwise." One corner of Manius's mouth lifted. His own Julia had always been gifted at persuading him to see the wisdom of what she proposed. "What can she do besides teach?"

"She can draw really well, and her handwriting is pretty. She's made special codices for friends before. I've seen one, and it was a thing of beauty. I heard her tell Kaeso she could make others to sell for private libraries."

"I suppose you'll be wanting me to buy some of them for mine." He tried not to smile. "And persuade your grandfather to do the same."

"I wasn't going to suggest it, but since you have…"

"Let my steward know when she has some ready."

"Thank you, Father."

Manius rolled his eyes for effect and got the expected grin from Septimus before he left the room.

He rubbed his jaw as he stared at the door through which his generous son had gone. He didn't mind having the brother and sister in his house. He rather enjoyed his tribune cousin, who was coming because the sister was there. From all he'd seen, he'd be willing to bet Kaeso had no desire to take advantage of Septimus. Theirs was a true friendship, a rare thing in the political circles of Rome.

He had wealth, power, and a large circle of friendly acquaintances. But he couldn't name a single true friend. It was probably too late to find one, and although he was content with his life, that was cause for regret. He would never enjoy what his son already had.

The Arcanus town house, morning of Day 12

It had been hard to sit in Rufinus's atrium, listening to conversations about mundane matters when Arcanus was expecting Vulpis at his own house later. But he was finally home, sitting at the desk in his own library, trying to read but finding it impossible to focus.

When the quiet tap on the door finally came, he jumped as if someone had struck a gong behind him.

"Enter."

With a satchel slung over his shoulder, Vulpis came in and closed the door. He strode to the desk as if he owned the room. The eyes of a well-fed predator contemplated Arcanus before he placed the satchel on the desktop. Arcanus stopped a shudder before the killer could see it.

"I take it you were successful."

"Yes, but there was a complication."

"A complication?" Arcanus leaned back in his chair. That didn't increase their separation much, but somehow it felt safer.

"We got him off his horse and cracked his skull, but one of his friends came and rode down my…assistant. He was coming after the two of us, so we dropped the body and left." He shoved the satchel toward Arcanus, but he didn't release his grip. "You hired me just in time. I took this off him. It holds wax tablets from Titianus's investigation. It's surprising what the tribune knew already. You probably want to know." He wiggled the satchel. "And you can find out for an extra fifty denarii."

Arcanus stared at the satchel. He did want to know…desperately, but an extra fifty? "With Titianus dead, his notes aren't worth anything extra. But I'll take those off your hands."

He reached for the satchel, and Vulpis pulled it back. "It's worth something to the urban prefect. He'll probably pay more than fifty denarii for something I found in a trash heap that was stolen from his dead tribune. The next man to take up the case will find them invaluable."

Arcanus rubbed his lip. Without knowing what was in them, he couldn't let the tablets get in Saturninus's hands.

"All right. Fifty plus the five hundred we agreed on." He opened his desk drawer and pulled out the sack of twenty aurei." He tossed the sack of gold coins to Vulpis, then pointed at a chair against the wall. "Sit over there, and I'll get you the fifty."

Vulpis sauntered to the chair and lowered himself into it. He placed the satchel on his lap, dumped the coins onto it, and counted them before shoveling them back into the sack.

From the strongbox bolted to the floor in the corner, Arcanus withdrew two more aurei. He locked it and dropped the key on its chain inside his tunic before walking over. He held out the coins in his closed fist as he reached for the satchel. The exchange was made, and Vulpis rose.

"It's been a pleasure doing business with you." His was a feral smile. "If you need my services again, you know how to reach me."

"Indeed." Palm up, Arcanus waved his hand at the door, inviting Vulpis to leave. A sneer curled Vulpis's lip before he stepped through the doorway and headed down the atrium to the front entrance. As he disappeared into the vestibulum, Arcanus's shoulders drooped.

Then anger at Lupus bubbled up inside him, and his back straightened.

If Lupus had dealt honestly with Rufinus, the freedman would be alive and the warehouse would still be standing. He wouldn't have had to kill Lenaeus, the boy wouldn't have seen him, and Titianus would never had been hunting him down.

But the boy would die soon, the tribune who always solved a case was dead, and he had the notes that would have let another take Titianus's place.

Gaius had proven himself a good friend in providing the means to solve his problems.

He closed and bolted the door, then dumped the contents of the satchel on his desk.

The first tablet held a list of twelve freedmen of Rufinus. Both his and Lupus's names were among them. The second contained sample seals of half the men, each made with their personal signets. Several were similar enough to Rufinus's seal that they might be confused by someone who didn't see the original often. But his own personal signet was quite different from his patron's. No one would think it could be used in a forgery. Only he and Rufinus knew he had an original.

What he'd bought wouldn't have been worth fifty denarii to the urban prefect. It wouldn't help whoever replaced Titianus identify him as Lupus's killer.

But the peace of mind from knowing that Titianus hadn't figured out he was responsible and that his replacement probably wouldn't either was worth every gold coin he'd spent.

The Sabinus town house, early afternoon of Day 12

Sabinus had just beaten Manius in their last tabula game before heading to the baths. It would be an afternoon of political alliance-building and gossip collection. He leaned back against the pillows lining the wicker chair in his son's library. "I'm not surprised someone finally tried to kill Titianus. I could name at least a dozen senators who could blame some loss on his obsessive pursuit of what he calls justice."

Manius picked up a silver game piece and placed it into the ivory-inlaid box. "Septimus's friends started spending nights with us until Titianus catches their father's murderer. Since then, he's dined here a few times. He's better company than anyone would think who only saw him on duty. He doesn't say much, but what he says is worth hearing. I like him."

"Hmph." Sabinus rested his hands on the arms of his chair. "I've never exchanged enough words with him to judge, and even I can't size up a man when he's sleeping. He didn't look too badly hurt. How long will he be here?"

"It's hard to say." Manius rubbed his chin. "He's got double vision and balance problems that could last a few days. Maybe longer. Keeping him here until those clear up is probably wise."

The slap of sandals on marble grew louder. One of the house slaves appeared in the library doorway and tapped on the open door.

Manius looked up as he dropped the last brass marker in and shut the lid. "Yes?"

"Prefect Saturninus just rode in and went straight up to see Tribune Titianus. Steward sent me to tell you quick."

Manius sent the messenger away with a wave. "Odd. Why would he come to see Titianus without speaking first with me?"

"More than odd. Worrisome. Last month at a banquet I overheard him talking about your injured guest after too much wine. It seems Titianus stopped some questionable dealings before one of his favored clients could get his share out. Our urban prefect was not happy with his best investigator's success." Sabinus stood. "We're going to join them."

As they climbed the stairs, Saturninus's nasal voice reached them. "The streets of Rome have become too dangerous when a tribune of the Urban Cohort can be almost killed in a robbery attempt. This must be addressed immediately. I've assigned Tribune Victorinus to investigate it and to take over your other cases. I'll send a litter to take you to the infirmary at the fortress. One of the Praetorian physicians can oversee your care."

Sabinus put his finger to his lips and softened his tread as they proceeded along the balcony to their houseguest's door and looked in.

Titianus sat up and swung his legs off the bed. "No need for that, prefect. I'll be well enough to resume my duties within a week. Reassigning my cases won't be necessary." He stood, but he was barely on his feet when he started to sway. He almost toppled before he sat down.

"Hmph." Saturninus's snort combined amusement and condescension. "It's obvious your injury is more severe than you think. I'll decide what's best for both you and Rome."

Sabinus's eyes narrowed. Best for Saturninus was what he meant. It was time to intervene.

"Saturninus. This is a pleasant surprise." Sabinus gave the prefect one of his most sincere fake smiles as he entered the room. "It's good to see such heart-felt concern for the recovery of your best investigator." He walked to the bedside and stood by his too-honest relative. "But he's my nephew, and I'm confident we can take better care of him here. We'll have him well enough to return to cleaning up Rome in no time."

He rested his hand on Titianus's shoulder. "It would be a great loss to Rome and a source of unhappiness for me if anything slows his recovery or if anything else happens to him. Catching whoever attacked him so it won't happen again should receive that tribune's full attention. It's undoubtedly related to another case Titus will solve as soon as he returns."

Saturninus's gaze moved from Sabinus's hand to his face. "Getting my best man back to work quickly is our mutual goal. He can stay here for now."

Sabinus had made a point of calling his nephew by his first name. He'd never done that before, and the way Titianus's eyes widened when he first spoke it was comical. Almost as amusing was the way Saturninus's eyes veiled at the affection it conveyed.

Two light pats, and Sabinus lifted his hand from the young man's shoulder. "Manius and I were just on our way to the baths. Would you care to join us? My nephew needs to rest if he is to return to duty as soon possible."

He smiled at Titianus, who'd recovered enough from the shock of their implied closeness to wipe all emotion from his face. "As you can see, Titus is eager to go back to work, even before it's wise. We've brought in an excellent physician, and he will decide when my nephew has healed enough to resume his duties."

The prefect's gaze shifted from Sabinus to his nephew and back. "Any other day, accompanying you would be most enjoyable, but I have a prior engagement." He took a step back. "Perhaps another time."

"Yes. Another time. *Vale*, Saturninus."

The prefect dipped his head to acknowledge the farewell and left the room.

Manius followed him to the door and watched for a few moments. "He's gone."

Sabinus's eyebrows dipped as he contemplated the nephew he'd never cared about…until now. "That one is not to be trusted. You'll stay here until you can defend yourself again."

Titianus drew a breath through his teeth. "He's my commander. If he orders me back, I must go."

"You needn't worry about that. Without my approval, he won't order it now."

"But I want to go back as soon as I can." Titianus scrunched his eyes before rubbing his forehead. "The trail I was following will go cold."

"No one knows head wounds better than the arena's top physician, and he says this needs time and rest. Remaining here will give you both." Sabinus let his smile turn suggestive. "That pretty teacher's daughter will keep you from getting too bored. Septimus tells me she's a smart one…just what you need to keep you entertained."

"Women are not just for entertainment. Pompeia is a gifted teacher in her own right and a philosopher."

"Philosophia…the love of wisdom. I can see where she might have that." Sabinus's lips twitched as he tried not to laugh at his nephew's obvious partiality. "From what I know of women, it wouldn't take much to get her to love a certain tribune as well. A woman who's independent and clever might suit you. Personally, I like my women pretty, compliant, and not too smart, but you and I have different tastes."

He turned before Titianus could answer, but he looked back over his shoulder. "Manius will keep an eye on you here, and I'll be keeping an eye on the noble prefect. Rest now."

He stepped onto the balcony, and Manius joined him. As they started down the stairs, he rubbed his jaw. "Your houseguest is not to know this and don't mention it to Septimus, either. I'll have Festinus look into the attack. He'll learn more than that incompetent tribune. I think Saturninus is counting on him not solving anything. Someone wants my incorruptible nephew dead, and Saturninus will do nothing to protect him."

Manius chuckled. "If your chief of spies can't find out who ordered his murder, not even Titianus could."

Sabinus answered with a grin. "If he weren't so inflexibly honest, Titianus would be unbeatable, but my man doesn't suffer from that handicap."

Chapter 29

A Welcome Change

The Sabinus town house, afternoon of Day 12

Even though Kaeso reported that Titianus had spent a comfortable night, Pompeia had been reluctant to leave him that morning. Would whoever was told to look after him only look on it as an added chore? At breakfast, Manius had laughed at her as he assured her his steward would check on "her tribune" while they were gone, but he still sent a second bodyguard with them so she could return to his town house as soon as she finished teaching.

She entered Titianus's room on tiptoes and stood by his bed, watching his chest rise and fall with the rhythm it had after they prayed. Someone had washed the blood out of his hair.

Galenos had said rest was what he needed most. Had the physician been back yet to check on his patient?

She hadn't moved four steps away when—

"Don't go." His voice was quiet, making it a request, not a command.

She turned to find him sitting up. "How are you feeling?"

"Better than this morning. Tired of lying here doing nothing."

He swung his legs off the bed and stood. But he started to sway and sat down again before she got close enough to catch him if he fell.

"Galenos said not to do that without someone beside you."

He squeezed his eyes shut, then focused them on her. "I'm still seeing two of you. Two of everything, and it's worse when something's up close."

"Seeing one of me is more than enough for anyone. But that should pass."

He closed his eyes and slowly shook his head. "I don't have time for this." He spread his arms and placed his hands on the bed to steady himself as he sat.

She moved closer. "At the moment, resting is the only thing you should be doing. Galenos said it would take a few days to get back to normal after you almost died. I'm going to make sure you rest like you should."

She stepped past him to fluff his pillow. "Lie down." She patted it. "I can read to you for a while so you won't get too bored. What would you like?"

◆

What would he like? He could think of a lot of things he'd like from her, but listening to her melodic voice as she read was a good start.

He swung his legs back onto the bed and lay down. The smile he gave her got one in return. "You pick something." A friendliness he'd never seen before lit her eyes. "Poetry's not my favorite, but if it's yours, then I'm fine with it."

"It's not my favorite, either. But I do enjoy history and natural history. Septimus says the library here is exceptional. I'll get something and be right back."

He started to rise again, but before he was halfway to sitting, she placed her hand on his chest and pushed him gently back onto the bed.

"What is it about men that you won't rest when you need to? Kaeso won't either."

It was the first time she'd touched him. The first time when he was awake, anyway. He almost rested his hand on hers to keep it there but stopped just before he did. She might snatch it away if he touched her.

Or would she? Before he could decide, she made her choice. She left it there, and the heat from her palm penetrated the tunic over his heart.

"Promise me you won't be trying to get up while I'm gone." She'd pursed her lips into a scold, but the smile in her eyes counteracted it.

"What will you do if I don't?"

"Hmm." She tipped her head back to look down her nose at him and tapped her chin while she thought. "As I see it, I have two options. I can get one of Manius's men to watch you. He could make you rest like you should, or I can say 'Please do it so I won't worry about you hurting yourself by falling and hitting your head again.' Then I could make eyes at you like women are prone to do to get their way." She batted her eyes at him. "But that would risk making you laugh so hard it would defeat my purpose. So, maybe I'll just say please and skip the rest."

He chuckled, and her eyebrows rose. "Your please is enough. I'll lie here until you return." He let a full smile curve his mouth. It felt good to let his guard down with her.

"Very good." Two light pats on his chest, and she left the room.

He laced his fingers and put them behind his head. It still ached some, but he could mostly ignore it. It was almost worth being hurt to have her treat him like she did Septimus. Perhaps she saw him as a friend now. He released a contented sigh. With time, maybe she would treat him as something much more than a friend.

Evening of Day 12

With Tutelus beside him, Titianus made his way down from the balcony, one step at a time. He was already tired before they reached the bottom, but ahead in the triclinium was a good dinner and the possibility of a conversation with Pompeia. A man who could complete a twenty-mile training march in five hours should be able to go another fifty feet for some time with friends.

By the time Tutelus guided him to his couch, determination alone kept his feet moving, and each step taken felt like a mile on that march. He settled onto the middle couch.

"Can I get you anything, tribune?" Tutelus stood before him with legs spread and arms crossed.

"We'll take care of him." Pompeia's lilting voice came from behind the bodyguard, and then she stepped into view. "Thank you for helping him down."

Tutelus bowed his head to her, and a smile like Titianus never expected on the Savage Syrian appeared. "I'll see you in the morning." He filled the doorway as he passed into the atrium, and Kaeso entered with Septimus.

"How are you feeling, cousin?" Manius was right behind them.

"Better than I ought to." Titianus tipped his head toward his young cousin. "Without Septimus, I'd be dead now."

Manius stretched out on his couch, and the others reclined on theirs.

"What exactly did you do, son?"

"I went after Titianus to ask him something, and I saw three men attack him. When one started hitting him with a club, I rode my horse into him. When I charged the other two, they dropped him and ran."

He looked at Titianus. "You were bleeding from your ear. I thought you were dying, but I got two men to help me get you on your horse and bring you home. Then Pompeia sent me for Galenos while she and Kaeso took care of you."

Bleeding from his ear? The only man he'd seen do that had died within minutes, even with a physician at his side. Galenos had expected to find him dead. Titianus shifted on the couch to face Pompeia. "What did you do?"

She blanched, then blushed, then gave him a friendlier smile than he'd ever seen in the dining room. "I'll tell you when it's time for you to know."

Manius raised an eyebrow, then a smile followed. "I'm curious about that, too. When you decide to tell him, perhaps you can tell me as well."

"Perhaps." She turned her smile on their host. "If it's time for you to know then, too."

Three young women entered with the salad course, and conversation quieted as they ate.

As the salad course was being cleared and the main course served, Manius engaged Septimus and Pompeia in conversations about nothing in particular.

As he had at their first meal together, Titianus mostly listened. But this time, when he glanced her direction, Pompeia rewarded him with a smile. Reclining on a dining couch wasn't physically demanding, but it wasn't long before his eyelids drooped, and his head jerked.

"Titianus?" Her voice was gentle, and he turned toward it. "Do you need to rest now?"

He wanted to say no, to stay and talk with his friends. But as much as he wanted that, he couldn't keep his eyes open. "Yes."

With a curl of his fingers, Manius summoned the wine server. "Find Tutelus."

He stood. "You need to rest, cousin, and I need to attend to something for Father. Perhaps tomorrow Pompeia will tell us the rest of your story."

With Tutelus on one side and Manius on the other, Titianus left the dining room. But when he looked back, the warmth of her smile followed him.

◆

Pompeia took a final sip and placed her goblet on the table before swinging her legs off the couch. "I'm glad your cousin felt well enough to join us tonight. He's much nicer than he seemed when we first met him." She folded her napkin, first in half, then in half again. "I'm so thankful God healed him."

"He'd be glad to hear you say that." Septimus bounced his eyebrows at her, then sat on the edge of his couch. "It does seem your god did something to keep him from dying, but…" He rubbed his jaw. "If your god is so powerful, why didn't he heal Titianus completely? Why leave the lingering problems with headaches, double vision, and dizziness?"

With a smile, she shrugged. "Why God does what he does…I don't always understand. But He'll do what's best for Titianus at the right time. You know He brought him back from the brink of death. The God who could do that could have easily healed everything at once."

She wiped her mouth and laid the napkin beside the goblet. "But maybe there's a reason He wants to keep Titianus here in your father's house for a while. Maybe for his safety." She lowered her voice. "Maybe so I'll get a chance to tell him about God and what Jesus did for us. If he wasn't still here because he's not well enough to leave, they might try again and kill him before he can choose Jesus over Rome." She tapped her chest. "I have a feeling deep in my heart that he's going to follow Jesus like we do."

Septimus snorted. "You think he'll abandon his dedication to Rome, betray everything he's devoted his life to, to follow your god?" He spoke softly as well. "If you expect that, you're counting on a bigger miracle than healing a broken skull."

"I do. That's my deepest prayer for him." She glanced at the couch where Titianus had reclined. If he did, what future might that open for them? She turned her eyes back on her almost-brother. "It's my prayer for you, too."

Septimus choked back a laugh. "If you can convince Titianus your god is the one true god and that he should surrender everything he values to follow him, that will be a miracle that might even sway me."

He wrinkled his nose and shook his head. "But it's not going to happen. When you try to tell him about your god, he's going to quote Seneca to you. 'Religion is regarded by the common people as true, by the wise as false, and by rulers as useful.'"

"Seneca was right about the gods of Rome and all the rituals for earning their favor, but it's not true of the only true God. I don't want Titianus to embrace a religion. I want him to see how much God loves him and decide to love Him back." She fingered the neck of her tunic. "Nothing is wiser than to give up our old way of living for someone we love, someone who loves us even before we decide to follow Him."

A slow shake of his head was Septimus's response. "He'll never do that."

"But if he does, will you?" Sitting on the edge of the couch beside her, she felt Kaeso tense. He wanted that more than anything for his best friend.

Her almost-brother's eyes widened, then narrowed. "I might think about it. No promises."

Kaeso took her hand and squeezed before they both stood. It was a clear signal she'd said enough…for now.

Septimus's shrug shut down the conversation for that night, and he rose from his own couch. He tapped Kaeso's arm and tipped his head toward the game table. "Play one game before bed?"

Pompeia stood. "I'll see you two in the morning."

"Are you going to check on him before you sleep?" Septimus grinned. "If he's awake, he'd like that."

"I might." She returned a playful smile. "But he needs his rest, so I might not." She wrinkled her nose. "Galenos wouldn't approve."

At the door, she looked back at her two little brothers. They never bet on their games, and Septimus was careful to avoid high-stakes betting with his other friends. But a person who put off thinking about what Jesus had done was playing a high-stakes game where eternal life was on the table. She and Kaeso would keep praying for Septimus to place his bet on God.

The Lenaeus town house, late morning of Day 13

Pompeia swung her legs off the couch in her family's triclinium and smoothed the front of her tunic.

"So, now you understand some of what you must do to arrange a proper Roman banquet. After your Latin lesson tomorrow, we'll talk more about how you decide which guest to put on each of the three couches. It can be a challenge at times so no one feels they've been slighted. Bring what you expect you would wear, and we'll practice reclining and rising without showing more of your body than is considered appropriate for upper-class Roman women."

She gestured toward the door. "I'll see you tomorrow."

Rezia and Talibah left the room, but Khepri lingered. When they and their guards were gone, she took something wrapped in red linen from her satchel. "I have a small gift to thank you for what you've shown us this week. It's what I would have worn to entertain my husband's guests if you hadn't taught me what was proper in Rome. It would have been very suitable to wear in Egypt." She smiled coyly. "My husband likes me to dress Egyptian when it's only the two of us, and I think your husband someday will enjoy the same."

"Words are always enough for thanking me, but it's kind of you to do more." Pompeia untied the knotted corners of the red linen. On top was a pleated cape that would not quite reach her waist. It was the same design as what Khepri wore over her strapped, ankle-length tube dress when she wasn't dressed like a Greek or a Roman, but the linen was so sheer, she could see her hand through two layers of it.

"It's exquisite. I've never seen fabric like this."

"The dress is better. It's called a kalasiris." As Khepri lifted it from its wrapping and held it up, the dress cascaded down, and Pompeia's eyebrows shot up. It was as sheer as the capelet.

Khepri's musical laugh was followed by a quick hug. "I think a Roman man would like it as much as my Egyptian does."

Pompeia steepled her fingers and raised them to her mouth. "I believe you're right." She returned the hug. "And when I wear it someday for a husband, I'll tell him he has you to thank."

She folded the kalasiris and held it to her chest. "I don't think we should let Kaeso see this."

Khepri's laugh wrapped her again in the affection that inspired the gift. "He'll want one for his wife, too."

Pompeia returned the dress to its wrapper. With arms held out, she invited the second hug Khepri was waiting to give her. "Thank you." She stepped back. "I'll see you tomorrow."

Khepri's bodyguard fell in behind her when she entered the atrium. She handed him the satchel and headed toward the door. With a final wave and smile, she disappeared into the vestibulum.

Pompeia held the capelet to her chest. She had nowhere to wear such things, but the friendship they proclaimed brought a smile.

What would Titianus think if she wore that on their wedding night? That thought triggered heat from her cheeks to the tips of her ears. Could she be so daring that she would wear it for him their first night together?

She shook her head as she laughed at herself. Even if he did decide to follow Jesus, an equestrian like him with family ties to the pinnacle of Roman society wouldn't choose a teacher like her as his wife.

As soon as she took Khepri's gift to her bedchamber, she'd be returning to Manius's house. Reading to Titianus yesterday had cheered him up. She'd always enjoyed reading to Kaeso when he was small, but the tribune was not her little brother.

She blew out a slow breath. She was no longer seeing him only as Septimus's friend or as the investigator who would catch Father's murderer. He was a smart, handsome man who could attract any woman, and she was no exception.

But if he was to be more to her than a friend, he had to follow her Lord. Before he was hurt, it would have been dangerous to speak to him of God. But now, he should be curious about the God who healed him. *God, please give me the right opening to tell him why he's really alive. Please let him listen and want to know more.*

She closed her eyes, and the stern face that used to frighten her changed into the warm eyes and smiles as he listened to her read yesterday.

Maybe he would choose her if, like her and Kaeso, he decided only a Christian wife would do.

God, please show Kaeso and me the way to reach Titianus so he'll want to follow You. I want him to know the joy of being Your child. I want him to have the hope we all have. I don't know yet if I'd want to be his wife, but if I find that I do, please make him want me, too.

Chapter 30

NEW POSSIBILITIES

The Sabinus town house, late morning of Day 13

With one arm draped over his eyes, Titianus waited for the salutation to end. He'd sent the boy who brought his breakfast to Manius's secretary. As soon as the last client left, Manius should come.

His uncle Sabinus might think he could control what Prefect Saturninus would do, but that was far from certain. If Sabinus was wrong and the prefect took his cases away, he'd be willing to bet a week's wages that one innocent person would be tortured and another would have her heart broken.

Manius could prevent both if he wanted. But would he?

"I heard you wanted to see me." Manius came to his bedside.

"I do."

This was not a request to make lying down, so Titianus swung his legs off the couch and waited for the swirling room to stop moving. "I need to ask an urgent favor of you."

"Urgent?" Manius's eyebrow rose. "What is it?"

"I want you to buy Kaeso's steward and free him. Today, if you can."

"Why?"

"Your father thinks Saturninus won't act without his permission, but the prefect doesn't like anyone telling him what to do. He might give me a week before he assigns Victorinus my cases, but he might do it right away. If he does, Victorinus will read the notes I took the first day."

Manius crossed his arms. "And that's a problem?"

"The boy who opens the Lenaeus door…he's the only one who saw the

194

murderer. Victorinus will take him right away to question. He'll want to impress Saturninus with his diligence in the matter, but Theo can't tell him more than what he already told me."

Manius's brow furrowed.

"It will break her heart to see what they'll do to him. He's a slave."

Understanding flashed across Manius's face, then his mouth curved down. "How would me buying Corax solve that?"

"Kaeso isn't twenty yet, so he's too young to make Corax a citizen. But if he's a citizen, he can buy and free his son to adopt him. Once the boy is a citizen, he can testify safely. When I arrest the murderer, Theo's testimony will ensure the conviction."

"You surprise me, cousin." One corner of Manius's mouth lifted. "I would never have expected a man with your reputation to try to circumvent an accepted legal procedure."

Titianus straightened and assumed his interrogator's mask, erasing all emotion from his face. "What's right and what's accepted often differ, and I choose what's right."

Manius's eyes narrowed. "Then why don't you do it?"

"If I find an important man is responsible, I don't want the truth the boy tells ignored because I saved him from torture myself." He squinched his eyes and rubbed his forehead. The end of the headaches couldn't come soon enough. "I'll pay you whatever it costs, but don't tell anyone, not even Pompeia."

As Manius massaged the back of his neck, a full smile formed. "I'll arrange it with Kaeso when he returns this afternoon, and I'll cover the expense." His eyes lit with silent laughter. "It's the sort of thing Father or I would do anyway." He slapped Titianus's upper arm. "Dining with me so often…it looks like I've started corrupting you."

"Or you've started making more honorable choices because of me." Titianus met smile with smile.

"Don't go spreading that rumor. I've worked hard to make some people afraid of what I might do, even though I'd never do it. You'll ruin my reputation." Manius's chuckle broadened Titianus's smile.

"You don't have to worry. Spreading that rumor would ruin mine as well."

Afternoon of Day 13

Titianus sat in a cushioned wicker chair, his arms lying on the arms of the chair, feet up on a pillow atop a game table. Manius had ordered a matched set of chairs and the table moved into his bedchamber to make it easier for Pompeia to entertain him. She'd be back soon from teaching, and he was ready to be entertained.

One corner of Titianus's mouth lifted. Between Manius's teasing attempts to get her to see his good points at dinner and asking her to keep him from getting too bored each afternoon, his cousin was proving invaluable. If someone had told him a week ago that Manius Sabinus would be playing matchmaker between him and his old tutor's daughter, even he couldn't have kept a straight face.

A tapping drew his gaze to the open door. Sciurus peered around the doorframe.

"Come in."

The youth came to stand by Titianus's feet, hands clasped in front of him. Worry widened his eyes, and his usually straight mouth had curved into a frown.

Titianus's own smile restored Sciurus's stressed expression to his relaxed but alert normal.

"You're the last visitor I expected. Is there a problem at the warehouse?"

"No, master, but you didn't come yesterday to get me, like you said. And when you didn't come today, we were worried. So, I asked Probus to let me look for you."

"I'm glad there's no problem." Titianus stopped the grin their concern for him triggered. "How did you find me?"

"I went to the Praetorian Fortress, and they said you hadn't been there for two days. They wouldn't tell me where you might be. So, I looked where I last knew you to be. At the station on the Via Patricius, they told me which way you went when you left two evenings ago. You were in full armor, so I didn't think you went to the baths. But maybe you went by Lenaeus's house after you finished whatever you were doing. So, I went there. I spoke with Kaeso Lenaeus, and he sent me here."

Titianus rubbed his mouth to hide the smile his helper's resourcefulness inspired. "Did you ride?"

"Yes." Sciurus blinked fast and swallowed. "I hope that was all right. It's a long way to the fortress. I was careful with the mule. The bodyguard watched him while I talked to Lenaeus."

"You did well tracking me down." The boy's eyes lit at those words. "When I recover, we'll resume where we left off." Titianus rubbed under his chin. "The tablet I had with the names has been stolen, but I'll have Optio Gellius make a new list. You'll take him my message on your way home. You can get something from Manius's steward for me to write on." He twisted his gold signet ring. "Gellius knows my seal, so he'll know you're my assistant. Ask when he expects to have it. You can pick it up then and bring it to me here."

"Yes, master." The dip of Sciurus's head was quick before his brow furrowed. "Lenaeus said someone tried to kill you." He rubbed the side of his nose. "If the one who attacked you finds his name in the tablet, will he have time to cover his trail more than even you can track by the time you're better?"

Titianus swung his feet off the table and started to rise. But the world swirled too much, so he sat again.

Sciurus's eyes widened. "You are going to get better, aren't you, master?" He bit his lip.

"I am. The gladiator physician said this usually clears after a few days."

"Or a few weeks." Both startled at Pompeia's words as she entered the room. "Galenos said not to try to do too much too soon."

"But if I wait too long, the trail will go stone cold. Even I can't track someone down then."

She'd reached his side, and he tipped his head back to look up at her smile.

Sciurus raised his gaze from the floor, and his eyes bounced between them. "Maybe I can track him if you tell me who."

Titianus rubbed his jaw again. "You could figure out what to do, but only a grown man and a free one at that would be able to do some of what's needed."

"I'm grown, and I'm free. Let me do that part." Septimus sauntered through the doorway. He scanned Sciurus and ended with a smile. "The two of us...we can do it all."

After drawing a deep breath, Titianus blew it out slowly. "There's a risk to that. I've made a few dozen enemies as tribune. More than one would like me dead. I don't know if the attack was related to Lenaeus's murder." He glanced at her and caught the fast blinks. "But it might have been. If you start making progress, you might become a target."

"I've trained enough at the ludus with sword and dagger." Septimus shrugged. "And at reading if and how someone is going to attack. I'm certain I can take care of myself."

"I wouldn't bet on it. I had all the training you've had and years of experience. I still wouldn't deliberately go some of the places you might need to without some of my men along."

He glanced as Sciurus and found too much eagerness on that face, too. "I don't want Sciurus going any of those places unguarded either. Probus would never forgive me if I got his assistant killed being careless. He's training Sciurus to replace him someday. I don't want to lose him either."

The youth lowered his head to hide his smile, but that just made the red tips of his ears more obvious.

"What if I get Father to give us a bodyguard, maybe two, to take along? Would that satisfy you?"

"More to the point, will it satisfy your father?" He glanced at Pompeia. What he said next might hurt her, but he had to say it. "Manius is not going to want you to put yourself in danger for a tutor, no matter how fond you were of him or of his family."

Rather than hurt, Pompeia's eyes declared her own worry. "I don't want any of you doing something on my account that would get you hurt." She touched Septimus's arm, drawing his gaze. "It would break my heart again if you were killed."

He patted her hand before she withdrew it. "I won't do anything stupid"—he directed a wry smile at Titianus—"like ride alone down a dark street where thugs lie in wait."

"You just proved my point. I've done that for years, and there's never been a problem. What looks safe can be deadly."

"But I've learned from your mistake." Septimus's smug smile raised Pompeia's eyebrows. "I promise I won't do anything that reckless." His mouth straightened. "But as you say, the trail will grow too cold to follow or someone will cover it up if it's not followed right now." He massaged his neck. "If I can get Father to give me a bodyguard for this, do you have any more objections? You'll need to guide where we look and tell me what questions I start out asking. I'm willing to do this if you are."

Sciurus's eager nod declared his agreement without Titianus saying a word.

A glance at Pompeia was all it took to know she was as worried about their safety as he was. But he wanted justice for her even more than she did. More than once, he'd opened his eyes because her voice trembled as she read him something that her father had once read to her. She flicked away the silent tears and smiled each time, as if nothing had just happened.

"If Manius approves, I'm willing to do anything I can to get justice for Lenaeus."

The smiles on Septimus and Sciurus were what he expected. He'd been young and eager like them once. There was potential for danger, but with Manius's bodyguards along, it shouldn't be too high.

"If you take the bodyguards and watch carefully yourself, it should be safe enough." He rubbed his forehead. This discussion hadn't helped the headache. "Word of me being laid up and Tribune Victorinus being likely to take over this case should make the killer less careful. Victorinus is known to be diligent only when the victim is important. His main goal is impressing the leading men of Rome who care about those cases so they'll help his career."

One corner of his mouth lifted. "He's also well known to have less than the sharpest mind in the Urban Cohort. The more important our quarry, the less likely that man is to expect he'll be caught once Victorinus has the case."

Septimus wrapped his arm around Pompeia's shoulders. "Father's in his library. I'll go talk with him now."

"Take Sciurus to your steward. He needs something for me to write a request to my optio, and I'll need some wax for my seal."

The two headed downstairs, leaving him alone with Pompeia. "Are you sure it's safe enough for them to do this?"

"It should be. I'll have them report what they find each day and tell them what to do next. I've taken Sciurus with me before. He sees suspicious things and reads people almost as well as I do. If I think it's turning dangerous, I'll stop them." He closed his eyes and massaged his temples. Somehow, that lessened the ache. "The attack…it probably had nothing to do with your father's death, and if it didn't, whoever my enemy is won't bother them."

"Does that help?"

"What?" He opened his eyes and lowered his hands.

"What you just did." She touched her temples and made small circles there.

"Some." He leaned his head back against the chair cushion.

She moved behind him. "May I do it for you?"

He tipped his head back until he could see her eyes. Concern for him shone there. But was it concern for a man she was growing to care about or only the concern she'd have for any person in pain?

"Please." He would have asked her himself if he'd thought she might want to do it.

As her fingertips made slow circles on his temples, he let every muscle relax. For as long as she wanted, whether it helped the headache or not, he'd welcome her touch. While it soothed the pain in his head, it stirred up regrets over what he'd been missing in the solitary life he'd chosen.

But when he'd brought Lenaeus's killer to justice and her period of mourning was over, he'd reclaim his town house and a life like other men. Maybe she'd want to be part of it.

The clearing of a throat opened his eyes. Sciurus stood in the doorway with a tray holding papyrus, pen and ink, and sealing wax.

Pompeia stepped away. "I'll leave you to prepare your message. I'll be back shortly to read to you."

Sciurus stepped back from the door to let her pass, then brought him the tray.

He'd ask for another massage when she returned. It worked much better when her fingertips replaced his. He tightened his lips and erased the smile.

When he finished his note to Gellius, he applied three drops of sealing wax and pressed his signet into it.

"Since you'll be my eyes and ears and guide Septimus in the hunt, I'll give you a choice. Would you rather be named after a squirrel or the squirrel hunter?"

"I can choose?" Sciurus raised his eyebrows.

"Yes. Have you ever seen a pine marten on the hunt?" The boy shook his head. "It chases the squirrel up and down the trunk, jumps from tree to tree after it, moves almost faster than your eyes can follow. It stays right behind the squirrel and doesn't stop until it catches it. Melis would suit you, but you can stay Sciurus if you want."

"I'd like to be the hunter, not the prey." His smile started slow and grew into a big grin.

"Then Melis it is. Ask Probus to change his records about you. Tell him I said you earned it."

He handed Melis the papyrus. "Come back tomorrow morning. Bring the mule, and I'll explain what you'll do first."

"Yes, master." Still grinning, Melis took the papyrus, bowed, and left.

Titianus laid his head back on the chair cushion and closed his eyes. A new name for Melis, new possibilities for himself. Sometimes the best thing that could happen to a man was almost getting killed.

Chapter 31

A New Level of Trust

How long Titianus dozed, he didn't know, but he woke to Pompeia's voice.

"Septimus said to tell you Manius left for the baths already, but he'll talk to him before dinner. He's gone to see if Kaeso and Tutelus want to go there as well."

"I expect he'll get approval." One corner of his mouth rose. "He has the Sabinus gift of persuasion. I haven't seen him fail yet. Melis will be coming in the morning, so if Manius gives them a bodyguard, they can start tomorrow."

"Melis?"

"My eager helper. The name of a rodent doesn't fit him. He's a hunter at heart, not prey. When I offered it, he liked the name change."

"I'm not surprised. Your praise lit his eyes like I see with Theo. When I walked in, he looked worried about you."

"That surprised me. Most of my people wouldn't care what happened to me as long as they weren't sold to a cruel master. Probus does, but I thought he was the only one. He's managed what comes and goes at the warehouse on the Tiber since I was a small boy."

He shifted in the chair to sit more upright. "He never failed to have a honey roll for me when Father took me there. He buys in bulk in Ostia, ships it upriver, then divides it to sell to merchants. I trust him to run the whole business without my oversight."

His smile dimmed. "I hadn't noticed how old he's getting until he helped fight the fire. He bought Melis to train to replace him. That was three years ago. I only met the boy when I used him to take notes as I collected names from the people who might have seen someone suspicious." His smile turned wry. "Probus found us a treasure. I doubt the wine merchant he bought him from had any idea what he was giving up."

"Our familia is like real family. They loved Father almost as much as I do." She shifted her gaze to the window. "I've told Theo so many times that it's not his fault, but I can't convince him. Corax was the same a few years ago when he wasn't able to pro—" She glanced at him as she froze midword, then looked down and away.

"Wasn't able to what? Was he trying to protect you?" Was this what she was afraid he'd find out? "Pompeia." Uncertainty filled the eyes she turned on him. "Whatever you say will go no further than me. I've seen what can happen through no fault of your own."

She drew a deep breath and held it. Solemn eyes locked onto his. When uncertainty was replaced by trust, he felt the full honor of it.

"I was barely sixteen, and I'd dined with the sister of one of Father's students. Flaccus's sister, actually. We were a little late starting home, and it was almost dark. Two men jumped us. Corax tried to stop them, but they knocked him out and kidnapped me."

He blanked his face. She mustn't think his disgust with men who would do that was disgust with her. It was too easy, even in Rome—especially in Rome—for a woman to disappear and never be found.

She offered a forced smile. "But I was rescued right away by Aulus Secundus and Marcus Drusus. They came with two of Brutus's gladiators looking for Secundus's sister. She'd been kidnapped, too, and they rescued me instead." Sadness filled her eyes. "I was spared what might have happened, but she was never found."

His head drew back. What were the odds? "Julia Secunda's kidnapping was the first important case I investigated, and it took me longer to find who was guilty back then. I was convinced Marcus and Aulus had something to do with her disappearance. Her father ordered the investigation stopped when he returned from Sicily. It was more than a month since she vanished. He said she would never be found alive after so long, and if she was dead, he'd rather not know how she died. So, he asked Prefect Verus to order me to close the case and spend my time on crimes where my efforts might produce something useful."

He snorted. "At least that was what he claimed. I suspected he knew what had happened to her, and he stopped my investigation to protect his son."

"Love can force an impossible choice. He didn't want to lose both of them."

"But she deserved justice. I would have kept searching until I found the ones responsible, even though Marcus Drusus was the younger brother of my closest friend. Lucius and I were like Septimus and Kaeso."

So long ago...it was over seven years since he'd seen his friend. He'd almost forgotten what it was to have a friend who truly knew and liked him, just as he was.

He closed one eye and rubbed his temple. One eye or two, he still saw double. "He's married and posted in Thracia now. He went first to Judaea, and rumor had it Marcus tried to kill him there. I wasn't surprised. Lucius has a scar"—he traced a line from ear to jaw—"where his brother cut him while they were sparring. Lucius insisted it was an accident, but I wasn't so sure. Marcus died in Sepphoris, and rumor was he forced Lucius to kill him or die himself."

He massaged his neck. "If I'd been allowed to prove him guilty here, Roman justice would have spared my friend that pain."

"Sometimes justice is the last thing you want because too many innocents get hurt on the way to it. Forgiveness and mercy can give more peace than full justice." She bit her lip. "If you catch Father's murderer and the only way to prove he did it is with Theo's testimony..." Her hand covered her mouth, and tears glistened in her eyes.

"That shouldn't be a problem now. Manius is going to make sure it won't come to that."

With her fingertips, she wiped off the tear that started down her cheek. "Manius?"

"Yes."

Her eyebrows lowered; then a knowing smile appeared. "Manius will do whatever it is, but I think I know whose idea it was."

His reply was silence and his emotionless mask. He hadn't wanted her to know the part he played, but it was too hard to watch her cry.

"I'm sure you've told Manius to give you no credit, and I won't say anything to anyone else." She touched his hand where it lay on the arm of the chair. "But you and I will know the truth of it." Her beaming smile warmed him like the sun breaking through the clouds on a rainy day. "There's not enough words to fully thank you."

She set the scroll on her chair and moved behind his. "But I can start by making your afternoon better. First, we make your head hurt less, and then I'll bore you to sleep with some reading."

He tipped his head back until he could see her smile. He might go to sleep, but being with her was never boring.

"Close your eyes and relax." The first circle of her fingertips drew his sigh. With each following circle, the pain faded and his whole body relaxed. A few more circles, and relaxation drifted into sleep.

◆

When Titianus's breathing slowed and deepened, Pompeia settled into the chair across the game table from him. She might not be reading to him today, but she found enough entertainment in simply watching him sleep.

As reserved as he was about talking at dinner, he'd stunned her with how much of his life he'd just shared. Living in quarters at the fortress, thinking only Probus cared what happened to him, the wistful note in his voice when he spoke of his friend being so far away, like he never expected to see him again—what a lonely life he'd been living.

She'd known what it was like to have no close friends. She could never tell the girls she'd been friendly with about her faith, and as they married and moved to their husband's homes, they soon had nothing in common to sustain their friendship. But with Lilia grown up and Ciconia, she had Christian sisters even if she didn't have her old friends.

The kidnapping was a family secret, too. She'd been gone such a short time that none of her friends had known, and Father said it was important to keep it that way.

She'd begged God for deliverance, and it came in the form of Aulus and Marcus and especially the gladiator Africanus, who'd known exactly what to say to convince the man who insisted he owned her to let her go.

If Aulus and the rest hadn't come...even after eight years that thought triggered a shiver.

When they brought her home, Father had told them he'd reported it at the nearest guard station but told no one else. The optio had taken notes, but he hadn't seemed to care.

Father was afraid two young men couldn't resist bragging to their friends about saving her, and cruel gossip about what must have happened would have followed. But they'd kept her secret, and it was almost as if it never happened.

In one unguarded moment, she'd started to reveal it. She stopped just in time.

Then that nudge in her spirit...like God wanted her to tell him, that it was safe to reveal it to this man who'd seen the ugliness behind the marble façades of Rome. She fingered her lip. That telling him would open a door...and it had.

Appius had said that Publius Drusus's son, Lucius Fidelis, had betrayed him to become paterfamilias and get the family wealth. But his grandson was also called Lucius, and he valued truth and honor like Publius did.

Since Lucius was his best friend, had Titianus ever met Publius? Would he want to know why his friend's grandfather chose death over denying his faith? The epistle Publius wrote had convinced Father and her to believe and follow the Lord. What might it do for Titianus if he read it?

He would have been sixteen when Publius died in the arena. Had Publius ever talked to him and Lucius about God, like Father used to talk to Septimus and Kaeso?

At dinner, he'd asked what they did before the physician came. The time to tell him wasn't right with Manius listening as well, and Titianus had been too tired anyway. He would ask again. But when she told him it was God who brought him back from the edge of death, would he scoff at the thought or be open to hearing more?

Chapter 32

THE NICEST MAN

Late afternoon of Day 13

Manius sat at his library desk, a scroll of Suetonius's *Lives of Famous Men* before him. The life of Fabius Quintilianus was summarized in two sentences. Brought to Rome from Spain by Galba. Had the first public school in Rome and was paid by public funds.

Suetonius had missed the essence of the man entirely.

He leaned back in his chair. He'd chosen Lenaeus to begin Septimus's rhetorical training because he preferred the Quintilian style of persuasion with straight-forward language to the flowery, extravagant style that was the popular alternative.

He hadn't considered what else Lenaeus would be teaching carefully enough. Quintilianus had insisted greatness as an orator was only achievable for a highly moral man. When Septimus started there at the age of nine, he never expected his son to take that lesson so deeply to heart.

He wouldn't have, so he never considered whether Septimus would.

Then Brutus had declared his goal was not just to teach swordsmanship but to help young men grow in honor and devotion to Rome. Father was devoted to Rome, as he was himself, and Brutus's trainers were the best. Those were only noble-sounding words often spoken by men who didn't mean them, but Brutus had delivered on his promise.

Now his son's best friend was Quintilian to the core, and his tribune cousin, the incorruptible product of both Lenaeus's and Brutus's teaching, was becoming his son's friend as well.

If Father knew the full extent of it, he wouldn't like Septimus's determination to be honorable in all things. He'd raised his sons to be shrewd and pragmatic, even ruthless when called for.

But if Manius could change how his own son approached life, he wouldn't.

It felt good to be part of the generosity both Septimus and Titianus were directing toward Kaeso and Pompeia. He'd bought the town house already. He'd buy two people today as he chose what was right over regular Roman practice.

A knock on the open door drew his eyes from the scroll.

"The doorman said I should come as soon as I got here." Kaeso stepped into the room. "Is there something I can do for you?"

"There's something we both can do for Pompeia and the rest of your familia."

Kaeso's brow furrowed. "What do you think I can do?"

"You can sell me Corax today so I can free him tomorrow."

Kaeso's head drew back. "Why do you want to do that?"

"So Rome's newest citizen can buy Theo and adopt him the day after. We need to do this before anyone decides to extract evidence under torture."

Kaeso stared at him; then a smile appeared. "Father never sold anyone. What do I need to do?"

"Very little except sign two bills of sale. I'll be paying you 750 denarii for your house steward today. My steward will record the sale tomorrow morning, and I can take him to one of my praetor friends for the formal manumission and conferral of citizenship in the afternoon. You will then sell my new freedman his son for 250 denarii. In the next day or two, we'll arrange Theo's manumission and adoption so he will also be a citizen."

"I never would have thought of that, but I agree it's an excellent way to protect Theo." Kaeso's brow furrowed. "But I can't take that much money from you."

"But you will. It's a price that will seem appropriate to anyone looking at the sale records. Suspicions about why we're doing this could be raised if the money exchanged is too little."

"Can Corax remain with us doing what he's doing now?"

"I have no need for another house steward. His freedman service to me can be rendered to you."

"It seems the perfect way to keep Theo safe. I don't know how we can thank you for this, for all that you've done to help us since Father died."

"Don't try. Your sister enlivens my evening meal with her cheerful conversation and by drawing amusing responses from my too-reserved cousin. Protecting your Theo should ensure that continues. I will expect the two of you to return occasionally to entertain me at dinner after my relentless cousin has tracked down your father's killer. I will notice your absence after you move back to your own home."

"We'd be honored to have you dine at our house as well."

Manius tipped his head as he smiled. He'd make no promise until he found out from Septimus whether their cook was decent.

"My steward has the bills of sale waiting for your signature." Manius unrolled his scroll. "Go now, before dinner. You can explain to your man what we're doing first thing tomorrow so he'll be ready when I come for him."

Kaeso's smile as he left the room was the biggest Manius had seen yet.

He adjusted the scroll to display the next panel. The listing of prominent rhetors continued with a sentence or two about each. The most important deeds of most men's lives went unrecorded. Saving the boy who was loved by his son's friends would be among them.

He hadn't finished reading it when Pompeia swept into the room.

"Kaeso just told me." Her eyes glistened with happy tears. "Thank you doesn't come close to what I want to say, but I expect you don't like gushing females, so I'll stop at that."

"It's not enough." Her eyebrows rose, triggering his chuckle. "I will expect occasional invitations to dinner to see how my freedman is doing." One corner of his mouth turned up. "I'll expect you to invite my cousin as well. I find it more entertaining when you're both with me."

"Of course. Whenever you want, you're welcome. If it were proper, I'd hug you right now for all you've done for us."

"My wife Julia gives me all the feminine affection I want, but you can give what you want to give me to Titianus, if you like. He's been lacking for some time." He raised his eyebrows at her. "But I don't expect that will last."

Pink swept across her cheeks, neck, and ears.

"He would enjoy watching you do that, too." He rolled up the scroll and stood. "Dinner will be served in half an hour or so. I'm sure he'd prefer you waking him early to Tutelus doing it later."

The pink had started to fade, but it surged again. "Perhaps you're right. I should at least give him the chance to find out." She flashed a smile at him. "Until dinner." Then she slipped out the door.

He returned the scroll to its cubicle. Kaeso should have finished signing. A few words with his steward would set all in motion.

He expected a satisfying dinner tonight, followed by contented sleep.

◆

As Septimus approached his father's library, Pompeia came out. She seized his hand when she reached him.

"Your father is the nicest man."

"He can be." His brow furrowed. What had Father just done?

Before he could ask, she squeezed his hand and headed toward Titianus's room with happy eyes and a big smile.

He entered the library to find Father by the scroll cubicles. When he cleared his throat, Father turned.

"Pompeia just told me you were the nicest man. What did you do?"

Father's chuckle was not what he expected. "Have you spoken with Kaeso?"

"Not since we returned."

"She's giving me more credit than I deserve. I'll let him tell you."

"Since you're such a nice man…" Septimus picked up a stylus from the desk. "I'd like to borrow one of your bodyguards."

Father crossed his arms and leaned back against the shelves. "Since Tutelus is spending most of the day at the school and Pardus is going there midday to escort Pompeia home, why do you need another?"

"This one's for me."

Father's head drew back. "Why do you need a bodyguard?"

"I want to do something that needs Titianus's approval, and he won't give it if I don't ask you for a bodyguard."

Father's scowl was what Septimus expected, but since Father would be imagining something more dangerous than what he would propose, it was a good beginning.

"What is it that your cousin considers it so dangerous?"

"It probably isn't dangerous, but since someone jumped him, he's turned cautious."

"As he should be. What is it?"

The scowl was gone. Time to put forth the request.

"He was making good progress toward discovering who killed Lenaeus, but he's afraid that will be lost if his balance and vision take more than a day or two to improve. I want to help him until he recovers."

"You don't know anything about tracking down killers."

"I don't need to. He'll tell me what to do. I'd just be running down some leads he had before the attack. He uses one of his people as second eyes and ears, and Melis will know what we should watch for. If we wait until Titianus is better, the trail will be too cold to follow. As soon as he can, he'll take over the hunt."

Father tipped his head back slightly to look down his nose. "Does Pompeia know what you're considering?"

"She was there when we discussed it." Septimus shrugged. "She had some concerns, but like any woman, she looks for the danger, not the reward."

"Danger that your cousin sees or he wouldn't send you to me for permission."

"But he said if you give me a bodyguard, there's no good reason not to do it. Melis offered to do it alone, but he's so young and only a slave. Titianus said Melis knew what to do, but only a free man can do all that's needed. If I help, that won't be a problem."

He drummed on the desktop with the stylus before locking his gaze on Father's eyes. "If he thought it likely we'd be hurt, he'd order Melis not to do it, bodyguard or not. He's training to be his next warehouse manager."

Father uncrossed his arms, and a slow smile curved his mouth. "Very well, but you'll be taking one of the Germans with you, and any time Titianus thinks it wise, you'll take both of them."

He walked to Septimus and placed a hand on his shoulder. "If there's something I can do to help, you'll let me know, too."

"Of course." Septimus made his mouth only smile, even though he was grinning inside.

"Your grandfather would be laughing now. You framed your request brilliantly. He would never had predicted you'd be hunting criminals for the Urban Cohort with your cousin."

With a squeeze and a pat, Father took his hand away. "But let me decide when to tell him. Dinner should be ready now, and I'm ready for another good meal relaxing among friends."

Chapter 33

What Happened Upstairs

Evening of Day 13

When Pompeia tapped on the open door and walked into his room, Titianus was lying on his back, staring at the ceiling.

When she reached his bedside, the faint scent of roses came with her. "You went to sleep quickly. How are you feeling now?"

"My head hurts less, but there are still two of you."

"That sounds like progress. Dinner should be ready soon." Her brow furrowed. "What were you thinking about when I came in?"

"Why I'm not dead." He shifted to a reclining position and fixed his gaze on her. "Yesterday at dinner, you were about to tell me what you did before Galenos came. Then you stopped. Why?"

Her smile froze, and the same caution he'd seen the first day cooled her eyes. Then, as quickly as it came, it was replaced by the warmth and openness he'd seen since his injury.

"I wasn't sure it was something Manius should know...not yet, anyway."

His eyebrows dipped. "Why?"

"There's some risk in telling you. Even more risk in Manius knowing as well."

The blanket he'd flipped to the side had slipped off the bed. She picked it up and folded it.

"Was sorcery involved?" One corner of his mouth lifted. He'd never believed in magical arts.

Her lips twitched as she fought a smile. "No. We would never do that."

"Then what?"

She held one finger to her lips before walking to the door. After shutting it, she returned to his bedside. "We prayed."

He flopped onto his back. She couldn't expect him to believe that made any difference. But when he turned his gaze back onto her face, there was no sign she'd said it in jest. He would have sworn she wasn't superstitious, that none of her family was since her mother died, but her eyes declared it was no joke.

"What god did you pray to?"

She drew a deep breath. "The only real God." As she gazed at his face, her eyes softened. "He's the only one with power to do anything." Her lips curved into a smile.

She must be joking. He'd just been misreading her. "What did you really do?"

"I told you. We asked God to keep you alive, and He did."

He wrinkled his nose. "Gods don't do such things. Seneca had it right. 'Religion is regarded by the common people as true, by the wise as false, and by rulers as useful.'"

She tightened her lips to stop a smile. "Septimus would laugh if he heard you. That's exactly what he expected you would say." She drew closer to the bed. "I agree with Seneca, too. But I'm not talking about religion. I'm talking about praying to the one God who's real. We didn't do some religious rite. We asked Him to save you, and He did."

"That's all?"

The religions he knew about had rites you had to perform perfectly for the gods to listen…except the gods weren't real and the rites did nothing.

"That's all. We just placed our hands on your shoulders and asked God to heal you."

"You and Kaeso. You just asked, and something happened."

"Yes." She swallowed. "We asked in the name of Jesus, and you started breathing normally again."

Jesus. He sucked a slow breath through his teeth, and her eyes widened as he did.

Twelve years ago, Lucius Drusus's grandfather had died in the arena for insisting that crucified Jewish teacher was a god. Not one god among many so he could keep offering sacrifices to the gods of Rome. The only god who demanded his followers worship none other than him.

They were both sixteen then. Lucius had been heartbroken when his

213

father turned his grandfather in, the grandfather who'd always made time to do things with Lucius and his brothers. He'd become a follower of the god of the Jews when Lucius was thirteen. Lucius's father didn't like him to spend time with his grandfather after that because he hated how Publius forced him to follow some of the Jewish laws about women and drinking.

But Titianus had dined with Publius twice at the villa where Lucius's father lived because his mother loved her father-in-law, and she'd picked the dinner guests.

The longer he went without speaking, the paler Pompeia became.

"There's no risk in telling me." She'd been holding her breath, and as she released the sigh, it brought his smile.

He hadn't meant to, but he'd blocked all emotion from his face. That had become too automatic when his mind followed a serious train of thought. It was an advantage as a tribune; it was a problem as a friend.

"Your secret is safe with me." How could he make her trust him still more? "My friend Lucius—his grandfather became a Christian. He died in the arena for it. Lucius always wondered why he didn't make the meaningless sacrifice to the gods of Rome and live. I wondered, too."

"I know about Publius Drusus." Her face brightened. "I know why he chose to die."

His brow furrowed. "You do?"

"If you still want to know, I have the answer for you."

"That's not possible." He raised himself on his elbow again. "You were a child then."

"I have a copy of the letter Publius wrote his son Titus in Thracia that explains everything."

His eyebrows lowered. "How did you get that?"

"Publius asked the person entrusted with getting it to Titus to read it before he sent it. The parts that weren't personal...he made a copy so he could think about it. Other copies were made, and I have one of those."

At the end of every letter, Titianus wrote the meaningless words everyone wrote—may the gods guard your safety. But since Lucius moved to Thracia, his ended differently—may the most powerful god guard your safety. He'd considered it a simple variation for literary effect, but could it mean much more? Did Lucius believe what his grandfather had? What Pompeia and Kaeso did?

"I'd like to read it."

"I'll be right back." She was beaming as she unbolted the door.

Why so eager for him to read it? When she stepped onto the balcony, she looked back at him with glowing eyes before heading toward her room.

He swung his legs off the bed and sat up. Sometimes that movement didn't make him dizzy now. At least not so dizzy that he couldn't handle it. He moved the short distance to the chair and sank into it.

With his elbows on his knees, he buried his face in his hands and closed his eyes. He would love to read the letter. Privately, slowly, with plenty of time to ponder what it said and whether it might be true.

He'd like to read anything, but the double images that he could almost ignore when he looked at something distant mocked him when he tried to focus on the letters of a written word.

"Titianus?"

Her voice so close to him made him jump.

"Don't sneak up on me."

She took a step back. "I'm sorry."

He smiled an apology. It was too easy to slip into his tribune mode of speaking. "You did nothing wrong. I shouldn't have snapped at you." Her eyes said she'd forgiven him already.

In her hand, she held several sheets of papyrus. When he reached for it, she hesitated before giving it to him. He leaned back in the chair and turned his gaze on the letters. Then he closed his eyes. Would this ever end?

When he opened his eyelids, she hadn't moved. Somehow, she always knew what he'd need from her. He handed the sheets back.

Was that sympathy or pity in her eyes? He didn't want her pity. But this time, he did need her help.

"Read it to me." A sigh drained his lungs. "Please."

"I'd love to." She settled into the other chair. "It wouldn't be a complete day without me getting to read to you."

As she lifted it in front of her, three loud knocks sounded.

"That will be Tutelus. It's time for dinner now, but there will be plenty of time tomorrow for this." With a small shake of the papyrus stack, she stood. "I'll put it back in my room and meet you downstairs."

She rested her hand on his forearm and squeezed. "I'm glad you know both my secrets now."

He was, too. Trust lit her eyes, and the satisfaction from that was beyond what he'd expected.

"You and your secrets will always be safe with me."

"I know." She hurried to the door and opened it before Tutelus knocked again.

The gladiator stepped into the room.

"Be careful with him." She glanced over her shoulder at Titianus. "He's just like my brother. You can't trust him not to do more than he should."

As she disappeared from sight, Titianus wasn't sure if he should frown or smile. Just like her brother? That wasn't the future he had planned for her...for both of them.

◆

In her room, Pompeia unlocked the small chest where she kept Publius's epistle and the blank papyrus sheets she was using to make a new copy. That Titianus would have met Publius was almost beyond imagining. That he would be so eager to read Publius's letter—she never would have expected it.

Reading and considering the way Publius came to recognize that the God of Israel was the true God of everyone was how she and Father and Torquatus came to faith. Surely the same could happen for Titianus.

And if it did...she tipped her head back. Eyes closed, arms raised, she twirled.

Thank you, God, for putting in Titianus a hunger to know more about You. Tomorrow, give me the words he needs to hear to join me in following You. And then, give him the words to speak to me that will make us husband and wife.

Chapter 34

How Things Could Change

Morning of Day 14

Only three days ago, Titianus had been visiting Rufinus's freedmen, riding through Rome with Melis at his side. The trail was getting hotter, and in less than a week, he'd expected to know who killed his old tutor and who ordered the killing.

He leaned forward in the wicker chair and took the last slice of cheese from the breakfast tray on the game table. If he tried to ride or even mount today, he'd end up in the dirt. But maybe the dizziness wouldn't last much longer.

The whole world didn't spin as much when he first got up. He wouldn't want to try the stairs alone, but walking across the room was possible now. And things at a distance were almost not double.

When the boy brought his breakfast tray, he'd told him to find the steward and ask if there was something with large letters he could try to read.

Three raps on the open door drew his gaze.

"Steward sent this for you." The boy handed him a short scroll, then picked up the tray. "He said Master Septimus used it when he started reading."

Titianus unrolled it to show the first panel. Aesop's Fables, and the letters were more than twice the usual size. "This will do."

A quick bow, and the boy left him.

With the scroll at arm's length, Titianus squinted. He could almost focus the letters…for a few lines, anyway. He set it aside on the table and lay his head back against the cushions.

When Pompeia returned after lunch, she'd be bringing Publius's letter to share with him. Anticipation of what he might hear matched the anticipation of seeing her again.

The death of his grandfather had changed things for Lucius. A group of the students from Brutus's ludus had often gone to the games together. But after his grandfather died in the lunchtime executions, Lucius always made some excuse, and Titianus had stayed with his friend instead of going with the group. The two of them still went to the races often, but never the games.

Lucius had wanted to know why his grandfather first became a follower of the Jewish god and then decided a crucified rabbi was that god in human form. But his father forbade him studying what the Jews believed or even talking about it, and Lucius honored his father's command. Though he and Titianus could talk about almost everything else, his grandfather and the faith that got him killed remained off limits until Lucius sailed for Judaea.

Distance and time had turned close friends into virtual strangers. The thoughts and feelings shared in deep friendship couldn't be conveyed by wax tablets or papyrus sheets sent through the military postal system.

When a man loses something, pretending it doesn't matter can make it hurt less. He rubbed both sides of his nose. His job made it easy to cloak his loneliness due to that loss. He'd perfected the emotionless mask when he interrogated. It made it easy to shut out anyone when he wanted to… and sometimes when he didn't.

But Pompeia had picked up on his loneliness. It was in her eyes when he said only Probus would care if he died. Only moments later, she'd trusted him with her first deep secret. That could only mean she knew he cared about her…and each circle her fingertips made to help with his pain showed she cared about him, too.

When she shared the secret of her faith that could get her killed, that proved it.

Today she would answer a question that had bothered him for years. He'd wondered why a brilliant scholar like Publius would even start worshipping the Jewish god. Like many of his intellectual peers, he would have known and agreed with Seneca's words: "Religion is regarded by the common people as true, by the wise as false, and by rulers as useful."

Titianus had been fifteen when he met Publius the first time at dinner.

Even at that age he could see what people tried to hide. Lucius's father hated his grandfather. He resented the respect and affection his wife had for her father-in-law. When word spread that son had betrayed father to the authorities, he wasn't surprised. But why embrace a religion that Rome had proscribed and follow it to his death?

But Pompeia said it wasn't religion that kept Titianus alive when his skull was broken. She spoke a few words to the Jewish god in the name of Jesus and got an immediate response. Had Lucius's grandfather seen something like that happen, and it convinced him their god was real?

It wasn't something most spoke of openly, but during his investigations, he'd found a few people, including some well-educated men, who believed in the god of the Jews. They went to the Jewish synagogues on their Sabbath and followed some of the laws set out in the Jewish scrolls that the synagogue leaders read aloud when they gathered.

But he hadn't found any that called Jesus the son of that god and were willing to die for that belief.

Lucius had written from Galilee that he'd became a God-fearer and married a Jewish woman he said had saved him, but he hadn't written how she did that. He also said nothing in the letters about what happened to Marcus, and Titianus didn't ask. He'd heard the rumors, and he didn't want to disturb the scar over the wound any good man would have if he'd been forced to kill his brother.

The letters from Thracia were shorter, less personal, and further between until they almost stopped. But if Lucius was now a Christian, was the loss of closeness because he was afraid someone else might see those letters? Surely Lucius knew he could trust him, like Pompeia had decided to.

Lucius was in the same town where his uncle had served and still lived. Had he read Publius's letter? Had it taken him from worshipper of the Jewish god, like Publius had been, to a believer in Jesus like his grandfather was when he died?

In a few hours, he'd have his curiosity satisfied on many counts.

A man of honor must accept the truth, whether he liked it or not. Even if the truth led where he didn't want to go.

The Lenaeus town house, morning of Day 14

With the air of a man who was in no hurry to go anywhere, Vulpis sat on the bench built into the wall across from Lenaeus's doorway. In his lap lay a sandal. He'd brought two unmatched shoes to the shoemaker whose shop was next to the school's entrance. When he asked the shoemaker to make another to match one, he made a show of waiting for it. It would take at least two hours. If that wasn't enough, he'd pretend to inspect the quality before asking for a matching pair.

The boy and the bodyguard switched back and forth for opening the door to the students. They were getting careless. He'd be able to complete the job soon.

The Syrian opened last, so the boy should be next. Vulpis had let his beard grow since he knocked on the door six days ago. It was thick enough now that the bodyguard shouldn't recognize him if he opened the door out of turn.

He leaned against the wall and crossed his arms. The shoemaker was cutting the sole leather using a short-handled knife with a half-circle blade. That was a shape he hadn't used himself, but it might be worth having one. It would be easy to conceal.

When he glanced to the south, a muscled-up German walked toward him. He stood half a head taller than the young nobleman beside him and a full head taller than the runty Greek slave. Vulpis had turned his eyes back on the shoemaker when the three stopped at Lenaeus's door. Three hard knocks by the German, and the Syrian opened it.

The nobleman and slave went in, but the German stayed out with arms crossed and legs spread.

"You must be bored half to death. I hate waiting around doing nothing all day."

A shrug accompanied the Syrian's half smile. "No. Theo is teaching me." He looked back into the vestibulum and curled his fingers. The boy who didn't even reach the neckline of his tunic came and stood in front of him. "Theo, this is Brummbar."

The German's eyebrows lowered; a chuckle followed. "What can one like him teach you?"

The Syrian ruffled the boy's hair as he smiled down at him. "To read and write."

Brummbar snorted. "Why?"

"Why not? I speak Greek and Latin. Writing is easy. Reading…" He scrunched his nose. "Knowing where one word ends and the next starts is tricky. But the more I do it, the easier it gets." He slapped Brummbar's upper arm. "Like sparing with you. I learn how you move before you strike. Practice makes it easier to get past your guard."

A laugh rumbled in the German's chest. "Not so easy yet. How often do you win?"

The Syrian's chuckle accompanied a grin. "Not often, but practice will change that." He rested his hands on the boy's shoulders. "Why are you here?"

"The young master is looking into what the tribune was investigating until he can do it himself again. But Titianus said Master Septimus had to take one of us along, and Sabinus said it would be me or Barin."

Vulpis's turned his eyes away to keep from staring. Titianus was still alive? He would have sworn the tribune's skull was broken when they dropped him. He'd already collected his final payment. How was his target not dead?

It was a threat to his professional reputation, so what should he do? Arcanus would find out the tribune wasn't dead soon enough, but perhaps he should report it himself. Maybe give back the second 500 until he completed the job.

Why had the young Sabinus taken over the tribune's hunt for Arcanus? How was the tribune related to one of the most powerful men in Rome? Why was the tutor's family protected by a Sabinus bodyguard?

No one in his right mind would deliberately draw the wrath of the elder Sabinus or of his son. It would be signing his own death warrant.

Maybe he should just cancel the contract and refund all the money. He hadn't killed the boy yet. He could refund that, too. He'd never complete the kill and get away alive with a Sabinus bodyguard on duty, anyway.

After he explained it, Gaius would still hire and recommend him. He would know that was the only possible decision. No one stayed alive who crossed a Sabinus, and neither of them wanted to die.

The Baths of Trajan, afternoon of Day 14

"Rufinus. Salve."

The nasal voice of the prefect startled Rufinus as he floated, eyes closed, just under the surface of the hot pool. He lowered his feet and stood so he could turn to face Saturninus.

"Always a pleasure to see you, prefect."

Saturninus tipped his head to acknowledge the compliment. "I was planning a small gathering next Friday, a banquet for a few of the top leaders of Rome. I was going to send you an invitation, but Fortuna has smiled to let me deliver it in person."

"She has, especially since I know that evening is free for me." He returned Saturninus's political smile. "My son mentioned his old rhetor, Lenaeus, yesterday. It seems none of the students Gaius studied with know he was murdered. I chose not to enlighten him since I thought perhaps you had a reason for keeping that private. Has your diligent tribune made progress toward catching his murderer?"

"He might have been closer than he knew himself. He was attacked three days ago, almost killed."

"Really?" Rufinus didn't even try to hide his shock. "But I suppose he's made many enemies in the past nine years."

"He's earned the enmity of many. One finally caught up with him."

"What happened?"

"Someone dragged him from his horse, clubbed him until Quintus Sabinus's grandson ran over one attacker and drove off two more. He almost died. He's staying at Manius Sabinus's town house now. The rhetor's children are staying there as well when they aren't teaching."

"Will he recover enough to work again?"

"He and Sabinus say yes and soon. I'm not convinced." Saturninus waved at a cluster of senators, and one gestured for him to come over. "Duty calls. My secretary will send the details of my invitation tomorrow."

"I'll look forward to it."

With a final nod, Saturninus strode toward his next conversation.

Rufinus settled back into the hot water and closed his eyes. First the tutor, now the tribune. Were the attacks related? Was Arcanus running scared and trying to kill anyone who could reveal his identity? Were his own son and his son's friend Tertius also in danger?

He dragged his hand down his face, flicking the water droplets aside. After the next salutation, he would find out.

The Sabinus town house, afternoon of Day 14

The door was open when Pompeia walked by Titianus's room on the way to her own. He was in his chair, dozing.

From her locked chest, she got Publius's letter. When she entered his room, she closed the door as silently as she could. She tiptoed to her chair and settled in.

He hadn't stirred. He probably needed the nap. She set the letter on the table and picked up a scroll. Had the double-vision ended? Would he still let her read Publius's letter to him? He might not understand parts if she wasn't there to explain.

Aesop's Fables.

Her hand went to her mouth as she silenced the almost chuckle. It wasn't at all what she'd expect Rome's most feared investigator to be reading.

She hadn't read them herself since Kaeso was little. She used to read them to him before he learned to read himself. She'd helped him sound out letters to find each word, but their copy only had the words. In this one, each fable had an illustration to go with the story. Septimus must have read this and loved it as a boy.

She was halfway through the scroll when Titianus stirred. His eyes opened gradually, followed by a slow smile.

"Improving your mind by reading, I see." One corner of his mouth lifted. Now that he was letting his show, their senses of humor were more alike than most.

"I loved these stories as a girl. It was interesting to read them again now that I know so much more about life. Some I'd still agree with; some... maybe not."

He shifted in the chair and pointed at the stack of papyrus on the table. "I'm more interested in the questions that will answer." He squinted and pulled at the side of one eye. "I can read a few lines of a fable now, but the letters are large and I mostly can predict the words." He leaned forward and tapped the top sheet. "I'll need you to read this, and I should warn you."

"About what?"

"I intend to stop you where I have questions and have you explain, when you can, what Publius meant."

She flashed him a smile. "That won't be a problem. I know the letter by heart."

His brow furrowed. "How many times did you read it to do that?"

"Not from reading. I've made a few copies." A few dozen, but he didn't need to know that yet. "Can I get you anything before we start?"

"No."

When he listened to her read before, he lounged in the chair with his eyes closed. This time, he sat upright and focused those all-seeing gray eyes on her face. No trace of a smile. A wolf on a blood trail...but this time something glorious awaited him at trail's end.

She placed the scroll on the table and picked up the papyrus stack.

God, please use this letter to answer his questions. Give me wisdom to explain where he's confused. Let him see why following You is the only wise thing anyone can do, and let him be willing to do it himself.

She cleared her throat. "The Epistle of Publius Claudius Drusus. By the time you read this letter, I will have been executed for refusing to deny my faith in Jesus of Nazareth and offer a sacrifice to Caesar. Everything I own will have been confiscated. This letter is my only legacy, but what it contains is worth more than all my estates, more than all the wealth in the Empire. I pray you will come to treasure it for the truth it contains."

Chapter 35

THE LEGACY

Titianus shifted in his chair. He hadn't been sure how Publius would start, but he hadn't expected so casual a statement, almost in passing, of his gruesome death. The Drusus fortune was greater than that of many kings, but truth was worth more than wealth. Truth was worth dying for. But was what Publius believed really true?

"I begin with how I decided the God of Israel is the one true God."

Philosophers usually played with words to create memorable phrases as they made their points. He liked straightforward, not elegant at the expense of clarity. He leaned back in his chair. He'd get answers to some questions today, but it was truth he sought, not just answers. The answers men gave were often wrong.

"The teaching of the great philosophers seemed true to me for a long time, but that was before I began to compare them to what my own eyes have seen of the world. After much thought, I came to the conclusion that a philosophy could only be of value if it described the way the world truly is. I discovered that the philosophers I had admired most contradicted what I had seen myself. I began my search for a new philosophy without those contradictions."

Contradictions. Titianus watched for those all the time. The smallest contradiction could show the way to the biggest lie and reveal who committed a crime.

> "I always considered Aristotle the wisest of philosophers, and I embraced his teaching wholeheartedly from my youth. At the core of his teaching was the existence of an effective cause for everything. I considered all I had seen of life, and if I looked deeply enough or back far enough in time, I could see the causes of almost everything. He also taught that nothing lasts forever, that everything changes over time. That was what I saw, too.
>
> "But I saw a terrible inconsistency in his teaching, and that disturbed me greatly. He taught that the universe was eternal, that it had no effective cause. But how could that be, that the universe as a whole was the opposite of all the parts within it?"

Pompeia paused as she leaned forward to set one sheet face down on the table.

> "Clearly, there was something wrong with this idea. The universe must also have an effective cause, so I began my search for a philosophy that taught the universe had a beginning and an effective cause that started it. I found it in the Jewish Scriptures. They tell how God created everything from nothing, how He is the effective cause of the whole universe."

She leaned back in her chair. "Did you want me to read any of that again?"

"No. It's clear...and surprising. Aristotle is held up as the standard of wisdom. But Publius was right about the glaring inconsistency. I should have seen it before."

"Father felt that way, too. Once we read it, it felt foolish to have overlooked that." She pushed a loose strand of hair behind her ear and held the stack to read again.

> "I also considered Plato a great philosopher, but the more I saw of men and how they lived, the harder it be-

came for me to agree with his teaching. He taught that cities and empires could be ruled by philosopher-kings: intelligent, self-controlled men who ruled based on wisdom and reason and placed the good of those they ruled above their own desires for power and wealth.

"But as I examined history, I found men like this have never ruled. Even Trajan, who provided food and education for orphans in Italia, led his legions out to conquer, killing and enslaving, making new orphans who would starve.

"From the histories of empires and kingdoms, we know that great rulers have always done so. Trajan condemns the men he has conquered to die like animals in the arena for the entertainment of the crowds. Where is the wisdom and goodness in that? Plato was wrong about the nature of man, so how could his philosophy be true?"

Titianus rubbed his temple. "It's not only the men at the top who want power and wealth. The thief in Subura will kill for a handful of brass coins."

Her eyes saddened. "Or kidnap a young woman or child to sell as a slave."

His mouth straightened. "You were one of the lucky ones. If it's more than a few days since a kidnapping, I seldom find the one who's been taken."

He would always wonder what happened to Julia Secunda because he failed to find her.

"I'd never been so terrified, but God brought me through it. I poured my heart out in prayer for deliverance, and He used Aulus and Marcus and the gladiators to deliver me, whether they knew it or not." She straightened the papyrus stack. "But I still wonder where Aulus's sister was taken, what her life is like now." She wiped at the corner of her eye. "Whether she's still alive."

Her eyelids closed for much longer than a blink, and when they opened, a strained smile appeared. "Shall I read on?"

"Yes."

"Man is not good and wise; he naturally chooses evil. There are a few who choose kindness and mercy, but it is cruelty and lust for power that rule. Rome is rotten at her core, and she rules vast lands with an iron hand. Man's love of violence led to the games.

"I expect to die in the arena tomorrow, killed by a lion or a gladiator's sword. Thousands of Romans, including many men whom I have known for years, will be watching and will consider it good entertainment. Again, I found this understanding in the Jewish Scriptures, that man is naturally evil, selfish, rebellious against God. Man is a sinful being."

He twisted his signet ring. "After Publius was killed, Lucius and I never went to the games." He raised his eyes to hers. "But before then, we thought it good entertainment. Not so much the executions, but the gladiators fighting to the death. We knew some of them who belonged to Brutus, but we still cheered for blood." He glanced at the closed door. "Tutelus is lucky Manius likes to buy his bodyguards out of the arena." One corner of his mouth rose. "I had to choke back a laugh when you said he was a nice man. I knew of him as the Savage Syrian. But you were right."

"Theo's teaching him to read and write, and Tutelus took over being doorman to protect him better. But no matter how nice we are, we're still selfish and want our own way. Being sinful means we make choices we know won't please God. We do things that make us unfit to be in His presence." She raised the papyrus stack off her lap. "That's called sin. Publius talks about that in the part that's coming up."

"Read on."

"In the Jewish Scriptures, I found the philosophy that explained everything I knew to be true about the world, but it is much more than a philosophy. In those same Scriptures, I met the God who made the universe. I discovered that He cared about men enough to reveal Himself to them so they could know Him. I learned of Abraham, Isaac, and Jacob, and how each of them had met God."

"Stop."

She set the stack in her lap and fixed her gaze on him.

"Met god. What does he mean? Met in the sense that they learned about him for the first time?"

"Partly that, but it means much more. Let me keep reading, and it might become clear. If it doesn't, we'll talk about it."

> "I learned of Moses, who was told by God Himself to
> lead the people of Israel out of slavery in Egypt because
> God had promised the land of Judaea to Jacob's children."

"Told by god himself—like his god talking to him directly? Like I am with you?"

"Yes. He told Moses to go to Egypt and tell Pharoah to free all the Israelite slaves."

"And this pharaoh just released them because Moses told him to?"

"God sent plagues on Egypt until the pharaoh gave in and let them go. There were many thousands of them. They followed Moses, and God gave them the land of Israel, where Judaea is now. The whole story is in the scrolls they have in Jewish synagogues, but I've never had a chance to read those myself. Publius probably did."

He raised one eyebrow. A god talking directly to a man…that was in many stories about the Greek and Roman gods. A god making a pharoah of Egypt release so many slaves? He'd never seen that in any history he'd read. A wry smile formed. But the loser never records his own crushing defeat for posterity to read.

> "God cared so much for His people that He gave Mo-
> ses the very laws by which they should live."

"Those laws. Are those the ones that Publius would have obeyed as a God-fearer?"

"Yes. He would have obeyed most of them. There are a few, like circumcision, that the Jews observe that the God-fearers don't."

That was a good one not to obey. "Go on."

> "I learned of the many men who were prophets to
> whom God Himself spoke so His people, who no longer
> knew and worshiped Him, would return to Him.
>
> "From the beginning, He always wanted men to know
> Him and love Him. So I became a God-fearer, worshiping
> the God of Abraham, Isaac, and Jacob, and I studied the
> Jewish Scriptures daily because I could learn about Him
> there."

She leaned toward him. "This next part about sin is the most important. It explains why Jesus came and chose to be crucified." She radiated excitement, but that made no sense. Had she never seen a crucifixion? It could take days to die. The men who died during the flogging before it were the lucky ones.

Titianus felt the frown form, even though he didn't mean to. Chose to be crucified? No sane man, no crazy one either, would choose that death.

Her smile met his frown. "I know that sounds odd, crazy even, but you'll see why it was necessary and why He did it willingly."

"He is a holy God, and He cannot tolerate sin in His presence. But sin is not just doing the things that He has forbidden or neglecting the things He has commanded; it is also choosing to treat God as if He didn't exist."

Titianus felt his frown deepen. If that was sin, he'd been guilty of it all his life.

"In the Law He gave to Moses, He told His people the way to approach Him by covering their sins through blood sacrifice in their temple in Jerusalem. For over a thousand years, His people made sacrifices so they could approach Him. That ended when the temple was destroyed by Titus when he was putting down the rebellion in Judaea.

"That created a terrible problem, or so I thought. God said the payment for sin always required blood sacrifice, but He let His temple be destroyed by Rome, so how was sin to be paid for? I was at a loss to explain how the true God, the one so powerful that He could make the entire universe, could allow Rome to destroy His temple and take away what allowed His people to approach Him."

She leaned forward. "Here's where he explains how he changed from God-fearer to Christian."

For no reason he could see, Titianus felt his heart speed up. He took a deep breath and willed it to slow.

"Then I met a man who could explain it all. He told me of Jesus of Nazareth and how He came from heaven to make the final sacrifice for sins. He was the Son of God. He was sinless, and He made Himself the perfect sacrifice for all sin when He was crucified."

With his fingertips, Titianus pressed on his temples and made the small circles that sometimes helped his headache. Jesus made himself the perfect sacrifice? No sane man would choose to be crucified as a sacrifice. At least not an ordinary one. But if he truly came from heaven, then he was no ordinary man.

"After three days, He rose from the dead, proving His claim to be God."

"Didn't the Jewish leaders claim someone stole the body?" Titianus rubbed his temple. Where had he read or heard that?

"The Jewish leaders who wanted Him dead did spread that rumor, but Prefect Pilatus gave them a guard of Roman soldiers to secure the tomb because Jesus had said he would rise from the dead in three days. Would a Roman guard have let anyone steal a body they were guarding?"

"No. They'd be put to death if they did."

"I have a copy of the writings by Luke. He wrote a careful history about Jesus and about the church after Jesus rose from the dead. He was a physician who traveled with Apostle Paul, who took the news about what Jesus did all over the northern half the Eastern Empire and to Rome as well. I can let you read that later."

His eyebrow rose. "I might want to see that." He'd never seen a bigger smile on her face. It would be worth looking at Luke's writings to see that smile again.

"The grandfather of my friend actually knew men who had been with Jesus after He rose. There could be no doubt of the truth that Jesus was the Son of God and the final perfect sacrifice.

"At last I understood it all. The temple could be destroyed because God had made the perfect blood sacrifice Himself—Jesus on a cross more than 80 years ago. The temple and its sacrifices were no longer needed, so He had Rome destroy it so people would no longer cling to the old ways.

"The coming of the Messiah, of Jesus, was foretold in the Jewish Scriptures hundreds of years before He came, and God kept the promise He made to His people. There was no need to continually sacrifice animals to cover my sin with their blood. To be saved from my sin, I only had to believe in Jesus as the sacrifice for all sins, including mine. It all made perfect sense, and I finally knew the truth."

"Stop." Titianus covered his mouth with his hand and rubbed his cheek. If sin did put a barrier between the real god and man, and if blood sacrifice was needed to remove the barrier, then the ending of the sacrifices with the temple's destruction would be as catastrophic as Publius thought.

He crossed his arms and blew a breath out through pursed lips. But if Jesus was the final perfect blood sacrifice, then the temple was a problem, not a solution, because people would keep going there and doing the same thing they always had, even if it no longer worked. Using Rome to destroy it solved the problem.

The way Publius described it all did make sense. He massaged the back of his neck. But making sense and being true weren't always the same thing. He glanced at her and masked his emotions. Her face glowed with excitement. She cared deeply about how he responded to this.

"Your question about what it means to meet God...he answers that next." She cuddled the papyrus stack against her chest like a baby. "Are you ready for it?"

Was he ready? Maybe not, but he wouldn't know until he heard it. "Read on."

"When I went the first time to worship with my friend, I actually met God myself. I felt His love surround me, and now He lives in me. I am never alone. That day when I decided to believe, to repent of my sins and commit myself to Jesus as my Lord, all the worry and sadness in my life was replaced by peace and joy. For the first time, I knew what it was to be fully alive.

"I want you to experience this yourself. For you to know this perfect love deep in your soul—that will be my dying prayer.

"Following Jesus is like a perfect marriage; denying

Him would be like committing adultery against the most loving, beautiful, faithful wife a man could have. I could never betray my Lord that way. I have chosen death instead."

"Stop." Titianus held up his hand.

A god living in a man? How could that be? Worry and sadness replaced by peace and joy? All from believing Jesus had chosen to be the final sacrifice?

Perfect love. Fully alive. What on earth did those mean?

She was leaning forward, eyes expectant. What Publius had described, did she know what that felt like, too? It sounded both wonderful and frightening. What happened at that first worship?

He rubbed his forehead. What did it really mean to meet god? He'd never met the emperor face-to-face, and he didn't want to. Being in the presence of that much power, no matter how benevolent, was never comfortable, and it wasn't safe.

"So, is that the end of it?" Part of him hoped it was; part wanted to know more, to know everything.

"There's a little more. It explains why he was content to die."

The final answer to the question he and Lucius had years ago. The question he still had, but did Lucius already know the answer?

"Finish it."

She settled back in the chair.

"I will die soon, but I have no regrets. I am content to die because it isn't death that matters. It is whether you have accepted Jesus as Savior. Death is terrible apart from Jesus. Without Jesus, I would be lost, in hell, forever separated from God. With Jesus as my Savior, death has no power over me, and I don't fear it. It will just usher me into life with Him in heaven.

"Jesus told us that He is the way, the truth, and the life. He promised if a man would believe in Him and follow, he would know the truth, and the truth would set him free. If you let Him, Jesus will show you what is true. Open your mind to Him. Open your heart. Know the truth and be free like I am, even in this prison as I wait to die. I will be praying for all my children to choose to fol-

low Jesus until I take my final breath and even after that,
for life with Jesus is eternal."

She closed her eyes and held the stack close again. What was she thinking? Was she praying?

"When you and Kaeso prayed for me, what exactly did you ask for?"

Her eyes opened, brimming with an emotion that looked like love and happiness mixed together. Was that what Publius called joy? "We asked God to heal your body first, and then..." The most beautiful smile yet brightened her countenance. "I asked God to open your heart and mind to Him."

"Like Publius prayed for Titus."

"Yes. Like what I did twelve years ago after studying this letter and asking God to show me the truth."

Through pursed lips, he blew out a long, slow breath.

Three hard knocks on the door made them both jump.

"It's Tutelus. Time for dinner." He'd never been happier to be interrupted in his life.

Uncertainty filled her eyes. She wanted an answer from him right then, but he wasn't ready to give one. He'd asked for facts. What she read had given him those, but the letter stirred up uncomfortable thoughts and uneasy ponderings.

"You've given me a lot to consider. I need time to think. But we'll talk about this later."

As he said "later," uncertainty was replaced by hope.

"Whenever you're ready." The smile he'd grown to love reappeared.

"Come in." At his call, Tutelus opened the door.

Pompeia gathered the sheets she'd placed on the table. "I'll see you downstairs." She placed her hand on his forearm and squeezed. As he rose to his feet, she disappeared through the door to put the letter away.

She'd answered more than the question about why Publius chose to die. But the answers only led to new questions. Until he could walk normally and see well again, he had plenty of time to think about them. He stopped the chuckle before it escaped. She'd probably say her god made him heal slowly so he'd have that time.

His smile vanished. Was she right?

Chapter 36

Upheaval

Night of Day 14

Moon shadows moved slowly across the wall, and Titianus rolled on his back to watch their companions on the ceiling. He'd napped much of the afternoon, but he was still bone tired. So, why couldn't he shut off his thoughts and go to sleep?

Manius had joined them for dinner. That left no opportunity for conversation about what was uppermost on his mind. Pompeia had delayed answering his question about what she and Kaeso had done when Manius was listening two nights before. Their faith was a secret, and until he knew who shared that secret now, he would follow her cue on when to speak or be silent.

But in the stillness of the night, when no one was with him to ask what he was thinking—or if he was, as Manius sometimes did when he put on his stone face without meaning to—Titianus's mind churned.

Two of the men he admired most had embraced the belief in the Jewish god. Lenaeus had gone on to believe in Jesus as well. Lucius…there was no way to know, but Titianus would almost be willing to bet he had, too.

He's asked for answers, and Pompeia had provided them. Answers she believed to be true, but were they?

When he worked a case, it was careful thinking about both the broad story and the specific details that led him to the truth. All had to mesh together with no key parts missing. But would that work for this?

The way men thought—good men, bad men, and the vast majority who were a mixture of both—that he mostly understood. But when one of

235

the players in the game was supposed to be a god, not a man, what does a thinking man do with that?

He rolled from his back to his left side. It still felt better to keep pressure off the side of his head where the thug hit. Where his skull was broken, if he was to believe Galenos, and the man should be as expert as they come on that.

Septimus brought him home dying…and then Pompeia and her brother prayed.

The world still swirled when he moved sometimes, his eyes saw two of everything, and the nagging headache never quite went away, but he wasn't a corpse. Not yet, and he wouldn't become one if he could figure out who paid to make him one.

He rubbed his forehead. That was a question that could wait while he recovered at Manius's house.

But pondering what Publius and then Lenaeus and Pompeia believed could not.

Lenaeus used to quote Seneca every day to his class. From Seneca's "There is nothing after death, and death itself is nothing" to believing death had no power over him because Jesus was his savior, the blood sacrifice for his sins so he could be with the god who loved him forever —why could the smartest man he ever spent time with do that?

Titianus had taken to heart another of Seneca's sayings: "The highest duty and the highest proof of wisdom—that deed and word should be in accord." He tried to live his life that way, and he mostly succeeded.

But so did Pompeia. She said she believed in her god, then lived as if he were real. She asked her god to keep him alive, and here he was, alive and soon to be well.

He drew a deep breath and released the sigh. She also asked her god to open his heart and mind to him. But if that actually happened, what would it mean for his future?

On his back once more, he closed his eyes and focused on taking deep, slow breaths. Tomorrow would be another day to question her. He would know when he had enough answers to decide what was true. As a man of honor, he should accept the truth. But what if it led where he didn't want to go?

The Rufinus town house, midmorning of Day 15

At the end of the salutation, Arcanus entered the tablinum and closed the door. Rufinus still sat in the throne-like chair, frowning.

"It was a quiet day, Patronus. I didn't hear any gossip of special interest."

Rufinus's eyes chilled. "I heard something at the baths yesterday, but it wasn't gossip. The man who told me knew it was true."

Arcanus clasped his hands in front of him. The silence as Rufinus stared at him was deafening.

"Saturninus said someone tried to kill Titianus."

"Who?" Arcanus raised his eyebrows in mock surprise. Then they dipped. Why had the patronus said "tried?"

Rufinus lips squeezed so tight they vanished from sight. "Stop lying and stop acting. Did you try to kill Titianus?"

"Yes." Arcanus sighed. It was a relief to admit it. Maybe his patronus could help with the complications that kept arising. "The tribune knew the murder of the tutor was tied to Lupus's death and the fire. He hadn't reached me yet, but he'd talked with half of your freedmen already, so he must have thought you were involved. If any of your political enemies or another candidate for consul got a whiff of that, you would never be elected."

A string of curses burned Arcanus's ears, even though they were spoken softly. "It's not my political career you're worried about. It's your own head. There was no proof of any wrongdoing on my part or yours before you killed Lenaeus. Not even Titianus could have linked you to what happened at the warehouse."

"I didn't trust the teacher to keep quiet about what Tertius Flaccus told him. The boy who opened the door at the school saw me." Arcanus squeezed his neck. "But I've hired a professional to take care of that. Once he's gone, no one can prove anything. Not even Titianus. I tried to remove Titianus before he ruined you. Truth doesn't matter once a scandal starts."

"The one for killing the boy...is he the same one you hired to kill Titianus?" Frustration coated Rufinus's words.

"Well, yes." His patronus rolled his eyes, and Arcanus cringed. "He's been delayed some by a bodyguard who's watching over Lenaeus's children when they're at the school, but he'll get the job done."

"I wouldn't bet on that. He didn't succeed with Titianus." Rufinus rubbed his face. "Now you've made Titianus want to find you for the murder of his teacher and for trying to kill him."

"The man I hired thought he left Titianus near death. Maybe he won't be able to return to his post as tribune. That's almost as good as dead. Or I could—"

Rufinus raised his hand. "Stop. I don't want to know anything you could do. I don't want to know what you've already done. But don't do anything else that might seem suspicious to anyone." He closed his eyes and shook his head. "We'll just pretend nothing out of the ordinary is happening. Keep doing all your usual tasks in your usual way. Maybe in time this will blow over…for both of us." He flicked his hand toward the door. "Go."

"Yes, Patronus." Head down, Arcanus went to the door and opened it. But he glanced over his shoulder before stepping through. Rufinus still sat in his chair, face buried in his hands.

The Sabinus town house, afternoon of Day 15

When Pompeia came back from teaching, Titianus waved as she walked by his open door. In her room, she took the gospel written by Luke from her satchel. After she got Publius's letter from the locked box, she held both to her chest and closed her eyes.

Please, God, open his heart and mind all the way. Give me the words he needs to hear. Let him decide today that he wants to follow Jesus as Lord.

She squared her shoulders and strode down the balcony to his room.

He smiled up at her. "Looks like I'm a student in the Lenaeus school again."

"But this time what you're learning about is the difference between life and death."

"Because you prayed and I didn't die?"

"There's more to it than that. That was just your body. For all of us, our body will someday die."

"But most people want to delay that as long as possible."

"True. It's hard to say goodbye, even when we're expecting it. It's harder when we don't get to say it, like with Father." She wiped the corner of her eye.

"I'm sorry." His smile vanished, leaving the straight-lipped man, but it was concern, not detachment behind his gray eyes. "I didn't mean for my words to cause you pain."

"It's not your words. Father is with Jesus. It hurts terribly right now, but I know our parting won't last. But my mother...she didn't decide to follow Him like the rest of us. She died when I was thirteen, and that parting was forever."

She wiped the other eye. "When I was kidnapped, death wasn't what I feared most." She looked away, then back with a tentative smile. "I wasn't scared only for what might happen to me. I was afraid Corax had been horribly hurt, maybe killed. The last thing I saw before they pulled the sack over my head was him crumpled on the ground with blood on his face."

She touched Titianus's hand where it rested on the chair arm. "Seeing you lying on the ground in the stableyard, so much blood in your hair...I was afraid I'd never see those thoughtful gray eyes again."

His mouth twitched, and he stopped the smile before it got loose, but not before she knew he was laughing at her.

He could laugh if he wanted to. She'd be laughing at the shock on his face if she told him how she really felt. But he had to make a decision before that could happen. *God, please let him make the right one.*

"I hadn't realized how much I cared before that moment."

He turned his steady gaze from her eyes. When it shifted back, it came with a smile. "You can hide your feelings as well as I do. Maybe we should both stop that."

"Perhaps." She hadn't hidden them. She'd just kept them in check for fear of what he might do if she let him get close enough to discover her secret. "I started praying for God to let you stay with us. I told them to bring you in here. Out there in front of everyone wasn't a safe place for how we prayed in this room."

"You knew what would happen when you prayed?" His eyes narrowed.

"I knew what I hoped God would do. I knew what He'd done many times in the past. The gospels tell of so many times Jesus healed. He even brought people back from the dead."

His eyebrow rose, and that made her smile. That would sound unbelievable to him now, but after he met God, it wouldn't.

"Luke was a physician who traveled with Apostle Paul, so he saw many healings. He wrote about a few of them. After Jesus rose from the dead, He appeared to Paul and told him to go everywhere telling people about how He'd saved us. Paul wrote a lot of letters. I have a copy of the letter he wrote to believers in Rome."

"I'd like to see that sometime, too."

"It's at our house, but I can bring it. Anyway, the history Luke wrote is full of times believers asked God to heal and He did. So is Apostle John's gospel. When you can read again, I'll lend you a copy."

"That might be soon. I could read the fables for a while today."

"Did that make your headache worse?"

"Would you rub my temples awhile if I said yes?" His raised eyebrow was a tease this time, not a challenge.

"I'll do it if you ask, whether it hurts or not."

He rested his head against the cushion. "Please."

When they first met and his mouth had always been straight, she would have sworn the playful smile he now wore was impossible for him.

She moved behind the chair and started the massage. "Apostle Paul even brought a boy back to life. He went to sleep when Paul was teaching and fell out of an upper-story window. His skull would have been broken, too."

"Paul was that boring when he taught?" His smile faded. "But you aren't like Paul. You weren't told to spread the news across the Empire. You're…"

"Ordinary? I am, but it wasn't Paul who did all those healings. It was the Holy Spirit. He only asked the Spirit of God to heal. We did the same. God listens to every prayer from those of us who believe. His kingdom isn't like Rome, where access to the emperor depends on rank and wealth. We're all His children the moment we believe in Jesus as our Savior. A good father listens to all his children, regardless of age or intelligence or beauty or skill. When what they ask for is what's best for them, He usually says yes."

"How long did it take…your prayer." He rubbed his jaw. "Tell me again. What did you say?"

Her heart beat faster. Surely a person who had felt God's power heal him couldn't resist following Him for long.

"It was short and quick. I told God you didn't know Him, but He already knew that. Then I asked for you to live so you'd get a chance to."

"That's not exactly what you said before. You said you put your hand on my shoulder and asked your god to heal me in the name of Jesus. Why did you end it that way?"

"Jesus said when we pray, to ask in His name. But we wouldn't have to be touching you for the Holy Spirit to heal. There's nothing magic about touching you." She rested her hands on his shoulders and leaned over to look in his eyes. "Not even when my fingertips are helping your headache."

"Maybe not magic." His smile reappeared. "But it is a useful treatment that shouldn't stop."

She squeezed his shoulders and straightened before returning her fingers to his temples.

By the third circle, Titianus's relaxed sigh drew her smile. "Then you said something about opening up to him."

"I asked Him to open your heart and mind to love Jesus and be filled with the Holy Spirit. I asked Him to do for you what He's done for me."

Chapter 37

A Different Kind of Love

Titianus twisted in the seat to look at her face. Two of the three things she asked for had happened. Publius's letter and her answers to his questions about it had opened his mind to the possibility that the Jewish god was real.

Open his heart…he wasn't sure how a man would do that to a god, real or not. But he'd opened his heart to her.

He'd planned for a comfortable partnership with the woman he married someday. She'd run his household, mother his heirs, and provide a dowry he could invest. He wasn't looking for a love match.

Pompeia was not what an equestrian would seek out. But if she agreed when he was ready to ask her, it was possible he would gain something of far greater value than he'd planned.

More than possible. It was almost certain.

"Open my heart…there are many who would tell you Tribune Titianus doesn't have one."

"They'd be wrong. Would a man without a heart have asked Manius to save Theo from torture? Or changed Sciurus's name to something he's proud of? Or kept the murder quiet so we wouldn't lose everything? I think you're a kind-hearted man who can seem heartless because you pursue justice so single-mindedly. I know that's your job." She moved from behind him to the side of his chair. "But sometimes mercy is better than justice, and forgiveness is needed with either."

She pushed back a strand of hair that had flopped forward as she massaged his temples. "The ability to forgive comes from God. It's an act of love, and love is a decision, not an emotion. It's more from your head than your heart."

His brow furrowed. That was an odd change of direction in their conversation, but it just opened a door.

Forgiveness was not something he gave easily, nor did he intend to change that. But love...two weeks ago he would have laughed at anyone who implied he could fall victim to it.

He rubbed his lip. She'd seen through the stern mask he wore on duty to the man underneath like no one else had. She even seemed to like what she found.

He wanted her with him when all this was over. Since the attack, he was almost certain she felt the same. But understanding women was a problem for him. She was warm and kind to everyone. Was he misreading her? Was it better to look at her eyes or not when he asked her? If the answer was yes, then eyes. But if it was no... His mouth twitched.

Only the bold man gained the prize. He focused his gaze on her face. "Do you think your head could decide to love me?"

Her eyes widened...but that was shock, not joy.

Why had he blurted it out like that? Since becoming adults, they'd known each other barely a week, and meeting again over her father's corpse had been a terrible way to restart their acquaintance. She'd only let her guard down with him three days ago.

"I already have, but not the way you mean. It's too soon for that."

She'd said "too soon," not impossible. Hope could hang on that.

"What do you think I meant?"

Her cheeks flushed. "Like a man and a woman, but maybe you only meant like friends."

"So, you love me as a friend?" Not what he wanted, but time and perseverance had been known to change that for others.

The shock was gone, and her eyes danced. Maybe he hadn't spoken too soon. Or had he? Was she pleased by his regard or laughing at him?

"I think so, but it's much more than that. God gave many commands to His followers, but whenever anyone asked Jesus what the most important commandments were, He named these two: to love God with all our hearts and minds and souls and strength and to love our neighbors as ourselves."

She settled into the chair across from him. "And by neighbors, He didn't mean only the people living next door. He also told us to love our enemies."

His mouth opened, but he closed it before speaking. Loving your enemies was not the Roman way. Enemies were to be destroyed, preferably in a way that made other enemies afraid to move against you.

What she described wasn't love like he'd ever seen it. He'd cared about Lucius almost as much as himself, but that was true friendship. To feel that way about other people…maybe for his future wife and children, but that was the limit.

He lay back in the chair and crossed his arms.

She leaned toward him. "You can see why it's a decision, and then I have to act on it. The love God commands isn't something people earn by what they do for me or to me or to those who are dear to me. Love is wanting what's best for someone, even when I'm tempted to want the worst. It's doing what I can to help, even if I'd rather not do it. It's also trying again and again until I truly forgive someone, even when they're to blame for something horrible, even when they aren't the least bit sorry. It might seem impossible at first, but God Himself helps me do it."

He rubbed the side of his nose. "Is this why you said you were trying to forgive the one who murdered your father?"

"I'm trying. I can't yet, but with God's help, I will in time."

Slowly rubbing his lip, he stared at her. Unperturbed, she looked back, waiting for him to speak next.

But what was he supposed to say?

If anyone but her had told him what he just heard, he'd think they were insane. But there was nothing crazy about her belief in her god. He was only able to watch her now because she'd prayed to the god with the power to stop a man dying.

But Lenaeus worshipped the same god that Pompeia said saved both her and him. So, why had his tutor died at one assassin's hand when he had been spared from another one?

"Staring in silence is a strange way to entertain each other." Manius's voice made both of them jump as he leaned against the doorframe. "But I have news that should please you both. Corax is now a freedman citizen who has purchased his son and freed him. Tomorrow the adoption will be completed and recorded."

He crossed the room to join them. As he stood by the game table, Pompeia took his hand in both of hers. "Thank you so much." She turned her smile on Titianus before looking up at Manius again. "Now an innocent boy won't have to suffer for the crime of another, and Roman justice won't be unjust."

"It was the obvious solution to everyone's problem. You don't need to thank me again." His eyes turned serious. "But you do need to leave us now. Unexpected company is coming, and I need to talk with my cousin."

"Of course." She picked up the letter and Luke's writings. "I'll see you both at dinner."

When she left the room, Manius settled into the chair she'd just vacated. "Saturninus just rode in. Since he came up here last time without first asking my permission, I think it best if I be here when he enters." He picked up the scroll and glanced at the first panel. "Aesop's Fables?" He raised one eyebrow. "Don't tell him we were discussing literature."

Manius's wry smile drew one of Titianus's own. "The letters are large. I can almost read it. Maybe in a few days…"

"Don't try to convince him you're more recovered than you are yet. You still can't make it downstairs without Tutelus's help. Let me do most of the talking. I've learned from the best."

"He's up here. I know the way." The prefect's nasal voice came from the balcony. Then his body came through the door with Tribune Victorinus two steps behind him.

"Good afternoon, prefect." Manius stayed seated. "Come to check on your best investigator's progress? Father's not here today. He'll be sorry you missed him." He tilted his head sideways to look past to Victorinus. "Who's this with you?"

"Good afternoon to you also, Sabinus. I'm sorry to miss your father as well." With a flick of his hand, Saturninus brought the tribune to his side. "Julius Victorinus is beginning his investigation of Titianus's robbery."

"Robbery?" Manius raised his eyebrows. "You mean assassination attempt. No one in their right mind tries to rob a mounted, fully armed tribune. Finding three such insane people to work together to attack Titus… that goes beyond the reasonable limits of what's possible."

He gestured, palm up, toward Victorinus. "As I'm sure an experienced investigator like Victorinus will tell you." He stared at Victorinus. "Even Titus's uncle, my father Quintus Sabinus, would know an attempted assassination from a botched robbery."

"Yes, well…" Victorinus cleared his throat. "It probably was an assassination attempt."

Manius turned a social smile back on Saturninus. "I knew your tribunes would agree on that point." He crossed his arms. "So, to what do we owe the pleasure of the two of you visiting today? I know you're both busy men with other places to be."

Saturninus's jaw twitched. "Victorinus needs the details of what happened to begin looking for the ones involved."

"One should be easy to find. His corpse would have been taken to the Praetorian Fortress to await someone claiming it. My son rode him down to stop him hitting Titus with the killing blow. You should be able to learn who picked the body up."

Manius uncrossed his arms and rested them on the chair. "Septimus isn't here at the moment, but I'll have him talk with Titus so they can write out an accurate description of the two who ran. You can pick it up tomorrow. That's all either of them know."

Victorinus cleared his throat again. He glanced at Saturninus and caught the slight nod. "That should be enough to get me started."

Saturninus turned off the frown he almost let escape and directed a smile toward Titianus. "So, are you still expecting to return to duty within the week?" He glanced at Manius. "Victorinus tells me he can close some of his own cases to take over yours if that doesn't happen."

"That's my goal, prefect." Titianus's mouth twitched. Manius was as skilled a manipulator as his father. Keeping his straight face had taken some effort, but the thought of turning his cases over to an incompetent now made it easy. "I expect I'll reach it."

"I'll check on you later this week to see if you will."

"I'll look forward to that, prefect."

"Our physician says he's making excellent progress." Manius crossed his arms again. "Father has been most pleased with his knowledge and skill. Titus will be ready to resume his work as soon as possible under such care."

"Your father's interest in enforcing the law in Rome—I never suspected it was so great." Saturninus's smile was stiff.

"Anything of importance to Rome interests Father, as it does me." Manius's smile broadened. "As I'm sure it does you."

He stood. "If that's all you need today, I'll escort you down. I'm sure Titus will rest better now knowing the assassins will be found soon."

Manius gestured toward the door, and the two men passed through the doorway ahead of him. But before he stepped through himself, he winked at Titianus.

Titianus lay his head back on the cushion and closed his eyes. Father and son were master manipulators. But one was a much better man than he ever suspected. If anyone ever asked, despite his cousin's reputation, he could say Manius Sabinus was a friend he could rely on.

Chapter 38

The Next Step

The Sabinus town house, evening of Day 15

Titianus awoke to the thud of a gladiator's fist on his door. He'd missed his chance for a private conversation with Pompeia. She must have come back to find him sleeping and decided not to disturb him.

"Come in."

As Titianus rose from the chair, the room tilted, then straightened and held steady. It was a big improvement.

"How's your balance today, tribune?" Tutelus's question sounded as if he cared what the answer was.

"Better, but not perfect. I can try walking alone, but you'll need to watch me on the stairs."

A warm smile accompanied Tutelus's nod. The Savage Syrian had become a gentler man after only four days under Pompeia's influence. Did she have that effect on every man of her acquaintance?

At the base of the stairs, Tutelus donned his guard face again. Masks were as wise a precaution for Tutelus as they were for him.

He walked into the triclinium to find her reclining, but she rose and came to his side. "I hope you rested well after your visitor left."

"Because of Manius, they didn't stay too long."

"I'm famed for my hospitality." Manius's amused voice came from behind him. Regrettably. Titianus had hoped for some conversation with her before the arrival of his host, who was too observant by far. The questions he still had would go unanswered tonight.

248

"They left quicker than I expected. I thank you for that, cousin."

"It's a host's responsibility to make sure visitors stay as long as is good for the guests in his house and no longer." Manius sat on his couch and swung his legs up.

Titianus reclined, and when everything settled, he turned to Pompeia. "I think I'll able to read some tomorrow. Did you bring something from the school you think I should read next?"

Her eyes danced even though her smile started slowly. "I brought exactly what should suit you. I'll put some ribbons in the places I think you'll find especially enlightening."

Three girls entered and placed some fruit bowls on the table. Manius picked up a grape. "I hope it's something at least as profound as Aesop's fables."

"At least as profound." The smile she directed at Titianus promised much more. "I'm sure he will enjoy it even though it doesn't have any pictures."

Pompeia set down her pen and read what she'd written. Tomorrow might be the day Titianus's barriers came down—barriers between him and God. Once those were gone, there would be no barrier between him and her.

She put her note to him face down on the bed. She added the copy of Publius's letter to it. Then she took two hair ribbons, one blue and one red, from the dressing table.

His vision still bothered him. Even though he'd been able to read some today, he'd never make it through the whole gospel written by Luke tomorrow. He mustn't stop before he reached the parts that would answer his deepest questions.

She started adding Luke's writing to the pile, sheet by sheet, scanning each before placing it facedown. As she found each section that he most needed to read, she cut a length of blue ribbon to mark its place, but she marked two special places with a length of red. Her favorite investigator would know what that meant.

God, please help him find what he needs here to decide to follow You. If something confuses him, please make him ask me. Please guide my explanations if he needs more.

After straightening the stack, she took the runner he gave her from the dressing table. He'd shocked her when he gave her a gift. What frightened her then had become precious.

She stroked the red flower before placing it facedown and centering the papyrus stack over it. A few folds and tucks and the runner became the perfect wrapping to give back to him.

If he did what she was praying for, it would be hers again. She closed her eyes and tipped her head back as her smile grew. The sooner that happened, the better for both of them.

He left his door open when he slept. He was usually still sleeping when she walked by in the morning. But in case he woke early, she crept down the hall and left the packet on his chair.

Then she returned to her room and slipped into her own bed. Tomorrow she'd keep praying for God to open his mind and claim his heart as he read. If that happened, as soon as he wanted, he could claim hers.

The Arcanus town house, evening of Day 15

His chef had prepared one of Arcanus's favorite dinners, but it had tasted like wood shavings. He'd been sitting at his desk for some time with an aching belly, eyes closed, face in his hands. A flagon of wine sat next to his half-empty goblet. Wine usually helped, but it only made the stomach pain worse this time.

Starting with when he struck Lupus, his life had gone downhill. He'd done it for Rufinus out of loyalty. But from the moment that accursed friend of Gaius overheard them talking, Rufinus hadn't taken the risk seriously.

He'd killed the teacher to protect them both. But did Rufinus see that? No!

Arcanus ground his teeth. He'd done his utmost to protect his patron. If what he'd done came to light, would his patron do anything to protect him?

"You lied to me." The voice was soft, but it still dripped venom.

Arcanus startled and dropped his hands to the desktop. Vulpis stood in the doorway with a satchel hanging on his shoulder. He stepped into the room and closed the door.

"I certainly did not." Arcanus straightened his spine and slid his chair back. "Would you care for a drink while you explain what you mean?" He opened the desk drawer to take out a second goblet, then left it open beside him. A dagger lay in that drawer, but whether he could use it before Vulpis used his was a question he didn't want to try answering.

"You told me I was killing a meddling tribune and an unimportant slave of a dead tutor. You knew they were both important to Manius Sabinus, and you said nothing. A deliberate omission is the same as a lie."

"But I didn't know that."

When Vulpis reached into the satchel, Arcanus lowered his hand into the drawer. It would take only a moment to bend enough to grab the dagger.

But the killer only pulled three small bags from the satchel. One by one, he dropped them on the desktop. Each clinked, declaring there were coins inside.

"I'm canceling the contracts. There's two hundred for the boy, a thousand for the tribune. Whoever draws the wrath of a Sabinus ends up dead, and I'm not planning to join that group."

He stepped back from the desk. "You will never tell anyone you hired me. If you're wise, you won't try to hire anyone else. It will likely be the last thing you ever do."

"I didn't lie to you. I truly didn't know, but I thank you for telling me. I know Sabinus's reputation, and I'll act accordingly."

"Hmph." Vulpis's sneer spoke volumes before he turned and let himself out of the room.

Arcanus slumped in his chair. Maybe he should be glad Vulpis canceled the contracts. If Titianus were to track his assassin down and Vulpis named him, he could insist that the assassin produce the money he supposedly paid him. When he couldn't, it would be a murderer's word against his own.

But there was still the problem of the boy who could identify him. If he couldn't hire a professional to dispose of him, how should he do it himself?

He crossed his arms and leaned on the desk. When he rested his head on his arms, the same curses Rufinus used that morning escaped his own lips.

Chapter 39

NOT WHAT HE EXPECTED

The Lenaeus town house, morning of Day 16

Each morning as soon as Pompeia and Kaeso arrived, they gathered their familia in Kaeso's bedchamber and closed the door. With Tutelus downstairs as doorman, there was little risk he'd hear them praying.

"I have a special request for prayers for Titianus today." Pompeia fought to suppress a grin. "He's been asking about our faith since I told him God kept him from dying. We already talked about Publius's letter, and he wants to know more. He still has some problems with his vision, but I left him a copy of Luke's gospel with ribbons marking a few of the most important sections for him to read."

She couldn't stop it any longer, and the grin leaked out. "After what he reads today, he should be asking about Jesus's sacrifice for his sins and how Jesus will save him, not just from a broken skull, but to give him eternal life. Please pray for him to be open to the Holy Spirit, to hear God's call, and to decide to follow."

Kaeso put his arm around her. "I haven't talked with him about God yet, but he asked at dinner if Pompeia had brought him something to read. He seemed eager for it."

They formed a circle and held hands. Kaeso now led them in their prayers, as Father always had. There was both pleasure and pain in that remembrance.

When they finished and exchanged hugs all around, Ciconia spoke softly in Pompeia's ear. "May I speak with you privately?"

252

"Of course. Let's go to my room."

While the others headed downstairs, Ciconia closed the door behind them. "Since your mother isn't here to ask you, may I ask what she would?"

"What do you think she would ask?"

Ciconia took her hand. "Have you grown fond of the tribune as more than Septimus's friend?"

"Yes." The remembrance of his eyes when silent laughter lit them brought a smile to Pompeia's lips. "He's a man I could spend a lifetime with if he chose to follow Jesus. We wouldn't have to worry about the future of the school if he asks me to marry him."

"Do you think he plans to?" Ciconia's mouth straightened.

"He almost did, or at least that was where he seemed headed when I was telling him that love was a decision of the head, not just an emotion of the heart. He asked if I could love him with my head, but he meant as a man, not a friend. I told him it was too soon for that, and he accepted that answer for now."

Ciconia's lips tightened. "I remember him as a quiet, serious young man. I've only seen a hardness in him since he's grown up. If your father were here, would he think him suitable? Not just because he's a wealthy man, but because he would care for your heart as well as your needs?"

She drew her breath between her teeth. "He's so cold and aloof, and a woman needs a man with a heart that can show her love to be happy." She glanced at the door and smiled. "A man like Corax and your father."

"That's just the mask he wears when he works. There's a caring heart behind that mask. It was his idea for Septimus's father to buy Corax and Theo as soon as possible and set them free. He wanted to protect Theo from torture. Manius is a nice man, so he was happy to do it once Titianus asked him to."

She took Ciconia's other hand. "I only told him it was too soon because my head tells me he must believe in God and be well on the way to believing in Jesus before I agree. I'll speak the love my heart already feels toward him as soon as that happens."

"Are you sure it will?"

"Oh, yes. He's a man who loves truth, and once he sees the truth about what Jesus did, he won't be able to keep himself from deciding to follow Him."

Ciconia dropped Pompeia's hands and pulled her into an embrace. "Then I'll be praying for him to decide to believe in our Savior and start loving Him today. If he's the man you think he is, you deserve a chance to love each other."

The Sabinus town house, morning of Day 16

When Titianus opened his eyelids, a patch of red on the chair caught his eye. He swung his legs off the couch, and for the first time the room didn't swirl. He grinned at the improvement.

On the cushion sat something wrapped in the runner he'd given her. She'd snuck in and out without him waking. Good thing she was a friend, not a foe.

From the shape and size, it might be one of her copies that he'd asked for. He lifted it from the seat and settled in. He'd been unable to read Publius's letter two days before, but today might be different. When he unrolled the Aesop's scroll, it was a little blurry, but still easy enough to read.

But what about the smaller letters she would have used? He'd have to read what she'd brought in short sections, but he would be thinking about the pieces as well as the whole, like Lenaeus taught him. As Publius had written, the parts and the whole have to be consistent to be true. Would he find the ring of truth in what she'd given him?

A light breakfast of bread, fruit, and cheese had been left for him on the game table. He gobbled it down, glancing often at the red flower that beckoned him.

When he finally pushed the empty plate away, he leaned back in the chair and removed the wrapping. He thumbed through the stack of papyrus to find a note from her, Publius's letter, and a sheet labeled "the gospel according to Luke." Many more sheets lay below it. He kept her note in his hand and placed the rest on the table.

Titianus, my dear friend.

Dear friend. It was a good way to describe what they were to each other at the moment, but it wasn't where he intended them to stay. Quintus Sabinus had been partly right when he said a woman like her would suit him. He didn't want a woman *like* her. He wanted her.

I hope you feel up to reading today. As I promised, I've left something to entertain you while I'm gone. Perhaps entertain isn't the right word, although there's nothing I enjoy reading more than these. Like Publius's letter, I've made copies of other writings. If you want to keep these as your own after you read them…I can think of nothing that would please me more.

Her letters were beautifully formed and easy enough to read. His double vision was no worse than a little blurry now. If he took frequent breaks, he could ignore that.

I know it might be too hard to read the whole with your vision still not perfect, so I marked some important places with ribbons. All of it is important, and I hope you'll want to read every word when you feel up to it. But for now, the marked spots will give you a good start.

Some history before you begin.

History? Wasn't she going to give him something to explain her religion? Something more like what a philosopher wrote than the work of a historian?

Apostle John was one of the twelve men who was with Jesus from the start when He began teaching, and he was there at Jesus's crucifixion. He saw Jesus die. He saw Jesus many times after He rose from the dead as well. Apostle John was filled with the Holy Spirit (you'll understand what that means later), and he spent his life telling people about what Jesus had done for us all.

I almost left you the gospel he wrote because he shares so many of the words Jesus spoke in private with His close followers. But as I read parts to myself again, I realized I understand it and love it so much because the Holy Spirit, who is always with me, helps me. So instead, I'm leaving you the history Luke wrote after talking with many eyewitnesses of what Jesus said and did. When you know what happened, what I will tell you later about what it means for me and for you will make sense.

One corner of his mouth lifted. She was her father's daughter and a teacher to the bone. Lenaeus always started with the background of the writer before presenting what the man taught.

> As you read, you will find reports of unexpected things and of true miracles. Some will be very different from what you expect, but do keep in mind that the God who could create the universe from nothing, like Publius described, isn't limited by what you or I think might be possible. Who would have thought a man dying with a broken skull would be reading my note today?
>
> Whether you believe in God now or not, please ask Him to show you what the truth is. Publius prayed for his son. Maybe he prayed for Lucius, too. Today, I will be praying for you to open your mind to see the truth and your heart to embrace it. If you let Him, the Holy Spirit will guide you to the truth. Ask Him to do that. He'll be listening. Nothing is better than being God's child once we believe in Jesus.

His eyebrow rose, and he stopped a wry smile. Ask her god for something? He couldn't remember the last time he asked a god for anything. Characters in stories couldn't listen.

But—he rubbed his lip—she and Kaeso asked her god to stop him dying, and he had. The Roman gods weren't real, but that didn't mean hers wasn't. The evidence he'd seen himself suggested he was.

He cleared his throat. The asking—did it have to be aloud? Maybe, but a real god could hear a whisper. If Manius walked in, he didn't want to be thought crazy for talking to an empty room.

"God of Pompeia and Publius, I don't know if you're listening, but I'm asking you to let me discover the truth about you."

Silence answered him, but there was something… He couldn't put his finger on what it was, but it felt like he wasn't alone.

He set her letter aside and picked up the stack. Page by page, he set Publius's letter on top of hers until he reached a sheet proclaiming what remained were the writings of Luke.

Her note and Publius's letter were Latin. Luke had used Greek. Not what he expected, but it made sense for something from the Eastern Empire. Her Greek letters were as easy to read as the Latin ones. Leaning back in his chair, he set the pile of sheets in his lap and picked up the first one.

"Inasmuch as many have undertaken to compile a narrative of the things that have been accomplished among us, just as those who from the beginning were eyewitnesses and ministers of the word have delivered them to us, it seemed good to me also, having followed all things closely for some time past, to write an orderly account for you, most excellent Theophilus, that you may have certainty concerning the things you have been taught."

He rubbed his jaw. She'd promised him a history written by Luke, but he hadn't expected a real history. Not something starting like Tacitus or Suetonius would write.

As he read on, he hit the first thing she might have had in mind as unbelievable. A virgin having a child without ever lying with a man? That didn't even happen in the stories of the Roman gods. They always took their pleasure before a demigod was born.

He shook his head. Those were only children's stories; the Roman demigods lived in the imagination only. But her Jesus was a man out of history. At the very least, a real man, even if not what she and Publius thought him.

Then he shrugged. As she said, if a god could create the universe out of nothing, starting a human child in the belly of a woman was easy. The story was pinned to a fixed point in history. One of the censuses in the reign of Augustus—you couldn't get more specific than that.

He scanned ahead, and his eyes were caught by the words *Holy Spirit*. An old man had been waiting in the temple for Israel's consolation, whatever that was. But the Holy Spirit was on him and had told him he wouldn't die until he saw the lord's Christ.

Pompeia spoke of this Holy Spirit healing him and guiding her. What did it mean to have the Spirit on him? Something to ask her later, but it was the prophesy the old man spoke that made Titianus draw his head back.

"'Lord, now you are letting your servant depart in peace, according to your word; for my eyes have seen your salvation that you have prepared in the presence of all peoples, a light for revelation to the Gentiles, and for glory to your people Israel.'"

Lucius had told him how any non-Jew was a Gentile and how any devout Jew considered them unclean. Disdain for every Gentile blossomed into full-blown hatred for any Roman. Yet the old man said Jesus was a light for revelation to the Gentiles. Even though he said Jesus was the savior of Israel, that salvation was for all peoples.

But why wouldn't the god who created everything want all people to worship him, not just one small group in a backwater of the Empire?

Silence about most of Jesus's early years and young manhood followed, but it picked up the story thirty years after Jesus's birth, in the fifteenth year of the reign of Tiberius while Pontius Pilatus was governor.

Titianus smiled at another solid date set in the history he knew. In Tacitus's report on the Great Fire of Rome during the reign of Nero, he reported that Christus had been executed by Pontius Pilatus, procurator of Judaea, during Tiberius's reign.

The story resumed with a public baptism with the Holy Spirit in the physical form of a dove landing on Jesus and God's voice proclaiming him God's son.

God, Jesus as God's son, the Holy Spirit…how did these three fit together? The Holy Spirit overshadowed the virgin so Jesus was called the Son of God. But if Jesus as a man and the Holy Spirit as a dove were at the river, whose voice came from heaven? He must be the father since he called Jesus his beloved son, but hadn't the Holy Spirit been the father?

He closed his eyes, and with both hands, he massaged his neck. Maybe that would be explained later by Luke. Or maybe the explanation was in the writing by John that she loved. He'd ask her later.

Titianus scanned past the list of the stepfather Joseph's ancestors and a story about a devil tempting Jesus. Then Jesus started teaching.

Teaching and healing. So many healings. No wonder he drew crowds. But Publius's letter didn't speak about him as a healer. It talked about him being a sacrifice for the sins of men that put a barrier between them and God.

About a quarter of the way through, she'd placed a blue ribbon. It was at the story of a paralyzed man whose friends made a hole in the roof to reach Jesus. They believed Jesus would end the paralysis if they could just get their friend in front of him.

> "And when he saw their faith, he said, 'Man, your sins are forgiven you.'
> And the scribes and the Pharisees began to question,

saying, 'Who is this who speaks blasphemies? Who can forgive sins but God alone?'"

The obvious answer: no one. If he spoke the words like he was the one forgiving the sins, it was an invitation to trouble. Had her Jesus just publicly declared himself to be God?

Titianus blew out a slow breath. Blasphemy…that's what it would be if he was only a man. That's what the Jewish leaders considered it, too.

> "When Jesus perceived their thoughts, he answered them, 'Why do you question in your hearts?
>
> "Which is easier, to say, 'Your sins are forgiven you,' or to say, 'Rise and walk'?
>
> "'But that you may know that the Son of Man has authority on earth to forgive sins'—he said to the man who was paralyzed—'I say to you, rise, pick up your bed and go home.'
>
> "And immediately he rose up before them and picked up what he had been lying on and went home, glorifying God.
>
> "And amazement seized them all, and they glorified God and were filled with awe, saying, 'We have seen extraordinary things today.'"

Extraordinary things…what an understatement. But they couldn't see what had really happened when Jesus spoke that forgiveness. So how could they know whether Jesus's words had done something or not? Did the man himself feel something? If your sins were suddenly forgiven like that, would you know it?

> "After this he went out and saw a tax collector named Levi, sitting at the tax booth. And he said to him, 'Follow me.'
>
> "And leaving everything, he rose and followed him. And Levi made him a great feast in his house, and there was a large company of tax collectors and others reclining at table with them."

Any tax collector would be a man who became rich working for Rome. Lucius had said they were frequent targets for attacks by rebels, who called them traitors. They collected more than Rome required and kept the difference. They were thieves, really, not men of honor. He wouldn't invite such men to dine at his own table, and he wouldn't choose to dine at theirs. What had Jesus seen in Levi that he singled him out to become his follower?

> "And the Pharisees and their scribes grumbled at his disciples, saying, 'Why do you eat and drink with tax collectors and sinners?'
>
> And Jesus answered them, 'Those who are well have no need of a physician, but those who are sick. I have not come to call the righteous but sinners to repentance.'"

There was the answer. He called a sinner to repent, and Levi had. A thief, approved by Rome or not, had plenty to repent of. But Publius had said he needed to repent, too, and Lucius thought his grandfather was the finest man he ever knew.

He closed his eyes and rubbed his temples. He was maybe a third of the way through the stack, and his head was hurting. Maybe it was too soon to read so much, but she'd be disappointed if he didn't make it to the end.

He set the stack face-down on the table and rested his head on the cushion. A few moments with his eyes closed should help.

The Lenaeus town house, late morning of Day 16

Pompeia watched her Egyptians write on wax tablets what they would be doing that evening. It was an exercise in using the proper endings to show it was in the future.

But her thoughts were on a man at the house in the Fagutal. What might the future hold for him...and for her?

God, please let his head recognize the truth today. Please let his heart embrace it.

It took her and Father some time to make that decision, and they became God-fearers first. If you don't know you're a sinner against God, you can't realize you need a savior. Was he going to take the same path?

Had he been able to read much? Had he even started?

She moved to the back of the room by the door and closed her eyes.

Holy Spirit, please guide him into the truth.

Ciconia was walking past the door, but she turned and slipped into the room. She cupped her hand by Pompeia's ear. "Lilia and I are praying for him, too."

A quick embrace and Ciconia returned to the atrium.

Pompeia strolled back to the desk and half-sat on the edge. "Who would like to read what you wrote first?"

Chapter 40

WHAT TRUTH DEMANDS

The Sabinus town house, midday of Day 16

Titianus awoke to find Manius sitting in the chair opposite him. He glanced at the face-down stacks of papyrus. They were exactly as he left them. She'd entrusted him with her dangerous family secret, and his carelessness had almost betrayed it. Without doubt, Septimus knew it. Whether Manius could be trusted with it...that was not something he wanted to risk without talking to Septimus first.

He might be dangerously close to having a secret he needed to keep himself.

"Father is coming midafternoon to enjoy a private bath and a few games of latrunculi or tabula before we go to a banquet." Manius stretched out his legs. "Consul Camerinus has a town house here in the Fagutal. Did you want to join us for a soak before we leave?"

He picked up the runner and felt the flower. "Or would you rather finish reading whatever Pompeia gave you this morning?"

He reached for the stack, but Titianus beat him to it.

With a chuckle Manius settled back into the chair. "I thought that too long for a love letter, but perhaps not. She is a teacher's daughter. I'm sure she can find many delightful ways to express her feelings. Greek and Latin, poetry and prose."

"It's not a love letter." At least, not one addressed to him personally. But it did talk about God's love. "It's a history of some events in the Eastern Empire a hundred years ago. Not something to interest you." He offered a wry smile. "Not something that would have interested me before I met her."

But nothing intrigued him more now than the question of what he should do about her god and especially Jesus.

"I'd like to finish it before she returns." He put on his interrogator mask. "I believe your father will find it more relaxing if I'm not there."

Manius mimicked his face, then chuckled as he rose. "He's only just beginning to appreciate you. In time, he'll like you as much as I do. I'll see you tomorrow."

He strolled out the door, and Titianus turned the papyrus stack over to read once more. He scanned through several more healings and some words about blessings that would follow times of suffering.

> "'But I say to you who hear, love your enemies, do good to those who hate you, bless those who curse you, pray for those who abuse you. To one who strikes you on the cheek, offer the other also, and from one who takes away your cloak do not withhold your tunic either.'"

So this was where she got the idea she should love her enemies, although how she could ever have one was hard to imagine.

He inhaled sharply. Except for Rome. Rome had declared Publius its enemy because of his faith, and he died for it. The same could happen to her.

A strange thought wormed its way into his mind. A man of honor couldn't deny the truth. If Jesus really was who the Christians claimed, he'd have to believe and follow, no matter the risk.

He snorted. The man who'd single-mindedly enforced Roman law might be condemned for violating the proscription against Christians. If that's where the truth led, it could happen. Would it be worth it?

> "'But love your enemies, and do good, and lend, expecting nothing in return, and your reward will be great, and you will be sons of the Most High, for he is kind to the ungrateful and the evil. Be merciful, even as your Father is merciful.'"

Merciful. It wasn't the Roman way, and no one had ever accused him of it. It was justice, not mercy, that he always strove for.

> "'Judge not, and you will not be judged; condemn
> not, and you will not be condemned; forgive, and you will
> be forgiven; give, and it will be given to you. Good mea-
> sure, pressed down, shaken together, running over, will be
> put into your lap. For with the measure you use it will be
> measured back to you.'"

Judging, condemning, never forgiving. Those described him perfectly. If God's greatest command was to love even your enemies, he'd built a barrier high and wide between them. She said everyone sinned, and he could name these as his.

To follow the god who kept him from dying, he'd have to change. But what would that mean for what he did as tribune? He hunted down and arrested thieves and murderers to protect innocent people. Surely protecting others from evil was something God would approve.

If Lenaeus were alive, he could ask him. Some questions were too hard to figure out yourself when you were just starting to learn.

He rubbed his eyes and blinked hard a few times. Almost back to normal, but not quite. He wouldn't be able to read it all today, but he'd at least read what she marked. He scanned down the sheet, and "centurion" caught his eye. A Roman officer asked Jesus to heal his sick slave, but he didn't ask Jesus to come to him. He assumed it took only a word, spoken at a distance, to heal. Like any Roman in a legion, he understood how authority worked, and he knew it when he saw it.

And Jesus praised his faith. That triggered a crooked smile. Praise for a Roman...guaranteed to upset many of the Jews. But if God was the God of everyone, faith worth praising could be found in anyone.

He tucked that sheet at the back of the stack and moved to the next place she'd put a ribbon.

> "'The Son of Man must suffer many things and be
> rejected by the elders and chief priests and scribes, and be
> killed, and on the third day be raised.'"

Titianus massaged the back of his neck. Jesus knew what would happen long before it did. He knew he was going to Jerusalem to be the final sacrifice. A perfect blood sacrifice, for God had said only a blood sacrifice could remove sin. But how he could do that, knowing a Roman cross was waiting?

To save someone he cared about deeply, someone like Lucius, Titianus would have been willing to give up his own life. But that would have been quick, like in battle. A man could take days to die when he was crucified. The stronger the man, the longer it took. Could he have done that, even for his closest friend?

> "And he said to all, 'If anyone would come after me, let him deny himself and take up his cross daily and follow me. For whoever would save his life will lose it, but whoever loses his life for my sake will save it. For what does it profit a man if he gains the whole world and loses or forfeits himself?
>
> 'For whoever is ashamed of me and of my words, of him will the Son of Man be ashamed when he comes in his glory and the glory of the Father and of the holy angels.'"

He closed his eyes for a long blink. Exactly what Publius had written. Exactly what he had done as he stood in the arena because he wouldn't deny Jesus was his lord.

But once a man knew the truth, he couldn't deny it. If that meant dying—he drew a deep breath and released it with a sigh —then a man of honor had to choose to die.

He flipped to the next ribbon. She'd used red, not blue. Did that mean anything, or had she just used up all of the first one?

> "'And I tell you, ask, and it will be given to you; seek, and you will find; knock, and it will be opened to you. For everyone who asks receives, and the one who seeks finds, and to the one who knocks it will be opened.'"

It meant something. Here were specific instructions for what he should do. He sucked air between his teeth. He'd already started the asking and seeking. What he needed was the answers to those questions. Answers he knew to be true.

"God. Jesus. Holy Spirit." His voice was a whisper. "However I'm supposed to address you, I'm asking you to show me what's true. I'm seeking to understand what all this means." His mouth twitched. "Pompeia said she would pray for my mind to be open to the truth and for my heart to embrace it. I guess that's my prayer as well."

He scanned the room. He didn't see anyone, but the sensation when he whispered the first prayer, the feeling that someone was in the room, had just become more intense.

> "'If you then, who are evil, know how to give good
> gifts to your children, how much more will the heavenly
> Father give the Holy Spirit to those who ask him!'"

When the old man Simeon spoke of Jesus being the one who would die for Gentiles, Luke wrote that the Holy Spirit was upon him. Could that be the Holy Spirit Titianus was feeling? She said he was always with her, even in her, however that worked. It wasn't clear how a god could be inside you and outside at the same time, but there was a lot that confused him.

Luke kept writing about the Father, Jesus the Son, and the Holy Spirit, but it was like the three were the same but also different. Confusing, but she could explain it to him later.

What was clear was that God had kept him from dying in the ambush, and God wanted to give him an eternal life if he'd only believe Jesus broke down the barrier he'd built with his sins. But how exactly had Jesus done that?

With eyes closed, he rubbed his temples. When he opened them and squinted, the letters were clear enough again.

The next red ribbon was near the end. With regret, he moved the unread sheets to the back. When his eyes worked better, he'd come back and consider every word.

> "And he took bread, and when he had given thanks,
> he broke it and gave it to them, saying, 'This is my body,
> which is given for you. Do this in remembrance of me.'
> And likewise the cup after they had eaten, saying,
> 'This cup that is poured out for you is the new covenant
> in my blood.'"

There was the answer. Jesus declared himself the blood sacrifice, and he went willingly to a Roman cross to complete it.

One more blue ribbon lay on the last sheet.

> "Then he said to them, 'These are my words that I

spoke to you while I was still with you, that everything written about me in the Law of Moses and the Prophets and the Psalms must be fulfilled.'

Then he opened their minds to understand the Scriptures, and said to them, 'Thus it is written, that the Christ should suffer and on the third day rise from the dead, and that repentance for the forgiveness of sins should be proclaimed in his name to all nations, beginning from Jerusalem. You are witnesses of these things.'"

His fingertips stroked the underside of his jaw. What would it have been like to be there while Jesus himself explained everything in their scriptures so they truly understood? But even with what little he knew, he was ready to believe in the truth he'd been shown. Repentance and forgiveness…exactly what that meant he would ask Pompeia. He had no doubt she'd love to tell him.

As he straightened the sheets, he read once more the ending of Publius's letter.

"I will die soon, but I have no regrets. I am content to die because it isn't death that matters. It is whether you have accepted Jesus as Savior. Death is terrible apart from Jesus. Without Jesus, I would be lost, in hell, forever separated from God. With Jesus as my Savior, death has no power over me, and I don't fear it. It will just usher me into life with Him in heaven.

Jesus told us that He is the way, the truth, and the life. He promised if a man would believe in Him and follow, he would know the truth, and the truth would set him free."

Titianus didn't know all he wanted yet, not even all he needed to be a follower of Jesus. But he'd felt the truth of what he read, and he was ready for what came next.

Ask, seek, knock. God had certainly delivered on the promise of providing the answers to anyone who would.

He wrapped the stack in the runner once more. It wasn't as pretty as the way she'd done it, but it would keep prying eyes from finding out what might put her in danger. He stretched out his legs and placed the package against his chest with both hands on it.

When he closed his eyes, he heaved a contented sigh. He'd asked God to show him the truth. Now that he'd seen it, choices he'd never expected lay ahead.

A man of honor must follow where truth leads, and he was ready and willing to go.

Chapter 41

A PROBLEM TO SOLVE

A shop in Trajan's Market, late afternoon of Day 16

When the two men entered his spice shop, Marcus Siricus barely glanced at them. He stayed at the worktable on the back wall behind the counter. The newly purchased cumin seeds he bought in bulk had to be divided into the small packets he would sell. He'd paid good money for the woman who ran the shop when he was removing an unwanted person for someone. She would take care of them.

"Marcus Siricus?"

He glanced over his shoulder when one spoke his name. Then he turned to face them. Neither looked like a cook. One looked Roman and wore a toga. The other was red-headed like a Thracian and looked too much like a bodyguard. "Yes. Can I help you?"

"I come with condolences."

Siricus's head drew back. "You've come to the wrong place. No condolences are needed here."

The Thracian moved close to his slave. "You want to leave for a while." He held his closed fist out. When she put her palm under it, he opened his hand to drop two small brass coins into it. "You need to go get something to eat. Close the door behind you, and don't hurry back."

Her eyes saucered, and she looked at Siricus for permission.

A dip of his head sent her through the doorway. As the door closed behind her, his heart rate rose. "I think you have me confused with someone else."

He'd worn his dagger, as always, but even with his skill, one against two could be a problem.

"I think not. The wife of your...friend whose body she claimed at the fortress told us we could find you here. She was sure you'd want to know of his...untimely death because someone rode him down."

Siricus half-sat on the table and crossed his arms. That put his hand near the dagger's hilt for a quick draw, if it came to that.

"I'm very sorry to hear that." He tightened his lips and shook his head. "A man should be able to walk the streets of Rome in safety."

"Yes, he should." The visitor's mouth curved into a fake smile. "Especially if he's a tribune of the Urban Cohort riding home from a quiet dinner with friends." His mouth hardened. "Especially when he's the nephew of one of the most powerful men in Rome."

The Thracian blocked the opening in the counter, and his hand settled on his dagger.

Siricus uncrossed his arms. He knew a willing killer when he saw one, and he was probably seeing two. Words could be better than swords when you were outnumbered.

"The tribune and his uncle don't have to worry about his safety anymore."

Sometimes the best thing to do was tell the truth, and this time was one of them.

"I was hired to kill a slave who witnessed a murder. When Titianus was getting too close to finding the murderer, I was hired to kill him, too."

Siricus cleared his throat. "But that was before I knew of his ties to Sabinus. I cancelled the contract on the boy and the tribune and returned all the money. Titianus is under no threat from me."

The Roman picked up a small bag from the counter and sniffed. "Dill. Hmmm." He dropped it back in the basket and stared at Siricus. "Fortuna smiled on you when you failed the first time. We wouldn't be talking now if you hadn't. But if there's another attack on Titianus or if someone tries to hurt the master's grandson or his friends...any thinking man would assume you hadn't returned the money and you completed the contract."

He swept his hand toward the shelves of packaged spices. "From all over the Empire, I assume, so you know how big it is." His eyes turned icy. "But the Empire isn't large enough to hide a man from Sabinus's wrath."

"I'm no fool. I would never risk that."

The Roman raised one eyebrow. "Who hired you?"

Siricus had never revealed the name of an employer before, but this time... "Faustus Rufinus Arcanus."

"Why?"

"The door slave saw him when he killed the teacher Lenaeus, and he was fool enough not to kill the boy before he left the school." Siricus fought the urge to rub his mouth and won. "He was afraid to go back and do it himself. I figured he'd end up hiring me to kill the tutor's children, too. I was surprised when it was Titianus he wanted killed next."

The men before him were paid killers, too. They'd know what a normal kill cost. "But Arcanus was willing to pay a thousand denarii, so I agreed." He shook his finger at them. "But only before I knew Sabinus would care. I refunded as soon as I knew that."

The Roman rubbed his lip with his middle finger. "So you say. But if Arcanus hires someone else to complete the job, I won't be able to convince Sabinus it wasn't you."

Siricus drew a breath and blew it out slowly. "He could do that, but I can resolve the problem permanently for you for five hundred denarii."

An explosive snort was followed by a chuckle. "Sabinus doesn't pay someone to kill a citizen, not even a freedman. But..."—the laughing eyes chilled with a single blink—"he remembers those who take care of a problem for him. A reliable man can have repeat business of an appropriate kind. But Sabinus has to know the man is reliable before he hires anyone."

Siricus crossed his arms. "I'll make certain no other contracts are set on the boy, the tribune, the grandson, or his friends."

The Roman's mouth relaxed into a friendly smile. "I'm glad to hear that. I'm sure you'll find a suitable way to solve your own problem. The wise man takes care of such business quickly."

A tip of the Roman's head, and the Thracian moved back from the counter.

The Roman picked up the dill again and bounced the bag in his hand. "A sestertius for this?"

"That seems fair." But anything would sound fair to Siricus if it got these two to leave.

"I'll be watching to see if you know your business well. If you do... I'm always looking for reliable men."

The two left the shop, leaving the door open behind them.

Siricus held his right hand out. The conversation had left it with a slight tremor, but that would pass soon enough. He'd used that hand many times to solve someone else's problem. He'd use it tonight to solve his.

Chapter 42

A Change of Location

The Sabinus town house, late afternoon of Day 16

When Pompeia entered Titianus's room, he was dozing in the chair. His fingers were clasped as his hands held the runner and its precious contents against his chest.

Had he opened it? Did he read it? Did God reach him while he read?

Patience was a virtue, and self-control was the mark of a mature Christian. Maybe she should let him sleep until he woke naturally, but…

"Titianus?" Her voice was barely above a whisper, not enough to wake him if he really needed to sleep.

His breathing changed, and he stirred.

"Titianus." The name was louder but still softly spoken.

He opened his eyes, and they warmed as a slow smile appeared. "You're back early."

"I couldn't wait." She rested her fingertips on the package. "Did you read any of it?"

He moved his hand atop hers. "I read enough. Where you put the red ribbon—where it said to ask, seek, and knock—I did that, and what Jesus promised happened."

Joy flooded her heart and mind. *Thank you, God, for making him Yours. Now, please make him mine.*

"All day I've been praying that would happen. The same thing happened to me."

One corner of his mouth lifted. "I'm living proof He listens to your prayers. Two times that I know of and maybe more. I still have questions, but I see the truth of it." He wrapped his fingers around her hand and squeezed. "It's like your father always told us. Once a man knows the truth, he has to admit it. After he does that, he has to act on it."

He leaned forward to place the package on the table. "I think Publius made the right decision. I'm ready to do the same."

"Kaeso will be as happy as I am."

She felt her cheeks warm. That wasn't quite true. Kaeso would be happy, but not for as many reasons. Titianus deciding to join them wasn't the dearest desire of her brother's heart.

"There are some things that confuse me. God, Jesus, Holy Spirit—I wasn't sure how to address Him." He ran his fingers through his hair. "Maybe I scanned past the parts that explain it, but I don't understand how God as Father, Jesus as Son, and the Holy Spirit are both different and the same, but I figure you can explain that."

His eyebrow rose at her chuckle.

"I can share what I've figured out, but I don't understand it completely. I do know Jesus said He would send the Spirit to be with us after He returned to the Father, and I feel His presence with me."

"Like someone is in the room watching, but you can't see him? I felt that when I started reading."

"That and more. Soon you'll feel Him in you, not just watching you. The gospel by John is full of what Jesus taught His disciples, and part of the explanation is there. There are vital things you need to know about confessing your sins and repenting, too. I'll guide you through that when we read it together and talk about it, like we did Publius's letter. But I only have the mind of a mortal person, and some of the things of God are beyond what people like us can ever understand."

He rested his head on the cushion. "In a day or two, I should be able to walk and ride like before. It will be safer to do that at your home than here. I'd put the sheets face down on the table while I rested my eyes for a few minutes. I woke to find Manius watching me. I almost betrayed your secret, but he hadn't looked at the sheets." He glanced at the precious package before refocusing on her. "Does he know you're Christians?"

"Not that I know of."

"Is Septimus one of you?"

"Not yet, but he knows we are. I think he will be someday." She looked at the runner wrapping the treasured words, then raised her eyes to his. "I'm so glad you decided you want to believe in Jesus, too. That's been my prayer since the day we asked God to keep you from dying. There are more important things in life than staying alive, and I want that for Septimus as well."

"He reminds me of myself when I was young. I never had a brother. Then I met Lucius. We were like Septimus and Kaeso, where there was no need for secrets between us. But it's more than seven years since I last saw Lucius. I doubt I'll ever have a friend like that again. It's only the young who form such bonds."

"That's not so. Publius and Appius were good friends from childhood, but Appius, Father, and Glyptus became deep friends only a dozen years ago."

For the first time ever, he looked sheepish. "After the way he hugged you when he brought the toga, I wanted to know what Glyptus was to you, so I checked into him. Twelve years ago was before Glyptus was freed. A teacher, a senator, and his slave were close friends? How did that happen?"

"When they became Christian brothers. It started when Appius went to the arena to tell Publius he could get him a new trial. He didn't understand why his best friend would refuse to make a meaningless sacrifice to stay alive. Glyptus was with him, so when Publius wanted to write a final letter to his son, he went for the papyrus and ink and stayed with Publius while he wrote."

She picked up the package and caressed the rose. "Publius made Appius promise to read the letter before he sent it on, and he copied the parts that weren't personal to study later. He brought it to our house to discuss it with Father, and the four of us decided to become children of God."

"Your whole familia...are they Christians?"

Knowing it was safe to tell him now...that triggered a smile. "Yes. Ciconia was already when Father bought her and Lilia for Mother, but she kept it secret until Mother died. Glyptus knew Corax was, so when we needed a steward, Appius bought him for Father."

"So, if I want some Christian slaves, could Glyptus find them for me?"

"Probably. Why?" His tribune mask was back. Was it real or fake this time?

◆

"I've been living in quarters at the fortress, but I need to change that."

He'd planned this conversation before he slept. If it ended as he hoped, he'd be a doubly blessed man today.

"Is Manius going to have you stay here?"

"He'd probably let me, but I'm going to tell my renters to find another place."

"That can be hard in Rome. There have been several people offer to pay more than we do for our town house. That's why Kaeso is so worried about losing too many students."

"He won't have to worry now."

"Why?" Her eyes narrowed, then relaxed as her eyebrows rose. "What have you done?"

"Nothing." Nothing yet, but that was about to change. "But you're going to be moving the school to someplace larger."

She shook her head. "We can barely afford where we are."

He stood. Lounging like an invalid wasn't how he'd envisioned asking her. "The new home of the Lenaeus School will be rent-free. The owner has to take out some walls to combine some of the smaller rooms off the atrium to make classrooms, but that shouldn't take long. It even has a stableyard so new students can come by litter or horseback."

"We can't afford something like that."

"Perhaps not right now." He moved closer to her. "But your future husband already owns the perfect place for the school."

"Future husband?" Her head drew back. "Are you asking me—"

"To be my wife. Tradition says a man should ask the paterfamilias first and negotiate the dowry. But you don't need a dowry with me, and I think you can make up your own mind."

Her hands flew up to cover her mouth. Wide-eyed, she stared at him, and his stomach clenched. He'd never understood women. Had he asked too soon? Had he been too clumsy in how he put it?

Then her eyes warmed, and her beaming smile made him laugh at those questions.

"I often told Father only a Christian man would do for me, and God would bring me one if He intended me to marry." She stepped toward him, and he placed his hands on her waist. "He always liked you. He thought you would grow into a fine man." She rested her hands on his shoulders. "I think you grew into the best man I know, and I'd be honored to marry you."

He drew her against him and inhaled the rose scent in her hair. But it was scarcely a moment before she pulled back. "What's wrong?"

"If we have students coming and going all the time, what if one of them discovers you're a Christian? I don't want to risk what that could mean."

"I'm not worried." He stroked her cheek with the back of his fingers. Softer than he'd even imagined. "If it's been safe enough for twelve years in your rented town house, it can be safe enough in mine. You were already teaching Roman elite like Septimus and Rufinus's son. Manius should be willing to recommend the school to some of his friends to keep a supply of students coming. Being in my house will enhance the prestige for a senatorial father looking for the right school for his son."

He caressed her cheek again. "After all, I'm the nephew of Quintus Sabinus, and some who don't know what's really important will think that adds value."

He leaned down to kiss her forehead. "Will you want to keep teaching?"

"I do enjoy it, so yes."

"That's another good reason to use my house. I'll only be hunting criminals for a few more months. Then I'll want you close when you have breaks between classes."

"I'd like that, too." She traced his lip with her fingertip. "I'm teaching my Egyptians how to entertain Roman men. You can watch our practices in the triclinium and tell me if I'm doing it right."

"If they watch us together, I might teach them more than you want to tell them." He bounced his eyebrows, and her cheeks reddened as she glanced away.

"I have no house staff at the moment. I assume Kaeso will move in with the school, so I'd like Corax to be my steward. If he and Glyptus find me other Christians, we can make our familia a real family like you have now."

"You seem to have thought of everything." She pushed back a strand of his hair, and her fingertips left a tingling trail behind. That and rubbing his temples—he could stand a lifetime of both. "When shall we do it?"

"As soon as I get my house ready." He drew her against him, and she slipped her arms around his chest. "There's no dowry contract, but I'd like a kiss to seal the betrothal."

"I think that's a fine idea." She closed her eyes and tipped her head back.

◆

Pompeia held her breath as he lowered his lips to hers. The kiss seemed to last forever, yet it was still too short. When he finally drew back, he placed his hand on her cheek and caressed her with his eyes.

In the chest in her bedroom at the school was the sheer kalasiris Khepri had given her. She would ask him to don his tribune mask before she stepped into view. What would his eyebrows and lips do when he first saw her on their wedding night?

"What are you laughing at?"

"You'll find out soon." She managed to wipe the silly grin from her face. "You're in for some teasing. You know Manius will take credit for this."

"He can think that if he wants. Someday, when it's the right time, I'll tell him God planned it for us, but his help made it easy." His mouth straightened. "He'd only laugh if he heard that now, but I'll get him to think about God and what Jesus did. I expect he'll be my brother as well as my cousin before God's through with him."

"He is a nice man. I'd love for him to join us."

"That's probably been Septimus's influence. I always thought Manius was like his father. Quintus Sabinus is as ruthless as they come, but he cares about Rome. Behind his back, people call him the crocodile, but he'd think it was praise, not an insult."

He pushed a strand of hair behind her ear. "Sabinus told me you would suit me the day after the attack, but I already knew that after our first dinner with Manius."

"Manius won't be at dinner tonight. Shall we keep it secret until we can tell him, too?"

Titianus put on his interrogator's mask. "I can hide what I'm thinking with the best of them. If you want to wait, it's fine with me. But as soon as we tell him, will you move from Kaeso's dining couch to mine?"

She stroked his stubbly cheek, and his cold, straight lips curved into the warmest smile. "Of course, and we'll share one for the rest of our lives."

Chapter 43

An Honorable Man

The Rufinus town house, late morning of Day 18

As Rufinus entered his library, his brow furrowed. He'd just finished the salutation, and Arcanus had failed to appear. He hadn't shown up the day before either. He'd never been absent two days in a row. What might have caused it?

He rubbed his mouth. He'd ordered Arcanus not to do anything else without asking him first. Surely he hadn't...or had he? What if he'd decided Tertius Flaccus was too dangerous as well?

He heaved a sigh. In an hour or so, he would go to the baths. At each visit, he nurtured the alliances that would help make him consul. Maybe there was nothing to worry about. Sometimes he saw Arcanus there. Perhaps he would today.

As he scanned his scrolls for something to fill that hour, three knocks drew his gaze.

"Excuse me, master." His doorkeeper clasped his hands and bowed his head. "You have a visitor."

"Tell him to come back tomorrow during the salutation. I'm about to leave."

A large hand came into view and pushed the doorkeeper aside. It was attached to a muscular blond man with a scar on his cheek.

"It will take only a few moments. You have the time." Quintus Flavius Sabinus stepped past his bodyguard into the room, and Rufinus's stomach knotted. That was anyone's natural reaction to an unexpected visit from the power broker who had Hadrian's ear and knew every senator's pressure point.

Sabinus looked over his shoulder as he strolled toward Rufinus. "No one is to disturb us."

The German took his post in the open doorway, facing out, legs spread, arms crossed.

"Welcome, Sabinus. What a delightful surprise. If this is a private matter, your man should close the door."

"Hmph." Sabinus's snort was followed by a humorless smile. "Closed doors can mean safety or danger, depending on who's in the room. We'll leave it open."

Rufinus gestured toward the guest chair. "Please sit. I always have time for a man who has served Rome so well for so long."

Sabinus walked to the chair and gripped the back with hands both wrinkled and muscular, but he remained standing. "I'll stand, but you can sit."

Handling power plays was second nature to Rufinus, but this was one it was wise not to challenge. He settled into his chair. "What may I do for you today, Sabinus?

"I came to offer you condolences."

Rufinus's head drew back before he thought to stop it. "But I've suffered no losses."

"Interesting that you think so. It would appear Fortuna is frowning on you without you even knowing it. First your warehouse burns with your freedman Lupus in it, and now the man who looks after your other illegal businesses seems to have been waylaid by thieves on the way to a late dinner with a friend."

Arcanus murdered? Despite the mess he'd created since the fire, he didn't deserve that. Rufinus tried to freeze his face so Sabinus wouldn't see that news hurt.

The old man clicked his tongue. "Rome has become dangerous of late. Even my nephew, Tribune Titianus, was attacked. On his horse and in full armor, no less."

Rufinus furrowed his brow. "I heard that from Saturninus. Robbers are so brazen at times. I trust he's recovering?"

"He's recovered and was going back on duty today, I think. Possibly tomorrow. Perhaps he'll track down the ones who killed both your men."

"I hear he's the best investigator Rome has. Perhaps he will." Rufinus stopped himself from swallowing. The eyes of this old predator missed nothing.

Sabinus crossed his arms and stared at Rufinus. Rufinus returned the fixed gaze with a political smile, but his heart beat still rose.

"Titus knows Arcanus set the warehouse fire. He knows your man hired someone to kill him. Perhaps Fortuna did smile on you when the robbers struck. Any direct link back to you died with him." He tipped his head enough to look down his nose. "But only a fool strikes at someone important to me. With Arcanus gone and my nephew recovered, you might think you got away with it because your involvement can't be proven. But I don't need evidence that will stand up in court to pass my own judgment."

Sabinus's snort was like a fist in the stomach, and the crocodile's icy gaze locked onto him. "No one who wants to be consul of Rome would be fool enough to risk the opposition of my allies and clients. You need people to think you're an honorable man. We both know that's not true. Still, you've served Rome well, and you might make a good consul. Since Titus recovered, I might let what you did pass this time."

The cold eyes flamed with anger. "But don't cross me again."

"But—"

Sabinus raised his hand. "Don't lie to me. I don't want to hear it." He stepped back from the chair. "We both have places to go and people to see. You don't want us to have this conversation again."

Sabinus strode out the door, and his German followed.

Rufinus listened as the slaps of their sandals on the marble floor faded away.

He clasped his hands to stop the slight tremor. With his elbows on the desk, he rested his forehead against his hands. He would miss his daily talks with Arcanus. He'd been a loyal servant he could always count on. He'd truly liked him, and he'd be impossible to replace.

But if Titianus knew he'd started the fire, his faithful client would have burned in the arena. Nothing he could have done could have stopped it. It was better to die quickly at the hand of a robber...or whoever really killed him.

If he were a betting man, he'd bet Sabinus had something to do with it. He slowly shook his head. No one in his right mind would risk Sabinus learning he had made that bet.

But the crocodile couldn't object to him having Arcanus's ashes put in his family mausoleum. It was expected for a faithful client, no matter why he died.

He clenched his jaw. He'd do it even if Sabinus did object. It was the least he could do for a man who'd always tried to serve him well.

The Titianus town house, three months later

At the desk in his library, Titianus was reading a scroll of Seneca's most quoted sayings. He'd loved that scroll when Lenaeus had read from it when he was a boy. He'd thought Seneca the wisest of men because the tutor he admired thought so.

Some of the quotes were sound. Others were utter foolishness now that he knew the Creator of the universe, the one true God who loved him so much He'd died on a cross to save him. Pompeia had told him the Spirit of God would live within him after he confessed his sins and declared his faith in Jesus. The Holy Spirit would give him wisdom to discern what was true and what only seemed to be. She was right.

Now each week, he reveled in worshiping with Glyptus, Appius, and the whole Lenaeus familia. But especially with his precious bride, who'd guided him to where he would see and embrace the truth.

Three raps on the open door announced the arrival of his cousin. Manius had a standing invitation to dinner, and he often showed up unexpectedly when his social schedule had an opening.

"Come sit, cousin. Join me for a drink before dinner." Titianus rose as Manius settled into the guest chair. He brought two gold-lined silver goblets from the cabinet with carved grapevines on the doors. He returned for the red glass decanter of wine and a blue one of water

Manius scanned the scroll. "Seneca? I suppose anyone trained by Lenaeus would keep reading him. Septimus still quotes what he learned from Pompeia's father."

Titianus rolled the scroll and set it aside. "Some of what he wrote is wise. Other things…not so much."

"You look like married life is treating you well." Manius leaned back in the chair and crossed his arms. "I thought Pompeia would be as good for you as Julia is for me."

"And you were right. I should thank you for letting me stay where she could decide she wanted me." He poured some amber wine into each goblet and diluted it with water. Then he handed one to Manius. "I also thank you for taking care of the whole Lenaeus familia before I took over that task."

Manius waived the thank you away and picked up the goblet. "I enjoyed every minute of it." He tapped the glass decanter with its swirls of red and orange that made it look like flames. "This is pretty."

"Pompeia got it for me. I needed something for the wine I keep in here." He raised his goblet as he tipped his chin toward the one in Manius's hand. "I think you might like it."

Manius swirled it and inhaled the aroma. "Different, but very nice." He took a sip, and his eyes widened. "This is the best wine I've ever tasted. Where can I get some?"

"You can't. Not yet, anyway. It's Brutus's special vintage for the honorable. The way you helped Kaeso keep renting the town house without letting him know, how you bought Corax and freed him so he could protect Theo—Brutus would agree those are the acts of an honorable man. He would agree you deserve at least one goblet of it."

Manius blew out a breath between pursed lips. "Everything I've heard about it is true. I've never tasted its equal."

"I'm glad you like it." Titianus's smile grew as his cousin took a second sip and closed his eyes as he rolled it around his tongue. "There is one thing..."

Manius's eyes opened, and he swallowed. "What?"

"Don't tell your father I have it or that I gave you a taste. It's in that glass decanter so no one will know Brutus gives it to me."

Manius full-throated laugh echoed in the room. "There's no danger of that. Father would never trust me again if he thought I was turning into an honorable man."

Titianus raised his goblet, and Manius did the same. "To truth and honor."

His cousin wasn't ready to hear about Jesus yet, but Titianus would watch for the right time to tell him. Duty and honor had anchored his own life before he met Jesus. But the truth of God's love meant much more than honor, and he didn't need an anchor anymore. He was now a child of God, and the truth had set him free.

I'd Love to Hear from You!

If you enjoyed this book, it would be a real gift to me if you would post a review at the retailer you purchased it from. A good review is like a jewel set in gold for an author. Other great places to share reviews are Goodreads and BookBub. If you've read others in the series, it would be great if you post a review of those, too.

I'd also love to hear from you at carol-ashby.com or directly at carolashbyauthor@gmail.com.

Want to hear about upcoming releases in the Light in the Empire series and free gifts only for newsletter subscribers?

For free gifts and other special offers, advance notices of upcoming releases, and info about my latest writing adventures, please sign up for my newsletter at https://carol-ashby.com/newsletter/.

LIGHT *in the* EMPIRE SERIES

Dangerous times, difficult friendships,
lives transformed by forgiveness and love.

More Than Honor is the tenth volume in the Light in the Empire series, which follows the interconnected lives of six Roman families during the reigns of Trajan and Hadrian. Each can be read stand-alone. The twelve novels of the series will take you around the Empire, from Germania and Britannia to Thracia, Dacia, and Judaea and, of course, to Rome itself.

COMING IN DECEMBER 2021 AND IN 2022: PLEASE HELP ME CHOOSE!

Who would you like to see in a future story?

I grew to love several of the characters in *More Than Honor* while I was writing. That usually happens, and sometimes a future story takes shape in my head even before I finish. But more often the next hero or heroine is chosen because readers tell me who needs to come back as a story lead.

Readers who loved Galen as a teen in *Blind Ambition* wanted to see him as a grown man, so he became the hero in *Faithful*. People who asked for Brutus and Africanus to have their own story found out what happened to them in *Honor Bound*.

Since people kept asking what happened to Leander's beloved but long-lost sister in *True Freedom*, it was clear Ariana would need her own story in *Hope Unchained*. People who met Ursus in *Hope Unchained* asked what happened to him, so he returned with his childhood name of Matti in his quest to know God better in *Hope's Reward*.

In *More Than Honor*, Septimus, who was rather like a Great Dane puppy in *Honor Bound,* comes back three years older, and Tribune Titianus from *True Freedom* got his own story because readers thought he should. I'm SO glad they did. I hadn't planned on Titianus being a lead without that input, and I loved giving him and Pompeia their own happy ending.

But there are many more characters in the books of the series that I would like to spend more time with, and I hope there are some for you, too. Who would you most like to see in a future story? What was it about them that made you want more of them? I'd love to hear what you think. It will guide what I write next.

Some possibilities:
Aulus of *True Freedom?*
Septimus or Manius of *Honor Bound* and *More Than Honor?*
Someone else I haven't mentioned? (I can't wait to see who shows up here!)

Please tell me who you'd love to see again as a comment at carol-ashby. com or directly at carolashbyauthor@gmail.com!

I'm thinking about writing a short story or novella about someone from Sextus's or Calvia's households in *Honor Bound* or Gracchus of *Hope Unchained* and *Hope's Reward* to give to newsletter subscribers. Which would you rather have?

Please go to my website, carol-ashby.com, and share your thoughts in the comment box. Sign up for the newsletter, and you'll get the story when I finish it. Looking forward to hearing from you!

Historical Note

LAW ENFORCEMENT IN THE CITY OF ROME

Today, the government is expected to maintain a police force to protect people from attacks on their person and property. That was not always the case in Roman times. During the Republic, it was a do-it-yourself activity. If someone suffered a physical injury or loss of property, they had to capture the criminals themselves, often with the help of friends or family, and bring the accused perpetrator before a magistrate for trial.

During both Republic and Empire, the streets of Rome were notoriously dangerous at night, and anyone of means traveling in the city after dark took their own force of slaves and often armed bodyguards with them.

During Augustus's rule, the emperor was the first to create military units in the city of Rome to maintain the peace and protect the city from fires. These were divided into the Praetorian Guard (*cohors praetoria*), the urban cohorts (*cohortes urbanae*), and the vigiles (*vigiles urbani*). As in the regular legions, the Praetorian Guards were freeborn citizens of Rome. The rank-and-file members of the urban cohorts and vigiles units were mostly former slaves who received their citizenship when they were freed.

The Praetorian Guard was the elite military unit in Rome itself. After defeating Antony and Cleopatra, Octavian (later called Augustus) assigned them their role as political and criminal police of Rome. Augustus originally placed the Praetorians under the control of two praetorian prefects of equestrian rank, but later emperors reduced that to one. Part of the Guard traveled with the emperor when he left Rome, and part remained in Rome to discourage attempts by political rivals to replace the emperor in his absence. They often played a crucial role in deciding who would be the next emperor.

There were originally nine praetorian cohorts, but Caligula added three. Nero added two more, and Vespasian reduced the number to ten. A cohort was assigned to keep order at the Circus Maximus on race days, at the amphitheater while the games were in progress, and at the theater during performances. The city prison was run by the Praetorians, and executions decreed by the emperor or the Senate were their responsibility. A centurion and detachment of Praetorians might be sent far from Rome to carry out an execution, bringing the head back for public display in Rome.

In AD 10, Augustus formed a less prestigious unit that would serve as the daytime policemen and city gate guards. Urban prefect was a very prestigious position, and he was in charge of Rome when the emperor traveled. In many ways, he functioned like the mayor of Rome with important administrative responsibilities, including the free grain distribution to citizens. Under him were three and later four urban cohorts with numbers XI to XIV after Vespasian reduced the number of Praetorian cohorts to ten.

Some units were stationed in the city while others were sent to other cities where they would protect imperial assets, such as guarding grain shipments from Carthage. One cohort guarded the imperial mint at Lugdunum (Lyon) in Gaul. Each cohort was commanded by a tribune who reported to the urban prefect. Under each tribune were six centurions. The organization of each century paralleled that of a regular legion. The urban cohorts shared the praetorian fortress (*castra praetoria*) with the Praetorian Guard. Their number and size varied with time, but in AD 120, there were four of them with 500 men under six centurions in each cohort.

Perhaps the most essential were the Vigiles, whose full name meant "cohorts that stay awake." Originally formed in AD 6 by Augustus, they were both the nighttime police force and the fire brigade. They were under the command of the urban prefect. Rome was divided into 14 precincts (*regios*). Each of the seven cohorts of Vigiles served two precincts and were quartered in barracks in one of them. A cohort consisted of a thousand men under a tribune and several centurions.

Every precinct had cells and a torturer for extracting confessions from slaves and noncitizens. Most of the accused were tried at the stations by the Prefect of the Watch (*praefectus vigilum*). He was an equestrian who reported to the urban prefect, and he ranked second in power in the city. For some serious crimes and for accused people of the higher classes, some might be taken to a central jail or be allowed to post bail before a formal trial by the urban prefect.

The Vigiles patrolled Rome at night, watching for fires and criminal activity. Equipped with hand-pumped fire engines, grappling hooks, ladders, axes, shovels, and coiled-rope buckets sealed with pitch, they especially tried to keep fires from spreading to adjacent buildings.

With all wheeled traffic within a mile of the gates to Rome restricted to the late evening and nighttime hours, they also served as traffic police. Detachments were stationed in Rome's port towns of Ostia and Portus as well.

In *More Than Honor*, Titianus is an equestrian tribune who has been serving for more than eight years in the XI Urban Cohort, reporting to the urban prefect Saturninus. He excels at investigating major crimes, and he has more than one murder and attempted murder to keep him busy in this story.

For more about life in the Roman Empire at its peak, please go to carolashby.com.

Historical Note

THE PATRON-CLIENT RELATIONSHIP IN IMPERIAL ROME

The patron-client relationship underpinned much of Roman society. Clients were free men who were under legal obligation to a patron who had bestowed some benefit upon them. While not all clients were former slaves who had been freed by the patron or his father, when a slave was freed, he automatically became his former master's client. When his former master died, his obligations transferred to the master's son.

Being a slave in the Roman Empire meant having the legal classification of "mortal thing" (*res mortales*), and a slave's murder was legally nothing more than property damage. But when a Roman citizen over twenty freed a slave over thirty, the newly created freedman (*libertus* as an individual, *libertinus* when considering him part of the freedman social class) became a Roman citizen as well. Younger slaves could also become citizens under special circumstances.

In the Republic and Early Empire (until AD 212), being a Roman citizen gave a person many rights and privileges not accorded to noncitizens, no matter how rich they might be. The right to appeal a judicial action, the milder forms of punishment for crimes (exile instead of the arena, beheading instead of crucifixion), and the opportunity to enlist in the legions or serve in many government positions were restricted to Roman citizens. To go from "living thing" to the highly prized status of "citizen of Rome" in a single day lacks parallels in other slavery-based societies.

The only major drawback was the 5% inheritance tax charged only to Roman citizens. The historian Cassius Dio claimed Emperor Caracalla's real motivation in AD 212 in awarding citizenship to all free men within the empire was merely to increase the tax base.

A freedman's citizenship rights were somewhat restricted. He couldn't hold political office, but his children had all the rights and opportunities of freeborn citizens. Pertinax was the son of a freedman who started as a military tribune under the sponsorship of an equestrian (possibly his father's former owner and now patron). He rose on his own military and political merits to become senator, provincial governor, urban prefect, and finally emperor of Rome.

In legal texts, a freedman's obligations were often equated with the obligations of a son. A freedman couldn't bring a lawsuit or be a witness against his patron, just as a son couldn't against his father. Both were supposed to honor and obey their patron or father at all times. It was common to bury a freedman with the members of his patron's family.

But there were freedman obligations that went beyond that of a son to a father. Some were unwritten requirements of loyal behavior (*obsequia*) and others were legal requirements continuing the relationship of obedience and duty like a slave (*officia*). Some were written obligations to perform certain tasks and services (*operae*).

The nature of the operae depended on what the freedman did for his master while still a slave. It might be a specific number of hours spent on tasks for the patron. Slaves who were freed were often highly skilled men who had operated businesses for their master. They might continue in that capacity. Their patron might provide money for them to start new businesses for a share of the profits. The details depended on each patron and freedman, but in all cases the freedman was expected to deal honestly with his patron and always show his patron respect and loyalty.

Many patrons held a salutation in the early morning, where clients and others came to pay respects and ask favors. Some had so many come that they had extra seating outside their homes where those seeking an audience could wait.

In *More than Honor*, Rufinus had set his freedman Lupus up in a business that senators weren't supposed to be in. Lupus violated the requirements of loyal behavior by embezzling profits and cheating customers. Arcanus was another of Rufinus's freedmen who monitored his patron's businesses, both legal and illegal, and it was Arcanus's attempt to get Lupus to fulfill his freedman obligations that started all the problems.

For more about life in the Roman Empire at its peak, please go to carolashby.com.

The Epistle of Publius

How One Man Came to Faith

In *The Legacy*, Publius Drusus was a scholarly man who loved philosophy and history and taught his sons that the Roman gods were only characters in stories. But his desire to understand the world and why it was the way it was led him first to belief in the creator God of the Jews and then to believing that Jesus was his savior. As he sat in a cell under the Flavian Amphitheater awaiting his execution for his faith, he wrote a final letter to his son Titus, who was serving as a tribune in Thracia. He hoped to explain how he got to that point and to convince Titus to embrace the Christian faith as well. With the personal portions meant only for Titus removed, here's the version of the Epistle of Publius that Pompeia copied for Glyptus to deliver to other believers around Rome.

THE EPISTLE OF PUBLIUS CLAUDIUS DRUSUS

By the time you read this letter, I will have been executed for refusing to deny my faith in Jesus of Nazareth and offer a sacrifice to Caesar. Everything I own will have been confiscated. This letter is my only legacy, but what it contains is worth more than all my estates, more than all the wealth in the Empire. I pray you will come to treasure it for the truth it contains.

I begin with how I decided the God of Israel is the one true God.

The teaching of the great philosophers seemed true to me for a long time, but that was before I began to compare them to what my own eyes have seen of the world. After much thought, I came to the conclusion that a philosophy could only be of value if it described the way the world truly is. I discovered that the philosophers I had admired most contradicted what I had seen myself. I began my search for a new philosophy without those contradictions.

I always considered Aristotle the wisest of philosophers, and I embraced his teaching wholeheartedly from my youth. At the core of his teaching was the existence of an effective cause for everything. I considered all I had seen of life, and if I looked deeply enough or back far enough in time, I could see the causes of almost everything. He also taught that nothing lasts forever, that everything changes over time. That was what I saw, too.

But I saw a terrible inconsistency in his teaching, and that disturbed me greatly. He taught that the universe was eternal, that it had no effective cause. But how could that be, that the universe as a whole was the opposite of all the parts within it?

Clearly, there was something wrong with this idea. The universe must also have an effective cause, so I began my search for a philosophy that taught the universe had a beginning and an effective cause that started it. I found it in the Jewish Scriptures. They tell how God created everything from nothing, how He is the effective cause of the whole universe.

I also considered Plato a great philosopher, but the more I saw of men and how they lived, the harder it became for me to agree with his teaching. He taught that cities and empires could be ruled by philosopher-kings: intelligent, self-controlled men who ruled based on wisdom and reason and placed the good of those they ruled above their own desires for power and wealth.

But as I examined history, I found men like this have never ruled. Even Trajan, who provided food and education for orphans in Italia, led his legions out to conquer, killing and enslaving, making new orphans who would starve.

From the histories of empires and kingdoms, we know that great rulers have always done so. Trajan condemns the men he has conquered to die like animals in the arena for the entertainment of the crowds. Where is the wisdom and goodness in that? Plato was wrong about the nature of man, so how could his philosophy be true?

Man is not good and wise; he naturally chooses evil. There are a few who choose kindness and mercy, but it is cruelty and lust for power that rule. Rome is rotten at her core, and she rules vast lands with an iron hand. Man's love of violence led to the games.

I expect to die in the arena tomorrow, killed by a lion or a gladiator's sword. Thousands of Romans, including many men whom I have known for years, will be watching and will consider it good entertainment. Again, I found this understanding in the Jewish Scriptures, that man is naturally evil, selfish, rebellious against God. Man is a sinful being.

In the Jewish Scriptures, I found the philosophy that explained everything I knew to be true about the world, but it is much more than a philosophy. In those same Scriptures, I met the God who made the universe.

I discovered that He cared about men enough to reveal Himself to them so they could know Him. I learned of Abraham, Isaac, and Jacob, and how each of them had met God.

I learned of Moses, who was told by God Himself to lead the people of Israel out of slavery in Egypt because God had promised the land of Judaea to Jacob's children. God cared so much for His people that He gave Moses the very laws by which they should live.

I learned of the many men who were prophets to whom God Himself spoke so His people, who no longer knew and worshiped Him, would return to Him.

From the beginning, He always wanted men to know Him and love Him. So, I became a God-fearer, worshiping the God of Abraham, Isaac, and Jacob, and I studied the Jewish Scriptures daily because I could learn about Him there.

He is a holy God, and He cannot tolerate sin in His presence. But sin is not just doing the things that He has forbidden or neglecting the things He has commanded; it is also choosing to treat God as if He didn't exist.

In the Law He gave to Moses, He told His people the way to approach Him by covering their sins through blood sacrifice in their temple in Jerusalem. For over a thousand years, His people made sacrifices so they could approach Him. That ended when the temple was destroyed by Titus when he was putting down the rebellion in Judaea.

That created a terrible problem, or so I thought. God said the payment for sin always required blood sacrifice, but He let His temple be destroyed by Rome, so how was sin to be paid for? I was at a loss to explain how the true God, the one so powerful that He could make the entire universe, could allow Rome to destroy His temple and take away what allowed His people to approach Him.

Then I met a man who could explain it all. He told me of Jesus of Nazareth and how He came from heaven to make the final sacrifice for sins. He was the Son of God. He was sinless, and He made Himself the perfect sacrifice for all sin when He was crucified. After three days, He rose from the dead, proving His claim to be God.

The grandfather of my friend actually knew men who had been with Jesus after He rose. There could be no doubt of the truth that Jesus was the Son of God and the final perfect sacrifice.

At last, I understood it all. The temple could be destroyed because God had made the perfect blood sacrifice Himself—Jesus on a cross more than

80 years ago. The temple and its sacrifices were no longer needed, so He had Rome destroy it so people would no longer cling to the old ways.

The coming of the Messiah, of Jesus, was foretold in the Jewish Scriptures hundreds of years before He came, and God kept the promise He made to His people. There was no need to continually sacrifice animals to cover my sin with their blood. To be saved from my sin, I only had to believe in Jesus as the sacrifice for all sins, including mine. It all made perfect sense, and I finally knew the truth.

When I went the first time to worship with my friend, I actually met God myself. I felt His love surround me, and now He lives in me. I am never alone. That day when I decided to believe, to repent of my sins and commit myself to Jesus as my Lord, all the worry and sadness in my life was replaced by peace and joy. For the first time, I knew what it was to be fully alive.

I want you to experience this yourself. For you to know this perfect love deep in your soul—that will be my dying prayer.

Following Jesus is like a perfect marriage; denying Him would be like committing adultery against the most loving, beautiful, faithful wife a man could have. I could never betray my Lord that way. I have chosen death instead.

I will die soon, but I have no regrets. I am content to die because it isn't death that matters. It is whether you have accepted Jesus as Savior. Death is terrible apart from Jesus. Without Jesus, I would be lost, in hell, forever separated from God. With Jesus as my Savior, death has no power over me, and I don't fear it. It will just usher me into life with Him in heaven.

Jesus told us that He is the way, the truth, and the life. He promised if a man would believe in Him and follow, he would know the truth, and the truth would set him free. If you let Him, Jesus will show you what is true. Open your mind to Him. Open your heart. Know the truth and be free like I am, even in this prison as I wait to die. I will be praying for all my children to choose to follow Jesus until I take my final breath and even after that, for life with Jesus is eternal.

Discussion Guide

1) When the story starts, Titianus was a highly intelligent, honorable man who always tried to get to the truth and do the right thing. He knew his best friend's grandfather had decided to become a Christian and died in the arena for it, but he agreed with the philosopher Seneca that thinking any god was real was foolishness. Have you known someone like Titianus? How did they react to you if they knew you were a Christian?

2) For years, Publius Drusus, Appius Torquatus and Gnaeus Lenaeus shared their scholarly interests and thought the Roman gods were mere stories. Then Publius let himself be killed for believing in Jesus. He asked his best friend to read the letter explaining his faith before sending it on to his son; then Torquatus was eager to share it with Lenaeus. How did these two highly intellectual men respond to what it contained? Why?

3) Pompeia was twelve and pagan then, but she studied Publius's letter with her father and understood the logic that led Publius to believe. Are there teens in your life who would say they are Christians but have never spent time thinking seriously about what and why they believe? Are they ready to resist society's attempts to lead them away from God?

4) Pompeia and her father had been Christians for twelve years when she discovered he'd been murdered. How did she respond? Do you think you would have responded the same way?

5) Kaeso accepted Jesus as a child of six, but he'd always followed his father's and sister's lead. His father's murder shook his faith, and he shared that with Pompeia. What did she tell him? Has anyone you know had their faith shaken by something that made it seem God didn't care? Were you able to help them? How?

6) Why was Pompeia afraid of Titianus's attentions when she first met him? What changed that?

7) Arcanus was deeply loyal to his patron Rufinus, the man who'd owned and then freed him. That loyalty led to the first accidental death. What should he have done then? What did he do? Where did it lead? Why do you think he made the choices he did?

8) Rufinus was politically ambitious and mostly honest, but he made money off his secret businesses that senators weren't allowed to own. When it looked like his law-breaking might be exposed, what was he willing to have Arcanus do? Could he have done anything to change Arcanus's fate?

9) In *Honor Bound*, Manius Sabinus was a pragmatic, often ruthless man like his father until his 15-year-old son Septimus embraced honor as his personal code. In the three years since then, how has Manius changed? How does his time with Pompeia and Titianus change him more? Have you had the chance to influence someone like Manius?

10) *More Than Honor* is a story of keeping the faith and sharing it even after tragedy strikes, of loyalty leading to good decisions and bad, and of how what people value most can change when they decide to seek the truth. What touched you most? What made you think about what your own choices would be?

WHO WOULD YOU LIKE TO SEE
IN A FUTURE SHORT STORY OR NOVELLA?

I grew to love several of the characters in *More Than Honor* while I was writing. That usually happens, and often the next story for a character takes shape in my head even before I finish. Sometimes it's requests from readers that reveal who should be the focus of a future story. There are many people in *More Than Honor* that I would like to spend more time with, and I hope there are some for you, too. Who would you most like to see in a future story? What was it about them that made you want more of them? I'd love to hear what you think.

Please go to my website, carol-ashby.com, and share your thoughts in the comment box. Sign up for the newsletter, and you'll get the story when I finish it. Looking forward to hearing from you!

Glossary

Aquarius: the *vigiles* soldier who supervised the supply of water while fighting a fire

As: in Imperial times, a copper coin worth 1/16 denarius, 1/4 sestertius, 1/2 dupondius

Aureus: a gold Roman coin worth 25 denarii

Atrium: the open central court of a Roman house with enclosed rooms on all sides

Centurion: 1st level officer over 80 men; rises through the ranks based on merit

Client: one with obligations to a patron; could be of same or lower status as patron. When slaves were freed, the former owner became their patron.

Cognomen: the third name of the 3-part Roman name, the surname or family name

Damnatio ad bestias: condemned to the arena to be killed by beasts

Denarius: silver Roman coin worth 1.13 drachmas; worth about one day's living wage

Domus: town house of the upper classes and wealthy freedmen with indoor courtyards (atrium and peristyle), many rooms, and a garden

Dupondius: Roman brass coin worth 1/2 sestertius or 1/8 denarius

Equestrian order: 2nd highest class of Roman citizens; required personal wealth greater than 100,000 denarii

Familia: the Roman family unit consisting of the paterfamilias, his married and unmarried children regardless of age, his son's children, and his slaves

Freedman: a freed slave who owes support and service as a client to his former owner

Gladius: short thrusting sword used by the Roman military and some gladiators

Ignosco: I forgive, pardon, excuse, overlook

Kalasiris: a close-fitting Egyptian tube dress with straps

Lanista: the head trainer of a gladiatorial school

Lararium: household shrine, often a niche in an atrium wall

Legate: commander of a legion

Legion: unit of the Roman army consisting of about 6000 Roman citizens

Ludus: (plural *ludi*) gladiator training school; also rents bodyguards

Optio: Roman junior officer ranked below centurion

Palla: rectangular cloth wrap worm by Roman women

Paterfamilias: Oldest living male of an extended Roman family, the patriarch who owns everything

Patronus: patron; expected to provide some material benefits for their clients, both freeborn and freed

Peregrine: a person who is not a Roman citizen

Praetor: a Roman magistrate ranking below consul, serves as a judge

Quintilian rhetoric: taught the good orator must also be morally sound, i.e., be good man

Rhetor: a teacher of rhetoric or oratory, which was used in court, public speeches, and writing

Rhetoric: the art or persuasion, including the concept, style, memory, and delivery

Salutation: daily ritual during which prominent citizens received clients and others seeking favors

Salve: hello, standard Roman greeting

Senatorial order: highest class of Roman citizens; required personal wealth greater than 250,000 denarii

Sestertius: (plural sesterces) bronze Roman coin worth 1/4 denarius

Salve: hello, the standard Latin greeting

Solis: Sunday

Sui iuris: independent of their paterfamilias, most often through his death

Taberna: tavern or shop selling prepared food

Tablinum: the main office and reception room for the Roman master of the house

Thermae: a Roman bath complex, the "baths

Tribune: high-ranking officer from equestrian or senatorial order

Triclinium: dining room with couches arranged along three sides of a low table

Urban Cohort: one of four military police units under the urban prefect; had 1 tribune over 6 centurions and about 500 men

Urban prefect: quasi-mayor of Rome with administrative and judicial powers to maintain order in the city; commander of the Urban Cohort

Vale: goodbye, the standard Latin farewell

Vestibulum: passage between the outer door and the interior of a town house (domus)

Vigiles Urbani: "watchmen of the City," firefighters and night watchmen of Rome

Scripture References

Chapter 7: When Pompeia is copying Scripture. Acts 20:6-12

Chapter 16: When Pompeia talks with Torquatus at his estate after her father's murder. Romans 8:28; Luke 10:3

Chapter 17: When Pompeia talks with Kaeso. "What Jesus said: How he was going to prepare a place for those of us who love him. How he told the robber crucified beside how that they'd be together in Paradise that very day. How those of us who believe in Him can never truly die." John 11:26, John 14:2, Luke 23:43

Forgiveness isn't a feeling. It's a decision, and Jesus told us we can't refuse to give it if we want God to forgive us." Matthew 6:14-15

"I keep reminding myself Jesus asked the Father to forgave the soldiers as they were crucifying Him. He asks us to forgive those who hurt us." She sniffed. "Commands, actually, not asks. I'll keep trying, and with the Spirit's help, I'll be able to obey." Luke 23:34

Chapter 19: Pompeia's comment to Kaeso as he worries about their finances. Matthew 6:34

Chapter 24: When Pompeia is worrying in her bedroom. Isaiah 41:10

Chapter 27: After Titianus is healed, Pompeia's thoughts about him finding out they are Christians. Matthew 10:17-20

Chapter 36: When Pompeia begins answering Titianus's questions about God. John 14:13, 15:16, 16:23-26; Luke 10:27; Luke 6:27

Chapter 39: When Titianus is reading Pompeia's copy of Luke. Quotations in the text are from the English Standard Version (ESV).
Luke 1:104, 2:29-32, 3:21-22, 4:16-24, 5:17-26, 5:27-32, 6:27-38, 9:22-26, 11:9-10, 11:13, 22:19-20, 24:44-48.

Acknowledgements

Most of all, I thank God for this opportunity to tell the story of a self-sufficient man who lived his life based on duty and honor without realizing what was more important and a woman who was willing to share her faith with him, even though it could be dangerous for him to know she's a Christian. I loved writing how God brought Titianus to see the truth about Jesus and become a child of God. What could be better than getting to write about lives being transformed by faithfulness and love?

No one can write the best book possible without the help of many others. I want to thank Andrew Budek-Schmeisser for being my critique partner, prayer partner, and good friend as I've written so many of these books. Whenever I needed prayers for something that was giving me problems, I could count on him. Despite serious health problems, he's always been willing to share his knowledge of good writing, his spiritual insight, and his expertise with horses, combat, and low-tech field medicine. With his artistic background as a painter, his comments on most of the covers have helped guide us to images that were just right for each story. He's also helped me with *The Legacy, Faithful, Second Chances, True Freedom, Hope Unchained, Honor Bound,* and *Hope's Reward* and with many brainstorming sessions about characters for future volumes. None of the books would have been the same without him.

I'm especially thankful for Lisa Garcia, my top alpha beta and dear friend. Her ability to spot places that need additional work to get the story right is invaluable. I wouldn't be able to write the spiritual scenes well without her prayers and her feeling for exactly how they should be to seem real. She's so good at spotting typos that I'll never need a copy editor. Her prayers always bless me in writing and in life.

I want to thank Sherril Stinnett, who's also been my invaluable alpha beta for *Honor Bound* and *Hope's Reward.* I can always count on her to tell me when something isn't quite right so I can fix it. I can tell she's praying when I'm writing the hard sections, especially where faith decisions were being made.

Christine Dillon, the inspiring author of the Grace series, was a wonderful beta reader for this book. With an author's eye and the spiritual insight of a missionary, her help in getting things just right was a blessing.

Terry Shoebotham is my local writing buddy and prayer partner for writing and so much else in life. She beta-read part of the manuscript and gave me sage advice for getting the right feeling for a cover with broad appeal. She's a joy to talk books with, and I'll be so glad when we can meet again in person.

I love getting a man's eye view of these novels, and Ray Warters, a fellow writer, shared his insights on part of the manuscript.

I also want to thank Katie Powner, my long-time critique partner, for her prayers and wise editorial comments. She is an award-winning author herself whose debut novel, *The Sowing Season*, released in October. For a wonderful contemporary read, you can't beat it.

Thanks also to Mesu Andrews for praying with me for inspiration and for meeting deadlines when they got way too close. As a leading writer of Biblical fiction, she shared her author insights on important spiritual scenes, too. Plus, I can always count on her to share my fascination with Biblical and Roman archeology. Ancient history nerds belong together!

My line editor, Wendy Chorot, has once more brought her editorial skill and her deep spiritual insight to bear to make the spiritual scenes feel like real life. Working with her is always a delight.

Roseanna White has designed another gorgeous cover that captures the location of the story and the relationship between Titianus and Pompeia when they first meet. My son tells me this is the best cover yet, and I think he's right.

I didn't need to have my son, Paul, or my daughter, Lydia, serve as body models in Roman attire I've sewn this time, but they were both willing to help if Roseanna decided we needed that. I can always count on my kids!

But my special thanks go to my wonderful husband, Jim. Even when he's heard something twenty times already, he listens to the variations in my plot ideas and scene details because it helps me to think as I talk. His humor, kindness, and patience are the model for the best of my heroes. I'm blessed to be with him every day.

About the Author

Carol Ashby has been a professional writer for most of her life, but her articles and books were about lasers and compound semiconductors (the electronics that make cell phones, laser pointers, and LED displays work). She still writes about light, but her Light in the Empire series tells stories of difficult friendships and life-changing decisions in dangerous times, where forgiveness and love open hearts to discover their own faith in Christ. Her fascination with the Roman Empire was born during her first middle-school Latin class. A research career in New Mexico inspires her to get every historical detail right so she can spin stories that make her readers feel like they're living under the Caesars themselves.

Read her articles about many facets of life in the Roman Empire at carolashby.com, or join her at her blog, The Beauty of Truth, at carol-ashby.com.

LIGHT *in the* EMPIRE SERIES

Dangerous times, difficult friendships,
lives transformed by forgiveness and love.

The Light in the Empire Series follows the interconnected lives of four Roman families during the reigns of Trajan and Hadrian. Join them as they travel the Empire, from Germania and Britannia to Thracia, Dacia, and Judaea and, of course, to Rome itself.

Forgiven

Are some wounds too deep to forgive?

With a ruthless father who murdered for the family inheritance, Marcus Drusus plans to do the same. In AD 122, Marcus follows his brother Lucius to Judaea and plots to frame a zealot for his older brother's death. But the plan goes awry, and Lucius is rescued by a Messianic Jewish woman. Her oldest brother is a zealot and a Roman soldier killed her twin, but Rachel still persuades her father Joseph to put his love for Jesus above his anger with Rome and hide Lucius until he heals.

Rachel cares for the enemy, and more than broken bones heal as duty turns to love. Lucius embraces Joseph's faith in Jesus, but sharing a faith doesn't heal all wounds. Even before revealed secrets slice open old scars, Joseph wants no Roman son-in-law. With Rachel's zealot brother suspecting he's a Roman officer and his own brother planning to kill him when he returns, can Lucius survive long enough to change Joseph's mind?

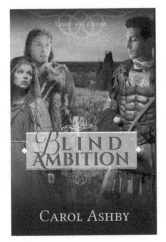

Blind Ambition

Sometimes you have to almost die to discover how you want to live.

It's AD 114 in the Roman province of Germania Superior, and being a Christian carries a death sentence. Tribune Decimus Lentulus is on the fast track for a stellar political career back in Rome. When he's robbed, blinded, and left for dead, a young German woman who follows the Way finds him. Valeria knows it's his duty to have her and her family killed, but she chooses to obey Jesus's command to love her enemy and takes him home to care for him.

It's not his miraculous recovery that shakes Decimus to his core. It's the way they love him like family and their unconcealed love for Jesus. In spite of himself, he falls in love with the Christian woman Rome wants him to kill. Can Valeria hide her faith to follow him into the circles of Roman power? Or should he abandon his ambition to help rule the Empire and choose to follow a different way?

The Legacy

When Rome has taken everything, what's left for a man to give?

Betrayed by a ruthless son who'll do anything for power and wealth, Publius Drusus faces death with an unanswered prayer—that his treasured daughter, Claudia, and honorable son, Titus, will someday share his faith. But who will lead them to the truth once he's gone?

Claudia's oldest brother Lucius arranged their father's execution to inherit everything, and now he's forcing her to marry a cruel Roman power broker. If only she could get to Titus—a thousand miles away in Thracia. Then the man who secretly told her father about Jesus arranges for his son Philip to sneak her out of Rome and take her to the brother she can trust.

A childhood accident scarred Philip's face. A woman's rejection scarred his heart. Claudia's gratitude grows into love, but what can Philip do when the first woman who returns his love hates the God he loves even more?

Titus and Claudia hunger for revenge on their brother and the Christians they blame for their father's deadly conversion. When Titus buys Miriam, a secret Christian, to serve his sister, he starts them all down a path of conflicting loyalties and dangerous decisions. His father's final letter commands the forgiveness Titus refuses to give. What will it take to free him from the hatred poisoning his own heart?

Join the people you met in *Second Chances* eight years earlier in this tale of betrayal, hatred, love, and forgiveness, where even bad things can work together for good.

Faithful

Is the price of true friendship ever too high?

In AD 122, Adela, the fiery daughter of a Germanic chieftain, is kidnapped and taken across the Roman frontier to be sold as a slave. When horse-trader Otto wins her while gambling with her kidnappers, he entrusts her to his friend and trading partner, Galen. Then Otto is kidnapped by the same men, and Galen must track them half way across the Empire before his best friend loses a fight to the death in a Roman arena.

Adela joins Galen in the chase, hungry for vengeance. As the perilous journey deepens their friendship, will the kind, faithful man open her eyes to a life she never dreamed she'd want?

A trip to the heart of the Empire poses mortal danger to a man who follows Jesus, especially when he must seek the help of an enemy of the faith for Otto to survive. Tiberius hunted Christians when he governed Germania Superior and banished his own son when he became one.

When Tiberius learns sparing Galen offers a chance at reconciliation, he joins the trio on their journey home. Can his animosity toward the followers of Jesus survive a trip with the Christian man whose courage and faithfulness demand his respect?

Follow the continuing saga of the people you met in *Blind Ambition* from the frontier of Germany to the heart of the Empire.

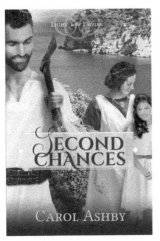

Second Chances

Must the shadows of the past destroy the hope of the future?

In AD 122, Cornelia Scipia, proud daughter of one of Rome's noblest families, learns her adulterous husband plans to betroth their daughter to the vicious son of his best friend. Over her dead body! Cornelia divorces him, reclaims her enormous dowry, and kidnaps her own daughter. She plans to start over with Drusilla a thousand miles away. No more husbands for her. But she didn't count on meeting Hector, the widowed Greek captain of the ship carrying her to her new life.

Devastated by the loss of his wife and daughter, Hector's heart begins to heal as he befriends Drusilla. Cornelia's sacrificial love for Drusilla and her courage and humor in the face of the unknown earn his admiration…as a friend. Is he ready for more?

Marriage to the kind, honest sea captain would give Drusilla the father she deserves…and Cornelia the faithful husband she's always longed for. But while her ex-husband hunts them to drag Drusilla back to Rome, secrets in Hector's past and the chasm between their social classes and different faiths erect complicated barriers to any future together. Will God give two lonely hearts a second chance at happiness?

Join the people you met in *The Legacy* eight years later in this tale of hope and a future never imagined until God opens the door.

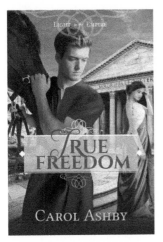

True Freedom

The chains we cannot see can be the hardest ones to break.

When Aulus runs up a gambling debt to his father's political enemy, he's desperate to pay it off before his father returns to Rome. His best friend Marcus suggests they fake the kidnapping of Aulus's sister Julia and use the ransom money. But when the man they hired kidnaps her for real, Aulus is catapulted into a desperate search to find her.

Torn from his childhood home by Rome's conquering armies and sold as a farm slave to labor

-until he dies, Dacius's faith gives him strength to bear what he must and serve without complaining. After a deadly accident makes him one of Julia's litter bearers, he overhears Marcus advising her brother to kidnap her. When Dacius almost dies thwarting the kidnapping, a Christian couple pretend Julia and Dacius are their children to keep her brother from finding them before her father returns.

But pretending to be free again makes returning to slavery more than Dacius can bear, while acting like a common woman opens Julia's eyes to dreams and destinies she never knew existed. With her brother closing in and her father almost home, can she find a way around Roman law and custom to free them both for the future they long for?

Find out what happens to Ariana's brother Diegis twelve years later in this tale of hope and a future never imagined until God opens the door.

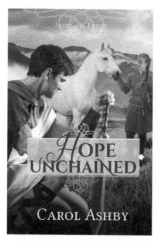

Hope Unchained

Can the deepest loss bring the greatest gain?

Rome's conquering army took Ariana's family and freedom, but nothing can take her faith in Jesus. When she rescues a tribune's wife from certain death, her reward is freedom and a chance to free her brother and sister. But first she must catch up with the slave caravan before they vanish forever, and tracking them from Dacia to the coast seems impossible for one woman alone.

Discharged from the legion with a hand crippled by a Dacian knife, Donatus faces a future without hope. When the tribune asks him to escort Ariana on her quest, it's the only work he can find. It means four weeks with a Dacian woman and a gladiator bodyguard, but it takes money to eat. A man without options must take what he can get.

But a lot can happen in four weeks. Even battle-hardened men can be touched by love and forgiveness, and it's easier to face an enemy with a sword than to face the truth. When his moment of truth comes, what will Donatus choose, and what will that mean for both of them?

If you read *True Freedom* and wondered what happened to Leander's beloved sister Ariana, you can find out in *Hope Unchained*.

Honor Bound

Can the deepest loss bring the greatest gain?

Marcus Brutus owns estates, ships, and gladiator schools that increase his fortune daily, but his greatest treasures are his honor and his wife. When she reveals her faith in Jesus before dying after the birth of their son, he's consumed by hatred for the unnamed Christian woman who led his beloved to abandon the Roman gods, making him lose her in this life and the next.

For fifteen years, Licinia's father hid her Christian faith. But now her father is dead, and a ruthless political enemy is hunting for anything to destroy her brother. When she becomes the target, her brother sends her to their estate in Germania. But is that far enough to protect her from an evil man who will stop at nothing?

When a carriage accident leaves Brutus injured and his best friend near death after rescuing Brutus's son, Licinia welcomes and cares for them. But her strange habits and his friend's unexpected recovery make Brutus suspect she's the Christian who corrupted his wife. When her brother's enemies come for her, does honor require him to protect her or turn her over as an enemy of Rome? And when Licinia's heart is drawn toward the pagan man who makes money off death, can she reconcile her growing affection with her love for Christ?

If you read *True Freedom* and wondered what happened to Africanus and Brutus, you can find out in *Honor Bound*.

Hope's Reward

Must the secrets we hide destroy our hope for a future?

For a gladiator slave, each time you step on the sand, it's kill or die. When Ursus decides to follow Jesus, he must choose to die the next time he's ordered to fight...or run away. He runs, taking again his childhood name, Matti. But he isn't just trying to escape. He's running to Thessalonica, where he hopes to find other Christians like the woman who led him to faith.

When Felicia's new husband, Falco, almost kills her in a fit of rage, her uncle won't help her end the marriage with his business partner. He will send her to her sister in Thessalonica, but only if she tells no one she plans to divorce Falco and demand her dowry back before she gets there. When Matti interrupts a robbery too late to save Felicia's money for traveling by sea, he offers to bodyguard and escort her overland to their mutual destination.

After Matti risks everything to save her from Falco's assassins, Felicia fears taking the danger to her sister's family. When his Christian friends take them in, she discovers the deepest desires of her heart. But will the secrets of Matti's past make a future together impossible?

If you wonder what happened to Ursus in *Hope Unchained*, he's the hero in *Hope's Reward*.

I'd Love to Hear from You!

If you enjoyed this book, it would be a real gift to me if you would post a review at the retailer you purchased it from. A good review is like a jewel set in gold for an author. Other great places to share reviews are Goodreads and BookBub. If you've read others in the series, it would be great if you post a review of those, too.

I'd also love to hear from you at carol-ashby.com or directly at carolashbyauthor@gmail.com.

Want to hear about upcoming releases in the Light in the Empire series and free gifts only for newsletter subscribers?

For free gifts and other special offers, advance notices of upcoming releases, and info about my latest writing adventures, I hope you'll sign up for my newsletter at carol-ashby.com.

Who would you like to see in a future story? Help me pick what to write next!

I grew to love several of the characters in *More Than Honor* while I was writing. That usually happens, and sometimes a future story takes shape in my head even before I finish. But more often the next hero or heroine is chosen because readers tell me who needs to come back as a story lead.

Readers who loved Galen as a teen in *Blind Ambition* wanted to see him as a grown man, so he became the hero in *Faithful*. People who asked for Brutus and Africanus to have their own story found out what happened to them in *Honor Bound*.

Since people kept asking what happened to Leander's beloved but long-lost sister in *True Freedom*, it was clear Ariana would need her own story in *Hope Unchained*. People who met Ursus in *Hope Unchained* asked what happened to him, so he returned with his childhood name of Matti in his quest to know God better in *Hope's Reward*.

In *More Than Honor*, Septimus, who was rather like a Great Dane puppy in *Honor Bound*, comes back three years older, and Tribune Titianus from *True Freedom* got his own story because readers thought he should. I'm SO glad they did. I hadn't planned on Titianus being a lead without that input, and I loved giving him and Pompeia their own happy ending.

But there are many more characters in the books of the series that I would like to spend more time with, and I hope there are some for you, too. Who would you most like to see in a future story? What was it about them that made you want more of them? I'd love to hear what you think. It will guide what I write next.

Some possibilities:

Aulus of *True Freedom?*

Septimus or Manius of *Honor Bound* and *More Than Honor?*

Someone else I haven't mentioned? (I can't wait to see who shows up here!)

Please tell me who you'd love to see again as a comment at carol-ashby.com or directly at carolashbyauthor@gmail.com!

Please go to my website, carol-ashby.com, and share your thoughts in the comment box. Sign up for the newsletter, and you'll get the story when I finish it. Looking forward to hearing from you!